A NEW ORLEANS MURDER MYSTERY: HORIZONTAL GARDEN

A Novel

by

Donald Patrick O'Callahan

Disclaimer

This book is lovingly dedicated to the memory of my mother, Yvonne.

ACKNOWLEDGEMENT

Many thanks to my Amazon team for helping to bring my dream and this book to fruition, every step of the way.

Contents

SYNOPSIS

The novel takes place during a mayoral runoff election in New Orleans in 1994, the year the murder rate reached 424, giving the city the dubious distinction of being the nation's "Murder Capital." The novel's main characters are Ashley Georgina Tarleton, Wyatt Terranova, Xavier Chenier, Keiffer Conright and Ashley's father, George, and mother, Evelyn.

Ashley, a 30-year-old socialite and entertainment reporter for TV 3 News, is given the opportunity to cover the "hard news," regarding the mayoral runoff election. The candidates are Chenier, 55, the African-American incumbent who was once a civil rights activist, and Conright, 55, a politically ultraconservative, allegedly racist businessman who may have ties to the American Nazi Party. Ashley teams with Wyatt, 30, her cameraman, to report the race.

However, when they meet at the Café du Monde in the French Quarter to discuss their tactics, a drive-by killing of a young Creole woman occurs only a few feet away in front of Jackson Square. Ashley is first to reach the woman who is dead on the pavement. Disturbed by this, Ashley is determined to investigate the woman's life, and cover the election. They set off on an adventure in newsgathering, taking the reader inside a mansion on St. Charles Avenue and inside a public housing project, and many other unique places in between, revealing a side of New Orleans Ashley never knew existed. On this journey Ashley gathers news about the candidates, civil rights, the removal of Confederate monuments, the Holocaust, her father, ghosts, the goodness of her ill mother, and her mother's well-kept secret regarding her own identity. Ashley comes from "old money" and has led a pampered life. But her life is changing, and she is becoming stronger as a result.

CHAPTER 1

New Orleans
***Anno Domini,* 1994**

They wanted a woman. The two young men could have stolen the car and made it across town an hour ago. But they didn't. They waited for the owner, so they could collect the keys in person. More fun that way, and a woman would be easier to subdue than a man, they thought. The men, like commandos on a night raid, crouched alongside a red pickup truck parked against a blonde brick wall of this suburban shopping mall. Both men wore black: one in a Los Angeles Raiders jacket with a tattooed cross between his thumb and index finger; the other in loose-fitting shirt and jeans. Though it was September, the night air was hot and humid, and a light southerly breeze was no comfort to the two young men who were burning up from without, and within. Sweat, like rain, rolled down their faces; they tasted salt; their eyes opened wide; their ears heard every sound; their breathing was deep and rhythmic. Ready. Wired.

They checked their watches: 8:45 p.m.; closing time was near. Their object of desire was a new black Mercedes-Benz E Class Sedan with tinted windows, parked in the next lane, T-tag still taped to the inside of the rear window. They could almost smell the cognac-colored leather. Perfect, they thought.

Just after 9:00 p.m., the squeaky skipping sounds of tennis shoes, mixed with the more evenly paced sounds of leather soles, were heard approaching the parking lot from the long, narrow main entrance corridor. Two children, their parents and the children's grandmother emerged from the corridor onto the parking lot where the two men finally caught sight of them. The boy and girl each held their grandmother's hands. The girl spied the men, waved her hand and innocently, smilingly said, "Hi!" Frightened by the child, the men quickly moved totally out of sight behind the truck before the father looked their way. The men then tracked the family and watched as they all climbed into a blue Dodge mini-van a few spaces removed from the Mercedes. They drove away, the boy howling at the moon through a small vent in a rear window.

The two men again focused their predatory stare on the end of the corridor from where they heard the hard echoing of a man's gait. The oversized man nearly fell down when his black, wing-tip shoes contacted the parking lot. He clumsily balanced two large boxes under his arms as he walked to his car. Though they preferred a woman, they were ready to take on this man if he owned the Mercedes. Their breathing grew deeper. The right thumb of one twitched uncontrollably. Their fingers separated, and then tightened to clenched fists. The man, however, did not walk to the Mercedes, but to the white Ford SUV to the right of it. He positioned one box between himself and the SUV, and the other between himself and the Mercedes. He tunneled into his pant's pocket and pulled out the keys. He opened the driver's door, quickly threw in the packages, and then jumped in, making the SUV rock up and down. The men watched him speed away. They were getting closer, they thought.

A sharp sound down the corridor immediately captured their attention. The two men readily recognized the pointed, reverberating sexy sound of a woman's high heels on smooth concrete. Each felt an adrenaline rush and a lightning-like impulse from their brains to their groins. Ten seconds later an attractive woman with short frosted hair, carrying three red shopping bags appeared and headed for the Mercedes. She sported a chic look: gold mule high heels, skintight black knit tunic and black jeans, and a gold crescent-shaped, Egyptian-styled necklace. She had a self-assured look about her, straight and tall, and obviously accustomed to a life of luxury. They tracked every step and knew she was the one. In this mostly white suburb of New Orleans, Louisiana, a car like that could only belong to a woman like her.

The Mercedes was parked directly under one of the tall lamps across the parking lot with flying bugs orbiting its globe. As she neared the car, she put all three shopping bags in her left hand and disengaged the car alarm by pressing the remote with her right hand. Everything was set. No words were spoken. Each knew what to do.

The men waited for her most vulnerable moment. Like two powerful Pit Bull Terriers, they ran and overpowered her from behind as she opened the car door and was about to sit down, her left foot on the ground and right foot in the car. The man in the Raiders jacket pulled the woman's right arm behind her and grabbed the keys, while the man in the tee shirt threw her shopping bags ten feet into the air like fireworks, tightly pulled back her hair, and rammed her face into the window. Blood quickly shot from her nose and covered the glass like a red ink blot. She was too disoriented and shocked to scream. The man in the tee shirt jumped into the driver's seat and started the car. The man in the Raiders jacket caught his jacket in her jewelry and tried to pull it free.

"Come on!" the man in the tee shirt shouted, after hearing footsteps from the corridor. "Come on!" he shouted again as he put the car in reverse, dragging both a few feet. "Hey, man, come on! Get in!"

The man in the Raiders jacket finally tore free, threw the woman onto the hood of the pickup, and jumped into the Mercedes. They backed out so quickly, that they hit the truck. Then the long, black Mercedes shot into the thick night air like a bullet. Lightning flashed across the thunderous sky and the rain fell like tears from heaven.

Two teenagers ran to the unconscious woman who was bleeding from her nose and mouth. Her legs were bent as if running, while her head was bent back. The glimmering light from the tall lamppost shone over this tragic tableau of white and black and glistening red.

"Jesus, she's dead!" one teenager said.

"No. Call an ambulance," the other said.

The woman groaned and lifted her shoulder as the boy removed the necklace stuck in her back. Her makeup was mixed with blood and her neck was now adorned with crimson.

Across town in the French Quarter, Wyatt Terranova stepped onto Chartres Street from the rear garage exit of WONO-TV3 television station. The last thrust of a warm, humid Gulf wind wrapped around him as he tried to light a cigarette, and quickly snuffed the flame. He moved closer to the corner of the old stucco building and lit another match which momentarily spotlighted his light olive skin, and the words "NOPD KILLS" written crookedly on the wall.

He ran his hand through his medium-length thick black hair, as he crossed Chartres, sidestepping a pyramid of garbage on the curb. An evening rain shower had just ended. The air was thick with crowd noises and the musical sounds of jazz and blues from Bourbon Street, two blocks away. Heavy humidity covered his skin like plastic wrap. He was thin and stood five feet, eight inches tall. He breathed in smoke, and with it the disturbing smell of urine.

He walked another short block past shops full of clothing and antiques to St. Peter Street where Chartres became a pedestrian walkway between the front of St. Louis Cathedral and the north entrance to Jackson Square, the heart of the French Quarter. The off white-colored cathedral was lit by soft white floodlights from several angles, looking as if the church itself was the source of light. One tall, cone-shaped steeple and two similar but smaller steeple-towers on either side below, pointed towards the heavens, giving direction to the prayers, released like birds, by all those who ever sought still and silent sanctuary there from a city that never sleeps, and a world without end. Amen.

A rebel yell shot into the night over Bourbon Street. A group of tourists stood near the cathedral listening intently to their tour guide, a man dressed in black boots, pants and vest draped loosely over an open-collar white shirt with billowing long sleeves. His eyes grew wide and he pushed back his long black hair, as he told tales of horror and ghosts. Everyone knew the French Quarter was haunted, as were some of its living residents. Two young lovers were embraced in a passionate kiss under an entrance archway to the Cabildo next to the Cathedral – her hands in his back pockets and his hands in hers. Two elderly ladies sitting on a cast-iron bench looked on, shaking their heads disapprovingly, though their husbands' envious eyes were transfixed. Two men held hands and shared an ice cream cone as they walked. Four kids tap danced as tourists gathered around them. Three transients in worn clothes stood near a corner of Jackson Square and lit their cigarettes, three on a match.

The Chicken Man waved to Wyatt as he rode his 1959 black Schwinn Phantom bicycle toward him. He was a voodoo priest who wore chicken bones on a string around his neck. He sometimes kept a live thin, black snake inside the band of his black, straw multi-feathered cowboy hat that he always wore. Some people said he used the snake for his voodoo rituals and to startle tourists by taking off his hat, and letting the snake crawl out. When walking, he always carried his tall staff with feathers and raccoon tails hanging from it. His black skin was coarse, stretched and old, burnt by the heat, and burnt by time. The passing of many years had left their tracks across his face. Like lashes across a slave's back, time had whipped him into submission that there was little time left. He was ill, but did not tell anyone. He just carried on with the incantations of his ancestral Haitian voodoo in his mind, the rattling of chains in his memory, freedom in his blood, and love of New Orleans and life in his heart. He was the Chicken Man, voodoo priest, and guide to the spirit world.

"Hey," Wyatt said, waving his hand.

"Peace be with you," the Chicken Man said, as he slowly peddled past.

"And with you," Wyatt added.

Wyatt turned onto the walkway block of St. Peter Street where a young woman in a long black dress and red beret was leaning against the black wrought iron fence of Jackson Square, playing guitar and doing her very best version of Rickie Lee Jones: Coolsville. A strong smell of marijuana whirled around her and two young men kneeling before her.

To Wyatt's right was one of two red brick, three-story Pontalba apartment buildings on either side of the square, and the most desired real estate in the city with a years-long waiting list for occupancy. The first floor was rented as gift shops, like many first floors in the French Quarter. Tourists stopped and gazed at the simple but elegant architecture, photographing history and past lives, never realizing their own lives were becoming history with each passing moment. The stale mildew smell of history, hung inside and near the building, as in most buildings in the Quarter.

Wyatt and other locals moved quickly between and around tourists who were busy taking photos of street people, as if the

French Quarter was an animal sanctuary. Suddenly, he heard a duck's quacking ahead of him. Ruthie the Duck Girl, dressed in a faded 1940s' formal gown and yellow Sou'wester fisherman's hat with the front folded up, was sidestepping tourists, too. A lifelong Quarter resident, elderly Ruthie could be seen walking her pet duck on a leash any day or night. She was the only surviving member of her family. Ruthie was a free spirit, free from all the weights and responsibilities that anchor most people to their homes. But the cost of freedom sometimes meant sleeping on the sidewalks and in doorways. She was even arrested one time, kicking and screaming all the way to the police district station. But her friends in the Quarter came to her rescue and gave her shelter so she could walk or roller skate the streets she knew so well. Residents of the Quarter always stood by each other.

"Watch yourself, darling. Jesus and that kid are fighting again," Ruthie said to Wyatt, as she pointed toward Decatur Street at the other end of Jackson Square.

"Okay, Ruthie," Wyatt said, as he continued walking.

For Ruthie and all the locals, the French Quarter was their "lost world." On any street outside of the Quarter, Ruthie would have been harassed. However, the Quarter was a safe haven for people who would have died and become extinct elsewhere for being considered too weird or different. Here in this old-world island refuge, they flourished. The Quarter did not look disdainfully on anyone. Like a church, it took in all orphans, saints and sinners alike.

Lining the walkway were ten Tarot card readers seated at small card tables, with short flickering candles on each. The cost for a glimpse into the future was $10. And when it came to the tarot, voodoo and hauntings, the French Quarter made believers of most. Some tourists became nervous during a reading, looking all around themselves, as if ghosts were near.

Angeline, wearing her trademark purple bandana on her head, was in the middle of reading the cards for a short pants-plaid shirt clad newlywed couple from the Midwest whose future – Angeline thought – was as predictable as New Orleans rain. She sold them the dream of a house with a white picket fence, SUV, 2.3 children and a dog running through amber waves of polyester. Though she may have seen something sinister in the cards, it was not Angeline's nature to reveal bad news. Angeline herself once had hoped for the same dream. But in her dream, she became a prisoner. Her lawn was her exercise ground and her white picket fence was ten feet tall. She had spoken freely to and confided in her husband while dating, and he in her. But, apparently, his wedding vows included one of silence because her confidant and lover became her warden, and her house became her solitary confinement. She finally worked up the courage to escape and came to the French Quarter, like so many other exiles. Wyatt winked at her as he walked by and she raised one eyebrow to him.

An argument was in progress when Wyatt reached St. Peter Street and Decatur Street, the last street before the Mississippi River, known to locals as only the "River." The French Quarter Jesus, known simply to locals as "Jesus," was screaming at Dennis Mena, nicknamed "Dennis the Menace," because he regularly terrorized the homeless, many of whom hung out on Decatur.

"Hey, Jesus, what's my name? Tell me, Jesus, what's my game?" Dennis said, laughingly, as he taunted Jesus with Mick-Jagger moves, while some tourists backed away.

"Leave my people alone! Leave my Garden!" Jesus shouted.

"Make me!" Dennis commanded.

"My Father has instructed me to punish you to eternal damnation for unleashing evil on His Earthly Kingdom," Jesus said.

"But you got to catch me first, schizoid!" Dennis said, as he turned and ran. "You got to catch me!"

Jesus ran after Dennis up Decatur, but couldn't keep up. Usually, Decatur was packed with tourists at this time of night. But crime kept many of them away this year and shop owners were upset. Decatur Street, the only two-way street in the French Quarter, still attracted most visitors because it was wide and there was strength in numbers there. Most made their way to Bourbon Street three blocks away. But beyond that, the streets were empty and dangerous. Hotel staffers freely admitted that and urged tourists to stay on the beaten path.

Up Decatur, the House of Blues attracted many people, as did

Margaritaville at the opposite end. Laughter and talking were heard from all directions on street level. Most buildings in the French Quarter were no more than four stories tall and most had balconies. Almost all were conjoined by sharing common walls. A short block in the Quarter was really a solid block of buildings patterned after buildings in Paris. Intimacies and secrets were short-lived in the Quarter. Residents and tourists intermingled peacefully. However, some locals disliked the tourists because some tourists saw the Quarter as nothing more than a place to get drunk, soil the streets, disturb the peace, and moon the world.

Wyatt looked to his left as he was about to cross the lanes of traffic. But he stopped when he noticed a young woman standing outside the south entrance to Jackson Square. She was about twenty-five, about five feet six inches tall, dressed in preppie fashion, and her long black hair was pulled back and clipped behind her head. He could see she was attractive with a somewhat exotic look. He continued to stare as she began looking up and down Decatur. She was obviously waiting for someone, he thought. Her eyes met his for a moment, and then she quickly turned away. Wyatt decided not to act on impulse and talk to her, though he felt a strong desire to.

He stepped off the curb to cross the street and nearly ran into a horse drawn carriage that had approached him, hoping he was a tourist. He sidestepped a car and jaywalked to the other side next to the old Jax Brewery now converted to small shops and restaurants.

Wyatt was headed for the Café Du Monde for coffee and doughnuts, a few feet away on that same side. But he loved to watch the River flow, so he walked up a couple of flights of concrete stairs and ended up on the Moonwalk, a short boardwalk with a few benches that extended several hundred feet next to the Mississippi River. He passed two lovers on a bench and walked down the short embankment to the River's edge. He came near three teenagers with shaved heads and in dirty clothes, who were passing around a jug of Wild Irish Rose wine.

"Hey, man, got some change for a boy on the run?" one said, his head tilted and hand extended.

"What are you running from?" Wyatt asked.

"Authority," the teen said.

"Yeah. Me, too," Wyatt said, dropping a couple of quarters in his hand.

He reached the River and watched the dark waters rolling silently by, and took a deep breath of damp, cool River air. A slight chill filled his nostrils and was a refreshing relief from the heat. He remembered visiting the French Quarter every Sunday with his parents when he was a child. They would park their new used car on Decatur, and then walk around and enjoy the sights, sounds and smells of coffee shops, praline shops, and the unique smell of imported meats and cheeses at the Progress Grocery. At Central Grocery and Deli in the same block his dad would buy muffaletta sandwiches before returning home. Just before that final stop, Wyatt would walk to the River's edge and become mesmerized by its flow. Many were. And many were afraid.

But this was not "Old Man River," that most people thought it to be. This was not the "Father of Waters." This River was a bitch, lonely and heartless. It gave life to everything around it but cared for none. Engineers tried to contain her waters when she would rather roll over all land and life in search of the sea. She was a thief who pick-pocketed bits and pieces of the shoreline as she silently ran her crooked thousand-mile course. She carried waste, chemicals, mud, blood, life and death, in her belly. If anyone swam or fell in her waters, he or she would turn up stillborn on her shores. This was no lady, no loving mother. She was a hag whose children stayed near her for nourishment but who feared her. She had alligator eyes, low in the water and half-opened. Men, women and history rode her back. But only time could tame her.

As Wyatt turned to walk away, another piece of earth broke away from the shore and sank into the dark waters.

Wyatt turned and started walking up the incline to the Moonwalk. Several tourists were strolling the walk, followed by a homeless old man dressed in brown, pushing his shopping cart with all his belongings, and beyond him a thin, young man dancing with himself, shouting "I'm tripping! Come join me! The spirits are here!"

When Wyatt reached the top of the walk, he stopped and looked out across Decatur. A photographer was setting up his camera on a tripod. This was the best view of the heart of the city in perfect symmetry: Jackson Square with its garden, flanked by the Pontalba Apartments, St. Louis Cathedral centered beyond the Square, flanked by the Cabildo and the Presbyter buildings. A beautiful sight, but Wyatt didn't notice this. He simply wanted to check his watch with the clock below the cathedral's center steeple. A silent lightning flash lit up nervous rolling clouds and a bruised, blue-black El Greco sky.

Wyatt noticed that the young lady he spied was still standing at the entrance to the Square. Though he was headed for Café Du Monde a few feet away to meet with TV entertainment reporter, Ashley Tarleton, he decided to take a closer look. He sidestepped cars as he hopped across Decatur. He stepped onto the sidewalk near her, took a few steps, and then looked in her direction. He was stunned by her beautiful light skin, high cheek bones and raven black hair. He was slowed down, as if being pulled toward her.

"Hi, I'm Wyatt. You look familiar. Did you . . . " She quickly shook her head no, as she eyed his black tee shirt, blue jeans and worn, chocolate-colored suede boots. "Because I . . . ," Wyatt continued, trying to hang in there. Now she refused to look his way at all. As if she released him from her pull, he walked on, wiping away beads of sweat from his temples. He had been rejected before, but never without a word being spoken. But he knew the risks of chasing Beauty.

He walked on to the traffic light at St. Ann Street, the next corner, where a solo saxophonist, nicknamed Tune, played his blackened blues. Rain water, like sweat, rolled down the faces of the buildings. While waiting for the light to change, a red Camaro convertible with four young men drove by. They whistled at the mysterious beauty by the gate. The Doors' "Back Door Man' was cranked up on the stereo.

"Hey, baby. . . I want to be your back door man!" one guy shouted in time with the music. "Ow! Oh, yeah!" They laughed as they drove away. The lady in waiting did not acknowledge them. Wyatt smiled and crossed Decatur behind a very slow-moving group of Swedish tourists who looked like they were ill from the heat.

When Wyatt stepped up to the curb, he could already smell the rich aroma of coffee and fried beignets from the Café Du Monde.

Fifty or so, small, square tables were arranged in six rows in the exterior half of the café which had a roof, and archways on two of its sides. Most of the tables were taken and most of the patrons were drinking this specially brewed coffee and chicory, despite the heat of the night. He sat at a table by an arch next to the sidewalk, the same place he and his family sat on those Sunday mornings. A young Vietnamese woman in a white waiter's coat walked up to him and placed a glass of water on the table.

"You order," she said, in broken English.

"Yeah. One coffee and one order of beignets. Thanks," Wyatt said.

She quickly moved into the enclosed half of the café where the orders were prepared. Wyatt sat back in his chair and felt the breeze coming from one of many ceiling fans. He took out a cigarette from his box of Marlboros and lit it. He moved a round, tin ashtray closer to his hand. He surveyed the café and could see that most there were tourists, marked by their shorts, sneakers, bags and cameras. He heard various dialects from all over the world coming from people with a myriad of skin colors. He also noticed a local whom he had never met. The man was a middle-aged Vietnam War veteran. He always wore his army boots, army shirt or tee shirt, with Purple Heart and his green beret. He had served among the army's elite, protecting the south Vietnamese from communism nearly thirty years ago. Now, here he sat under the green and white striped awning at the far end of the café, like a sentinel looking out across Decatur Street, as if it was the DMZ and he was still protecting the sons and daughters of the refugees who followed him home after the fall of Saigon in April 1975, and who now waited on him, serving coffee and memories of war in southern Vietnam, where the torrential rains were not cooling; they were crushing.

He looked directly across the street at a sight more unusual than most in the French Quarter. A small man, dressed in black, was rapping with drumsticks on a cardboard drum. Over his head was a huge, white sphere with two black eyes, one larger than the other, a black mouth and a tan cone on top. He looked like a demented jack-in-the-box. He continued his rapping motions as he looked up and down Decatur. Another orphan had found a new home. Very strange even for the Quarter, Wyatt thought, as he smoked his cigarette and listened to the low hum of the ceiling fans turning round and round and round all day and night.

The waitress returned with his order. She placed the *café au lait* on the table, then his order of square beignets. This French "delicacy" was part of growing up in New Orleans.

"Four dollar," she said as she exchanged a few words with another waiter in Vietnamese.

"There you go," Wyatt said, as he handed her five dollars. "You can keep it."

"Thank you," she said, as she turned away.

"Touch my heart!" a shadowy figure on the sidewalk said to Wyatt as he was sprinkling powdered sugar from a tin shaker on his beignets.

"What?" Wyatt said, looking up.

"Feel my heartbeat," the French Quarter Jesus said, as he moved into the light.

"No, no," Wyatt mumbled, when he saw Jesus.

The French Quarter Jesus was well known for stopping people on the street and asking for help, either for money or spiritual help in fighting Satan. Wyatt had managed to evade him until now. He wore a dirty tee shirt, soiled pants, sandals and a long dirty coat. His face was sweaty and unshaven; his hair long and matted. He had dark, wild, angry eyes that reflected a blitzkrieg warscape behind them. He pushed a broom for a few dollars at a bar on Conti Street called "The Grievous Angel." He sometimes slept there in a small room in the old slave quarters behind the bar and patio. Other times he slept wherever he fell when exhaustion overcame him and the bombing temporarily stopped. His age and origins were unknown.

"Our hearts beat together. All of us," the French Quarter Jesus said.

"Wait, Jesus. I don't have time right now. I'm waiting for someone." Wyatt raised his hands while speaking.

"You with me? He who is not with me is against me," the French Quarter Jesus said, moving closer to Wyatt.

"Hey, you know what. . . " Wyatt said, nervously.

"Help me drive Satan from the Garden," Jesus implored. "The killing must stop!"

Wyatt looked away for a moment to take a dollar from his pocket, as he said, "Here, take this." But the French Quarter Jesus was nowhere to be seen. "Good," he softly said, as he picked up his coffee cup and put his dollar in his pocket. He bit into his beignet and looked across the street to the Square. The young woman still waited at the closed gate, flanked by two tall broad-leaved banana trees just inside the black wrought iron fence. Around the St. Peter Street corner came Miss Ashley Georgina Tarleton dressed in a fine cream-colored linen suit with matching purse and shoes. She was born and raised an "uptown" lady, with an Ivy League Princeton University education, a taste for finery, affluence and social standing, and a certain arrogance she wore daily like cosmetics. Wyatt felt an uneasy, nervous twinge in his stomach. He had not worked directly with her as a cameraman, but had seen her in action as the entertainment reporter. She could be difficult. Here comes her royal highness, he thought, as he exhaled a long stream of smoke.

As Ashley walked toward the St. Ann Street stoplight, the carjacked black Mercedes Benz sedan with the T-tag still in the rear window was slowly heading up Decatur. Mega bass, boom-boom, coked-up, heartbeat rap music could be heard behind the tinted windows. It arrived at the stoplight the same time Ashley did, and stopped. When the pedestrian light turned green, Ashley stepped off the curb. Simultaneously, the Mercedes jerked forward, then stopped, alarming Ashley. She stopped and looked at the car, and then proceeded. The car again jerked forward, forcing her to stop again. She looked through the windshield and could see two figures, darkly. She pointed her finger at the driver as she stepped down with no intention of stopping. As she did, the car jerked slightly forward and she crossed the street. Something was wrong in that car. A Mercedes owner wouldn't do such a thing, she thought. She stepped up to the curb and entered the Café Du Monde. She spotted Wyatt who had turned around to signal her.

"What was that all about? I was about to go out there," Wyatt said.

"I don't know. Kids in daddy's car, I guess," she said in an angry tone of voice, still a bit upset.

"There they go," Wyatt said, nodding his head forward. They both looked at the car as it passed slowly by Jackson Square. "Joy riding."

Ashley then took several napkins from the tin dispenser and wiped the seat of one green vinyl padded aluminum chair where she placed her handbag. She wiped away powdered sugar off another and sat down.

"Did you have to sit next to the street?" Ashley asked, with an unpleasant look on her face, eyeing a passing public transit bus. "Those fumes. And must you smoke?"

Already the attitude, he thought, as he smashed his cigarette in the ashtray.

The waitress brought her a glass of water and said, "You order?"

"No. Me no order," she said condescendingly, while raising her right hand as if to push away a flying insect.

Wyatt rolled his eyes and looked away. The waitress stared at Ashley for a few moments, and then backed away.

"She has feelings, you know," Wyatt said.

"What do you mean? I don't want anything. I only have a few minutes," she said.

"Forget it. What did Darryl say?" Wyatt inquired.

"He said you will indeed be my cameraman for the next seven days, through the end of the mayoral run-off election" she replied.

"So, you're now news reporter and not entertainment reporter," Wyatt asked.

"Yes," she said.

"How did you manage that?" Wyatt wondered.

"Well, it's time. I've been with the station eight months. I've proved myself during that time. I can handle real news," she declared.

"Real news?" Wyatt asked.

"Yes," Ashley said, puzzled by his question.

"Do you know anything about the candidates?" Wyatt suspiciously inquired.

"Well, of course, I do," growing more irritated with him. "Chenier is the incumbent under much fire, and Conright is a local businessman with a shady, possibly far right past. Is this an interrogation? If you don't want to work with me . . ."

"I do. It's just that when you cover a news story as important as this, you've got to know what questions to ask," Wyatt said.

"I'm educated, Walter," Ashley asserted, staring straight at him.

"It's Wyatt."

"Yes. I'm sure I'll do just fine. I want to make the best of this opportunity. I can do this. And Jennifer said she would help with all aspects. She had her baby tonight and is unable to work," she said.

Aha!, Wyatt thought. There's the reason she's been promoted; the station is suddenly short-handed during the busiest and nastiest runoff election in years. He knew she was too inexperienced in hard news reporting. He knew she knew it, too. But he had to give her credit for wanting to try. But why try? She could have declined the offer and continued to live very comfortably on her salary and father's wealth. No one expected anything from her.

His first job had been as a photographer with the Times-Picayune newspaper. His assignment was to photograph the socialites in their natural habitat of stately homes on and off St. Charles Avenue, and society gatherings where he had photographed Ashley and her parents, though she failed to recognize him. He photographed their smiles, their toasts, their own little world where ice could almost be seen hanging from their faces, he thought, and outsiders were unwelcome. He did this for a year until he couldn't stand to be in their presence any longer. They either coldly stared at him, as if he was an animal in the zoo, or ignored him completely, as if he was a black man. Yet, he felt a desire to hold Ashley, though he was not of her class. She was so very pretty, neat and clean with long auburn hair, smooth porcelain-like skin, manicured fingernails, wrapped in linen and adorned with a Cartier tank watch, diamond ring and pearl necklace. He really wanted to know what it would be like to kiss such a woman, though he was almost certain it would probably be like kissing an ice sculpture.

"Alright, then. We're on for tomorrow. Conright's press conference is set for eleven. We'll meet at the station for ten," Ashley said, checking her watch. "I've got to run."

"Okay. See you tomorrow," Wyatt said. She stood and jumped back a bit as lightning lit the sky. A sudden whirling gust of wind blew through her and into the café, carrying with it napkins and dust. A waitress dropped a tray of coffee cups, and then shouted something in Vietnamese, her left hand bleeding. Wyatt moved to help her but the Vietnam War veteran made it to her first. He wrapped her hand in two cloth napkins and led her to the restrooms. "She'll be okay. See you tomorrow."

"Yes," Ashley said as she quickly stepped to the curb, so she wouldn't have to walk with Wyatt. She heard, then saw the new black Mercedes returning up Decatur. The bass beat was so loud now, sounding as if the car was the instrument. She waited to cross as the car rolled slowly by. She hurriedly crossed, sidestepping a few tourists and turned left to retrace her steps to the TV station's parking garage.

The Mercedes stopped in front of the Square. The passenger's window was lowered, revealing a black Tech 9 semi-automatic pistol. Bullets and sparks shot out of the barrel as the gunman moved it left to right. Everyone in the area fell to the ground. Screams and the sounds of bullets striking the iron fence were heard. The two banana trees inside the gate were shredded. Pieces of their fronds fell to the sidewalk. Some landed on top of the exotically beautiful young woman at the gate who was motionless on the pavement and bleeding from her chest and head, as the Mercedes sped up Decatur toward Canal Street, the wide main street of downtown New Orleans.

Moans and muffled words of disbelief rose with the crowd. Some people moved slowly toward the center of the scene of the crime. Others did not move at all. A few tourists snapped photos of the newest piece of New Orleans history. The shooting had obscured time. The Mercedes had left the scene at a high rate of speed and was gone. But all movement at the scene was in extreme slow motion. The horrific event had disturbed the peace of the night, history, and the lives of all the people present. This time and place had been marked by blood and would be forever linked to the murder of the young woman at the gate. The people there would never forget it. The people of New Orleans would wake up to the shocking news, and those yet to visit the city would be made aware of it for years to come. It would soon join the ranks of the many shots heard around the world and the haunting silence they caused.

Then, a vacationing doctor, dressed in plaid shorts and polo shirt, pushed through the crowd.

"Please, let me through. I'm ER-trained," the doctor said, as she moved toward the young woman at the gate. She placed her hand on the girl's throat, and then on her wrist. "She's gone."

"Over here, doctor," a tourist said, pointing to one of the other four people wounded.

Ashley had inched her way through the crowd and could now see four bullet holes in the young woman – in the forehead, left cheek, at the base of the throat, and chest. The bottom half of her right front tooth was gone. Dark red blood rolled snake-like from her nostrils down each side of her face, as blood from the exit wounds collected in a pool on the pavement under her head. She had JFK-Parkland eyes, opened wide and seeing nothing.

"Jesus!" Wyatt said, after working his way through the crowd. It was difficult for him to believe the young woman he thought so beautiful was now dead. Change was usually thought of as taking place over a great many years. But drastic irreparable change, he realized, took only seconds. He felt a strong sadness, as if he knew her. Even black bullet holes could not diminish her beauty.

Father Ulloa ran from the Priest's rectory down Pere Antoine Alley next to the St. Louis Cathedral, and made his way to the scene just as the ambulance and police arrived. He noticed a thin, gold cross around her neck.

"Clear the way! Clear the way!" a cop said, as he tried to part the crowd.

"Get your camera," Ashley said, tugging at his arm.

Wyatt was temporarily stopped from leaving so the paramedics could squeeze in. The crowd backed away and revealed the French Quarter Jesus kneeling by the young woman's body. Two policemen helped him up. "Her spirit . . . I spoke to her spirit . . . Gone now . . . with all the others," the French Quarter Jesus said. "She has seen the face of God." As he was turned around he came face to face with Wyatt. The flashing red lights of the ambulance and police cars were reflected in his weeping, sorrowful eyes. "Do you see? Do you see?" Thunder cracked the night. "Listen! God is angry! He sees us . . . all of us. The stars are His eyes," Jesus said, as he became lost in the crowd.

Father Ulloa had just administered last rites and made the sign of the cross over the body. The man in black was so often taken for granted until the two most important times he was needed most: entering into this life and crossing over into the next.

Wyatt moved away from the crowd to return to the station for his video camera, and bumped into Angeline.

"Is anyone seriously hurt?" ironically asked the fortune teller.

"One dead. Four wounded," Wyatt said.

"My God, what is happening to this city?" the fortune teller asked.

"I don't know," Wyatt said, with a look of dismay on his face.

Angeline moved in closer to the scene. Ruthie the Duck Girl, with her duck under her arm, ran up to Wyatt.

"I heard shots. I got scared but I had to see for myself," Ruthie said.

"Don't go up there, Ruthie. You don't want to see it," Wyatt said.

Wyatt was about to turn right onto St. Peter Street walkway again when he noticed Tune across Decatur Street. He had stopped playing his sax. He was now sitting down, his head tilted back, his shaded eyes possibly opened, possibly closed.

CHAPTER 2

The Avenue

It was just before midnight when Ashley drove her white BMW 325i convertible out of the French Quarter, following the same path as the killers, up Decatur to Canal Street, the wide main street of downtown New Orleans, separating the French Quarter from the Central Business District. While stopped at that red light, she looked to her left at the huge, gray granite U.S. Customs House. Sitting four feet off the ground, inside one of the niches that were carved out of the granite to hold never-received statues of American heroes, was a homeless man soundly sleeping between the earth and sky, above the curious tourists passing by him. Wine from an overturned bottle in his hand flowed to the sidewalk below. She was then drawn within herself to the photo flashes of the crime scene that were continually going off in her head, becoming permanent memories. How could such a brutal killing occur amid so much activity, so much life and in the heart of the city, she thought? Her mind's eye zoomed in like a camera on the murdered young woman. She wasn't dressed like a tourist. She must have been a local. And why a drive-by murder? Those were usually reserved for retaliations by gangs. The risk for capture was too great. She felt nauseous and noticed a slight tremble in her hands, so close was this horrific crime to her. A few more seconds and she would have been at that gate, she thought. Her mind was racing, images flashing of herself bleeding on the sidewalk. She closed her eyes and shook her head as if to loosen the image and send it down the river in her mind. Unknowingly, she had eased off the brake pedal, allowing the car to creep forward until it hit the leg of a homeless man crossing the street in front of her.

"Hey!" he shouted. Ashley opened her eyes and was startled to see the man looking at her, pointing to his leg. He moved toward her door. She quickly rolled up the window and said nothing, remembering one of her father's rules of life: never accept blame for anything. But she had the top down, so he looked over the window and down at her, as she nervously stared straight ahead. "You owe me one," the darkly clad man said, smiling and pointing his finger at her as he walked away.

She saw him moving away out of the corner of her eye and felt relieved. She closed her eyes, and her body relaxed. The driver behind her honked his horn. The light had changed. Ashley opened her eyes, hit the gas pedal and turned up the air conditioning, four clicks. She drove across Canal Street into the Central Business District where Decatur became Magazine Street, changing names, like all the other French Quarter streets, as they crossed Canal. She drove four blocks to Poydras, turned right and drove two blocks, then turned left on St. Charles Avenue. On the next four blocks stood many four-and-five-story buildings, including law firms, small businesses, a cheap hotel, a restaurant or two, and the Greek Revival architecture of Gallier Hall, the city's first City Hall.

She felt nauseous and pulled into a Texaco station on the right at Lee Circle. She thought she would vomit, and opened her door. She sat motionless, and then looked up at the dark bronze statue tinged with green of General Robert E. Lee atop a Doric stone column sixty feet tall. The general stood defiant in full military dress with arms folded, his back toward the north and looking out over the city, the population of which was over sixty-percent African American, as he had stood since the monument's commemoration on a Friday, February 22, 1884, a stormy day in New Orleans that foreshadowed the current storm in the city regarding the statue's removal. She never gave much thought to the statue which was as major a landmark of the city, as was St. Charles Avenue that encircled it. She felt a tightening sensation in her chest and a fire up her throat. Her entire body then involuntarily jerked back in the seat, as if someone pulled her back. She looked around her and saw a dark figure crossing the street.

She quickly started the car and drove halfway around Lee Circle, and then continued up St. Charles Avenue on the other side. She drove past old three- and four-story buildings, some still businesses and some vacant or boarded up to keep out vandals and hide the shame of urban blight over the past thirty years when a city, like an aging beauty queen, sadly says, "Don't look at me in this light. Remember me as I was." Like other cities, only certain areas of New Orleans were in decline. Ten blocks away, the Grande Dame of Avenues was aging beautifully with dignity.

Ashley passed by the old but elegant Pontchartrain Hotel where her wedding reception was held, and where she and friends had finished off many an evening with Cristal toasts. She crossed over Jackson Avenue where the appearance of civility and tranquility was seen and even felt from the grand homes and gardens on both sides of the Avenue, as if signs saying "Do Not Disturb" were posted. Traveling the Avenue was like going back in time. Many houses were one-hundred fifty years old. The architectural styles were varied in this historic Garden District: Georgian Revival, Greek Revival, Italianate, Queen Anne, Romanesque, French Second Empire, Victorian, and many combinations.

She drove up the oak tree-lined Avenue past one beautiful home after another. The twisted branches of the majestic two-hundred-year old oak trees reached up and over the Avenue creating a natural canopy that made this one of the most dreamily elegant avenues in America. She passed a streetcar traveling the neutral ground, separating the two sides. It emitted a low-level hum as it rolled down street tracks, enhancing the hypnotic look and feel of this scenic wonder, this brilliant conspiracy of co-existence made of man and nature.

The Academy of the Sacred Heart High School appeared on her right. The statue of an open-armed, welcoming Jesus stood at the end of the long entrance walkway. This was her welcoming world of wealth, power, privilege and exclusion. This was New Orleans society at its grandest. Few had the means to live on or just off the Avenue, but most New Orleanians would like to. And many were very curious about these particular people photographed having much fun at social gatherings and seen in the society pages of the newspaper every day. Where did they get their money? Was it earned or inherited? Were these wealthy families like any other families? Or were they a special breed, immune to life's difficulties? And were they as arrogant as they were thought to be? After all, from these families came the kings and queens of the carnival krewes each year at Mardi Gras. Perhaps they really thought that to be their station in life. And there was a feeling among some that these people were having all the fun in life while the rest of the city watched, exemplified best at a carnival ball where people outside this realm were seated far and away to watch the evening's activities of men dressed as king and dukes, and women dressed as queen and maids, who paraded about the auditorium dance floor as if it was the court of the palace of Versailles, before the Revolution.

She looked through the many twisted branches of the oak trees for her parents' home to come up on the right. Her mother had always left the light on in Ashley's second floor bedroom, as a guiding light through the trees, even though Ashley did not live there anymore. The trees beautified the Avenue during the day, but made it eerily dark at night. And this night the twisted branches appeared menacing to her, like the hands and fingers of a dark force.

She slowed down and finally came to the entrance. She knew her father would be awake because he was to return late from a business trip. She pointed the remote gate opener at the black wrought iron entrance gate and pressed down. The capital letter "T" was intertwined and encircled in the middle of the gate. It slowly swung open and gave entrance to one of the most glorious homes on the Avenue.

It was a large, white, three-storied house built one-hundred and twenty-five years ago of the Greek Revival style. Twenty steps led up to a porch that stretched the width of the house. The second-floor balcony sat atop the porch and was supported by four Corinthian columns. The balcony's railing was simply designed with elegantly detailed posts every six feet. Two large front windows to the left and right of the doorway were recessed and topped by arches. The front door was mahogany with a large, oval crystal glass running almost its entire length with a crystal fanlight above the door.

Ashley drove up the semi-circular driveway and parked behind her mother's British Racing Green Jaguar XJ6 sedan, which was parked behind her father's white Rolls Royce Corniche convertible, his throne on wheels.

She took her key from her purse and unlocked the door. She entered and immediately felt the cool air surround her body as she stepped onto the black and white checkerboard tile floor in the foyer that extended to the wooden staircase and hallway several feet forward where a long, lustrous hardwood floor continued to the kitchen in the rear. Befittingly, a mahogany-framed print of Jan Vermeer's "The Piano Lesson," having the same checkered floor, hung on the hall wall.

She had stepped through a crystal door into a crystal world. To her right was a large living room also having a hardwood floor, as did all rooms except the kitchen and bathrooms. A huge crystal chandelier and a crystal candelabrum-adorned grand piano dominated the room. Four green and white awning-striped chairs of mahogany and a similarly styled couch were at the opposite end. A Queen Anne mahogany cabinet containing a crystal decanter and long stem crystal glasses stood against one wall directly across from a marble fireplace with crystal figurines of English maidens running along its mantel. Hanging on the wall behind the piano was a large family portrait of Ashley and her parents.

The connecting room was Mr. Tarleton's study with imported English walnut paneling and large table-sized walnut desk, brass lamps, leather furniture, and floor-to- ceiling wall bookshelves full of leather-bound classics, indicating either a man of true intelligence, or one who feigns intelligence, dwells here.

To the left of the foyer through an arched entrance way was the dining room. The walls were forest green, topped with intricately carved cornices that included small, oval acanthus leaves. An eight-foot long Queen Anne mahogany dining table occupied the center of the room. Atop a short chest of drawers of the same style was a sterling silver tray and pitcher. On the wall above was an imposing portrait of the British Cavalry Officer Sinclair George Tarleton standing in full uniform, a forest green military jacket, white vest and white trousers, and black boots, with a foxhound at his feet. Having fought the Colonial Army in the American Revolution, the only thing this commanding lifelike figure lacked to make it convincingly real was speech, though he could almost be heard saying, "Kill all wounded!" a command the officer allegedly shouted after some victories in battle, and the reason for the nickname "Bloody Sin." Ashley's father was of a long line of descendants of Tarleton's only child, an illegitimate daughter, Banina Georgina, who insisted on keeping the Tarleton name for her children. A few of these descendants became cotton and sugar merchants, and land speculators, leading one, Percival George

Tarleton, to the United States, and Louisiana after the Civil War in 1865, when the French Creole Planter Society had collapsed, land was cheap, and desperation among Louisianians was on the rise. Percival was Ashley's father's great-great-grandfather.

Ashley continued down the hall toward the kitchen where she thought she heard her father. "Father?" she inquired.

"Yes. I'm in the kitchen," she heard him say.

Her father was standing at the island counter preparing a cup of Café du Monde coffee when she walked onto the checkerboard floor of the solar white kitchen. She slipped her arm around his waist for the warmth and reassurance she had always felt when close to him, and kissed his cheek, feeling beard stubble against her lips. The scent of his Polo Sport Ralph Lauren cologne mixed with dancing ribbons of smoke from the cigarette in his right hand. "When will you ever stop?" she scolded, as she took the cigarette from him, ran water on the tip, and dropped it in the ashtray next to the red box of Dunhill cigarettes and slender platinum lighter bearing the initials GBT, also visible on his white button-down shirt and belt buckle around his dark gray slacks.

George Banastre Tarleton was a good-looking, square-jawed man six feet tall who spoke with a resonating tone of voice, and, by his very presence, commanded a certain degree of respect. His silver-gray hair and age of sixty-three years belied his physical fitness and youthful enthusiasm for life. The lines on his face were more of character than age, he thought. His eyes at times could be penetrating and his face unnerving to a competitor. He was a shrewd businessman and well-known figure around town, and feared by some. People stayed out of his way. And those who didn't were at risk. He was a destroyer of men, and families, if need be. He employed a legion of spider-lawyers who wove a web around him, his family and his businesses, wherein all foes were attacked, cocooned and slowly eaten alive. Ashley was a poor driver. She had been involved in three accidents in as many years and was at fault in all. But Tarleton's lawyers immobilized the other drivers by dredging up their pasts and entangling them in expensive lawsuits. He cared nothing of right or wrong. Might was right. He was a man of no shame. In the many thousands of years of human evolution and the slow dawning of enlightenment, some dark interior parts of his mind were still lit by primitive fires, illuminating painted scenes of the day's hunt and carnivorous cousins of modern man, eating bloody meat on a stick.

Buying and selling was the Tarleton family tradition. Land was always a desirable acquisition. The land his magnificent house stood on was purchased by Percival Tarleton from a sectioned plantation when New Orleans was dragged into the nineteenth century. He was an opportunist and no friend to the evicted or failed businessman. It was rumored that some of his deals involved shady characters. Some called his home "the house that greed built" but he was admired for his wealth, and the rule of wealth was always: don't ask, don't tell.

"You look tired," he said, placing the pots on the stove.

"You're not going to believe this. I just witnessed a murder," she said.

"Oh no! Where?" he exclaimed.

"Right in front of Jackson Square. It was unreal. I walked across Decatur and was headed that way. A black Mercedes stopped right there at the gate, shots rang out, and a young woman was dead. In a matter of seconds . . . right in the middle of everything . . . with people everywhere. It was incredible! It was something out of a movie," she said.

"My God! Who was she?" he asked.

"I don't know. Police took her I.D. I'll find out tomorrow" she said.

"Tourist?" her father asked.

"She didn't look to be," Ashley said. "But four others were wounded. And I could tell they were."

Mr. Tarleton took a glass from one of the windowed cabinets, and then pressed against the "ICE" lever in the icebox freezer door. When it was halfway full, he pressed against the "WATER" lever until the glass was full, then handed it to Ashley.

"Thank you," she said.

"You know you're very lucky. A few more seconds and you might have been hit," he said, and noticed her hands were trembling slightly. He brought her to a stool at the counter and she sat down.

"I know. I've been thinking about that," she said. He hugged her and kissed the top of her head. "I'm okay."

"When is the killing in this town going to end?" he asked. He poured sugar in his coffee, and then stood opposite her on the other side of the counter. "The mayor has got to go. That is a definite. The city is out of control. He's proven time after time that he simply cannot handle it. We shouldn't have to hear about murders every day. This city wasn't like this when I grew up. What kind of life do we have? How do you find peace of mind with such intrusions every day? A killing in the heart of the city . . . right before the eyes of tourists, sad . . . very sad. Just what a city dependent on tourism needs. Wait until the networks broadcast this all across the country. Just wait. How embarrassing."

"I filmed it. We're an NBC affiliate. Darryl will want to give it to them. I was the only newscaster on the scene," she said, as she drank from her glass, monogramed with the letters GBT.

"You're reporting hard news now?" he said, with a surprised look on his face.

"Yes, as of tonight," she said.

"So, this murder was your first news story?" She nodded her head. "I don't know whether to congratulate you or feel sorry for you."

"Father, it's what I wanted. We talked about it," she said, with a concerned look on her face.

"I know. But in light of what happened tonight and all the other bad news we hear every day, don't you think reporting entertainment news is really the better choice? Stay your distance from all the madness. You won't like what you find. I promise you that. You will not like what you find," he said, with strong conviction.

"I understand that. You were very concerned when I divorced John. You told me to think about it for a long time. And I did. You said he was a good man. But you didn't live with him. I was right from the start. I'm learning. This is the first time I've been on my own . . . and I like it. But sometimes I'm frightened . . . like tonight. But I'll face it . . . and I'll fight it . . . and I'll learn," she stubbornly said. "I've got to learn."

"I just think you're making life more difficult than it is already. Tell that station manager, Darryl, you can't do this," he said.

"I can do this, I think. I've got to do this. It's what I want," she said. He saw in her face a determination that he had never seen before. He thought that maybe turning thirty years old had something to do with it, and that she would return to her normal self when that alarm stopped ringing in her head. But maybe she was more like him than her mother, and that drive was just beginning to kick in. "You pulled a few strings to get me hired there. But now I want my talent to take me further, if, in fact, I have talent."

"Sure, you do. There isn't a Tarleton who isn't gifted in one way or another," he said, pridefully, raising his cup as if to toast her and any Tarleton ghosts that might be hanging around. "But you won't like what you see. I promise you that."

"Ashley? Ashley is that you?" her mother called from her upstairs bedroom.

"Yes, Mother. I'm coming," she called back. "How's she feeling tonight?" she inquired from her father.

"I spoke to her when I returned about an hour ago. She's in better spirits than a couple of days ago. But she's still very weak," he said.

They looked at each other in silence. A feeling of dread ran the entire length of her body as if someone had poured it over her head. Ashley then walked over to her father and they embraced. She exited the kitchen and climbed the stairs. Two paintings of Monet's water lilies and one of Van Gogh's daisies hung on the stairway's taupe and cream-striped wallpaper. To the left at the top of the stairs, was her old bedroom with the light on. To the right and down the hall was her parents' bedroom. She walked the hall as she had for a month now, knowing she would find her mother in bed suffering from some mystery illness the doctors could not accurately diagnose, and knowing she would struggle to fight back her tears.

"Hello, Mother," she smilingly said, as she entered the room. She took her mother's hands in hers, bent over and gave her a kiss on the cheek. "You look well."

"Oh, I do not," her mother said, returning the smile.

"You do, really!" Ashley turned to the round and short black nurse and said, "Hello, Beverly."

"Hi, Miss Ashley," Beverly said.

"How's mother doing?" Ashley asked.

"She's doing just fine. She ate all her dinner tonight, not like last night when she was fussy," Beverly said, laughingly.

"Oh, I was not," Ashley's mother said.

"You were a little fussy when the cook brought you those carrots and greens you didn't want," Beverly said.

"Maybe a little," Ashley's mother said.

"Aha! I told you so," Beverly said, with a smile that lit up the room, while shaking her head. "All right. I'll leave you two to talk. I'll be in the kitchen."

"You can have those vegetables I didn't want," Ashley's mother said.

"No, I don't want them either. I'm going to eat a cake," Beverly said, laughing loudly as she left the room.

"How are you feeling?" Ashley said, still holding her mother's hand.

"Well, today was much better than yesterday. I had a lingering pain in the middle of my back," her mother said.

"Did you tell Beverly?" Ashely asked.

"Yes. She wanted to call an ambulance but I asked her to wait a while. It finally went away," her mother said.

"Mother, don't ever do that again. The moment you feel pain like that, tell Beverly to call for an ambulance and then have her call me and father." Ashley spoke in a gentle but serious tone of voice, as if chastising a child. "I'm serious." She looked down on the ruins of her mother's once beautiful face that had been ravaged by time and illness. She recalled the photo of her mother as queen of a carnival krewe taken at the ball forty-five years ago, and how stunning she looked as she danced with the king. Ashley herself was also a queen once when she was twenty years old. The Avenue had once been her world, as with Ashley now. She had been a member of social clubs and devoted much time to charity organizations when time was endless. But now her world had recoiled to her house, her bed, and her memories. She knew there was a new city awaiting her mother's entrance, a city where royalty and paupers were equal.

"I will," her mother said, appreciating Ashley's concern and love.

"I've got good news. I was promoted to news reporter, the real deal," Ashley said.

"Oh, wonderful! That's what you wanted," her mother said, with a big smile and a mother's genuine joy. "I'm very proud of you."

"Thanks," Ashley said, beaming with pride. "I start tomorrow. Well, actually I started tonight . . ." She was about to relate the horrible incident in the French Quarter, but stopped so she wouldn't upset her mother. "Father didn't like the move up too much."

"Don't worry about him," her mother said. "He's used to keeping people in their places. It's the natural reaction of a very competitive person. Do your job, and do it well. Show everyone that you're not only pretty, but smart, too."

"That's what I want to do. I feel as if I have something to prove," Ashley said.

"I wish I had done the same. But your father wanted me home," her mother said.

"Why?" Ashley asked, curiously.

"I was offered a position as a journalist for the Times-Picayune," her mother said. "But your father said 'no', and I obeyed. That's the way it was done then."

"I never knew that about you," Ashley said, with a surprised look on her face.

"I had some talent there that I never did follow up on. Who knows what would have happened?" her mother wondered. Her eyes drifted upward as she recalled the memory of a young, very beautiful Evelyn Linet Etiene Tarleton. "I was gorgeous in my cobalt blue gabardine suit and white silk blouse. *La femme extraordinaire!*"

"I bet you were," Ashley said.

"I was actually hired and worked three days. But when your father returned from a business trip, he put his foot down and I had to quit," her mother said.

"Oh!" Ashley said, in response to her mother's forlorn look on her face.

"But it was fun and exciting, if only for a few days," her mother said. "So, you keep with it. You be the successful 'Lady Tarleton' of the family." She smiled, as Ashley pulled her closer and kissed her cheek.

"Mother, you were successful . . . in caring for and teaching me. Don't think you were not," Ashley said, holding her mother's hands. "I love you."

"Thank you. *Je t'aime, ma precieuse fille,*" her mother said.

Ashley noticed the fatigue setting in as her mother's eyes began to close. "You rest now, Mother," she said as she kissed her cheek. She stood up and slowly moved away from the bed, but stopped to make sure her mother was still breathing. She felt a nervousness in her stomach as she watched the bedspread over her mother's body gently rise and fall while her mother drifted off to her own personal dreamscape world where cities made of memories are built and razed all in one night, night after night. She picked up a photo framed in silver of her father, mother and herself, taken at her wedding when she was twenty-one. What a bright day that was when her marriage was new and her mother healthy. The excitement shone on her face and the promise of dreams brightened her eyes. There was so much her young mind didn't know at the time.

She walked up the hall and into her childhood bedroom. She surveyed her past by thumbing through books and looking at photos marking her growth from child to adult. She picked up her Madeline doll and smiled, recalling the day her mother gave it to her. She opened the closet door and smelled the faint scent of her mother's perfume on old dresses that still hung there, again recalling when she and her mother picked them out together at D.H. Holmes, Godchaux's, Gus Mayer's and Kreeger's, all of which had closed their doors and become part of the city's history, pushed aside by the cruel, sweeping hands of time. She began to realize the importance of her mother in her life. She had always revered her father, while often taking her mother for granted, until now.

She stepped out onto the small balcony facing the Avenue and took a long breath. She put her hands on the railing and looked out beyond the sidewalk through the oak branches to the Avenue. A rolling hum sounded the passing of a streetcar with several riders. They appeared like phantoms in the night, as she glimpsed their faces through the holes between the branches. She then noticed a dark figure approaching on the sidewalk. He paused in front of the house to light a cigarette, then lingered. Ashley stepped back inside her bedroom, as the man moved on.

She stopped at her mother's door to look in on her before leaving. A few tears rolled down her face. She noticed that it was 1:00 a.m. on the crystal clock near the bed. A wave of anxiety and fear rolled down her brow as she stared at her mother and realized possibly for the first time that she was getting older, too. And, thinking about what the future would eventually bring, she wished she could make time stand still. It seemed that anything was possible but that.

She got a much-needed goodnight hug from her father, got into her car and drove much farther up St. Charles Avenue, passing grand homes on both sides, and Loyola University and Tulane University which stood next to each other on the right. Directly across the Avenue was Audubon Park designed and landscaped by John Olmsted in the late 1800s and named after John James Audubon, the naturalist and artist. Ashley was quite fond of the Park where her father took her on many walks as a child. She especially enjoyed feeding the ducks that swam on a pond deeper in the Park. The pond was surrounded by tall, Spanish moss-laden oak trees that blocked a substantial amount of sunlight, creating a dimly lit, calmingly quiet, primeval-like sanctuary for Ashley and her father, and a special place to which she returned frequently as an adult in person, and in her mind.

When the light turned green at Broadway, Ashley passed St.

Mary's Dominican College on the left and proceeded two blocks to Lowerline Street where she turned left, crossed over the streetcar tracks on the Avenue and continued up Lowerline which was one of the streets of this small uptown neighborhood called "Black Pearl," so named because one cross street was Pearl and in previous years this neighborhood was home to mostly black families, though now it was well over fifty percent white. Lowerline was a narrow, quiet street, lined with tall trees which created a lot of shade over the sidewalks and houses. Ashley's house was midway down the block between the Avenue and Leak Avenue which ran parallel to the River. It was a quaint, pale yellow Victorian cottage much longer than it was wide, with red brick steps leading to a covered porch, and a red brick chimney attached to the right side of the house and extending seven feet above the roof. She bought out her husband's share of the house in the divorce settlement, and she was quite proud to be a homeowner, and proud of her independence.

She pulled into her long, narrow driveway on the right side of her house and parked next to the chimney. She stepped out of her BMW and started toward her front porch but stopped when she heard a noise like footsteps from behind. She opened her cognac-colored leather Christian Dior saddle bag purse and put her hand on a can of mace. She turned around but saw no one. She walked toward the door but heard something or someone down the driveway. She walked to the edge of the porch and looked down its length. She saw nothing. She was shaking slightly. The highest murder count in the city's history flashed across her mind. Would she appear on tomorrow's newscast as a reporter or a statistic?

She quickly opened the door, stepped in, turned on the inside and outside lights, and then locked the door. She parted the French blue curtains and looked outside. The floodlights lit up the brilliant pink Cherry Blossom tree near the sidewalk, but she saw no one. She backed up a few steps until she bumped into the couch. The weight of fear and fatigue made her legs collapse. She fell back onto the blue and white striped French Provincial couch. Her purse fell from her shoulder. Crystal and porcelain angels stared at her from every direction – on the mantel and on the coffee table, surrounding family photos on the *etagere*. The memories of the murder scene and the visit with her mother seemed to occupy her mind simultaneously. She cupped her head in her hands and tears rolled down her face. She felt nauseous. Her heartbeat quickened. She was suddenly startled by her cocker spaniel, Georgia, which jumped onto her lap. Her stomach was twisted while the nausea seemed to climb up her throat. She bent over to rest her head on her knees and noticed a jagged line of blood at the bottom of her left pant leg. She knew it was from the murder scene. She closed her eyes as a replay of the whole incident unfolded in her mind. She was unable to stop it. She became more nauseous as she remembered the woman's face . . . the bullet holes . . . the eyes. She recalled thinking "someone close her eyes." She then remembered that she had closed the woman's eyes. She had blocked it out until now. She had knelt down very quickly and closed the eyes when the French Quarter Jesus was helped to his feet. That is how she got a spot blood on her clothes. She remembered the terror revealed in those eyes. She had seen the face of death. She remembered touching the eyelids, and the pool of blood behind the head . . . and those eyes . . . touching those eyes. She even thought the young woman had whispered something in her ear. But that would have been impossible.

The nausea was overwhelming now. She ran to the bathroom and threw up in the toilet, spotting her linen suit. She wiped her face with a washcloth. She threw up again, and then sat back against the wall with enough force to knock a crystal angel off a shelf, breaking the angel into three pieces. She bent over, head in hands.

"Why?" she whispered.

CHAPTER 3

Roxanne, Brandi, and Dr. Cocaine

"You don't have to bother with those, Rox," Brandi said, noticing her roommate slipping on pantyhose. "Everything comes off for Dr. T, except the heels. He likes toe cleavage."

"What kind of guy is he? Does he freak out or anything like that?" Roxanne asked with a sideways glance, as she slipped off the hose and slipped on her black mini skirt.

"Well, some doctors I've been with were weirdos. What they carry in their little black bags isn't medicine. They like to explore the body. They've got some hang-ups about the body. This guy isn't weird like that but he is strange. But he does give good tips," Brandi said, with a smile and a nod, as she buttoned her white satin blouse.

"Really?" Roxanne asked.

"Yeah. I've already gotten as much as a thousand dollars," Brandi replied.

"Come on!" Roxanne exclaimed, in astonishment.

"Yeah. He's a doctor. He's loaded," Brandi said, checking her look in the mirror and adjusting her red leather skirt around her curvaceous figure. "But this is the last time for the doc."

"Why?" Roxanne asked.

"Because of this," Brandi said, as she showed Roxanne a tiny camcorder lens.

"What's that? A camera?"

"Yeah," Brandi said, reaching for her purse. "The lens goes right under the zipper. I'm doing a little favor for a friend who's involved in politics. The doc's a nice guy but he's no friend of mine. Besides, I'm getting two-thousand dollars for it. I'll give you five-hundred plus your share of the date. I know you've got a little boy to take care of now."

"Thanks. Who's the friend in politics?" Roxanne inquired.

"Let's just say he'll probably be the next mayor of New Orleans," Brandi said, with a wink.

"Oh," Roxanne said, after thinking about it a while.

"It may seem like a mean thing to do. But it's the way of the world, Rox. You're just starting out in life on your own. You'll need money and lots of it. Do what I do. I'm getting out of this business. I want to reacquaint myself with daylight. Take a vacation and lie on my back without a man on top of me for the first time in years. Then maybe open a naughty little dress shop or something," Brandi said, as she took off her turquoise cat eye eyeglasses and put on her contacts after pulling back her long, black hair.

"That sounds good. And you can hire me," Roxanne said, pulling Brandi in front of the mirror. "We'll call it 'Leather and Lace'."

"Done," Brandi said, as they both laughed. "Alright. Let's hit it. Oh, don't tell Lou at the agency about this. We get all the money tonight. He'd break our legs if he found out."

"Okay. What does the doctor want us to do?" Roxanne asked, eagerly awaiting an answer.

"It's a surprise. You'll see." Brandi turned off the lights and closed the door to her apartment. The sharp sounds of their stiletto heels announced the coming of Brandi and Roxanne from the second floor of the building to Brandi's gray Nissan Stanza. They threw their purses on the back seat. Brandi reached under her seat, pushed aside a Ruger .38 handgun, and withdrew a small clear bag of pot. She rolled a joint and put it in her mouth. "Let's rock and roll," Brandi said, as she lit it and took a long drag, and then passed it to Roxanne. She slipped Stevie Nick's *Bella Donna* cassette into the player. The relentless jackhammer riff of the electric guitar from "The Edge of Seventeen" song echoed loudly in the car from four speakers. Brandi rolled back the sunroof. Sound and smoke shot into space like a bomb blast, as they sang along.

They left their suburban Metairie apartment on Lake Avenue and headed toward uptown New Orleans. They drove the interstate, rocking out and waving to people all the way. They exited I-10 at St. Charles Avenue, the second to last exit before crossing the River. They drove the Avenue for fifteen blocks, turned left on Third Street, and stopped in front of a white two-story, renovated wooden house with gas lanterns on either side of the door and two tall floor-to-ceiling windows facing the street. It was one-hundred and fifty years old. It was not as large and impressive as some of the mansions on and around the Avenue, but it was still a much-desired house and one that would make any uptowner very proud. Two or three blocks of houses off the avenue were similarly renovated, and owned by white professionals. The houses beyond these blocks to the River were largely owned or rented by blacks for whom the past was the present and the future with no plans for renovation any time soon. A new, red Porsche 911 Carrera Cabriolet was in the driveway, license plate DOCS911.

Brandi blew the doctor a kiss when she saw him looking at her through the window. Balding and overweight, Doctor Terrance Leonidas Polk Whitfield opened the door slowly and gave each a kiss as they entered, and then tied his navy blue silk robe as he felt the warm night air hug his bare legs, like a cat trying to get inside.

"Hello, Brandi. You're looking lovely as always," he said, as he moved closer to Roxanne. "And who might you be?" he inquired. "My guess is Aphrodite herself."

"Who?" Roxanne said, looking puzzled.

"Terry, this is Roxanne," Brandi said.

"Hi," Roxanne said, somewhat nervously.

"Hello, Roxanne. It's very nice to meet you," he said, kissing her hand. His eyes widened and he felt a surge in his groin when he spotted the high-heeled shoes showing toe cleavage he liked so well. "Love those shoes," he said, thinking how he would love to devour the pretty young woman.

"Oh, I know that. I remembered. And I brought Roxanne along because last time you told me to bring a friend," Brandi said.

"Oh, absolutely. Step right this way, my fair young maidens," he instructed.

The girls wiped away a few beads of sweat from their foreheads, as they moved from the foyer into a large, cool living room with a fireplace and mantel separating the room from the dining room. Beautiful hardwood floors and tall ceilings made each room grand. Hanging on the walls were paintings by American expressionist artists, Pollock, de Kooning, Rothko, and Kline. The music of Johann Strauss's "The Blue Danube" waltzed through the air. "Have a seat, ladies," the doctor said, as he sat down on his taupe and cream awning-striped couch, again exposing himself. Roxanne dropped her purse on the floor near the coffee table. Brandi strategically placed hers on one of the two taupe-colored Queen Anne chairs opposite the couch, making sure the camera inside was aimed straight at the doctor. They then both sat down on either side of him. "Ladies, I would like to offer each of you a snifter of the finest cognac money can buy." He picked up the Baccarat crystal decanter and poured the cognac into two glasses, and then his own. "And at three-thousand dollars a bottle, it's quite a sniff. Ladies, I give you royalty, Louis XIII de Remy Martin."

"Wow!" Roxanne said.

"Indeed!" the doctor added. "Savor the bouquet, ladies. Let it breathe, like this . . ." The doctor slowly swirled the cognac in his glass. Brandi did so successfully. However, Roxanne put too much force behind it and some cognac flew out to the floor.

"No. No. Slow swirl, not a whirlwind."

"I'm sorry," she said.

"Not so hard," Brandi said, laughingly.

Roxanne followed Brandi's lead.

"Yes, that's it," the doctor said. "Now sniff and taste." All three slowly sipped the cognac. "Now swallow." He gently placed his hand on Roxanne's throat. "That's it."

"Oh!" Roxanne said as she quickly spit out her drink. "I'm sorry, but that's awful. My mouth is on fire! Water!"

The doctor pointed beyond the fireplace and dining room to the kitchen.

"Sorry, Terry. She's young," Brandi said, apologetically.

"This cognac is older than she is. But maybe she'll like this," he said. He uncovered a sterling silver tray on the coffee table with a pyramid of cocaine on it. "Roxanne, come see what the doctor has prescribed for you."

"Oh, Rox! It's your favorite," Brandi said, in a raised voice.

"What's that?" Roxanne said returning to the room. "Oh! Now this I like," she said, sitting down.

"You're not going to sneeze, are you?" the doctor inquired, as they all laughed. "This is the finest coke Peru has to offer." He handed Roxanne a sterling silver cocaine spoon. "Snort away, my fair young maiden," he said, as he caressed her thigh with his hand. Roxanne took a spoonful and snorted it, and then took another for the other nostril.

"Oh, that hit the spot!" Roxanne declared, as her eyes rolled back.

"Those Indians down there can sure pick those leaves. Poor savages. If they could only see us now," he said, with a Cheshire cat smile, as he passed the spoon to Brandi. He wrapped his arm around Brandi's waist and pulled her closer. "Oh, baby."

"I can't hold the spoon steady," Brandi complained.

"Give me a kiss," the doctor demanded.

Brandi kissed his cheek and snorted two spoonsful. "Oh yeah! That is good. It's got to be pure coke."

"Or close to it," the doctor added, as he lifted another napkin off another silver tray. On it was two-thousand dollars in hundreds. "Okay, ladies, do your stuff!"

Brandi put the money in her purse. "Aren't you going to do some?" she asked the doctor, as she motioned for Roxanne to take off her clothes as she was doing.

"Right now!" he said, as he dug in the pile with his spoon. "You can leave your shoes on."

"What do we do? Do we have sex?" Roxanne whispered.

"Maybe. Just follow my lead," Brandi instructed.

The giggling, naked girls ran around the room three times, and then sat next to the doctor. They fed him cocaine and cognac, and ran their hands under his robe while kissing him.

"Yeah! More!" he said.

"Yes, Big Daddy!" Brandi said, in a southern accent.

"Yes, Big Daddy!" Roxanne quickly added, looking at Brandi and puzzled by all of this.

The girls got up and ran around some more. This time, however, the doctor chased them after slipping out of his robe.

"Oh, Big Daddy!" the girls shouted.

Brandi led him back to the couch and reclined, spreading her legs, as the doctor jumped on top of her.

"Ow! You're crushing me!" Brandi said.

"The doctor is in!" he exclaimed.

Roxanne stood in the way of the camera, so Brandi motioned for her to move away and give the doctor cocaine. Roxanne, holding a spoonful of cocaine, then mounted the doctor. Before he had a chance to snort it, they all fell off the couch, while the camera recorded everything, including date and time.

CHAPTER 4

Look Away, Jesus

The twenty-year-old, brown Panasonic clock-radio's alarm sounded at 9:45 a.m. when the white plastic number "5" replaced the "4" with a quick hammer-of-time jolt. Tune opened his eyes as he lay in bed and listened to David Lerner on the radio.

David Lerner was the newest shock jock on the airwaves in New Orleans. He was a New Yorker who left his native city to begin his career in smaller, inferior stations, hoping one day to return to NYC and land a job in big-time broadcasting.

Lerner cleared his throat and said, "All right. Before we get to the serious matters of murder and mayhem plaguing the little city of New Orleans, called 'Crescent City' or the 'City That Care Forgot' – whatever that means – or as it's currently known across this great country of ours, 'The Murder Capital.' But before we get to that, I want to throw out a question to all of you who couldn't care less about what's happening in and to your city . . . the question is: what was the name of Race Bannon's old flame in the 1960s' Jonny Quest cartoon? You remember, don't you? She was sometimes a little more butch than Race himself. And while we're on that subject, what was Hadji all about? Was he a playmate for Jonny, or a plaything for Dr. Quest? I don't know. Anyway, the ex-girlfriend was seldom seen and went by a single short name. Be the first caller with the correct answer, and I'll give you a big wet kiss. We'll be right back after these messages."

The phone rang and activated the answering machine. Tune's voice was rough and deep. "Leave a message." A beep sounded, and then a girl's voice.

"Hi, Daddy. You said you'd come see me. Please call me. I'm worried about you. I just wanted to wish you a happy birthday. I hope I can see you tonight to give you my present. And I'm baking a cake for you. Bye."

There was no reaction on his face. An old black Emerson oscillating fan on the dresser continued to blow cool air over his face. He sat up on the edge of the bed, pressing his feet on the hardwood floor which still retained some of the night's dampness. He raised his hands and stared at the cracks and lines on his palms, rivers of time leading to the edge of existence. He looked closely at his rough, fifty-four-year-old, dark-as-mud brown skin on his hands and arms, noticing the bumps, bruises and two bullet hole scars near a dark blue tattoo of a cross. On the wall opposite him was a 3D drawing of Jesus weeping under a crown of thorns.

Naked, he rose and walked down the hall of his narrow 150-year-old, Creole Cottage. One third the way down the hall, he stepped right and into the small bathroom. He checked his face in the medicine chest mirror while he urinated. The telephone rang. He turned his ear to the door.

A man's voice said, "A photo finish last night, Tune. More later, my brother."

Tune walked up the hallway to his front door, passing the kitchen, a smaller bedroom and his living room. None of the rooms had much furniture, and what was there was old, as if from an old motel. He grabbed the crystal-like handle and applied force to open the white door, revealing an iron-braced screen door. He unlocked, then twisted the loose doorknob, and stepped onto short granite steps. This was Tune's home in the neighborhood known as "The Treme" situated just across Rampart Street at the rear of the French Quarter.

He picked up the morning's newspaper. Several children, cooling themselves by watering each other with a hose, looked up at their naked neighbor. They giggled, then pointed the hose toward Tune. Though some water reached his leg, he didn't notice. He was too busy reading the front page which included a photo of last night's shooting victim at Jackson Square.

He stepped inside, walked down the hall, and stopped by the bathroom door. He looked at himself in the mirror. He rubbed his fingers over tattooed flames that ran up his neck. A fierce pain raced up his neck and grabbed the back of his head like a claw. As he stepped back into the bedroom, he threw the paper against the wall. He upped the speed on the fan and sat down on the bed, staring at his saxophone in the corner and listening to the radio.

"All right," Lerner said, "the answer to our trivia question is Jade, Race Bannon's ex-girlfriend. No one got it right, you morons. She's only a cartoon character but I'd do her. How about you? Listen, you all . . . how's that for a little southern accent? Today's business is last night's shooting. Or should I say shootings because several people were murdered last night, making the year's total so far to be over 400, an insanely high number, considering the number of people who live within Orleans parish. Can you believe it? An all-time record for the city. Congratulations. Let me hear from you, New Orleans. You're dying. We'll take a break. More in a minute."

Tune turned Jesus' bleeding face to the wall, and then fell back on the bed and closed his eyes. A stack of one-hundred-dollar bills on the dresser suddenly blew up from a burst of air from the fan. The bills silently sailed through the air and landed all about Tune.

CHAPTER 5

A Nazi by Any Other Name

"Hurry! Hurry! Hurry! It's ten o'clock," Wyatt said to Ashley, as she pulled into the parking garage of TV-3.

"I know! I overslept," Ashley said, stepping out of her BMW and into the TV-3 Chevrolet sedan.

"How could you oversleep today? Conright's probably already there," he said.

"I had a bad night," Ashley said, pulling her brush out of her Dior handbag. "Don't tell me you slept soundly after last night."

"You're right. Okay, let's hit it," he said.

Wyatt quickly backed out of the garage onto Chartres Street, drove down one block to St. Peter and turned left, just missing a couple of tourists.

"Why are you going this way? You should've taken Decatur to Canal or Poydras," Ashley said disapprovingly, removing her tortoise shell Ray-Ban Wayfarer sunglasses and combing her hair in the visor mirror.

"Too much traffic. We'll shoot up Basin to Tulane," Wyatt said, as he came to a stop at Royal Street, thinking this girl's got attitude problems first thing in the morning as well as late at night. He quickly looked to his right, and then crossed.

"Crossing Bourbon takes time . . . all those tourists," Ashley admonished.

"Not the way I do it. If I have to take down a few tourists, I will," he said, laughingly.

"That's not funny anymore, Walter," looking for tourists ahead.

"It's Wyatt. I'm joking, of course."

"Stop! Watch those people," Ashley said, gripping the door handle and touching the dashboard.

Cars were allowed on Bourbon Street during the day, making the sidewalks crowded with tourists. But crossing Bourbon in a car at any time of day or night was difficult and slow-going. Wyatt rolled to a stop at Bourbon and St. Peter.

"I see them." Wyatt blew his horn a few times and began rolling slowly again. Tourists began touching the car and telling him to stop. He took a paper towel from under his seat and waved it out the window. "I've got a sick girl here. Can we get through?"

"Don't say that!" Ashley exclaimed.

"I've got to get her to the hospital. She needs an emergency attitudinal removal. Can we get through?" Wyatt shouted.

"That's not funny. We don't know each other well enough to make jokes like that. I don't appreciate it," she said.

"Who's joking?" he softly said. Wyatt then noticed Ruthie the Duck Girl in his left side view mirror, roller skating up St. Peter Street with her duck under her arm and a can of beer in one hand. He stuck his head out of the window. "Hey, Ruthie, help me out here."

"Okay, baby." Ruthie put her duck on the sidewalk and barreled into the crowd. "Hey, watch where you're stepping. This is a duck crossing here!" Ruthie shouted.

Ashley put on her sunglasses and tried to hide her face. She had always thought Ruthie was mentally ill.

The crowd stopped to witness this strange woman who looked a little like Popeye the Sailor, dressed in western wear and red heart-shaped sunglasses, stopping traffic to walk her duck on a leash across Bourbon Street. One tourist shouted "Mardi Gras!" Ruthie put out her hand and stopped a taxi. Wyatt crept alongside her as she parted the crowd, Moses-style, on the other side of the street.

"Thanks, Ruthie. I owe you one," Wyatt said, smiling and pointing to the beer.

"Yeah. 16-ounce!" said Ruthie, in a raspy voice.

"Okay." After he cleared the other corner, Wyatt turned to Ashley and said, "Only in the Quarter, Leslie, would you ever see that."

"It's Ashley." Wyatt smiled and turned on the radio to David Lerner's show. "Must we listen to him? He's so vile. And roll up your window. I'm sweating."

"Yes, we must," he said, rolling up his window and turning up the air conditioner. "He's controversial. He sparks debate about the city. That's what I like."

Wyatt stopped at the next street corner, Dauphine Street, and then drove quickly across, as he turned up the volume.

"So, you think the National Guard is not needed on the streets of New Orleans. Is that correct?" Lerner said, in his deep, perfect radio voice.

"That's right," the caller said.

"The city has the highest murder rate per capita in this country right now, and you say the New Orleans Police Department can handle everything themselves," Lerner said, disbelievingly.

"The NOPD is doing everything it can . . ." the caller quickly added.

"Obviously, that's not enough!" Lerner shot back. "So, allowing over four-hundred murders this year in a city of under half a million people, you call 'doing everything it can' . . . you're an idiot! What kind of moron would defend a police department with a record like that and with accusations that some officers are corrupt and that some have actually killed innocent citizens. I'm from New York City where there's a lot of crime, too, and where you grow up quick because you have to . . . and even I am afraid to walk the streets of this city."

"Well, go back to New York," the caller angrily said.

"Hey, my friend, my time will come. But you have to live here all your life. I would think you'd be more concerned about your own safety and that of your children," he said, forcefully. "Jesus!"

"I am concerned," the caller said.

"Then admit the NOPD can't do the job, and let's bring in the

Guard. I'm done with you. Next caller. You're on," Lerner said.

"Yeah, David . . . . If the Guard is on the streets, no one in their right mind is going to visit the city. We need the tourists' dollars," the caller said.

"But you need a safe city to get them. Tourism has already been affected, my friend. Ask the hotels. The media picked up the story and is spreading it all across the country. New Orleans is a joke," Lerner said, with disgust in his voice.

"That's why we need Conright in office to get back our self-respect. Mayor Chenier has got to go. Absolutely," the caller said.

"Conright's a racist and a fascist. They've got photographs of him wearing a Nazi uniform. Is this all this town has to choose from – a weak incumbent and a Nazi?" Lerner said, with mock outrage and laughter.

Wyatt pointed to the radio and said, "Remember to ask Conright about that."

"I was thinking the same thing," Ashley said.

"You see, Ashley, we do think alike," Wyatt said, with a half-smile. You must be joking, she thought. "Listen," he said, pointing to the radio again.

"If anyone has a photo of Conright in a Nazi uniform, I'll give you one-thousand dollars for it," Lerner said. "You got that? One thousand. I don't want to see this creep get into office. First thing he'll do is round up all the Jews – and that means me!"

"Hey, Lerner, there are no photos like that because it never happened. They're just trying to discredit him," the caller said.

"Discredit? This guy celebrates Hitler's birthday, for crying out loud! It's a known fact. What's your name?" Lerner asked.

"Frank."

"Your last name," Lerner said.

"I don't have to tell you my last name," the caller said.

"What do you have to hide?" Lerner asked.

"David . . ." the radio producer interrupted.

"Yeah, John . . .," Lerner said.

"His name is Goebbels. Callers have to tell me before we let them speak on air," the producer said, beginning to laugh.

"Oh, my God! We've got the son of Nazi propagandist, Josef Goebbels, on our show. Hey, if anyone has a photo of Fritz Goebbels in a Nazi uniform, I'll give you two-thousand dollars," Lerner shouted, screaming with laughter.

Wyatt turned down the volume on the radio after reaching Rampart Street, the last street before leaving the Quarter.

"So, what were you planning on asking Conright?" he said, looking left for oncoming cars.

"I'm going to listen and take notes," Ashley said.

"Pin him down on something, like the Nazi photo or racism. I'll shoot you asking the question, and then get a good closeup reaction shot of Conright," Wyatt said, slipping in a quick look at Ashley's shapely legs.

"I see. All right," Ashley agreed.

"The whole purpose of his press conference is just to make the evening news while bad-mouthing Chenier," Wyatt said. "But you've got to light a fire under him to get him to slip up and expose himself for the liar he is. That's where the real news will be. The press conference itself is of little importance."

"Do you think he's really a closet Nazi?" Ashley asked.

"I don't know. But I'd like to look in that closet for a photo or two," Wyatt said.

"Yes, that would be helpful. Wouldn't it?" Ashely added.

Wyatt looked at her, wondering what she really meant by that.

As Wyatt turned right from Rampart onto Basin Street by the Municipal Auditorium, Ashley locked her door. This was a poor part of the downtown area. Ashley was an uptown girl and had no use for this part of town, except during the Mardi Gras season when she was chauffeured to the auditorium at night to participate in Carnival Balls.

She looked right and noticed the St. Louis Cemetery No. 1 on the corner where the dead are buried above ground, sometimes on top of each other in crypts, as in all cemeteries in the city. The roofs of miniature mausoleums and crypts crowned with crosses could be seen above the white wall surrounding the cemetery, giving it the look of a "city of the dead," wherein legendary voodoo priestess Marie Laveau and civil rights champion Homer Plessy, and other notables, were interred. Wyatt slowed down to allow five black children to run across the street and into the Iberville Housing Project in the next block. One child waved to Ashley, as she watched them run down the worn gray-dirt paths separating the many two and three-story, red brick buildings. Their clothing appeared old and dirty, like the buildings themselves. But the children's laughter transcended the poverty around them. Around the corner of one of the brick buildings came five young black men dressed in gangster clothing – low-riding baggy jeans exposing boxer shorts, open shirts, large gold chains, sunglasses and bandanas around their heads. Ashley felt a chill run down her spine.

Ashley had once heard of Storyville, the infamous red-light district of 100 years ago. She didn't know it once stood on the site of this housing project on Basin Street, purportedly the birthplace of jazz. Many young black musicians sounded their trumpets with a rat-a-tat jazz in the many houses of ill repute in the Tenderloin district, four blocks in length and five blocks deep ending near St. Louis Cemetery No. 2, at Claiborne Avenue. Names like Kid Ory and King Oliver hit their marks in smaller houses and cabarets, whereas Jelly Roll Morton, a "professor" piano player, could work in the larger more ornate houses that served the wealthy and "civilized," like the legendary Mahogany Hall. Owned and operated by Lulu White who offered the "sporting" man beautiful "octoroon" girls to deliver the pleasures of the flesh. These girls had one-eighth black blood with fair skin, some of whom could have passed for white or "crossed over." Mahogany Hall and a few other houses offered men a taste of this much desired forbidden fruit. The patrons could be seen with these girls in the houses, but not on the street.

The days in this forbidden city of sin were hot and languid; the girls fanning themselves, playing with their children and pets, thinking fondly of loved ones in photos on the mantel, or sitting in the doorways and windows mimicking the act of fellatio on their fingers to entice passers-by, and waiting for the nightfall of irony that the seed of so many men would go unused, quickly washed away by women who thought not of time and love as eternal, but time as money and love as non-negotiable. This area, once rich in pleasure and cash, now stood bankrupt in both. Storyville had been razed to the ground in the 1930s and the men who frequented it had long since turned to dust. But the two cemeteries that bordered it still stood as memorials to time and futility.

"Hold on. I'm going to blow this light," Wyatt warned.

Tension and fear gripped Ashley's entire body. Her heartbeat quickened and her eyes widened as Wyatt sped through the red light at Canal Street and Basin.

"Watch those black people! They're all over down here!" Ashley pointed to the dozen or so black men and women beginning to cross at the corner, next to the blonde brick Krauss department store building which had recently closed its doors forever after 100 years, another casualty of the economic decline in the downtown area.

Wyatt crossed Canal Street onto Elks Place past a bus stop where ten blacks stood waiting for the only transport they could afford. One person stepped off the curb, causing Wyatt to swerve left. Ashley was thrown over to his side. Wyatt reached out to help her and unintentionally put his hand on her knee. They both glanced down, then at each other with raised eyebrows. Wyatt quickly removed his hand and Ashley slid back to her side.

"Slow down!" Ashley commanded.

"I can't slow down. I was born to rock," Wyatt jokingly said, although knowing she didn't have much of a sense of humor. He figured her type usually laughed at people and not with them.

City Hall and Civil District Court lay straight ahead. But Wyatt and Ashley were headed for Criminal District Court where Conright had scheduled his press conference; so Wyatt turned right onto Tulane Avenue which put them right in the midst of Tulane University Hospital, Louisiana State University Medical Center and the fifty-five year old Charity Hospital, providing medical care to the city's poor.

Wyatt tried to beat the light at LaSalle Street but had to stop short due to pedestrian traffic. He looked to his right and noticed a homeless woman under a covered bus stop who was stooped over her shopping cart containing her life's work. He looked to his left at Charity Hospital where a black woman was lying down on the sidewalk near the front steps. Her pose was not that of someone writhing in pain, but that of someone relaxing. She was lying on her side with her right arm bent, and resting her head on her hand. She said to everyone passing by, "Hello, Doctor." He started across LaSalle on the green light not hearing the siren of an approaching ambulance.

"Stop!" Ashley shouted.

Wyatt hit the brake just as the ambulance sped across Tulane, headed to the rear entrance to Charity marked EMERGENCY. He glimpsed the ambulance's interior and saw a paramedic administering care to someone, as another person inside wiped away tears.

"Straight from the front lines," Wyatt said, shaking his head.

"No doubt," Ashley added.

"Hold on!"

Wyatt hit the accelerator and raced up Tulane past old motels, small storefronts with trash bags piled high outside, and a boarded-up Tastee Donuts. Seeing that sign reminded Wyatt of the Hubig apple pie slice he bought on the way to the studio. He reached down into a brown bag and pulled out the pie in its opaque pouch with the large round chef on it.

"Oh, please don't eat now. Put that thing away and watch what you're doing!" Ashley said these words in disgust as she watched him bite into the pie. She looked him over – tee shirt, jeans, boots – and shook her head thinking him foolish. No manners, she thought. None at all. And who wears boots in the heat? Who wears boots at all?

"It's too good to throw away. I'll wolf it down. I'm starving," he said. He swerved to the right to miss a car turning left at a NO LEFT turn sign. Ashley squealed. "There he is," Wyatt shouted as he neared the intersection of Tulane and Broad.

"Where?" she asked.

"Just getting out of his car," he said. "I can see his big white head. Looks like a white BMW. You two have the same tastes."

Ashley searched the large crowd of reporters and curious onlookers of whites and even more blacks gathered in front of the Criminal District Court to see and hear Keiffer Conright, the Republican candidate in the mayoral runoff election with the incumbent mayor, Xavier Chenier.

"Yes. I see him. Where can we park?" Ashley inquired, looking around her. Noticing black people on every corner, she became a bit anxious.

Cars and news vans encircled the courthouse on one corner. Wyatt pulled into the E-Z Serve convenience store on the opposite corner. A Popeye's Fried Chicken and a McDonald's occupied the other two corners. Beyond and well above the McDonald's was a large billboard twenty feet across that read: THOU SHALT NOT KILL, in bold black letters. Paid for by the Reverend Josiah Ishmael Johnson and his congregation at the First Mount Zion Baptist Church, it faced this well-traveled intersection and the Orleans Parish Prison behind the courthouse. And if the Lord couldn't set a prisoner free of his chains, then maybe one of many bail bondsmen whose offices fronted that intersection could. On the neutral ground between McDonald's and the courthouse stood a large sign on which was printed "Prisoner Crossing," placed there as a joke due to recent prison escapes and to those prisoners set free because of erroneous paperwork.

Wyatt jumped out of the car and grabbed his camera on the back seat. Ashley, right behind him, said, "Watch that garbage!" Wyatt hopped over a line of ten large E-Z Serve trash bags on the curb, as they ran across Tulane Avenue to the steps at the courthouse – a dirty sandstone four-story, castle-like fortress of justice with fifty steps, two big urns and twelve Corinthian columns marking its entrance, and four tower-like corners, as if designed for sentries to search the horizon and sound the alarm at first sight of the enemy's army. Carved in the granite above the columns was a promise to the public of: 'No Impartial Administration of Justice, the Foundation of Liberty.'

It appeared the court was under attack due to all the people in the street, on the sidewalk, and gathered around the podium midway up the steps. Ashley and Wyatt inched their way through the back of the crowd, past a Japanese news crew, and then became wedged between a German news team and a short, round elderly woman who was trying to glimpse Conright by looking through any available opening.

Conright's PR spokesman, Alphonse St. Amant, approached the podium as Conright shook hands in the crowd. A bodyguard accompanied Conright while two others watched the crowd.

"Is it hot enough for you?" St. Amant said, wiping his face with a handkerchief. "Well it's about to get a lot hotter. We're turning up the heat on Mayor Xavier Chenier and his rat pack. We'll chase them from City Hall and down to the River. We're tired of a rat-infested city. We want to be proud of our city again. We want our city back! And the only man who has the courage to lead the crusade . . . the next mayor of New Orleans . . . ladies and gentlemen . . . I give you . . . Keiffer Conright!"

Scattered applause was heard from the crowd as Keiffer Conright stepped up to the microphone. Conright had recently been called the "Aryan poster boy" because of his tall, Nordic appearance and his supposed ties to neo-Nazis. Another detractor said, "He would have made Hitler proud." Someone else said, "He's a white man's white man." A gust of hot air tousled his short blonde-brown hair, and lifted his red paisley tie over the shoulder of his light blue seersucker suit. He had a youthful, slender face that belied his fifty-four years, though the tracks of time had left their marks around his eyes and neck. He had a wide mouth, pearl-white teeth and a killer smile. Everyone had an opinion about Conright. He was a devil to some and a redeemer to others. But everyone knew he was slick.

"This city is in a . . . ." Conright began.

Conright was stopped short in his opening sentence by a black passenger in a slow-moving car who yelled, "Hey, Conright, you suck! You racist bastard!" Everyone turned around to look at the car. The Japanese cameraman struck Ashley in the back of her head with his camera. The passenger flipped Conright the bird, as some people laughed. One of Conright's bodyguards wrote down the license plate number. Suddenly, the car came to a screeching halt as it rounded the intersection to avoid a police car heading up the wrong side of Broad. The cop turned on his siren, turned right and took off down Tulane Avenue.

Conright, trying to overcome this embarrassment and regain control of the moment, said, "People! People of New Orleans . . ." Once again, all eyes were on him. "This city is in a state of emergency! Sirens are sounding off every few seconds, citizens are in distress . . . and the police can't even stay on the right side of the road or on the right side of the law to answer those calls of emergency!" Applause was heard. "Ladies and gentlemen, there is an evil loose in our city that stalks every one of us. Terror has grown like a cancer in our hearts and minds . . . and it is destroying us all. We must watch our blacks . . . I mean our backs, everywhere we go now. Peace of mind no longer exists here. Crime is killing us – literally. We're not through all of September yet, and over 400 murders have already occurred this year. This is outrageous. A young woman lies in the morgue beneath this courthouse. She was gunned down last night in Jackson Square and in full view of hundreds of people," he said, pointing to the courthouse and in the general direction of a three-prisoner work detail assigned to picking up trash. They wore orange jumpsuits with "OPP" on the backs, for Orleans Parish Prison.

One black prisoner muttered, "Don't point at me. I didn't murder anyone. I been framed for drugs, you fucking white Ku Klux Klan motherfucker. But I wouldn't mind shooting you."

"This insanity has got to stop! We've got the highest murder rate in the country. New Orleans is at the bottom of every list but at the top of the murder per capita list. This is outrageous! This is embarrassing! This is unacceptable!" Conright shouted. He was gaining momentum. He could feel it. But he felt anxious about questions concerning racism and his past that he knew would be asked. "We don't know what will happen from one day to the next in this town. The mayor is incompetent. He's given major city contracts to his cronies who are equally as incompetent. They're bleeding the city dry. Your city! The city is filthy. He can't even get the garbage picked up. How will he ever stop the crime? Hell, police officers themselves are even being arrested. Ours is the most corrupt police department in the country. Why do you think all these reporters from around the world are in old New Orleans?"

"Because you're a Nazi!" someone in the crowd shouted.

Conright's bodyguards scanned the crowd with their death-ray-vision eyes for the subversive practitioner of free speech. Conright wiped the sweat off his forehead and kept going.

"It's because our beloved Crescent City has become a joke," Conright said. "And all the news shows are coming to see for themselves – including *60 Minutes*. When that show investigates a person or a city . . . well, then, folks, it's all over but the crying."

Ashley looked around and noticed most reporters were white; although, there were some black and Asian reporters, too. She then looked behind her and noticed that the crowd had grown to include about twenty-five blacks who happened to be on the street. They wanted to see the "white devil" up close. Ashley felt her skin tingle, her body tighten and a nervousness invade her bloodstream, as if injected. "And we've done a lot of crying here, haven't we?" Conright continued. "Even God cries tears of sorrow on New Orleans. The only thing you can count on in this city is that someone will die a violent death every day. Now that's a hell of a statement to make . . . but you know it's true. I ask the good people of New Orleans: do you feel safe?"

"No!" a few people shouted.

"No! Exactly. We can't live like this any longer," Conright said emphatically, with fist held high, clenching his handkerchief next to his red face dripping with sweat. "We want our city back! The city we grew up in . . . the city we love. It's a war zone now. It's not a free city. It's a city under siege! I'm the only candidate, the only real man to do something about it! The mayor even wants to take down our beloved Confederate monuments, especially General Robert E. Lee at Lee Circle, an iconic focal point in our great city for the last one-hundred and ten years. He can't stop crime, he can't stop the murders; he can't stop the drugs; he can't pave the streets; he can't improve city services; he can't break the garbage strike, he can't stop the city from flooding; but he wants to take down monuments for his own political gain."

"That's right. Take 'em down," another black activist shouted.

"I will not let the mayor deface our city, erase history and disrespect my American heritage," Conright declared.

"Fuck your heritage! What about my heritage and my people's

suffering under white oppression?" a middle-aged black man in a dashiki angrily said.

"I am asking all New Orleanians to help me fight the new oppression of me and people like me, and the conspiring in our own city government to erase white history in our city. The school board has already changed the names of numerous public schools from white men of history to black men of no significance. They even changed the name of George Washington Grammar School. George Washington, the Father of our Country! This is outrageous," Conright insisted.

"He was a slaveholder!" a woman cried out.

"I will not let my American heritage be erased. I stand for truth, justice and the American way," Conright declared.

"Who are you? Superman?" someone shouted.

"No. I am a concerned citizen," Conright said. "I am concerned that the predominantly black City Council will not care about the white people's desires to keep the monuments, forgetting that most property owners are white and pay heavily in taxes. I am concerned that these people will not be represented and that their voices will be heard but not listened to. The mayor, who I call Boss Chenier, will cause an irrevocable division of the races. I am willing to compromise but Boss Chenier and the City Council are not. We refer to our city as historic New Orleans, rich in history, traditions and having a unique culture. We must not remove our history. If we remove four confederate monuments, where does the process end? Next, they will want to remove our beloved Andrew Jackson monument in Jackson Square, and others and street names. I propose adding monuments on Howard Avenue leading to Lee Circle and the Confederate War Museum around the corner from Lee, thereby creating another point of interest for tourists and New Orleanians alike. Let us not forget the great philosopher George Santayana who said, 'Those who cannot remember the past are condemned to repeat it.' No truer words were ever spoken."

"Except these words: you're a racist asshole!" a young black man said.

"That's the problem," Conright said. "If a white person disagrees with a black, he's considered a racist. There are two sides to every story and my side will be heard. So, do you want Mayor 'X' or the real thing, a real mayor and man of the people? I want to put those people responsible for the crime in this city behind bars for good.

"Yeah! The blacks!" a white person in the crowd shouted.

Heads began turning left and right to spot the man who spoke that remark.

Wyatt leaned in to Ashley and said, "Who is the village idiot who said that?"

"I don't know," she replied, continuing to look to her left and right.

"I heard that, you mother fucker! Fuck you, whoever you are!" a young black man shouted.

"That's right! Fuck you and all you Conright supporters! Racists! All of you!" a black woman screamed.

"He ain't gonna win. You can forget that! You ain't gettin' this city back! We slaved for this city. It's ours!" said Rory Toutant, a local black activist.

"Please, my friends, listen," Conright pleaded.

"We ain't your friends!" an old black man stated. "Jesus is my friend!"

"Say amen, brother," a woman added.

"Are you getting this?" Ashley asked Wyatt.

"Every angry word," Wyatt said.

"There are too many criminals on the street . . . too many guns," Conright roared. "It's the wild west all over again. Our city is turning into a ghost town. People are dying on our streets. The people of our city are afraid to leave their houses. Tourism is falling off. Conventions are canceling. Can you blame them? Just the other night four people in one house were murdered. This is insanity! Every newspaper, magazine and TV news show are spotlighting New Orleans. Instead of 'The Big Easy,' they're calling us, 'The Big Sleazy.'"

"What are you going to do about it?" a local TV reporter asked.

"Clean house. I'll weed out bad cops and hire men and women dedicated to law enforcement. I'll get them better pay. A police officer's salary is embarrassingly low. How can we expect someone to serve this city and endanger his own life on such a salary? And they need automatic weapons. And they'll get them. They're out-gunned. The criminals have better guns. I'll take many officers on desk duty and put them out on the streets in cars that work. Thirty percent of the police cars don't work. The parking lot is turning into a junkyard," Conright said, throwing his hands in the air in disgust.

A BBC reporter in a heavy British accent said, "Some say you will not have the cooperation of the City Council because most members are black."

"I trust the Council to look beyond race as I will," Conright said.

"Bullshit!" was heard from the rear of the crowd.

"Is your campaign a race war with Mayor Chenier?" a French reporter asked.

"A race war!" Conright exclaimed. "My remarks about the mayor are made of frustration over his incapability to run this city, not his color. You people in the media are making this race black versus white. This election is about a dying city. I am not a racist. I am a fair and honest man who is after the truth."

Wyatt nudged Ashley's shoulder with his camera. "Ask him something. I'll get you in the shot."

A bead of sweat rolled down her right temple. Ashley's shoulders and neck were stiff. Her hand tightly clutched the microphone and her mouth was dry as she began to ask him about his alleged Nazi past. "Mr. Conright, are you . . . "

Before she could speak the remaining words to her question, a local rival TV news reporter, John Fullilove asked, "Have you ever been a member of the Nazi Party?"

Ashley looked at him with widened eyes of alarm. But the Tulane Avenue bus was just leaving that corner and Conright had not heard the question. So, she jumped in and shouted, "Are you a Nazi?"

"I asked him that," Fullilove said.

"Sorry, John, I couldn't hear you," she said.

Conright looked down at Ashley and said, "Well, Ms. Tarleton, how could a beautiful, educated young lady like you ask such a ridiculous question as that? Shouldn't you be reporting on local entertainment?"

Feeling a little embarrassed, she nevertheless asked, "There's a photo of you in a Nazi uniform, isn't there?"

"Are you asking me or telling me? Do you have a photo?" Conright inquired.

"No, but . . . ," Ashley embarrassingly admitted.

"Because there is no photo," Conright pointed out. "I have never worn a Nazi uniform. In fact, my father fought in World War II. He died in battle."

"Then why do you persecute me?" spoke the small elderly woman standing next to Ashley. Everyone turned and looked for the woman who had the courage to accuse Conright. Ashley looked down at her, as Wyatt pointed his camera on her. Captivated by this little old lady, the crowd of reporters parted and allowed her to move slowly toward Conright. She pressed a photo of her family to her chest. That photo was her flag, her sword, her world. A silence fell over the crowd, as serious and shocking as the silence during the aftermath of a murder scene. No cat calls, no jokes. It seemed like the whole city had fallen silent. And up walked this stoic woman, as if out of the pages of a history book, as if through a portal in time. She was the witness to the crime, the accuser, the avenger from across the years – pointing her righteous finger straight at Conright, the new face of an old enemy. "Why do you persecute Jews?" the lady said, with a French accent and an impassioned voice. "I am Bella Blum and I accuse you!"

"I don't persecute anyone," Conright said with nervous frustration.

"But you say the Holocaust never happened." Bella continued. "I was in the concentration camp. Everyone in my family died there. I saw! I saw with these eyes!"

"Madam, this campaign is about the present . . . here in New

Orleans, not fifty years ago in Europe," Conright said, with a half-grin on his face.

"You won't let the dead rest in peace. You murder their memory! You're a grave robber. Stop changing history. Six million died . . . . Let them rest in peace!" Bella said, said with elevated voice.

"Are you a Nazi?" Ashley shouted.

Conright looked sternly at Ashley and said, "No!"

Alphonse St. Amant stepped up to the microphone and said, "Ladies and gentlemen, thank you for coming out today. It's been a great rally. And we'll see you at the debate."

Conright's bodyguards hustled him down the steps. But reporters crowded around him, making it difficult for him to get to his car.

"Mr. Conright, can you explain yourself regarding World War II?" one reporter shouted.

"Sir, do you honor Hitler's birthday?" another reporter said.

"What an asshole that guy is!" someone in the crowd said.

"Wyatt, over here!" Ashley shouted as she moved toward Bella, noticing she was left alone wiping tears from her eyes and holding on to history. Her clothes looked more 1940s' style than 1990s'.

Wyatt turned his camera away from the crowd and followed Ashley.

"Hi, Miss Blum, I'm Ashley Tarleton from TV-3 news. May I talk to you for a few minutes?"

"Yes," she said.

"Let's go inside," Ashley offered, motioning to the courthouse.

As Ashley, Bella and Wyatt stole up the steps and into the house of justice, the crowd of reporters filmed Conright and his party jump in their cars and speed off down Tulane Avenue toward the Central Business District.

"We can sit here," Ashley said, as she led Bella to a long bench under one of the huge front windows of this wide hallway-entrance between the actual entrance to the building and the entrance through huge black doors to the court and inner sanctum where the victim, or victim's family faced the criminal, begging the judge and Jesus for justice to be done. "This is my cameraman, Walter."

"Wyatt," Wyatt said, shaking his head.

"Hello," Bella said.

"Hi," Wyatt replied, as he knelt down and centered Bella's beautiful but sad face in his viewfinder.

"Can you tell us about your experience? You can begin whenever you're ready," Ashley said, positioning her microphone.

Bella looked into Ashley's eyes before closing her eyes to the present, so she could see the past, and then she began to tell her life story in a lilting French accent. "My father said during that time that it was as if the world had stopped turning, and Europe had turned into a frozen land where hungry wolves prowled and giant birds of prey flew freely in the sky. We were all frightened – even my father. He and Mother did everything they could to protect us. But everything wasn't enough. Number 25 Rue Jeanne d'Arc in Paris was our home – an apartment on the third floor. It was small but we were happy. Papa owned a café two streets away. Mother helped. We helped, too, after school." Bella showed the photo to Ashley, as she pointed to the eight smiling faces. "This is Daniel, the oldest. The second in line was Jacob, then Sara, then me, then Ruth, and the youngest, Leon, named after Papa's favorite statesman, Leon Blum."

"Was he a relation?" Ashley questioned.

"No. But you would have thought he was, the way Papa went on about him," Bella said. "He was a socialist and that's why my father admired him. Look at the smiles on my father's and mother's faces. They were so proud of us. Our whole world was that little area around the café. Mother came home to cook for us. Papa came home late, always tired but always open to help us with our little problems – usually school. On Saturday we went to temple. Sunday was the park. We were free and we were happy. Then the Germans came." Tears, like soft rain, dropped from her eyes and rolled down the cracks on her sagging but beautiful face, as if a lifetime of tears had carved those lines. Ashley took a monogrammed handkerchief from her dress pocket and gave it to

Bella. "Thank you." Ashley tried to understand the time and the pain that caused those tears from those brilliant blue eyes. "We were mocked, even by some people we knew," Bella continued. "Some who we thought liked us, forced us to wear the Star of David. All Jews. We were separated from all others like sick cows from the herd. They took the café away from Papa. Papa was quiet with his feelings. But we knew. Then they took away our school. Then came the roundups. At night it happened. Mama sent me to Miss Anna's for coffee, down the hall. We enjoyed talking to her. Lived alone. No children. Then German voices were heard. Boot steps. Heavy boot steps. Voices grew louder. Then the boot steps stopped on our floor. Miss Anna opened the door a little. Soldiers pushed open the door to our apartment. I heard Mama scream. Then loud, shouting voices. Papa and soldiers. They pushed my family into the hall. Mama looked my way. I wanted to run to her. Miss Anna held me back. Through that one-inch opening, I saw my family, my life, pass from view. After they took my family, I stood alone in the middle of our home. I never felt so cold."

Bella wiped away more tears as Ashley asked, "Do you want to stop?"

"No. The whole story," Bella said. "I lived with Miss Anna two years. A new family moved into my home. Their laughter stolen from my family. Miss Anna told me to say nothing. But one of them discovered me."

"How?" Ashley said.

"I don't know. Someone else living in the building must have said something. They came one night. Four soldiers and a Gestapo agent to arrest a fourteen-year-old girl. I was a week in Drancy," Bella said.

"Drancy?" questioned Ashley.

"An unfinished housing complex near Paris used to detain us for a while," Bella continued. "From there to Auschwitz by train. They packed us in cattle cars. All those people. And I alone. Human waste in the car. The smell. I asked God, why do they do it? Five people died in my car. An infant. I saw France and Poland pass by through cracks in wood. Then Auschwitz. Black and gray. Everything. No grass, only mud. Soldiers with giant dogs – barking, growling. We stood in line. Five-hundred or more. Prisoners in black-white striped uniforms took our luggage. One whispered to me, 'Tell them you can sew when they ask.' I did. I and some others walked toward our barracks. The others toward two towers, smokestacks. Gas chambers, crematoria. I was told the truth about Auschwitz. Death factory."

Ashley noticed a tattooed number on Bella's left arm. "Auschwitz?" she asked.

"Yes. The first thing they do to those kept alive for work," Bella said.

"What of your family, Bella?" Ashley asked.

"Yes. My family," Bella slowly said, as if stalling the story's tragic end would change it. "Mama was there. Her job was to help in making gunpowder. I didn't know her, at first. She lost so much weight. I didn't recognize my own mother." More tears came. Ashley and Wyatt exchanged concerned glances. Bella fought for her composure and began again. "She looked very old. And she was sick. We held each other and cried all night. I can still feel her embrace," she said, clutching the photo. "Two weeks later she died. She was selected for the ovens because she had a cough. No parting words. No kiss goodbye. The Nazis erased her existence. In their dark, twisted minds she was never alive. I never found my father, brothers or sisters again. And I think of them every day. Every day. I still don't know why they killed us. What harm did we do? And why does Keiffer Conright say it never happened? This is my pain – not only the deaths but the denial of all those deaths by people like him. I live in two worlds – past and present. And he makes both painful."

"When did you come to New Orleans?" Ashley asked.

"I met Saul, my husband, after the war. He was a survivor, too. We emigrated to the U.S., to New Orleans, and we have six children," Bella said.

"Just like your own family," Ashley smiled.

"Yes. To carry on. But Saul died three years ago, or he would be standing here with me today to fight Conright," Bella said.

"Maybe he is," Wyatt added.

"Yes. I hope so. Thank you," Bella replied.

"Do you mind if we use this tape on TV?" Ashley said.

"Use it. People must hear the truth. Conright is an accomplice to murder. That's how I see it. Anyone who says the mass murder of the Holocaust didn't happen is an accomplice to it. I was there. And I will not let this man have his way. This is how it starts. This is how it starts! No. Never again," Bella said.

Ashley saw a look of grave concern and conviction on Bella's time-worn face. She didn't know much at all about the Holocaust, but she could see and almost feel its aftershock like that of a catastrophic event in deep space of an exploding light from a dying star that had taken all these years to reach her dark, ignorant eyes. She now knew, however, that something terrible and real had happened to this woman, something so horrible that even time would not erase.

"I can see this is difficult for you," Ashley said.

"It's difficult to make anyone understand what happened then. Imagine your own family abducted and murdered," Bella suggested. "And now he's murdering the memory of all those who died in the death camps. All I have to hold are the memories of my family and dreams of what could have been."

Ashley made direct eye contact as she said, "I'm so sorry." Bella's eyes now seemed at rest after visiting and reporting that unforgettable landscape of personal history in her mind. They walked Bella to her car on Tulane Avenue and said goodbye.

Wyatt looked at Ashley, shook his head and said, "Powerful stuff."

"Yes. Very. I think Darryl will want to use it," she said.

"Positively," he said.

CHAPTER 6

Red for Murder

"Do you know anything about the Holocaust?" Ashley asked.

"Not really. Supposedly, millions died . . . murdered and cremated. I've heard of Auschwitz," Wyatt replied.

"Let's make a quick stop at the bookshop. I want to take a look at a book on the subject," Ashley suggested.

"All right. First, I want to stop in and see my friend in the DA's office. See if he can give us some news on last night," Wyatt said.

"Where's the DA's office?" Ashley inquired.

"A half block that way," he said, pointing down South White Street that bordered the courthouse. "You don't know where the DA's office is?"

"How would I know? I've never had to deal with the DA," she said, defensively.

"I didn't mean it like that," Wyatt said, noticing Ashley's how-dare-you look. "I just thought everyone . . . . Forget it. It's over here."

"All right. I can see, "Ashley said.

The building housing the District Attorney's offices was a white flat-faced, bunker-like stone block. Wyatt and Ashley entered and noticed five chairs in disarray in the lobby. "He's up there," Wyatt said, pointing to the third-floor tier of the upper three floors that overlooked the lobby. Before entering the elevator, Wyatt stuck his head in the door of a small room to his right. Sitting at the switchboard was an old friend, Janie, an attractive woman in her forties with her hair piled high on her head, her skirt hiked up, and her legs intertwined. "Hey, Janie."

"Hi, good looking," she said, with a pleasantly surprised face. "How have you been?"

"Pretty good," Wyatt replied.

"How's your little girl?" Janie asked.

Ashley looked at Wyatt, unaware he had a child.

"She's doing good. My mom watches her during the day. Hey, what's with these chairs in the middle of the lobby?" Wyatt inquired.

"One of the ADAs and his lover got into a fight after hours last night and started throwing chairs over the third-floor balcony. Joe didn't move them yet," she said.

"Professionals, Janie, when will they ever learn to behave?" Wyatt said, laughingly.

"You're right about that," Janie said, smiling. The switchboard lit up with an incoming call. "Got to run."

"Important call for a professional, no doubt," Wyatt said. "Talk to you later."

Janie waved goodbye as she directed her call. Wyatt closed the door. He and Ashley moved to the elevator a few feet away. "She's a sweet girl. We date off and on. Nothing serious."

"Hmmm. Seems like a nice arrangement," Ashley condescendingly said.

Wyatt looked at her disapprovingly. "She's nice."

The elevator door opened. Joe, the old black driver/runner, stepped out.

"Hey there, Wyatt," Joe said, extending his hand.

"Hey, Mr. Joe," Wyatt said, shaking hands. "How you been?"

"Can't complain. How 'bout yourself?" Joe asked.

"Oh, moving right along. This is Ashley Tarleton. She's a news reporter at the station," Wyatt said.

"Ashley, pleased to meet you," Joe said, extending his hand.

"Hello," she said, shaking his hand after hesitating. She had a quarter of a smile on her face, but was cringing on the inside.

Wyatt and Joe exchanged telling glances about Ashley's reticence.

"Okay, you all take care. I've got to move these chairs, and then pick up lunch for the crew. Take it easy, Wyatt. Pleasure meeting you, Ashley," he said, moving away.

"Yes. Pleasure meeting you," she said.

"Be careful out there," Wyatt warned.

"Oh yeah. You too," Joe said, exiting the building.

They entered the elevator. Wyatt pushed "3". Ashley immediately dug into her purse and retrieved a small plastic bottle of anti-bacterial gel. She vigorously spread it over her right palm and fingers. Wyatt shook his head.

The elevator stopped at the third floor. On exiting, Wyatt noticed Cindy, a secretary, at her desk. A pretty woman in her forties, she had talked to many prisoners as she typed their personal information on various forms in the many years she worked for the DA. Prisoners were regularly escorted by sheriff's deputies to the DA's office from the jail across the street. Often, they would tell their tales of woe to her that they had been framed, then ask her to intercede on their behalf with the DA. Some prisoners wouldn't cooperate. She would see prisoners' faces nightly in her dreams, as if she witnessed the crimes she recorded.

Ashley stood to the side while Wyatt walked up behind her and said, "I'm innocent, lady! I swear! I've been framed!"

Cindy turned around, laughed and said, "You look guilty to me. Hey, you. What brings you here today?"

"Came to talk to Jack . . . to see what's up on last night's murder," Wyatt said.

"Which one?" she said, raising her eyebrows.

"How many were there?"

"Three. The Quarter and two uptown," Cindy said.

"Jesus! What's happening to our fair city?" Wyatt asked, while shaking his head.

"I don't know. But I don't go out at night anymore. Got to keep my family safe," she said, pointing to a picture of her three children.

"Me, too." Wyatt noticed Jack lift his head above his cubicle walls, adjust his black wire frame glasses, and look in his direction. They pointed at each other and laughed. "There's Jack. Take care, Cindy. Keep safe."

"You too. Good to see you," Cindy said.

"Same here."

Ashley followed Wyatt to the cubicle of Jacques Edouard Daniel, an always smartly dressed young Assistant District Attorney, whom Wyatt had known for a couple of years. Jacques was the descendant of a slave captured on the western coast of Africa, brought to Senegambia's coast, then walked through the "Door of No Return," and then shipped to New Orleans in the mid-1700s.

Jacques quickly adopted a Jamaican accent and jokingly said, "Hey, man, pull up a chair and let's smoke us some giant ganja spliffs the NOPD just confiscated from some crazy negroes in the Ninth Ward."

Laughing out loud, Wyatt said, "What have you been up to, my friend?"

Ashley looked confused as Jacques reverted to his normal voice and said, "Just fighting crime. What about you?"

"Filming it," Wyatt said.

"Yeah, I heard that. You'll need lots of film," Jacques declared.

"Ain't it the truth! Jack, this is Ashley Tarleton. We're covering the election," Wyatt said.

"Nice to meet you, Ashley," Jacques said, moving forward to shake her hand.

"Pleasure to meet you," Ashley coldly said. Wyatt watched as Ashley lowered her right arm after shaking hands, and then rubbed those fingers together, as if trying to rub off something tangible.

"You must have caught the press conference," Jacques said.

"Yeah. Just now," said Wyatt.

"How was he? Any racist remarks?" Jacques inquired.

"Veiled remarks, like 'American Heritage'," Wyatt said.

"He loves using that one," Jacques conceded.

"Right. But there was a disturbance when a little old Jewish lady challenged him on his Nazi past and denying the Holocaust," Wyatt said, with widened eyes.

"Wow! Good for her. What did he do?" Jacques asked.

"Ran away." Wyatt said.

"All right," Jacques said with a big smile. "He can't win unless he buys many, many votes. I don't know what he's trying to prove. His is a lost cause."

Ashley noticed on Jacque's small desk a memo pad, mug, clock and statue of Jack Daniels, the trademark of the whiskey manufacturer. She also noticed three stacks of file folders – yellow, blue, and red, the tallest.

"What do the colored folders represent?" Ashley asked.

"Well, those are for the colored folk. They commit all the crimes . . . and you know the Africans like them bright colors . . .," Jacques joked.

Wyatt laughed but Ashley remained stone-faced. "He's joking," Wyatt said to Ashley. "No sense of humor," Wyatt mouthed to Jacques.

"Sorry, Ashley. A sense of humor is the only thing that makes all of this bearable," Jacques admitted.

"He goes to comedy clubs and performs," Wyatt added.

"Right. I'm going to Los Angeles this weekend. I'll do about twenty minutes as a warmup act" Jacques said, with a grin.

"All right!" Wyatt said, excitedly. "The big time."

"Yeah. A friend got me in. I like LA but always get lost. But anyway, Ashley, to answer your question . . . . The yellow folders are misdemeanors, blue are felonies, and red means murder," Jacques said.

"You need more of those," Wyatt added.

Just then, Cindy walked over, placed her hand on Wyatt's shoulder and tossed two red folders on top of the stack. "It never ends," she said, as she walked away.

"Yeah. I've got a robbery and attempted murder case where the attacker actually said to his victim, 'Here's something to remember me by,' as he thrust a knife in the guy's back," Jacques said.

"Jesus," Wyatt said.

"Yeah," Jacques continued. "And there's a murder case where the murderer, a drug dealer seeking revenge, actually dragged a guy out of his house one night, doused him with gas and lit him on fire. Remember that? About three months ago."

"Right. I remember," Wyatt said.

"What do you know about the girl killed last night?" Ashley inquired, as she retrieved her notepad from her purse.

"In the Quarter?" Jacques said.

"Yes."

"A terrible, terrible thing. I asked the DA for this one. I want to try this case and I want the death penalty. Her name is Yvette Lenieu. She lived on Nashville Avenue – an apartment," Jacques said, as he tapped his Jack Daniels notepad with his pen on which was the exact address. Ashley looked over and wrote it down.

Wyatt shook his head and said, "We were right there. Ashley almost got hit herself."

"Really? Wow! It's a strange case. Who would commit a drive-by in the Quarter right in front of everyone? Doesn't make sense," Jacques said, with a look of bewilderment.

"Any suspects?" Wyatt asked.

"The usual," Jacques said. "We're rounding them up. The Mercedes was car-jacked from the shopping mall in Metairie last night. The woman they stole it from was badly beaten. She's in intensive care. But the car's nowhere to be found."

"No trace of a big black Mercedes with a temporary tag?" Ashley wondered.

"No. You'd think it would be easy to spot. It will probably turn up in one of the housing projects. They usually do," Jacques said.

"What about the girl? Any idea why she was targeted?" Ashley inquired.

"We don't know that she was. Four other people were hit," Jacques said.

"But most of the bullets hit her," Wyatt pointed out.

"True. I've never seen anything like this before. Something's up with this one."

"Well, New Orleans has always been a violent port town, like other ports. My grandfather told me some stories . . ." Wyatt said.

"Is he still around?" Jacques asked.

"No."

"He'd be shocked, if he were," Jacques said.

"Absolutely."

"The people who've come and gone in old New Orleans wouldn't believe their eyes . . . over 400 murders, and the year's not done. There's another river running through our town . . ." Jacques said.

"Yeah. Blood red," Wyatt said.

The elevator door opened and the ghostly sound of chains rattling was heard. Three prisoners in orange jumpsuits, chained together at the wrists and ankles, and a Sheriff's Deputy made their way from the elevator to Cindy's desk. They sat down on three plastic chairs near the typewriter. Cindy placed a form in the typewriter. Though she had done this many times, she was always a little nervous so close to the prisoners. She looked out the corner of her left eye while typing.

Jacques stood up and said, "Our usual suspects have arrived."

They watched the prisoners, all black, from a safe distance. The prisoner nearest to Cindy was approximately 5'7" with short hair and a tattoo of a cross on his arm. He turned his head frequently, as if looking for an escape route. The smaller one at the other end looked down, shaking his head. The prisoner in the middle was a bodybuilder at 6' tall. His biceps were as big as his shaved head. He, too, had a dark blue tattoo on his arm – a heart with a knife in it. He had tattoos on his fingers of both hands. The left bore the word 'No,' the right, 'Fear.' He joined his hands together, as if praying, and his credo was plain for all to see, even to God. His angry eyes stared straight ahead as sweat rolled down his face. Occasionally, his arms twitched, causing the chains to rattle and the Deputy to jump. The room was quiet, except for Cindy asking personal data questions and typing answers.

"I think it's time for us to leave," Ashley nervously said, realizing she had to walk right in front of the prisoners to exit. She looked around for an alternate escape route.

"Yeah," Wyatt agreed, while pondering the idea of videotaping the three.

"Well, friends, one of those may have murdered Yvette Lenieu," Jacques said, looking sternly in their direction.

Ashley felt a chill run down her spine. She didn't know whether to move toward the elevator or hide.

"Your name," Cindy asked the first prisoner.

"C.T. . . . Calvin Tyrone Johnson. And I don't know nothing about no murder. I'm innocent."

A few minutes passed as Cindy finished questioning the first prisoner. She then looked at the middle and much more menacing prisoner and asked, "Can I have your name?" No answer was given as the prisoner stared straight ahead. "Sir, I'll need your name." No answer. The prisoner clasped his hands together and closed his eyes.

"Tell her your name," the Deputy commanded, stepping forward. No reaction came from the prisoner. After a few seconds the Deputy again said, "Your name!"

The prisoner opened his eyes and softly said, "She knows my name and so do you, especially you." He then raised his voice and startled everyone. "I am the black Everyman! I am the nigger of the world! Every white son-of-a-bitch points his boney finger at me and accuses me of every crime since the Fall of Man. The police are the bloodhounds of the new slave state." Hen then bellowed, "This is a slave planet! I will not be your nigger no more!"

"Oh, Jesus!" Jacques said.

Ashley was now very frightened and so was Wyatt who picked

up his camera and started taping. The prisoner shot up, towering over everyone like a bronze monument come to life. He raised his hands toward heaven, pulling the two other prisoners with him. "These chains are the only gift the white man has given to me!"

The Deputy lowered his head and rammed the prisoner in the stomach, forcing him to drop to his knees. The other prisoners fell face down. The NOPD policemen arrived to help. One jammed his knee on the prisoner's neck. A prisoner's foot slammed against a cop's crotch. One cop drew back his fist with so much force, it looked like Popeye's fist rotating. He let it go but hit the Deputy by mistake. The Deputy fell over backward. Cindy moved away from her desk. Ashley thought she could move around the heap of bodies but her legs were hit. Someone grabbed her purse and she fell down. Jacques and Wyatt rushed to help her up.

"God damn you! Get your fucking hands off me, you fucking enemies of the people. Fuck you! Fuck the system!" the rebellious prisoner shouted.

"You guys better go. We'll handle this," Jacques said, ushering Ashley and Wyatt toward the elevator.

"Are you sure about that?" Wyatt wondered out loud.

The out-of-control prisoner lifted his head and looked straight at Ashley who had turned her head around to get another look at this puzzling and frightening scene. "See this? See what they're doing to me? Do you see?" The prisoner loudly wailed.

As Jacques moved them closer to the elevator, Ashley noticed he walked with a slight limp. She thought the prisoner stabbed him. "Are you hurt?" she inquired.

"No. It's from an old accident when I was a kid," he said, as he pushed the elevator button. "It's nothing." The elevator door opened immediately. "I'll talk to you guys later."

"Yeah. Call me and let me know how this turns out. I'll buy lunch," Wyatt said.

"All right," Jacques said.

"Catch you later," Wyatt said.

"Yeah. Take care. Nice meeting you, Ashley" Jacques said.

"Nice meeting you too," Ashley said, as the elevator was about to close. She witnessed a last glimpse of a cubist-like entanglement of black, white, orange, and blue, and one face looking through twisted arms, mouth wide open screaming the age-old cry of the vanquished: 'Innocent!' Though the door closed, there was no escaping that sound.

"God, what a mess," Wyatt said.

"There's no escaping the violence in this city. It's outside, inside . . . all around us," Ashley said alarmingly.

"Yeah. But he probably thinks the same thing," Wyatt added.

They stared at each other with worried looks on their faces like two people hopelessly lost in a foreign city, knowing danger was out there but not knowing where.

CHAPTER 7

Black and White

"I want to stop at the Maple Street Bookshop," Ashley said, as they returned to the car.

"Where exactly is that?" Wyatt questioned.

"You don't know the Maple Street Bookshop?" Ashley snidely said, seeing a bit of revenge for his earlier comment about her not knowing the location of the DA's office. "Everyone knows the Bookshop."

"Excuse me. I'm not an uptowner," Wyatt said, placing his camera in the back seat.

"It shows," she mockingly said.

"Ha, ha," he said, with mock laughter. "Get in. Let's hit it, blue blood."

As they pulled away from the E-Z Serve heading south on Broad Street toward the River, Ashley took out her antibacterial gel and spread it over her fingers.

"What is up with you and that?" Wyatt insisted.

"I like to be clean and free of germs. What concern is it of yours?" she retorted.

"Kind of obsessive-compulsive, isn't it?" Wyatt asked.

"No. It's not. It's called 'cleanliness'," Ashley countered.

"Sure, it's not called 'prejudice'?" Wyatt questioned.

"And what does that have to do with this?" she said, scornfully.

"Well, you shake the hands of two black men and you pull out that stuff. I was wondering if you were going to do it in front of Jack," Wyatt said.

"I wouldn't do it front of someone. That would be impolite. And I am not prejudiced. Are you?" Ashley reprimanded.

"I don't think so," Wyatt said.

"What do you mean, you don't think so?" Ashley said, suspiciously.

Wyatt thought about it for a couple of minutes, as he continued down South Broad Street, flanked by old, small businesses on both sides and poor black neighborhoods behind the businesses.

"Well, sometimes under certain circumstances, people say things . . . mean things . . . . And you don't know if the person really meant to say that . . . if deep down inside, that's how they really felt," he said, with a raised eyebrow, hoping he made sense.

"I don't doubt that sometimes people say things they don't really mean and that they later regret," she said, confidently.

"But I was wondering . . . I heard some guy on some show . . . I think he was a professor . . . . He said there are three things that can mess up your perspective on life, and can cause you to be mean or prejudiced. But he said if you have a strong character or foundation or something like that, you can resist any thoughts of superiority over others and stay . . . I don't know . . . focused or something," Wyatt said, somewhat nervously and looking out the side of his right eye. He hoped that was understandable.

"What are the three things?" Ashley said, looking straight at him.

"Youth, good looks and money. And you've got all three," Wyatt pointed out.

"So, what are you saying . . . that I think I'm superior to others because I have the three traits?" she asked, leaning in to him a bit.

"No. I'm just saying the possibility is there in someone like you. I'm not saying you're that way." Yes, I am, he thought. "I don't really know you."

"You're right. You don't really know me." And you're not going to, she thought.

"Well, I guess we'll learn more about each other before the

election's over."

"I doubt it. Turn right on Fontainebleau," Ashley directed.

He dropped the issue, realizing this was neither the time nor place to undertake an exploration of her Arctic regions.

They had reached the intersection of South Broad, Napoleon Avenue, and Fontainebleau, the backdoor to the uptown area, Ashley's parade ground. Wyatt turned and proceeded up tree-shaded Fontainebleau, passing old white stucco houses, some with red tile roofs and elevated entrances; not nearly as large and stately as the inaccessible mansions on St. Charles Avenue, but proud with subdued elegance.

Noticing a folded piece of paper on the seat between them, Wyatt said, "Something fell out of your purse."

She picked up the note with one hand, as she returned the gel to her purse. She opened the paper.

"It's a note and phone number. It's hard to read. Looks like, "I'm innocence. 525-0005.""

"'Innocence.' Must mean 'innocent' . . . oh, the prisoner you tripped over . . . the guy next to Cindy . . . I saw him grab your purse," Wyatt said.

"That's why I fell."

"You going to call it?" Wyatt said, with a raised eyebrow.

"I've got to," she said, retrieving her portable phone. "You'll need to turn left at the stop sign on Broadway."

"All right."

Ashley dialed the number. It rang several times, and then a voice was heard.

"Yo! Speak!" a young man's voice loudly said.

"Hello . . . who is this?" Ashley inquired, unsure of what to say.

"Who's this?" the man said, angrily.

"I'm a reporter for TV-3 News."

Ashley heard the man say to someone, "White woman . . . TV reporter."

A calmer man's voice said, "Who is this?"

"I'm Ashley Tarleton. I'm with TV-3 News. I believe a young man . . . a prisoner at the DA's office slipped me a note. He said he was innocent and gave this number to call. Do you know him?" Ashley said with furrowed brow, trying to make a connection with whomever was on the end of this call.

"Yeah! That's my boy, CT," the man said. Fucking cops picked him up for that murder in the Quarters. He didn't have nothing to do with that. They're looking for me, too."

"Do you know who did it?" Ashley asked.

"I can't hang on the phone, baby. I got to keep moving. Meet me at the 'T' at two o'clock . . . in the 'Big Valley.' Not even cops go up in there. Bring your camera. We'll have a little press conference," he said, and ended the conversation.

Wyatt turned and looked at her. "What did he say?"

"He said to meet him in the 'Big Valley' at the 'T' at two. What's the 'T'?" she said, pressing 'stop' on her phone and slipping it into her purse.

"St. Thomas Housing Project. Oh, Jesus, that's a rough place," Wyatt said.

"Where is it?" Ashley asked.

"It's uptown. You didn't know that?" he said, with a look of amazement.

"I've heard of it. I didn't know it was uptown," she said, defensively.

"You don't know uptown as well as you thought. There's a whole other world all around you. You've just got to look over your fence," he said, with a smile.

Ashley looked back at him with a who-are-you-to-tell-me expression on her face and said, "Just keep driving down Broadway, oh wise one from the suburbs."

"You're not going to the projects to meet with that guy, are you?" Wyatt asked.

"Not alone," she said.

Wyatt's eyes widened as if being inflated, and a look of astonishment poured over his face. "Wait a minute! I'm not going deep inside a housing project. Are you kidding? That's suicide."

"We have to," Ashley said. "We have to film this guy, especially in the project. What a great story. Can't you see it? No one else will have this story. People will want to see this. Envision this whole thing. Use your mind."

"I am. And I don't want a bullet in the middle of it because I plan to use it often. You're not thinking of your own safety . . . or mine," Wyatt expressed.

"Are you afraid of your city?" Ashley wondered.

"Parts of it. Yeah. And you know I'm right," Wyatt quickly responded.

"We both witnessed that murder. We're part of this now. Don't you want to know who killed that girl?" she asked.

"Yeah."

"Something of what Conright said was true. It's our city . . . and it's being taken away from us," Ashley admitted.

"True."

"So, you'll come with me? I need you," she said, sounding like a good wife.

"Yeah," he said, acquiescing like a good husband.

They continued down Broadway, crossed Claiborne Avenue and passed a side entrance to Newcomb College. Next to Newcomb was Tulane University. They stopped at the red light on Freret Street, lined by residences and fraternity houses for Tulane University and Loyola University students. Wyatt saw students walking all about him. Tulane was just a block away down Freret on his left. A student pulled up in a red Porsche Speedster and parked in front of a frat house. Obviously, daddy was a rich doctor or lawyer to afford a car like that for his son, Wyatt thought. He looked down Freret again at the many students walking to and from the university. Then, he looked at Ashley's beautiful, floral face. She was a delicate flower and this was her uptown garden. Though she was only three feet from him, there may as well have been miles of fences between the two. Still, he felt that strong desire again to kiss her frosted lips.

He graduated high school, married and started his career as a photographer all in the same year, twelve years ago. His background and limited income did not afford the opportunity for monumental success bestowed on some uptowners. He could only capture their world of wealth and privilege on film. He was the photographer, not a member of the wedding or a guest at the party. Rather, he was the hired hand whose job it was to capture the fortunate ones on film for posterity as they toasted each other with Dom Perignon and sparkling smiles. But that was close enough for him. He thought all uptowners were arrogant, pretentious and abrasive. At least, that was the feeling he got. And Ashley had done nothing so far but reconfirm his assumptions.

"Go!" Ashley said, catching Wyatt in the act of staring at her.

"What?" Caught red-handed, he thought.

"You've got the green," she said.

"Oh, right," he said, looking upward through the top of the windshield.

"Turn right on Maple." He drove two blocks, turned right and proceeded up Maple, a narrow tree-lined street like most in the uptown area. He drove several blocks, pulled over to the right, and parked in front of the bookstore. "You can stay here . . . if you want. I'll only be a few minutes," Ashley said, not really feeling comfortable with Wyatt, unless in a work-related setting.

"I'll come in. It's too hot out here. And I want to see those photos myself," he said, wiping sweat from his temples.

"What about the camera? You can't leave it in the car," she said, searching for an escape.

"I'll put it in the trunk," he said.

"Oh, all right," she said, frowning and frustrated.

As Wyatt grabbed his camera from the backseat, Ashley quickly exited the car and pushed open the short black wrought iron gate that cleared a path through two banana trees with large green fan-like leaves on either side of the steps of the old narrow wooden house, converted to a bookstore in the 1960s. She hurriedly walked up the steps onto the porch and stepped aside to allow two customers with enlightened smiles exit. She opened the screen door and immediately felt cool air like feathers on her skin, as she stepped inside the main room of the shop wherein the walls were bookshelves floor to ceiling, and giving the appearance that those tall stacks of bound knowledge were actually holding up the walls. Photos of famous authors were everywhere.

"Hi, Rhoda," she said, as she approached the owner bending over a desk at the opposite end of the room, about a dozen steps away.

"Hi, Ashley," Rhoda said, pulling back her long blonde hair and resting her hand on her thin hips. "How have you been? I haven't seen you for a few weeks."

"Mother is ill," Ashley said.

"I'm so sorry to hear that. Nothing serious, I hope," she said expressing concern in her voice and a show of sympathy in her eyes.

"We're afraid it might be," Ashley said.

"Oh, I hope not," she said, now with sorrow in her eyes. "Here, Ashley, take her this book." Rhoda stepped into a tiny darkened room behind her and brought out a large coffee-table book entitled *Gardens of the World*. "I just got this in a couple of days ago. I was holding it until you and your mother could take a look. You've bought so many books on flowers. I thought you both would want this."

"Oh, it's beautiful," Ashley said.

"Take it to her. I want her to have it," Rhoda said.

"Oh, thank you so much," Ashley said with a smile.

Wyatt stepped into the bookshop and quietly moved in their direction.

"Tell her to get well soon," Rhoda said. "She's so sweet and thoughtful. I've seen her stop to talk to children playing outside. Black or white, rich or poor, she has a 'Hello' for everyone. I once mentioned that a Creole lady I know, Philomene, who works as a cleaning woman, was having a tough time financially. Her husband had lost his job . . . . They have six kids. They were having trouble paying utilities and buying food. Do you know your mother visited

Philomene and brought food, clothing and gave her money! She never said a word about it. But Philomene told me. She even gave Philomene her beautiful taupe-colored Anne Klein suit that your mother loved so much. Generous lady, your mother."

"I didn't know that. But it sounds like something Mother would do," Ashley said, nodding her head.

"Truly a beautiful lady," Rhoda said.

"Yes," Ashley said, as a picture of her mother standing tall, healthy, elegant and dressed in her Anne Klein suit flashed across her mind. "Truly beautiful." She then noticed Wyatt and turned toward him. "Rhoda, this is Wyatt, my cameraman. We're covering the election."

"Oh, how wonderful," she said, shaking hands with him. "You get to talk to the candidates. When you see Conright, tell him to please leave town. He's giving the city a bad name."

They all laughed.

"Some people said words to that effect during today's press conference," Wyatt said.

"The city will come to a halt if he's elected. And you know how slow it moves already," Rhoda said.

"Oh yeah," Wyatt said.

"We met an elderly woman at the press conference who challenged Conright on his denial of the Holocaust. I'd like to take a look at a book about it. I'm not too familiar with the subject," Ashley confessed.

"Sure. Follow me," Rhoda said.

She led them only three steps away into a small square room that contained books on art and on New Orleans. It took only six steps to enter the next room, rectangular and running the width of the house. They turned right at "Spirituality" which put them next to the "History" shelf.

"Here you go. You'll find what you're looking for here," Rhoda said.

"Thanks, Rhoda," Ashley said with a smile.

They were left alone in this matchbox-like room with a low

ceiling and uneven floors that squeaked with every move. Ashley cocked her head to the right as she scanned the titles. She pulled one book off the shelf and flipped through its pages. She saw the name Adolph Hitler speed by, as she fanned the pages documenting the world's most heinous crimes. More names passed by – Adolph Eichmann, Heinrich Himmler, Hermann Goering, Josef Goebbels. Pages were ablaze with names synonymous with torture, mass murder and hell on earth. She came across black and white photos of these men and others – Albert Speer, Reinhard Heydrich, Klaus Barbie, Joseph Mengele – all wearing suits and uniforms, looking official, honest and fatherly, but also wearing the smiles of devils. But where was photographic evidence of the crimes Bella spoke of, she wondered?

Wyatt opened another book full of photos of Nazi Germany: black and white street scenes crowded with excited, smiling faces; women wearing hats and holding flowers; boys and old men cheering and saluting the German army as it goose-stepped its way into the most hellish war ever waged and crimes unimaginable; then color photos of red and black swastika banners like billowy curtains draped over Baroque architecture. The Third Reich came alive as he turned more pages, more photos of troops marching to the military beat of drums, cymbals and horns. He turned a new page and looked over a night rally at Nuremburg that spanned both pages. Thousands of mesmerized young men and women holding torches, covered the entire stadium, not realizing that they were the sacrificial lambs for their high Nazi priest, Adolph Hitler, who stood at his altar preaching the irony of a greater "Deutschland" by condemning them all to death. *"Deutschland Uber Alles"* was the caption at the bottom of the page. Wyatt stared at the face of a mass murderer and what Bella called "pure evil."

Ashley had picked up a thick book, heavy with the weight of history and horror. She opened it to reveal the concentration camp, Auschwitz. Every page in the middle of the book had a photo or two on it, depicting madness in progress. One photo showed the arrival and unloading of people packed tightly in freight train cars. The photo below showed officers screaming orders to drop their personal belongings and form two lines. Ashley's eyes darted to the top of the right page where a group of women and children undressed, and then entered a one-story building with no windows.

The photo below it was a closeup of a gas canister marked "Zyklon B" with skull and crossbones above it. She quickly turned the page to see a photo of prisoners in vertically striped uniforms with the Star of David over the heart, carrying off corpses. Another photo showed where the corpses were unloaded: the crematorium, a brick building with tall smokestacks. The photo on the opposite page revealed the ovens inside the crematorium, and the charred skeletons inside the ovens.

"Look," a mesmerized Ashley said.

"Jesus! Are those . . . were those real people?" Wyatt questioned, astonished.

"Yes. This is what Bella was talking about. This was the fate of her family."

She turned the page and saw a photo of General Eisenhower viewing emaciated corpses inside a camp stacked like cords of wood. A few prisoners still alive at the time of liberation stood nearby. They were walking skeletons with dark recessed eyes.

"They don't look human," Wyatt whispered. "How could anyone survive this?"

"What made the Germans do it?" Ashley said. "Oh, my God!" she said, as she noticed four children in the same condition on the opposite page.

"Half her skin is stained with something . . . ink, maybe. I don't know," Wyatt commented, as he pointed to one girl whose skin below the chest had been permanently stained as result of one of Dr. Joseph Mengele's mad experiments. "Mengele," he said, pointing to the name below the photo. "Dr. Joseph Mengele."

"This one's missing his lower leg. God, this is ghastly but look . . . they're smiling," Ashley said.

Though they had experienced torturous experimental procedures performed by Dr. Mengele in the name of medical science, the children still retained their innocent smiles and held on to their joyful souls. But they were aware now of the demented, twisted world of adulthood where the key word was "survival." Mengele himself was the experiment gone wrong.

They returned to their car and got in. Ashley held the book

Rhoda gave her.

"That was a lesson in history I'll never forget," Wyatt said, as he started the car.

"Incredible," Ashley added.

"That's exactly what Conright thinks . . . that it can't possibly be true. But why would he say it didn't happen?" Wyatt asked.

"I don't know," Ashley said, shaking her head slightly. It doesn't make sense. It obviously happened."

"Right."

"I think I agree with what Bella said," Ashley confirmed.

"About what?" Wyatt said, as he pulled away from the curb.

"That if a person knows a crime occurred . . . but continues to deny it, then that person is also an accomplice to that crime. It makes sense, doesn't it?" Ashley added.

"Yeah. I guess so."

Ashley placed the book on the seat between them. She pulled a piece of paper out of her purse with an address written on it. "Turn left at Fern. We'll head down St. Charles to Nashville."

"For what? We've got to get this Conright footage back to the studio," Wyatt said, looking at his watch.

"I want to pass by Yvette Lenieu's apartment . . . just to take a look," Ashley said.

"Okay." Wyatt looked down at the book. "I guess your mom will like that book."

"Yes."

"She sounds like a great lady," he said, feeling a bit guilty of his assumption that all uptowners were insensitive.

"Great and gracious," she said.

"I hope she's feeling better soon."

"Yes. Thank you," Ashley said, as she turned her head away from Wyatt to wipe away a tear.

They drove down St. Charles Avenue past many mighty oaks, the most beautiful and largest flowers in this enchanted uptown garden. Swaying streetcars rolled up and down the neutral ground between the two slow moving single lanes of traffic on either side. A streetcar's overhead electrical cable popped and sparked as it came to a slow stop to pick up students in front of Tulane University's Gibson Hall, a wide, imposing building, designed in the Richardsonian Romanesque style, and built of blocks of Bedford limestone. Walking up its steps led one straight into the past one-hundred years of its historical existence.

Separating Tulane from Loyola University next door was the mammoth Holy Name of Jesus Church, standing very close to the Avenue itself. Its tall steeple touched the sky and the Mind of God. Its stained-glass windows were its eyes, seemingly sending light outward and downward to the people in the street. Its doors were its mouth, opening and closing, and whispering promises of eternal life to all passers-by.

The welcoming, forgiving, comforting arms of Jesus were raised high over his head in the center of the horseshoe driveway entranceway to Loyola. Imposing, its main red brick building looked like an English manor. But the lord who ruled this home was the Lord Himself.

Both universities stood rock solid next to each other, offering to their students secular and religious educations in preparation for a world of unknowns.

Across the Avenue, on Ashley's right, was pastoral Audubon Park. Old gray beards of Spanish moss hung from the sprawling limbs of the many ancient oaks throughout the park. They provided much shade, even darkness. One place near a pond remained a perpetually damp garden of darkness, like the heart of an undiscovered forest, virginal and untouched by man or sunlight. The park was a preserve, a repose, a tranquil part of the mind of the city gone mad by heat and hate.

Wyatt looked at what appeared to be a homeless man on a stone bench in the park. Next to him was a shopping bag overflowing with clothes. A red shirt lay on top. The man looked straight at Wyatt and pointed to the sky. Wyatt looked up through the windshield and saw only blue sky and some clouds.

They continued down the Avenue past homes grand and immense for New Orleans' standards. Ashley's parents lived farther down the Avenue. All the houses were just as intricately detailed with wrought iron fences and fine woodwork. Large windows provided a view of the grandest Avenue in New Orleans, and allowed canyons of sunlight to shine on the opulence within. Wyatt noticed that all the front doors had an oval or rectangular crystal center. He glimpsed crystal chandeliers in several homes and all the faces white, as they rolled at parade speed down New Orleans' Great White Way. Ashley looked like a queen in her carriage, as she waved to a friend outside one home, Wyatt thought. And if she was the queen, he was her chauffeur.

"Turn right on Nashville," Ashley said.

"Is it on the River side of St. Charles?" Wyatt said, as he made the turn.

"Yes. Since we're headed toward downtown, right would mean the River side. Would it not? And slow down," she said, as she eyed the addresses.

The attitude had returned, Wyatt thought.

Wyatt crawled down Nashville Avenue. Everywhere were prismatic crystal doors on beautifully architected houses sharing ground with enormous oak trees, shading large portions of these splendid homes. It looked like an enchanted forest where the houses seemed as natural on their sites as the trees, so close was the bountiful beauty of nature and the beauty of the hand of man.

"This is it," Ashley said.

"Ok," Wyatt said.

Wyatt pulled up in front of a dark wooden house with a large, curved awning-covered veranda. A middle-aged man was placing boxes in a Black Jade Pearl Lexus sedan just ahead of Wyatt.

"Stay here. I won't be long," Ashley dictated, before stepping out of the car.

"Yes, ma'am," he said, shaking his head. In a low tone of voice, he said, "Yes, ma'am, Miss Ashley. Anything you say. Pleasure to drive you, Miss Ashley. I'll just sweat my ass off. Yeah. No problem."

He turned on the radio to catch the tail end of David Lerner's radio show.

"I'm not kidding about this," Lerner said. "Someone or something or some ghost is stealing angels."

"What do you mean?" a listener asked, over the phone.

"They're disappearing from cemeteries. Some of the tombs and mausoleums have these granite or concrete little angels in front of them . . . put there by the families of the deceased. So far, at least eight or ten have been taken. They're gone. They're missing. Nothing's sacred in this town," Lerner suggested.

"Jesus! Incredible," Wyatt said in disgust, as he rolled down his window and wiped sweat from his face.

Ashley walked to the front door with neatly trimmed dark green Japanese yews on either side. She turned the crystal doorknob and walked through a crystal door into the foyer. She saw Yvette Lenieu's name and apartment number, 2C on one of six gold mailboxes in the wall above a mahogany table. She opened another crystal door and entered the interior of the house. A hallway with highly polished wooden floors led to three apartments to the right of a wooden staircase that she began to climb. Each step echoed throughout the house.

The young man in apartment 2A opened his door, startling Ashley as she reached the top of the staircase.

"Hi. I was waiting for someone. I thought you were her. Hey, you're that entertainment reporter on Channel 3. I like you," the man said.

"Thank you," she said, continuing down to the end of the hall.

The door to 2C was half open. She knocked twice, and then pushed it open to reveal a middle-aged woman sitting on a white couch. She was staring at an 8x10 silver-framed photograph.

"Hello," Ashley quietly said. The woman looked up. "I'm sorry to intrude. This is Yvette Lenieu's apartment, isn't it?"

"Yes" the woman who opened the door said.

"I'm Ashley Tarleton with Channel 3 News. I was wondering if you could put me in contact with her parents or friends . . ."

"I'm her mother, Yvonne."

"Oh!" Ashley was momentarily stunned because this beautiful

woman was African American. She had light brown skin and black wavy hair. Ashley thought the woman was there to clean the place. "I'm terribly sorry. I didn't know." But she did know that Yvette was white. At least, she thought she knew.

"I don't want to be on camera right now," Yvonne said.

"No. I didn't mean on-camera, necessarily. I am very sorry about your daughter's death. I wanted to talk to you because I witnessed the murder," Ashley said.

"Come in and sit down," Yvonne said, shocked by this admission.

"Thank you," Ashley said, as she entered the cool apartment and sat next to the woman who extended her hand.

Shaking Ashley's hand, Yvonne asked,. "What did you see?"

"Just the black Mercedes," Ashley said. "That's all anyone saw. I rushed to her side but there was nothing any of us could do. I'm so sorry."

"Who would want to kill my baby?" Yvonne gently touched the photo of Yvette, as if actually stroking her daughter's hair. "Look how beautiful she is."

"She is. She's very beautiful," Ashley said.

Ashley now saw some similarities between mother and daughter, especially the dark eyes, black wavy hair and high cheek bones. But the girl's skin was very light and her nose was straight. For all intents and purposes, Yvette in her graduation cap and gown looked white.

"So young," Yvonne said.

"How old was she?" Ashley asked.

"Twenty-eight," Yvonne said. "She graduated from Xavier University six years ago. She's in Loyola Law now . . . she was. I remember when she moved into this apartment. She was so excited. She always wanted to live uptown. I helped her paint this room."

Ashley surveyed the peach-colored room. A Queen Anne wingback chair occupied one corner, empty bookshelves at the opposite corner, two Monet water lily paintings stood on the floor against the wall. A box of compact discs stood beside a small mahogany table with a telephone and telephone directory on top. Two porcelain angels, one short and one tall, stood side-by-side on the mantle above a small, square fireplace. A crucifix hung above the front door.

"Do you think she was murdered or the victim of a random drive-by shooting?" Ashley asked.

"I don't know. But I can't believe anyone would want to kill her. I can't imagine it. She was a good person, a sweet girl," Yvonne said, as a sad smile appeared on her face like a momentary break in an overcast sky.

"Was she employed?" Ashley asked.

"No. Not in recent years. My husband and I have been supporting her while in law school," Yvonne said. The smile returned briefly. It was obvious to Ashley that Mrs. Lenieu's thoughts were fluctuating from present to past, sadness and remembrance. Her mind was drunk with grief. Ashley decided not to ask anymore pointed questions. "She loved flowers. I always brought her flowers every time I visited. Come see," she said, as she rose and walked to the balcony just off and beyond the kitchen. Ashley followed. "We planted these," pointing to the flower pots full of yellow marigolds and pink Gerber daisies. "I can smell her scent on these flowers. Isn't that something! It's like she's here but I just can't see her . . . like she's just around every corner and I am missing her. I've had that feeling all morning." A shaft of light rolled across Mrs. Lenieu's face, revealing makeup haphazardly applied over pale, light brown skin. Ashley saw the heavy weight of sadness in her brown eyes, the disfiguring scars of grief on her face, and the trail of liquid pain rolling down her cheeks. "She was my life. I brought her into this world. Now I've got to kiss her goodbye. Does a murderer ever think of the intense grief he causes? My husband told me not to come here today. He said I should rest. But I wanted to come . . . to touch her clothes, her bed . . . to feel her presence. I fell asleep for an hour this morning. I dreamt I saved her." A warm breeze suddenly rushed over them, blowing their hair high.

Ashley heard Samuel Barber's "Adagio for Strings" rising from one of the neighboring houses, beyond tall hedges. She turned and looked out over a beautiful, well-manicured verdant lawn and a garden of red and white roses. A yellow butterfly floated over them. She was reminded of her parents' backyard and its garden that she and her mother tended while discussing flowers, clothing, dating candidates, choice of colleges and carnival balls. Financial matters were reserved for talks with father. She hadn't had one of those talks with mother in a long time. She was slowly accepting the fact that they were history.

"Ow!" Ashley exclaimed, and looked down to witness two battling armies of ants at her feet. Some were crippled, dragging their torsos in a valiant attempt to save themselves. Ashley swatted at them, turned to reenter the apartment, and felt a cold rush of air over her face and arms. The crucifix above the door fell to the floor, landing near the phone stand. She bent down to pick it up and, on rising, noticed the top of the answering machine had popped up, exposing the cassette tape. Suddenly, she was tempted to take the tape. Her body tightened. She felt a pressure behind her eyes. She looked over her shoulder, ejected the tape, and put it in her purse. She turned around to be greeted by a tall man with short black hair in the doorway. Did he see her take the tape, she wondered? She then noticed the answering machine cassette lid was still open.

"Hello, I'm Philip Lenieu," the man said, extending his hand.

"Oh! Hello," she said, as she shook his hand. "I'm Ashley Tarleton from

Channel 3 News. It's a pleasure to meet you. Sorry it had to be under these circumstances."

"Yes. I don't know if we really want to give a statement at this time," Philip said.

"I understand," Ashley said, looking at his face and into his sad eyes, and seeing that his complexion was definitely white.

Yvonne stepped out of the bathroom. Philip walked toward her and said, "I've got the Lexus packed."

Ashley took two steps backward, bent downward a bit, and closed the lid. "I'll leave now. I appreciate your time," she said.

"We're leaving, too. We have a lot to do," Philip said.

"We'll talk another time," Yvonne said.

"Yes," Ashley said, knowing they probably would not. She tried twice to close the door behind her but it sprang open, leaving a crack through which she saw the Lenieus in a tender and desperate embrace. She walked toward the stairs. The man in 2A opened his door.

"I thought I heard those heels again," he said, smiling.

"Yes. Well, you heard correctly," she said, with a faint smile, and continued down and out.

"You're my favorite," he said.

Ashley opened the car door and stepped in, swinging her auburn hair over her shoulders.

"What took so long?" Wyatt said, starting the car.

"Don't be so insensitive," Ashley replied.

"I'm not insensitive. I'm not! It's non-stop sweat out here," Wyatt said.

"Turn on the air conditioner," Ashley said, then stared off into the distance.

"I did but I couldn't keep the car running all this time. What's up with you? You look dazed," Wyatt said. Ashley reached into her purse and pulled out the cassette. "How did you get that?"

"In the apartment," Ashley said.

"The mother gave it to you?" he asked.

"No."

"Don't tell me you took it," Wyatt said, with raised eyebrows and wide-eyed.

"I felt compelled. It was as if it was presented to me," Ashley confessed.

"Presented?" he asked, puzzled.

"Just drive."

"You've got to return it now. Her parents will see it's missing," Wyatt said.

"I will," she said.

"How will you manage that?" he asked.

"I don't know," she said, as Wyatt started to make a U-turn.

"You can't make a U-turn on Nashville," Ashley stated, with raised voice.

"Watch me," he said, defiantly. He made the turn, nearly missing a parked Fiat.

"Watch out for that car!" she squealed.

"You told me to just drive," Wyatt said.

"You're not funny. Show some respect for the law," Ashley insisted.

"You're the one who lifted a tape, not me," Wyatt said.

Ashley shook her head and stared straight ahead, as they turned the corner onto St. Charles Avenue.

"I take it you met the mother or father?" Wyatt inquired.

"Both. He's white – the man loading the Lexus; she's black," she said.

"She's black? So, the girl from last night . . ." Wyatt's words trailed off.

"Was black."

"Wow! She didn't look it," Wyatt said. "But you never know in this town. There's so much 'cross-over.' If one of the parents is black, though, then the child is definitely considered to be black, too – no matter how light the skin. Was she pretty?"

"The mother?"

"Yes," Wyatt said.

"Yes. I suppose she is," she said.

"Some white men find these women alluring, exotic, seductive, now as in the past," Wyatt mentioned.

"What do you mean?" Ashley asked.

"The Quadroon Balls in the French Quarter before the Civil War. The rich Creole men, the planters and businessmen, of New Orleans would take a mistress from one of those balls. That was the purpose – to parade these pretty young women who were a quarter black before those men who could afford to set up a love nest for the two of them on Rampart Street. They even had children by them but never married. That was not possible. You've heard about that, haven't you?" Wyatt asked.

"I know of the practice of *placage,* but the balls themselves, I read, are just a myth," Ashley said.

"I saw a Times-Picayune ad from the 1840s advertising Quadroon Balls every Sunday night at The Washington and American Ballroom on St. Philip street in the Quarter. That's what I read. And what's *placage?*" Wyatt asked.

"It was a legal agreement, a civil union, between a wealthy white man and a female free person of color," she said. "Study your New Orleans history."

"Well, I worked with a reporter from the newspaper on a story about the balls, and the cross-over thing . . . blacks passing for whites and blacks descended from lighter blacks. Maybe the mother is passing for white," Wyatt said.

"Maybe the daughter was, too," Ashley added.

"Yeah. I mean why not do that? It makes things a whole lot easier," Wyatt said.

"I guess it does," Ashley confessed.

"It definitely does. Theirs is a different world," Wyatt rightfully observed. "And, by the way, I saw two ads from the 1840s' Times - Picayune, not just one, when I worked with that reporter. So, you need to do your research, not me."

Ashley ignored his comment and inserted the cassette into the tape deck and pressed "Rewind." A winding sound was heard, then stopped. The "Play" light appeared. A woman's voice was heard. "Hi, Eve. Your father and I will pick you up at seven tomorrow for dinner at Antoine's. Love you." A pause preceded the next recorded message of a young woman's voice. "Hey, Eve, it's Jules. We're all meeting at House of Blues about six or so. Try to make it. There's a guy I want to introduce you to. See ya then. Bye."

"Maybe that guy was the perpetrator," Wyatt suggested.

Another recorded message, that of a man's somewhat raspy voice was heard. "Be at the Decatur Street entrance to Jackson

Square at ten o'clock. I'll pick you up and bring you to him."

"That's it! He's the one," Wyatt exclaimed.

Ashley felt a chill run down her spine. She was momentarily frozen, her eyes fixed on the cassette player.

"Yes. That could be the murderer's voice," Ashley said.

"You've got to bring this tape back. How are you going to manage that?" Wyatt wondered.

"I'll think of something," Ashley said. "But I've got to find out who these two men are."

"Wait. You're not Nancy Drew. A woman's been murdered — it appears. If not, it would be a hell of a coincidence," Wyatt declared.

Ashley looked straight into Wyatt's eyes and firmly said, "I know, Wyatt."

Ashley stared forward down the Avenue, seeing not its beauty, rather only disturbing images in her mind. Closing Yvette's eyes at the scene of the murder flashed across her mind, followed quickly by Mrs. Lenieu's face, followed by her own mother's face impacted by illness and the crush of time. At the beginning of the year her mother was not severely ill yet. She herself was still married, though not so happily. She had a nice job as entertainment reporter. All was well. She enjoyed afternoon teas with friends at the Windsor Court Hotel. She was witness to what was the good life. Now she was a witness to an apparent murder. Now she was in the middle of a maelstrom of changes that were pulling her down and around into a black vortex from which she couldn't escape. She couldn't close her eyes any longer to her mother's fate, her divorce, her life, her own city under siege. She looked out over the beauty of the Avenue that she thought would open up at any minute and swallow her, and the Avenue's thick canopy of oak trees would suddenly fall on her, extinguishing her existence.

CHAPTER 8

Reconstruction

"I'll meet you back here in an hour," Ashley said to Wyatt, as she got out of the car in the TV 3 News parking garage in the French Quarter. "We've got to be at St. Thomas by two o'clock."

"I take it you don't mean the Virgin Islands," Wyatt quipped, as he pulled his camera from the car's backseat.

"I don't mean the Virgin Islands," she said, placing her purse strap over her shoulder.

"Alright. Better wear some armor . . . and carry some, too," Wyatt warned.

"I'll have you to protect me," Ashley laughingly said.

"Am I supposed to do that, too?" Wyatt asked.

"See you here in sixty," she said, exiting the garage.

"If I'm not here, go without me. Say hello to the Bloods and the Crips and the Wu-Tang Clan," he said, shaking his head.

Ashley walked down Chartres Street toward St. Peter Street, at St. Louis Cathedral and Jackson Square. When she reached that corner, she saw a crowd of people to her right in the walkway between the Cathedral and the Square. The crowd was comprised of tourists of all ages and both genders. She heard someone screaming, so she joined the crowd and stood on her toes to see. She saw a young man standing next to the black wrought-iron gate, playing a black acoustic guitar and screeching the words to a song. He was dressed in a black tee shirt and black jeans and had orange hair cut in a Mohawk. He shouted...

You're so phony, you're so sick.

I'm so sick of you

Cause you're so full of shit!

All of you! You bourgeois hypocrites

I'm so sick of you.

You're so full of shit.

Here's what I think of you . . .

The young man dropped his guitar, dropped his pants, and defecated on the sidewalk. He then threw his feces at the crowd. The crowd exploded in a paroxysm of disgust and astonishment, and parted like a grenade had been thrown in its direction.

"Oh, my God!" people said, as they checked their clothing for stains. But many quickly looked at the young man to see what he would do next.

"Did you see that?" someone said, while others hurriedly left the scene.

Two policemen ran around the opposite corner of the Square. They pushed the young man to the ground, handcuffed him behind his back, and then led him to a nearby police car.

An elderly tourist said, "Lord, save us! What's this world coming to?"

"I assure you, ma'am, this behavior is not typical of New Orleans," one officer said.

Ashley turned to walk the half block to the Gumbo Shop and almost bumped into the French Quarter Jesus who was walking toward her with another homeless disciple.

"Oh, God!" she muttered, as she tried to steer clear of them.

"There were flames thirty feet tall that night. I saw them," the man said to Jesus.

"Yes. The Demon can take on many forms," Jesus said. He then spotted Ashley and said, "Hey! I know you. Woman, I need your help. Don't you want to save your soul? Leave your empty life. Join me. Are you a slave?"

Ashley's body tightened and she felt a chill down her spine as she sped up to avoid him, nearly tripping over several garbage bags blocking the sidewalk on the opposite side of St. Peter Street. In seconds she was at the doorway of the Gumbo Shop. She walked up the dim, damp entrance-alleyway, her arm brushing against the cool brick wall as she bypassed a line of people waiting for tables. She saw Darryl Delaney sitting at a small table in the small square courtyard. She walked through the glass door of the main dining room, and then left into the patio.

Courtyards, prevalent through the French Quarter, were constructed within these homes, providing quiet sanctuary away from street activity. The floor and walls of the Gumbo Shop's courtyard were brick. The left wall was that of a two-hundred-year old building, once a home, next door. The right and rear walls supported second-story offices that were once slaves' quarters before the Civil War when New Orleans was the "Belle of the South" and its largest port. Slaves from Africa and the Caribbean served their masters' every whim, and then retired to cramped quarters behind the main house. These quarters contained the kitchen downstairs and tiny bedrooms above. French doors opened to a small balcony overlooking the courtyard. Slaves from their bedrooms peeked through red-checkered curtains, fearfully unwilling to open those doors and enjoy the view because its beauty and serenity were not meant for them. Some people claim to have seen their ghosts, looking down from those rooms, still enslaved and unable to leave their joyless world.

Darryl was seated under a tall banana tree with large three-foot feather-like leaves bending down. He was short, overweight and forty-five years old. He had a bald spot on the crown of his head. His black hair was thinning in front, which he tried to conceal with a comb-over. His cheeks were red and the flesh under his chin rested over his unbuttoned white button-down collar. He had a voracious appetite for reading, work and food. Ashley took the seat opposite him.

"Hey. You're just in time. Want something to eat? Best Shrimp Creole in town," he said, scooping a large portion onto his fork.

"No thank you. I don't feel up to it. You should have seen what I just saw," Ashley said, in astonishment.

"What?" Darryl asked.

"A boy . . . by the Square . . . shouting about excrement . . . then he threw some in the crowd," she said, still exasperated by the event.

"Oh . . . that kid. He's done that before," Darryl calmly said, as he switched to his bowl of corn-crawfish chowder.

"Really?" Ashley asked, aghast.

"You've never seen him?" Darryl asked.

"No," Ashley said. 'That's insane!"

"Did they arrest him?" he asked.

"Yes."

"They'll run him out of town eventually," he said, breaking off a piece of French bread.

"Darryl, how can you be so complacent?" Ashley asked, tilting her head a bit.

"I only let the big stuff worry me . . . like what happened to you last night. Are you okay?" he asked, staring straight into her eyes. "I didn't get a chance to talk to you earlier."

"Yes . . . I guess . . . I don't know. It all happened so quickly. But I'm having flashbacks in slow motion. It's nightmarish. What's happening to our city? This is crazy. I never thought I would witness a murder," she said, despairingly and shaking her head.

"It's dementia. Anarchy. The heat. Some people have lost control. They're doing whatever they want. The criminals know the city is falling apart and NOPD is corrupt itself – at least part of it. Look at the police officer who murdered the very people she was assigned to protect. Remember her?" Darryl asked.

"Yes. She murdered some of the family members and stole the money from their business," Ashley said.

"Right . . . actually murdered the people she was guarding. Now, that's insane," Darryl said.

"But why, Darryl? Why all the murders? Why now?" she wondered.

"It's a simple collapse of order. It happens all the time. Happens on a molecular level, happens on a social level . . . happens to individuals, happens to societies – civilizations. In a city it's usually brought on by economic factors. And New Orleans has always been a poor city. Still is. After a certain period of time of suffering and decline, a new wave of people come in to the picture to reestablish order; or, no one comes and the house or city is abandoned. Comings and goings happen all the time. You don't always notice. But everything is in motion at all times," he said matter-of-factly, finishing his iced tea.

"Are you saying New Orleans is being abandoned?" Ashley asked.

"We're losing part of New Orleans, part of its identity, forever. Businesses are closing. People are leaving. Crime's going up with unemployment. New businesses will open. But the threat that a unique city like New Orleans faces, is that when it is rebuilt it might look like any other American city" Darryl explained.

"Why?"

"Because of chain stores . . . franchises that will come here to help rebuild and take away some of the city's originality in the process. They have the capital to rebuild in their images, not New Orleans'. We don't have the capital. We're at their mercy. It's Reconstruction all over again," he said, matter-of-factly.

A young waitress placed more French bread on the table.

"Thank you, darling," Darryl said, looking up to admire her pretty face.

"Is there anything else I can get you?" the waitress asked.

"Another iced tea and a big fan," he said, as he wiped sweat from his brow.

"I'll see what I can do," she said, smiling. "Ma'am," she continued, turning to Ashley.

"I'll have a Perrier with a twist of lime. Thank you," Ashley responded.

"It's hot out here but I love courtyards," Darryl said, leaning back and adjusting his belt.

"Yes, so do I. I've always loved the Quarter. It's a shame that it's buried under garbage. Imagine what tourists must think," Ashley said.

"And the Press, national and international. Nice for them to see this," he said sarcastically. "They already think we're lazy and backwards down here as it is. To them, we now wallow in our own filth, figuratively and literally."

"Yes," Ashley agreed.

"So, how did the Press treat Conright at his big PR rally?" Darryl asked.

"He was asked some tough questions about racism and his ability to control the city."

"What did you ask him?" Darryl wondered.

"I asked him about his denial of the Holocaust" she said.

"Good."

"But before he could respond, a survivor, Bella Blum, stepped forward and really let him have it. It was very emotional . . . and I've got it all on tape . . . and an interview with Bella," Ashley proudly offered.

"Wow! Your first day reporting the hard stuff. Fantastic!" Darryl proclaimed.

"Wayne . . ."

"You mean Wyatt?" Darryl asked.

"Yes. He's in editing. I'll do the intro at 10," she said.

"Excellent. This whole possible Nazi-KKK affiliation is why the world press is here, of course. So, it's particularly good that you got that incident today on tape. We'll lead with that," Darryl said.

"Okay. Are you friends with Conright or Chenier?" Ashley asked.

Darryl very deliberately said, "I don't know either for who they really are. I've met both at balls and galas and the Audubon 'Zoo to Do' . . . things like that. But if either is guilty of any wrongdoing, then we must report it. Same thing is true of any crime committed by anyone . . . or a racist affiliation . . . you must report it, even if that person is a stranger or a personal friend. Journalism is a quest for the truth . . . the whole truth . . . and nothing but. Shine the spotlight – in the deep of the night or high noon."

"I like that," Ashley said. "Who do you think is better for the city?"

"Neither," he said. "The mayor has lost control of the city and it's unlikely he will ever regain it. If Conright is elected, he'll allow any business with money from anywhere to come in and set up shop at whatever the cost to the city's identity and population. If they want to destroy landscapes or neighborhoods or break the law, he'll let them. For reconstruction. He may or may not realize that in doing so, little pieces of old New Orleans will vanish just as sure as the River removes soil from the banks of the city every day. Both are clever guys, though. Don't get me wrong. But Conright's no leader. And the mayor was once strong but not now."

"What do you mean?" she said, taking a linen handkerchief from her purse and patting her forehead.

"He was in the forefront of the Civil Rights movement in the 60s," Darryl said.

"He was? I didn't know that," Ashley admitted.

"Oh, yeah. Absolutely," Darry explained. "He marched with Martin Luther King. He took part in the Freedom Rides. He was a member of the Student Nonviolent Coordinating Committee. He was a strong leader – then. A number of those young pioneers went on to achieve some prominence, like the mayor. And a number of them have since fallen, like the mayor. As strong as they once were, they are no longer strong enough to stop their new foes: crime, violence, economic decline. The patient is bleeding and they can't stop it."

The waitress brought an iced tea with beads of water rolling down its sides, and a Perrier to the table. Darryl poured six sugar packets into it and held up his glass in toast and said, "Here's to the truth, Ashley . . . and an additional assignment for you."

Ashley held up her glass and said, "What additional assignment?"

"I need you to take Jennifer's place on the debate panel." Darryl said.

"The mayoral debate? Darryl, I can't do that," Ashley said, startled by such news. "I'm not ready for that kind of exposure. I'm afraid I'll fall flat on my face."

"Don't ever let fear stop you from achieving. You can do it," Darryl said.

"No . . ."

"Yes, you can. Don't underestimate yourself. You may think the only reason I gave you the entertainment reporter's position was because I've known your father for a long time. And, in part, that's true. I've seen you at functions around town. I've noticed that you're well-spoken, smart and gracious" Darryl assured.

"Thank you. But I'm not smart. You've got the wrong woman," Ashley said.

"Never put yourself down. One thing I noticed was your ex would give you a stern look whenever you spoke up about anything," he said.

"You're very observant," she said.

"Some women live the life of master-servant all their lives. And, little by little, it kills them. You've got to speak up. Now's your time," Darryl asserted.

"Well, I can't argue with you on that," she said, as a photo of her mother standing behind her father flashed across her mind. "Maybe you're right. But the debate . . ."

"Call Jennifer. She'll review some questions with you. She'll give you some pointers, and then you can go into that debate feeling confident," he said.

"I don't know about feeling confident," she said, hesitantly.

"You can do this. I'm counting on you. Just don't let them intimidate you," he said, and then took a big bite of Southern Pecan pie with vanilla ice cream on top.

Ashley's portable phone rang. She reached down into her purse and retrieved it. She swung her hair back and slipped the phone next to her ear.

"Hello . . . Yes . . . Did you? . . . Well, thank you . . . No . . . Well . . . I don't know if I should . . . . All right then . . . Yes, eight o'clock . . . Thank you . . . Yes, I'll see you then . . . Goodbye." She looked at Darryl. "Guess who I'm having dinner with this evening?"

"Who?"

"Keiffer Conright . . . at Antoine's. Is that permissible,

considering I'm reporting the election?" she said, as she squinted her questioning eyes.

"Sure. But nothing he says is off the record," Darryl advised.

"I wonder why he wants to take me to dinner?" Ashley asked.

"To influence your reporting . . . and to hit on you, probably," Darryl suggested.

"Do you think?" Ashley replied.

"He's a single guy. You're an attractive woman. He probably knows you're divorced. And your exchange with him today possibly got him excited," Darryl said.

"Oh, come on, Darryl."

"I'm serious. He wants you. No doubt," Darryl said, tilting his head.

"Well, he can't have me," Ashley forcefully said.

"A woman's refusal has never stopped a determined man," Darryl stated.

"Maybe he's never encountered a refusal from a determined woman," she said.

"*Touche!* You see, you are ready for that debate. Good luck," Darryl said, and paused. "Now, where's my second dessert?"

CHAPTER 9

Sunrise, Sunset

Ashley met Wyatt at the Channel 3 News car in the garage.

"Are you ready for this strange rendezvous?" Wyatt asked.

"Yes."

"Did you tell Darryl about this?" Wyatt continued.

"No."

"What about Yvette's mother?" Wyatt asked.

"No. I was afraid he would tell me not to pursue those leads," Ashley said.

"He probably would have," he said, starting the engine and catching a glimpse of Ashley's legs as she entered the car. "Load your weapons. Let's roll." As Wyatt backed out of the garage, he hit the brakes. "Jesus!"

"What?" Ashley said, as she turned around and looked through the rear window.

Wyatt had just missed hitting the "Mad Woman of the French Quarter." At one time she probably stood five feet eight inches or so, but now was old and bent over. She wore old pants and shirt with a tattered shawl. Her real gray, stringy hair stuck out underneath her silver-gray wig that hung over her forehead and recessed, dark eyes. Those ancient eyes, like fish eyes, followed anyone approaching her. Her name and destination were unknown. She walked the French Quarter streets at all hours, mumbling mad gibberish. But the only person she ever spoke to was herself.

"It's that old lady. She's off in some other world," she said.

"A few more feet and she would have been in the next world," Wyatt said. They exited the garage, turned left on St. Peter, left on Royal, and then left again on Toulouse to Decatur. Wyatt saw

Dennis the Menace running toward him, being chased by the French Quarter Jesus and his new homeless disciple. "Nut case is at it again."

"He's frightening," Ashley said.

"But then again . . . that kid he's chasing has beaten up some homeless people. One day Jesus will catch him and the wrath of the Almighty will descend on that kid's head," Wyatt said.

They continued up Decatur, across Canal Street, and onto Poydras Avenue, and then turned left onto St. Charles Avenue.

"Do you know where this is?" Ashley inquired.

"St. Thomas? Yeah . . . it's between St. Charles and the River . . . I think," Wyatt said.

"I thought you knew where," Ashley replied.

"I'll take a left up here – somewhere," he said, as he rounded Lee Circle and continued up the Avenue.

"We should ask for directions," Ashley suggested.

"I'm not going to ask directions to the projects. We're both born and raised here. We can find it. It's over by the River. Why did I even agree to do this?" he asked, frustrated and shaking his head.

"Yvette. Remember?" Ashley said, noticing the Pontchartrain Hotel on her right.

"Yeah, but we don't know her. And we're risking our lives," he said, as he slowed down to turn left on Jackson Avenue.

"Not here. Turn on Washington," Ashley directed.

"Why Washington?"

"I thought I heard someone mention it while on my way to Commander's . . . I was with friends," she said.

"What friends of yours would know about the St. Thomas Housing Project?" he asked, perplexed.

"I'll have you know my friends and I are well-schooled," she said, somewhat aggravated.

"Yeah. In what?" he mumbled.

"Just drive," she said.

"I'm not just your driver, you know," he said.

"Okay. Here's Washington," she said, noticing Chopin Florist on the left, while surveying the area. "I think you've got to go down one block and make a U-turn."

"Yes, ma'am," Wyatt replied, laughingly, while shaking his head.

Wyatt made a U-turn, and then drove down a block, and turned right onto Washington Avenue. They came to the white-walled Lafayette Cemetery No. 1 in the second block on the right, and then passed Commander's Palace Restaurant on the left. Once a home, the light blue building was now and had been for many years one of New Orleans' best restaurants and a culinary white rose in Ashley's uptown garden.

"Keep going straight," she said.

They drove by large, stately homes, mixed with smaller, less expensive homes, but equally refined, crossing over Coliseum and Camp streets. They crossed over Magazine Street and the houses became smaller and poorer, and the neighborhood moodier and less attractive, revealing its true age. Houses with old faces stared at them, suspicious of these intruders.

Wyatt, feeling very uneasy, said, "I'm getting out of here. Call that number and tell them to meet us." He turned left on Laurel.

"Wait! Don't you have a map in this car?" she asked, as she searched the glove compartment.

"Not a map of housing projects," he snapped.

"Slow down. Look at this," she said, opening the map and blocking the windshield.

"Watch out!" he said, turning right again. "Get that thing out of my face!" He turned right, then left once more and crossed over Jackson Avenue at Chippewa, and took a right on Josephine. Ashley unfolded another flap, totally obscuring his view. He hit the brakes, pushed the map away and looked up. "Jesus! This is a one-way street." He continued two blocks anyway and turned left on Rousseau and stopped. "Holy shit!"

Five young black men stood in the street about ten feet ahead of the car. Three had long baggy pants on that rode very low at the waist, exposing multi-colored underwear. Two others wore pants cut off below the knee. One was shirtless but held on to a tee shirt wrapped around his neck. Two wore long lime and yellow Fubu jerseys. One wore a black tee shirt with the word "FEARLESS" printed on it. Another one wore a tombstone photo on his tee shirt. The photo was of a young black man. "In Loving Memory of My Brother Calvin 'CK' Jefferson" was written under the photo; below were the words, "Sunrise 8-1-74 Sunset 8-8-94." They all wore gold chains, some close to the neck, others with long rope chains with medallions. Two wore black, polyester stocking-like caps that tightly fit over their heads. They all wore running shoes. Half-exposed handguns could be seen in their waistbands. Ten hidden eyes stared straight at Wyatt and Ashley from behind menacing-looking sunglasses.

Ashley felt a nervousness in the pit of her stomach. She pulled her skirt over her knees as every inch of her skin tightened. Her eyes frantically searched the area for an escape.

"Put it in reverse. Back out of here now!" Ashley commanded.

"I thought of that," Wyatt calmly said. "Take a look back there."

Three children on bicycles were directly behind the car. Parked cars lined the narrow street on both sides. Forward and behind the young black men, now approaching the car, loomed the mournful St. Thomas Housing Project. So bleak looking and in such a state of disrepair, it seemed to be in pain.

The men searched the car and their heads disappeared as they moved to the sides. Then, they lowered their heads and stared straight at Wyatt and Ashley. The shirtless man was opposite Wyatt's side window. Wyatt lowered his window.

"Don't do that!" Ashley exclaimed, excitedly.

"Hey . . . blood . . . bloods . . .," Wyatt nervously, haltingly said.

"Don't say that!" Ashley complained.

"How's it going? We're from . . .," Wyatt said, before being cut off.

"We want your wallet, your camera and the woman," the shirtless man, coldly said. Ashley's blood pressure surged. She pulled her skirt over her knees even farther and sat straight up. Wyatt's face was frozen by shock and disbelief. The man smiled and said, "I'm just fucking with you . . . blood."

"Oh! Yeah . . . sure," Wyatt said in relief, as Ashley nearly slid out of her seat. "Well, we're from Channel 3 News . . ."

"No shit! You got fucking 'Channel 3 News' written all over your fucking doors. Or, don't you think I can read? Follow me," the shirtless man commanded.

He walked ten feet, crossed a narrow street, then stepped onto the St. Thomas grounds. The other four walked alongside the car, two on either side.

"You want me to drive on the grounds? Shouldn't I park the car on the street?" Wyatt shouted, sticking his head out the window. His questions were ignored, so he jumped the curb and crept along over ground and brown grass. The scene looked like two rescue relief workers being escorted through a war-torn city. They continued toward dreary, three-story red brick buildings turned brown, burnt by the sun. This was Third World shelter, only minutes from the Avenue. This was, "The Land Time Forgot." This was the birthplace of fear and rage. This was the epicenter of a violent quake of the city's soul, felt daily throughout the town and measured in murders. "Now you know what I meant about our lives being at risk," Wyatt said to Ashley, who remained silent, rubbing her hands together. Women with small children at their feet and infants on their hips stared from half-opened doors, as the car was led deeper into the housing project. Some men were seen looking on from the shadows. They were led between two closely situated apartment buildings and came out into a courtyard, unlike the idyllic ones in the French Quarter. This courtyard was the size of two football fields and separated two unoccupied, uninhabitable buildings in severe disrepair; unhinged doors, broken windows, missing persons. This courtyard was removed from the street but did not offer sanctuary or a feeling of peace. It was anxiety-provoking. Wyatt and Ashley got the feeling they were in harm's way. This part of the housing project was known as "The Big Valley." "Jesus! Ground Zero."

The shirtless man commanded Wyatt to stop by pointing to the ground. Then he walked up to Wyatt and said, "Get your camera." Wyatt got out and grabbed his camera. Ashley followed. The young man walked next to Ashley and after looking her over, said, "Miss Polly Purebred. Let me show you to your table, Miss Polly. I'll seat you in the extremely white section."

Ashley's heartbeat quickened as the five men laughed. Wyatt and Ashley followed them into a first-floor apartment where they encountered other men – two standing and one seated on a small, stained mauve-colored sofa. The walls were covered with graffiti, mostly names, and "Kill the Cops." Broken glass and trash littered the floor.

The two standing men were dressed similarly to the others. The coolly confident seated man wore shiny black baggy jeans and a shimmering gold V-neck pullover shirt, with a kingly gold link chain from which hung a three-inch gold cross.

"Sorry I can't offer you a seat," the man said.

"That's all right," Ashley said, looking around, not knowing where to step.

"Are you TheRe?" Wyatt asked.

"That's what they call me," TheRe said, proudly.

"The Redeemer," one of the young men said.

"Why did you want to talk to me? And did you have anything to do with Yvette Lenieu's murder?" Ashley asked.

"Start taping," TheRe said to Wyatt who had begun taping before they entered. "I wanted you here to tell you exactly that. I had nothing to do with that drive-by . . . and neither did my boy CT. We were nowhere near the Quarters last night."

"Do you have an alibi?" Ashley asked.

"Shit!" They all laughed. "You think cops would believe my alibi? They want me dead or behind bars in Angola. Yeah, I've sold some drugs to my people but I didn't murder nobody," TheRe said.

"But a judge might . . .," Ashley added.

"You white people just don't get it!" TheRe said, and slammed his hand down on a small table before him. Ashley felt a tremor run the length of her body. But Wyatt smiled because he thought it was all a show for the camera. "Ain't no judge going to believe me. White man's rules don't apply to us colored folk. You're guilty until proven guilty here. Your laws are designed to keep me and my people from you and yours. Black men run from cops because the fucking cops kill black men – innocent men. You're a reporter . . . report that. Report the truth. It's the same here as all over the world. Open your eyes. This planet is a fucking slave planet."

"That's right," the apostles agreed.

"You think slavery is over?" TheRe asked. "It ain't fucking over! Black men are kidnapped by police who are supposed to 'serve and protect' them . . . they're framed and sent to rot in prison. We're treated like shit in your society. White men rule, black men suffer."

"Amen, brother!" his disciples said, in unison.

"White people just don't get it. When riots happen in cities in this country sometimes . . . . What do you think causes that? White people think we're animals . . . but it's blacks rebelling . . . they can't take it – the injustice anymore and they explode in rage . . . Rage! It's Us . . . and You," TheRe declared.

All eyes were on Ashley. She stood accused of all the crimes of the white race against each and every black, she felt. She was nervous and nauseous. She looked at the stone faces of the young black men. The only smiling face was that of the dead man on the tombstone tee shirt. She seriously thought about leaving but decided to stand her ground.

"Then why do you sell drugs to your own people?" she asked.

"Why? I'm a businessman. Why make $300 a week slaving in the white man's world when I can make $300 or more a day in business for myself? And I got to feed my family. I'm CEO of my own enterprise. I'm just like the man who owns Wild Turkey or Jim Beam," TheRe explained.

"That's right," a follower added.

"Drugs are illegal and ruin people's lives," Ashley quickly replied.

"And alcohol doesn't? See the people in the project?" TheRe

asked. "These are my people. I take care of them. Their lives were ruined by your society, not by me. If they want to relieve the pain they face every day living like this, why shouldn't they? I provide money, credit for drugs and other needs. I'm a fucking lending institution and general store. And my money I make from my people, I turn around and give it back in some way . . . or another. I'm doing the work of Jesus here . . . ."

"The work of Jesus?" she inquired, shocked by such a comparison. "So, that's what the 'redeemer' means."

Wyatt almost lost his grip on the camera.

"That's right. Jesus," TheRe asserted. "If Jesus was around today, he would live in a ghetto because He was a black man. Only a black man would be made to suffer that much," he said, turning to his left to allow Wyatt to film him head-on. "Same now as it was then. In desperate times, people look for a leader . . . a man of conscience . . . a spiritual and intelligent man to lead them . . . a man like me. I'm a powerful man. Me and my men could raze this town to the ground, if we wanted to. And sometimes we have cause to . . . like when the cops come gunning for us. But we would rather not play at that . . . because we are peaceful men, though people in this city and the cops in particular, don't want you to know that. They say we are a gang of dope-dealing murderers. We do work for the poor. Who's going to help them, if not me? You? That's why I need you to broadcast this news to the city and the cops, that we did not do that girl last night. We don't kill in cold blood . . . not our style. You understand?"

"Who did kill her?" Ashley asked.

"We don't know," TheRe said. "Could have been random . . . could have been on purpose . . . . It could have been some of the brothers from the other projects. Who knows? But everybody gets all upset when a white woman is gunned down and start pointing fingers at us . . . and saying 'the niggers did it!' We in here dying every day and nobody cares. It's like a dog fight in the projects . . . everybody on the outside looking in to see who wins . . . but not caring, just saying 'It's just another nigger dead . . . don't matter.'"

"Tell it like it is," one man said.

"She was black," Ashley said.

"Black!" he said, as if confused. "Shit! If she was black, my boy T-Bird here can really fly."

"I spoke to her parents this morning at the girl's Nashville apartment. Her mother is black," Ashley stated.

"Then that girl was passing," one member said.

"What?" Ashley asked.

"She crossed-over . . . passing for white. Ain't no sisters living on or right off the Avenue," another disciple said.

"No brothers neither," the man without a shirt said.

The other members laughed.

"When a sister is that white-looking, she cross over and don't look back," TheRe said.

"Well, I guess my work here is done," Ashley said, as she put away her notes.

"Lady, your work has just begun," TheRe said. "This is a violent world we live in . . . and sometimes the violence in my little piece of it busts out and innocent people get hurt, but we did not shoot that girl. I'm telling you true. You're a reporter. You're after the truth, right? So am I."

He rose and his gang of seven came to attention. Two walked to the doorway and peeked out, looking both ways for incoming anything. The others intensely looked on and listened like thieves. Ashley and Wyatt looked at each other with grave concern. Wyatt shook his head but continued to film. The men at the door motioned for all to come forward. They filed out, one by one, onto the elevated cement porch. As soon as Ashley walked down the few steps to the ground, gunshots were heard. Parts of brick rocketed off the building and dust rose like the igniting of miniature atomic bombs. Ashley fell face down onto the ground. Wyatt held his camera in one arm and grabbed Ashley with his other. He helped her up and pulled her close to the car, crouching low. He couldn't see the gunmen. He looked around and noticed the Sons of Jesus had disappeared.

"Looks like the Sons of Jesus aren't too brave. They're gone and we're screwed. Stay low," Wyatt advised. "Either you and I are extremely unlucky or someone's trying to kill us." Ashley's stomach was tight and getting tighter. She had never felt fear like this. Wyatt was right, she thought. They should not have come. Maybe she should not have taken this assignment. Maybe she should have stayed an entertainment reporter like her father instructed her to do, she thought. Wyatt looked around and saw a woman open the screen door of her apartment in the next building, motioning for them to come in. "We've got to run to that building. There's a woman motioning for us to go to her apartment."

"I don't know if I can," Ashley nervously said.

With his face right next to hers, and brushing against her hair, Wyatt said, "Pretend your life depends on it . . . except, don't pretend. Let's go." He helped her up and they moved forward. But she stumbled again as more gunfire was heard. "Come on!" he urgently said and helped her up again.

Wyatt and Ashley reached the bottom floor apartment and the woman flung open the tattered screen door. They rushed in and the door slammed shut, recoiling from the violent force that had opened it. Ashley jumped, thinking the gunmen were right behind them.

The apartment was dark and hot. The burgundy curtains were drawn. Neither could see well for a couple of minutes until their eyes adjusted. But they heard the sound of a fan and felt a slight breeze on their legs. A small hand slipped into Ashley's and guided her to a kitchen, no larger than a small car. In one corner were two other much younger children. Three feet from them was a hole in the wall. Wyatt followed.

"We stay here until the shooting stops," the woman said. "It's the safest place – away from the windows. You can sit on the floor if you want. We don't have room for a table and chairs."

"No. That's all right," Ashley said.

She looked down at the little girl holding her hand. Her pretty face was framed by two platted pigtails on either side. Pink ribbons were woven into her hair. The smiley face on her tee shirt belied an anxious sadness Ashley had never seen in a child. The other two children, she noticed, were mournfully frightened. She knelt down beside the little girl. She didn't know what to think of this surreal scene of a family huddled in a kitchen-bunker, hiding from an unknown evil on the loose just outside their door.

Ashley turned to the mother and said, "How often does this happen?"

"Lately, it's been almost every day," the woman said.

"How do you cope?" Ashley asked.

"I give it all up to God," she said, as Wyatt turned on the camera's light and zoomed in on her worried face. "My life is in His hands. I trust in Him to take care of us."

"And you find that comforting?" Ashley asked.

"Oh, yes. Very comforting. There's only so much a person can do. The rest is up to God," she said.

Ashley was dumbfounded by this statement of total resignation.

"Are you employed?" Ashley asked.

"Yes. I work for a janitorial service at night. We clean offices. In the morning I work as a housekeeper for one of the hotels downtown," she said.

"Who watches the children?" Ashley continued.

"Mark checks in on them. I can't afford no babysitter," she said.

"Who's Mark?" Ashley asked.

"The boy you just talked to out there. He's my son. I had him at 14," she said.

"Your son? Do you know the police are looking for him in connection with last night's murder?" Ashley informed the woman.

"Yes. He didn't kill that girl. He wouldn't do that kind of thing. I know he's been involved in shootings. But it's because of the other young men in the projects. They're all mixed up. He's trying to protect us. He saw his father shot dead when someone tried to rob him one day after work in broad daylight. It really hit him hard. He still cries about it. Now, he says he's got to fight fire with fire. But the fire's growing, and no one can put it out," the woman said.

Ashley was shocked. She could not begin to understand the violent world she had successfully avoided until now. But now she was in the midst of this whirlwind, this vortex of violent forces that were pulling at her, disturbing her own little world by rattling her mind and threatening her life.

"Is it okay now, Mama?" the little girl asked.

"I think so. I haven't heard any shots in the last few minutes," the mother said, as a strange reassurance. "I'll check."

She rose and opened the curtains, allowing sunlight to dissolve dark doom and anxiety.

"Take a look at the wall," Wyatt whispered to Ashley, who turned and saw three bullet holes randomly spaced about one foot apart above the couch.

The woman opened the door and looked out, as a young veteran of previous turf wars in a metallic purple wheelchair rolled hurriedly by, chasing the rolling thunder of the battle.

"It's okay now," she said.

"Thank you for helping us. We owe you one," Wyatt said, with a smile.

"Yes. Thank you. We don't even know your name," Ashley said.

"Betty Johnson. And this is my daughter, Alicia."

"Nice to meet you both," Ashley said.

Betty extended her hand which Wyatt quickly shook. "Very glad to meet you. Very glad." Wyatt then noticed that Ashley was a bit resistant to shake her hand. He felt like putting Ashley's hand in Betty's. But Ashley did slowly raise her hand and slipped it lightly into Betty's.

"Thank you," Ashley said. "I would really like to put you on the news tonight . . . if that's okay."

"All right," Betty said. "Maybe it will do some good. Maybe the mayor and the police chief will see how we struggle to live here."

Ashley saw sweat and anguish on Betty's round face. Her dark brown skin glistened in the sunlight. She used Kleenex to wipe away some sweat on her chest above her pink and white striped tank top. Ashley felt an odd anxiety come over her. She couldn't remember the last time she had actually spoken in person to a black person, not in her or her parents' employ as a maid or nurse, or in some other position of servitude like cashiers at K&B Drug Store or the counter help at the Camellia Grill, her favorite uptown diner for club sandwiches and homemade waffles. But even there she always sat at that part of the counter that Mr. Harry, the oldest and only white waiter served. She was always waited on by whites at her favorite French Quarter restaurants, Antoine's and Gallatoire's. She had no black friends and simply had no reason to associate with any on a personal basis, only professionally, as with the male news anchor at the television studio. But this desperately poor, fortyish black woman had quite possibly saved her life. She wasn't sure how to act or what to say.

"Can I give you any money . . ." Ashley suggested, as she began to open her purse.

"No need for that," Betty humbly said.

"Good-bye," Alicia said.

"Good-bye," Ashley said, bending down.

"Will you come back to see us?" Alicia asked.

"Baby, she's got work to do," Betty answered.

"I'm sure I'll see you again," Ashley said, knowingly lying, as she stared into the child's big brown eyes and wondering of her future. She straightened the bow in the girl's hair and stared into her sweet face. She smiled, revealing a slight separation between her front teeth. Ashley wondered how she could smile at all in such living conditions. Then she realized that the child was hopeful and still a child at heart, even in a war zone. "I like your name. It's pretty, like you."

"She watches you on TV," Betty said.

"You do?" Ashley said.

"Yeah. I want to be on TV . . like you. I want to do what you do," Alicia said.

"Well, I'm sure you will," Ashley said, not knowing what else to say.

But Wyatt, being a father of a little girl, stepped forward and said, "We'll talk to our boss. I'm sure we can arrange a visit for you."

Ashley, realizing this to be good and wishing she had thought of it, said, "Yes. We'll talk to our boss about that. Okay?"

"Okay," Alicia said, well pleased. "Friends."

"Yes. Friends," Ashley repeated.

"It's a date," Wyatt added.

"Thank you again," Ashley said, rising.

"That's okay," Betty said. "Just tell everyone that my boy did not kill that woman last night. He's not a murderer. He may get into fights with other boys in other housing developments over drugs and turf and all that . . . but he's not a murderer. That I know."

Wyatt opened the back door of the car to put his camera on the seat as Ashley opened the front door, and saw glass on the seat.

"Oh, shit! We've been hit," he said, sweeping glass off the seat with his hand. "The rear window's been shot out."

Ashley turned and said, "What do we tell Darryl?"

"Nothing," Wyatt said. "Remember, we're not supposed to be here. I'll get it fixed and submit the bill to Accounting."

"But he'll find out," she said.

"Then be creative," he said.

"How do you mean?" she wondered.

"Lie," he said, jumping in the front seat and starting the engine.

"I guess I'll have to," she said, as she plucked her tiny plastic bottle of anti-bacterial gel from her purse and spread it heavily on her hands.

CHAPTER 10

History

Mayor Xavier Chenier looked out the eighth-floor window of City Hall. He saw fifty or more protestors, mostly black, on the lawn and on the steps to the building. Some carried signs saying, "Stop the Murders," and "We Want Our City Back," and "Your Time Is Up." The city was under siege and so was City Hall, a modern rectangular building of glass that faced the New Orleans Public Library and Gravier Street on which Charity Hospital was just two blocks up. He moved his office from the second floor because the protestors, steadily growing in numbers, were too close and had thrown eggs and tomatoes at his windows. He rose above them, but not the city's problems. He looked to the sky and prayed for God's guidance as he wondered about the city, its history and his own.

His great, great grandfather, Pierre Auguste Chenier, once owned a 500-acre cotton plantation and 100 slaves before the Civil War. It was located up river about ten miles and called "Little Versailles." Pierre's father, Louis, was a wealthy Parisian who purchased the land during Napoleon's reign. Pierre was a Creole, a person of French (or Spanish) heritage born in Louisiana. He was educated in Paris, and then returned to the plantation to help his father oversee its operation, knowing he would inherit it. His life was one of mastery and privilege.

Pierre also purchased a beautiful home in New Orleans on Esplanade Avenue, one of the original boundaries of the French Quarter and the premiere street of Creole society. He entertained there weekly by giving lavish dinner parties. It was the place to see and be seen.

His wife, Josephine, and all the sophisticated Creole ladies in New Orleans were always elegantly dressed in fine floor-length silk and satin gowns with low, lace necklines, framing ruby and diamond necklaces on their white skin; their long dark hair gathered with bows behind their heads. The men, formally dressed, escorted their ladies from black-lacquered carriages through the tall front door where they exchanged pleasantries with other guests, as black servants immediately attended their needs. Those ambitious men were eager to make favorable impressions on Pierre and the other landholders by making insightful financial commentary on the cotton and sugar cane crops, or on the Americans who lived outside the French Quarter across Canal Street and down St. Charles Avenue, and who were singularly considered by the Creoles as an encroachment on their little world – the real New Orleans – ever since Napoleon sold Louisiana to the Americans in 1803.

The crops were always discussed, especially the bales of cotton and barrels of sugar that would cover the wharves in fall and winter. Also a topic of discussion was "Yellow Fever" that would significantly curtail port activity and significantly deplete the New Orleans' population by thousands, as many as 9,000 deaths in the summer of 1853. The changing face of the city spurred by the Americans, the waves of immigrants, and the rising crime rate were all feared. The men were anxious, as they sipped their absinthe, "the green fairy," because they knew that for all their present prosperity, they were losing control of their city. Bits and pieces of French Creole heritage were eroding away like the shoreline itself, and the ground on which they walked was no longer French, but American.

Candle flames fluttered, as servants holding sterling silver candle holders entered the dining room, lighting the way for a procession of foods on sterling silver platters – French onion soup, crawfish, oysters, shrimp, crabs, gumbo, chicken, beef, pork roast, jambalaya, sweet potatoes, shrimp-stuffed mirlitons, fried apples and cinnamon, pies, *mille-feuille* pastry, *beignets*, and pralines.

Though the hot air of the evening rose to ceilings twelve feet high, the night was still warm. Ladies and gentlemen exchanged furtive glances and smiles across the long mahogany table, and toasted beauty and the prosperous Creole way of life, though neither would withstand the weight of time, hanging like a shawl lined with lead on frail shoulders. Their houses, their furnishings, their clothes, their breaths, the sweet smell of camellias would, with time, become the suffocating stale smell of history; their books, dishes, spectacles, would become items on display for ignorant eyes of museum tourists whose own lives might one day be the source of casual curiosity of those yet unborn.

After dinner, the ladies and gentlemen would gather in the double parlor where a quartet played on piano, violins, and cello. Family portraits hung on the walls. The ladies glimpsed themselves in the large gold-framed mirror over the mantle as they moved from one room to another. Porcelain vases with palmettos in them flanked the mirror at either end of the mantle. The ladies laughed as they drank *café au lait* and ate pastries. The men moved into the adjacent parlor, or perhaps in the rear courtyard to discuss the newly opened French Opera House or the latest slave auction at the St. Louis Hotel, and rumors of civil war and the South's survival. Then the topic of conversation would turn to desire and the Quadroon Balls in the French Quarter where wealthy Creole men would meet young free women of color (non-slaves of light color and mixed blood) for the purpose of establishing a sexual relationship outside of marriage. The girls' mothers would also be in attendance to aid their daughters in introductions to men at the balls, many of which were held in the French Quarter at the Orleans Ball Room on Orleans Avenue behind St. Louis Cathedral, or in the Washington and American Ball Room on St. Philip street. These Creole men were already married but would purchase small cottages for the quadroon girls and maintain a lifelong relationship as man and mistress in civil unions. They would even have children together but would never marry. But those children did often inherit money or property from their fathers.

Pierre Chenier fathered a son with his mistress, Mazy, for whom he had purchased a Creole cottage just around the block on Rampart Street where he visited her weekly. Mazy was a beautiful sixteen-year-old quadroon who had entered into a legally binding civil union agreement known as *placage*. She respected Pierre but never really loved him. She would sometimes walk to Pierre's Esplanade Avenue house and stand in the shadows as she watched the private parties he gave, knowing she could never attend. She became more jealous with each visit, until she couldn't bear to watch any longer. Henri, Pierre's son from this union, lived and worked on his father's plantation in the tall shadow of his half-brother and half-sister from Pierre's wife, Colette. He slept in a small cabin between the "Big House" and the slaves' cabins; legally free but the South was still his Master. Pierre's children knew of Henri's mother, and purposely kept their distance from him. He envied them their privilege, especially during parties when he listened to chamber music not meant for his ears. His father gave him his name, employment and a small inheritance. But for the real love any child needs, Henri visited his mother as often as possible. She empowered him with the ability to think beyond social constraints of racial divides.

In the pre-dawn hours of April 24, 1862, Henri ran from his cabin to the levee and down river to see the final night of battle between Admiral David G. Farragut's Union fleet and the Confederates at Forts St. Philip and Jackson, a great distance away. He and others on the levee witnessed the night sky lit up by mortar shot and cannonballs exploding like shooting stars. Cannon fire ceased and only sniper fire from the shore was heard as Farragut's flagship, the sloop-of-war steamer named the USS Hartford and seventeen other ships, broke the blockade and sailed up river to capture New Orleans. Henri knew it was the end of the Confederacy in New Orleans, and the end of the French Creole Planter Society that had designed and installed a three-tiered society of segregation: whites, "free people of color" (*"gens de couleur libres"*), and the enslaved.

Shortly after the city was occupied, Henri joined the Union Army there. His father disinherited him and ended the relationship with Mazy by severely beating her. Pierre could not accept the fact that his slaves were no longer slaves and that his plantation was rapidly falling to ruin. On that fateful night, when he realized the South would lose the war, he drank a bottle of Cognac, walked outside and shot himself in the head so all the world could hear. His legitimate son and daughter moved to their father's Esplanade Avenue home but sold it to pay his debts. They then took an apartment on St. Ann street in the French Quarter and faded into history.

After the Civil War, Henri worked within the new reconstructed city government and was able to help his mother financially. She saw him later graduate from Straight University's Law School in New Orleans before she died, shortly after. He always remembered that among her last words were, "Believe in God and yourself. And remember me."

Frederick Douglas spoke at the University, founded in 1868 on Canal Street to aid blacks in their educations after the Civil War. Douglas's speech on freedom, equality and responsibility spurred within Henri the ambition to be a lawyer and a leader. He established a law practice in the city, one of a very few owned by a black man. In the 1890s he contributed to the defense of Homer Plessy, an octoroon who was racially discriminated against on a train in New Orleans, which led to Plessy's arrest at Press and Royal Streets. Henri later spoke at many colleges in the north and south. He fathered five children, all of whom became prominent citizens and activists in their own right. One son, Frederick, was the father of Xavier Pierre Chenier, the present mayor of New Orleans, a city under siege.

Mayor Chenier continued to stare out his office window atop his City Hall fortress, wondering if he could stop the city from bleeding to death.

"Mayor . . ." Guy, the mayor's public relations assistant, said.

Suddenly, siren sounds startled him. They grew louder as he searched Loyola Avenue. Then he saw an ambulance approaching from the Canal Street end of Loyola, near the Iberville Housing Project. People at the busy intersection of Tulane and Loyola jumped out of the way as the ambulance raced through. It slowed as it rounded the Gravier Street corner which bordered City Hall's lawn courtyard, named Duncan Plaza. The mayor saw it pass on its way to the rear "Emergency" entrance to Charity Hospital, two blocks down. He closed his eyes as another victim of violence was rushed from the front lines of battle to the overworked miracle-working Emergency staff already awaiting his arrival, like a patient nervously awaiting news about the severity of his illness. "My city is dying," he whispered.

"Mayor, are you alright? You look beat," Guy said.

"Maybe I am, literally," he said, walking toward his desk as large as his self-importance once was. He wiped sweat off his forehead and temples. "Is it me, or did the AC just go out again?"

"Yeah," Guy said, placing his hand near a vent. "No air."

"Must be three times in as many months," the mayor said, shaking his head.

"I think it is. I'll call the engineers," Guy said, picking up the phone.

"Tell them this time to engineer a solution. Turn on those fans," the mayor asked, as he sat down on his black leather chair.

Guy turned on two industrial-sized oscillating fans on tall stands. Papers blew off the mayor's desk. The mayor scrambled to retrieve them, placing them under the "I'm The Boss" paperweight.

"The engineers are on it," Guy assured the mayor, hanging up the phone.

"Yeah . . . on their asses. What about Sanitation? Has any progress been made on the strike? The city smells like a garbage dump for Christ's sake," the mayor said.

"Still stalled. They still want a pay increase of 7%," Guy said.

The mayor threw back his head and said, "That's unreasonable! We can't adjust the budget to meet that! We're facing possible layoffs next year as it is."

"I think the title 'Sanitation Engineers' has gone to their heads," Guy said, laughing. "They really think they're real engineers. And they want to get paid like a real engineer."

"You're right there," the mayor said.

"It's on today's agenda at the City Council's emergency meeting," Guy said.

"The emergency is money. The city doesn't have any," the mayor said.

"Maybe we need to open the old U.S. Mint on Esplanade and print our own damn money," Guy said, with a loud laugh, split into six staccato parts, each a little weaker than the one before it.

"Just don't tell the government," the mayor added.

"I won't, if you won't," Guy said.

Mayor Chenier pressed his hands against his temples and closed his eyes. He then unbuttoned his collar and loosened his green-black-orange horizontally striped silk tie. He massaged his scalp, then his face. His fingertips kneaded folds of fifty-five-year-old light brown skin which was sprinkled with moles and canyon-creased at the corners of his brown eyes. His jowls sagged and his cheeks were flatter because he no longer owned that firm face of four years ago when he took office. Fourteen-hundred stressful days of managing a city under siege had taken its toll and, like a river of time, had carved their tracks over the square-jawed once stone-like face, leaving scars only time and tragedy can make.

He ran his fingers through his wavy gray-black hair and looked at the framed photos on his desk. In the center was his family — wife, Eunice of twenty-six years, daughter, Clarice, and son, Justin. To the left was another photo of Clarice and her husband and baby daughter; to the right was a photo of a proud and smiling Justin in his St. Augustine high school cap and gown. On the wall behind him were many photos of the mayor taken during his career as a lawyer and his political career as city councilman, then mayor. Two were taken with President Clinton during trips to Washington. The wall also included a dozen photos taken during his youth in the 1960s as an active participant in the Civil Rights movement, standing with a friend in front of the Greyhound bus used for one of the Freedom Rides from Washington to New Orleans; another showed him shaking hands with Martin Luther King, Jr, just before the march across the Edmund Pettus Bridge in Selma, Alabama; another photo forever captured his religious-like fervor in his eyes as he delivered a fiery speech to other black students at the headquarters of the Student Nonviolent Coordinating Committee; and another photo showed him with one arm over the shoulder of good friend and fellow activist, James Armstead, who was also recently a mayor of a northeastern city but was imprisoned for twelve months for using cocaine while in office, captured on tape by the video camera, the world's all-seeing eye.

The mayor smiled as he looked at this photo. He and Armstead were the best of friends then. He remembered those days of rage and protest when the enemy, racism, was always in plain sight — in the eyes of an angry crowd, at the end of a policeman's billy club, or in the jagged jaws of German shepherds. Now, the enemy was subtle but still present behind closed doors and closed minds. New enemies of drugs and violence now claimed the streets. Xavier and Armstead had kept in touch by phone now and then. But those calls became fewer with the passing of time. He felt bad that he did not call Armstead about his prison sentence. He should have spoken out about the way Armstead was mistreated and disgraced in the press, and the fact that Armstead was set up by a government informant. But the once camera-ready Mayor Chenier fell back into the shadows and kept his distance. His own son was fighting drug addiction and he was fearful of exposure. But Mayor Chenier always thought a huge injustice that the press and the public did not remember the great strides made by Armstead as a civil rights activist. Instead, he would be forever remembered as the black mayor who was caught on videotape snorting cocaine, branding him with the scarlet letters, "D.A." for "Drug Addict."

"Mayor," Guy said, "I need your undivided attention."

"Yes, I'm listening," the mayor said, turning his chair around and wiping away sweat that clung to his face like a web.

"We could still lose this thing," Guy said.

"We ain't going to lose," the mayor said. Over sixty percent of the city is black. brothers and sisters who run this town, and not all the whites will vote for that white son-of-a-bitch. You've seen the polls."

"Many whites who say they won't vote for him, secretly will vote for him. And you can be sure Conright's thugs are out there right now buying votes from every one of every color," Guy said.

"Ain't no brother or sister going to sell their votes to him," the mayor said.

"You're forgetting that many brothers and sisters in this city are angry at us for all the crime and the crumbling schools and the crooked cops and every other damn problem that plagues New Orleans," Guy said, as he wiped away sweat from his upper lip. "Did you see the news last week? They found a colony of bats living in one of our schools. Bats!"

"I saw that. That's an isolated problem," the mayor said.

"All those isolated problems now number in the hundreds all over town. Shit!" Guy exclaimed. "New Orleans itself has become one big isolated problem. The whole country is staring at us in horror. Tourism is down because of crime. We're losing money.

We've been spotlighted by *60 Minutes* twice already. Magazines are calling us 'The Big Sleazy.' Reporters from every shit hole city in the country are here to prove New Orleans is a shittier hole than theirs. And we're giving them every opportunity to do just that. Don't think we can't lose."

"What can we do?" the mayor said.

"Well, not all of our people are registered to vote," Guy stated. "We can start by busing them to the Registrar's office to sign up. And we make it a media event. We also have to initiate a media blitz to expose Conright's white supremacist ties. There has to be some photos of him in a Nazi uniform somewhere."

"You'll have to catch him on video shaking hands with Satan himself. That mother fucking 'Con-White' son-of-a-bitch! That mother fucker was out there today on the steps of the courthouse telling the Press about last night's murder . . . and saying I can't control the city . . ." the mayor angrily said.

"We've got to shock the whites into seeing who this guy really is and that it would be a national embarrassment to have a Nazi for mayor," Guy declared.

"What else can we do?" the mayor asked.

"Kill that mother fucker! That's what we do. Or cut out his tongue so he can't give any more press conferences. He'll be doing sign language," Guy laughingly said, as he raised his hands and moved his fingers. "He'd be one silent fucking Nazi who couldn't say, 'Heil Hitler.' He'd have his arm in the air with nothing coming out," Guy said, opening and closing his mouth. They both laughed. For a moment, the mayor felt relief from the stress and pressure at the top of his head where an invisible crown of gold sat four years earlier, and where now sat an invisible crown of granite. "He's one evil mother fucker. And the way to fight evil is with righteousness and your fight is that of Good over Evil . . . the evil that is loose in this town and the evil that is Conright. We will ask the voters to use their power and elect you to another four years . . . in a sense, then, empowering you to continue this crusade against crime."

"But some people think I am the reason for the crime. Didn't you read those protest signs down there?" the mayor said.

"The people want real solutions," Guy offered. "So, we'll give them those solutions, like revamping the Police Department and arresting crooked cops, and getting federal funds to change this city around. But we must raise the stakes first. We must make this an all-out war on Evil. We'll put you on the news with priests, ministers, rabbis and say you are doing God's work. And that with His Divine Guidance, we will win this war. And we'll spotlight your Civil Rights work . . . your ties to Martin Luther King . . . the beatings you took in the Movement . . . the fact that you've been a fighter from the very start . . . a real American fighting for Good, fighting for Righteousness, and not an evil person with anti-American, Nazi racist ties and beliefs."

"I don't want it to look like I'm presenting a false front," the mayor said.

"You're not doing that. You're the same person you were back then. You've got the same fight in you," Guy said.

The mayor softly said, "Do I?"

"You still need to mention more examples of how the city would be hurt if Conright became mayor. We need more of the 'here and now,'" Guy suggested.

"I intend to," the mayor said.

"It's a fact that the city would lose revenue if Conright won," Guy said. "His election would cause a slow-down in tourism and convention cancellations. We have contacts all across this country. I can get any number of organizations to state on paper, by phone, on videotape, that they will cancel if Conright is elected. We will strike the fear of God in every voter in this city. And I need you to hold a press conference ASAP."

"I don't know . . ." the mayor said, looking very anxious about the subject.

"You have to, mayor," Guy said. "Conright's holding press conferences every few days . . . the one today . . . one a couple of days ago when he attacked the Police Department and announced the names of indicted officers . . . another before that, citing statistics of just how many people are leaving town due to unemployment and crime. And you can be sure there will be another in the next couple of days. You must face the Press and the people. And, of course, there's the debate. You did agree to do one this Thursday."

"That was probably a mistake," the mayor said, regretfully, as he rose and walked to the windows.

"It's a necessity," Guy insisted.

The mayor looked down at the crowd. Drops of sweat fell from his face onto the windows and meandered down the glass. Could he face those people, he wondered. Did he really deserve another term? City Hall had become a shelter, retreat and bunker away from the war on the streets. But now his fortress was usaid whispered.

"And I think it's advisable that your son leave town until after the election, because attacking your family is not beneath Conright," Guy said. "Nothing is."

The mayor looked at his son's photo, then looked out the window again. The evil had invaded his own home and he knew it. "I'll talk to him."

The phone rang. Guy answered it.

"Mayor's office," Guy said. "Oh, Christ! Yeah, I'll tell him." He hung up the phone and said, "A tourist was just shot and killed in the French Quarter on Bourbon, near Esplanade. Some guy out to rob an easy target . . . saw a couple walking alone at then end of Bourbon . . . backed his car up the street . . . got out and at gunpoint made them lie down . . . but the woman wouldn't . . . so he shot her . . . in the head." The mayor closed his eyes as if a black veil of grief had descended over his mind. "Mayor, I think we should drive over there and be on the scene when the TV crews arrive. It will show your deep, real concern about the murder."

"No," the mayor said. "I'll look like a cold calculating opportunist . . . or . . . the total failure that I am. Maybe I should resign."

"Don't say that. This city needs you," Guy insisted.

"Needs me? This city needs a savior. And I don't have that power within me," the mayor conceded.

The phone rang. Both stared at it, as if they were afraid to pick it up.

"I'll get it," Guy said.

"Hold them off for a while," the mayor said, as he grabbed his coat and moved toward the door. "Tell them I'm in a meeting."

"Where will you be?" Guy asked.

"Dooky's," the mayor replied, exiting the office.

"You said you weren't going to drink during the campaign," Guy said, with raised voice. "You've got to talk to these people downstairs."

"Maybe you're right. Maybe we could lose this. Maybe it's lost already," the mayor said, vanishing from sight.

CHAPTER 11

Wolf's Lair

Keiffer Conright's office and campaign headquarters were in his home, a large, white and brown two-story wooden house with ten rooms and thirty medium and small-sized windows, located near Pontchartrain Lake and Pontchartrain Boulevard, and having a peaked, steep roof, Bavarian style.

The house was built in 1936 by Conright's father, Gustav Von Konright, in a rural area of New Orleans that was sparsely populated at the time. Gustav had fought as a German soldier in World War I. In 1918, rumors were as numerous as rats in the trenches on the front lines that Germany was close to surrendering. The advent of the Americans into the war in 1917 on the side of the French and British was quickly bringing the first modern war to its end. Gustav knew that Germany would pay heavily for the war. Its economy would be in ruins. His father died when Gustav was fourteen. He taught Gustav of Kaiser and Country, a strong work ethic, and blacksmithing to earn his living. His mother died of influenza on his last leave home two months earlier. He watched her take her last breath. He had been depressed ever since. During that short time home, she held his hand and told him to honor always God and the Church, and to rebuke sin and Satan. He fed her her last meal of soup; then, she slipped away. Her death was more grievous to him than any horror or headless torso witnessed in the war.

One night, while sitting in the trenches and watching rats crawl through thick, wet mud, he heard moans coming from the battlefield before him. He crawled onto the field not knowing who the soldier was because moans are of a universal language. He crawled low and slowly, sometimes dragging his chin in the mud and tasting the land for which he fought. He finally came upon Karl, a German soldier badly wounded in the chest during the day's battle. He saw steam rising from the wound. He told Karl to be quiet. He removed the olive-colored uniform from a nearby dead American soldier, and wrapped Karl in it to keep him warm and stop his trembling. He dragged Karl back to the trench and lowered him down. He removed the American uniform, wrapped Karl in blankets, and carried him several hundred yards to an ambulance.

Gustav then returned to his little corner in the trench and lit a cigarette. Soldiers patted him on his back and said he deserved a medal. He said he wasn't a hero, just a soldier helping another soldier. Karl, he said, deserved the medal. He hoped the Kaiser would honor those men with holes in their chests. He looked down and saw the American uniform still there where he dropped it. Suddenly, he saw his future, too. He scraped the mud from the uniform and stuffed it inside his coat. He would not return home.

On Armistice Day, November 11, 1918, the German Army was ordered to lay down its weapons and return home. The vacant stare of the vanquished was on the face of every German soldier as they climbed out of the trenches and walked to trucks to transport them to trains that would bring them to the cities of the once proud, now defeated Germany.

But Gustav did not board one of those trucks. He stayed behind in the trenches until they were deserted. Then he took off his own uniform and put on the American uniform with the dead soldier's identification papers in its pocket. He felt strange and anxious about his transformation. He poked his leg with his knife to draw blood. He tore off a long piece of undergarment, pressed it against the wound, and then wrapped it around his neck. He ran across the battlefield and jumped into the trench, well behind a line of American soldiers. He followed them to a truck, and was the last to board. His pulse quickened and his skin tightened as he looked out the rear of the open-ended truck. An American soldier asked him what Company and Division was he with. But Gustav just pointed to his fake neck wound and shook his head. The soldier across from him asked about his boots, and if he had taken them off a dead German. Gustav feigned a smile and shook his head affirmatively. The soldier laughed and said, "The only good German is a dead German!" Other soldiers agreed, one saying, "Yeah! And we made damn sure of that! Didn't we, boys?" The thunderous roar of the victorious exploded inside the truck and shot out the back, like a fireball, melting his pride. The significance of all those deaths over four years was quickly reduced to nothing but a loud laugh that forced Gustav to turn away and watch the blood-soaked battlefield and distant Germany vanish from his sight. He never wished to disobey his parents or the Kaiser, but his parents were dead. He hoped the Kaiser would understand his actions. Though he never met the Kaiser, he still felt guilty leaving Germany because the Kaiser was Germany and Germany was the Kaiser.

The troop train rolled into Paris where Gustav heard jubilation in the terminal as troops disembarked. Listening to jokes on the train and now hearing loud laughter as it echoed in the terminal, reinforced his opinion of the French that they were buffoons and pigs. His anger was contained within the thoughts that they would meet again on the battlefield and that their victory was due solely to American intervention.

The train took him, with the remaining wounded British and American soldiers, to the northeastern French coast and the small township of *Etaples-sur-Mer* for embarkation. He stayed to himself, pretending he was sleeping most of the way. A ship took them to England. He walked the streets of Portsmouth, waiting for a ship to take the Americans to New York City. Just as he had thought, the British appeared humorless and pretentious. He thought the only way to teach and change these people was to replace their Union Jack with the Iron Cross.

He grew forlorn while waiting. He looked to the sky but thought of the sky over Germany. He looked into shop windows but saw his reflection clothed in an American uniform. He had misgivings about his plan and thought about returning home. He then began to feel weak and feverish. Reluctantly, he boarded a ship with hundreds of American soldiers and set sail. He and other men on board were sick the entire crossing. One soldier died. He was on deck to get some fresh air when the ship sailed into New York Harbor. He saw the giant Statue of Liberty, the American Colossus, with raised torch, welcoming the returning heroes. He felt envious. When the ship docked, he and hundreds of other soldiers on board were taken to the nearest hospital and quarantined. The great Spanish influenza pandemic of 1918 had begun.

Soldiers began dying in numbers, civilians too, as the pandemic spread through the city. Gustav listened intently to every word spoken and began to absorb the English language. As he lay in his hospital bed, he overheard two soldiers talk about the closing of Storyville, New Orleans' notorious red-light district, due to the demands of the U.S. Government. One soldier commented that "Sin City" wouldn't be the same without the sin. Gustav took this to heart as his mother's warning to rebuke sin surfaced from his memory. He was certain he would grow strong again, as he was certain he was meant to hear those words that directed him to his new home, New Orleans.

When he was discharged from the hospital, he walked around New York for a few hours and was amazed by its new world architecture and sky's-the-limit hugeness. He hitchhiked from New York to New Orleans, still wearing the uniform and still feigning a throat wound. His encounters with Americans helped him form a favorable opinion of them. They were certainly not buffoons or pretentious. They were honest and strong, he thought.

On his arrival in New Orleans, he changed his name to Gus Conright. When asked about his accent while looking for work, he swore it was Swedish. He finally found work with a small wrought-iron company in the French Quarter, enabling him to use his own talent in metal sculpture. Within ten years he took over management of the shop when the owner retired, and eventually bought it from him. He had many clients because wrought-iron fences and balconies were synonymous with the French Quarter, the surrounding area and uptown on St. Charles Avenue. Business slowed down in the 1930s during the Great Depression. He worked a second job with the Works Progress Administration, refurbishing buildings and building roads.

Gustav lived in a rented room in the French Quarter on the third floor of 632 1/2 St. Peter Street which had a skylight, through which he imagined looking at a German sky. He he met a German girl, Elle, employed as a waitress at Kolb's Restaurant on St. Charles Avenue, just off Canal Street. She was escaping economically ravaged Germany where fighting in the streets was commonplace. She told him about a rising star in politics, Adolph Hitler, who wanted to make Germany strong again. About this,

Gustav was especially interested. They would drink a glass or two of beer after her shift and talk of the Fatherland. They eventually married in 1936 and with their savings they built the house near the lakefront that now belonged to his son. Gustav built there, because he wanted to escape the ever present and escalating crime in the city. He realized a short time after arriving in New Orleans that though Storyville had been forcibly closed because of its sinful nature, sin and sinners were still plentiful in other areas of town.

Gustav read all he could find about Hitler. He was convinced that this was the man who would rebuild Germany and unite its people – his people. On September 1, 1939, at 4:43 AM, Germany invaded Poland. Gustav told Elle, who was pregnant with Keiffer, that he had to return to Germany and fight for the Fuhrer and the Fatherland. He reminded her that they were Germans, and Germany was the Fuhrer and the Fuhrer was Germany. Tearfully, they said good-bye. He promised to send for her and their child soon because he was certain it would be a short, limited war to re-establish German prominence in Europe. He retraced his steps from New Orleans to New York to England to France and by railway to Berlin. She never saw him again. When asked about her husband, Elle said he joined the army and was killed in the war. She never said which army.

In 1946, about a year after the war ended, she received a letter postmarked Argentina. In it was a note and cash. The letter stated that the anonymous sender was a friend of Gustav and that they served together in the war. The sender assured Elle that Gustav had fought hard and died an honorable death. The sentiment of his last words to her were – to remember him, to remember he lives on within their son, and to forgive him for leaving her to fight in the war. The sender stated that she would receive money every month. It was also Gustav's wish that she should remarry. She never did, and died of a heart attack on what would have been their 37th wedding anniversary. Keiffer buried her in the grave marked with both his parents' names, though his father's body was never recovered. Mother and son had grown close over the years. She had taught him the doctrines of Lutheranism, stressing the might of Good over Evil, and that sinful thoughts were to be crushed, not just dismissed. He held back his tears at her funeral. But that night, alone in that big house, he got drunk and cried until grievous exhaustion razed his tall German frame to ruins.

Keiffer Conright sat in his desk chair that had a tall ornate back, like a king's chair. On the wall behind him was a solitary frame within which the words "A MIGHTY FORTRESS IS OUR GOD" were written in three-inch black letters. He stared at the fifty-five-year-old photo of his parents that stood in a gold frame on his desk. He wished his mother was alive to see him run for mayor. He knew she would be proud of his efforts to clean up New Orleans and chase Evil off its streets. He unbuttoned the first button on his white shirt, loosened his tie, and rubbed his fingers over the tips of long red welts that climbed up his back like flames.

Les Himm, Conright's bodyguard and assistant, walked into the room. He was six feet tall with an eighteen-inch neck and dressed entirely in black – pants, shirt and lace-up military boots, like those worn by the Monster in *Frankenstein*. His hands were large like bear paws; his fingers thick with dirt under the nails. He emitted a body odor. But his teeth were perfectly white. He brushed them three times each day, as if a nice smile was the only thing of consequence. A skull-and -crossbones tattoo about the size of a dime was tattooed to the upper center of his forehead.

"Les, get the good doctor on the line," Conright said.

Les picked up the phone on Conright's desk, next to the paperweight-sign that read, "No Pain, No Gain." He punched seven buttons and put it to his ear. After a couple of rings, he said in a pseudo-sophisticated voice, "Doctor Goodnight, this is Les Himm from the Conright campaign. How are you doing today, sir?"

Doctor Goodnight was driving down St. Charles Avenue in his red Porsche 911 Cabriolet with the top down. He was driving from his uptown practice to his uptown home. "What's this in reference to?" he said on his portable phone, somewhat aggravated.

"Well, we would like your support in Tuesday's election. You are a very successful man. Let us drop off some signs for your front lawn . . . some bumper stickers and pins to pass out at your cocktail party this weekend," Les said.

"Are you out of your mind? I don't support Nazi racists! And I don't know how you got my phone number, but don't ever call me again!" the doctor shouted.

With the speed of a lunging rattlesnake, Conright hit the speaker button on his phone. "Doctor, Conright here. Are you on your way home by chance?"

"Yes, I'm turning down my street now," the doctor said.

"Good. Check your mailbox for a special present," Conright said, with a Cheshire-Cat grin.

Doctor Goodnight pulled into his driveway, exited his car with his large portable phone in hand, and headed straight for the brass mailbox by the door. He quickly lifted the hot cover and retrieved a large yellow envelope. He opened it and pulled out a videotape. On its label was printed "Surprise, Doc. You're on Candid Camera!" He hurriedly unlocked the door and tripped while running to the VCR under the wide-screen TV, striking his head on a cabinet. A meandering trickle of blood slowly made its way down his right temple as he inserted the tape. He then witnessed his own Jerry Springeresque late night romp with Roxanne and Brandi the night before. "Oh, Jesus!" he moaned.

"Got yourself a good front row seat there, doc? Videotape is an amazing invention, isn't it? And it has many uses. You'll notice the date and time are there at the bottom for all the world to see. I do believe you performed surgery this very morning at 8:00 A.M. Am I right?" Conright asked.

"You know I did. What do you want?" the doctor said.

"Just your support. It would be nice and would touch my heart to see a man of your esteem on my team. A tall 'Conright for Mayor' sign in your front yard would be appreciated. A small price to pay, I think, considering the consequences should this video find its way to the AMA and local newsrooms," Conright said.

"You evil son-of-a-bitch!" the doctor exclaimed.

"Watch what you say, doctor. You're the one fueled on coke and brandy who performed life-threatening surgery this morning. We're all sinners, doc. And one day we'll have to pay for our sins. You start paying immediately. And we'll have lots of handouts for your party. See you in hell!" Conright said and turned off the phone.

"The nerve of that bastard! Telling me I'm evil. He's a fricking quack! His patients are nothing more than science projects to him,"

"Yeah. I'll send Frank over there today with our largest sign," Les said, smiling.

"Good. Send the one that reaches the sky. Who's next?" Conright asked.

"Ginsweet. But he hasn't returned my calls. He owns several large manufacturing businesses round town. Very influential. If we could get him to speak to his employees and people he does business with, we could maybe pull in a couple of thousand votes or more. He's got a weakness," Les said.

"Really?" Conright said, with a surprised look.

"Oh yeah," Les said. "Listen to this . . . I know a girl who is a secretary at one of his businesses. He makes his rounds weekly and has asked her to join him and others at his home near Lakeshore Drive. Just about every Saturday night, he has those women over . . . about a half dozen . . . and everybody gets naked . . . and they do stuff to him . . . kinky, sexual stuff. She wasn't sure exactly what. But she can tell from the way he talks and looks at her, that there's some weird shit going on out there."

"That might make a pretty picture – whatever it is," Conright said, smiling.

"Yeah! That's what I'm thinking," Les said, enthusiastically. "And she said she'd go to his house for the campaign and some cash. Her name is Loretta. But the problem is hiding the video camera. If she can make sure a curtain is left open, someone on the outside can video it."

"Make sure someone does," Conright said, shaking his head up and down. "That video will be worth a thousand favors."

"That's just what she said," Les said, flopping down in a mustard-colored Naugahyde 1950s' chair, and raising his arms. "But she didn't say 'favors.' She said 'dollars.' She ain't no fool."

"Well, pay her out of the 'I ain't no fool' slush fund. Cash," Conright said.

"Right. There's got to be something kinky going on there. I hear he's a real ruthless bastard, when he's not entertaining the young ladies," Les said, laughing.

"That's the only way to get ahead in this world; so, he should appreciate our tactics," Conright said.

"True. I might go down there and take those pictures myself. See what's happening in that big house," Les said.

"But don't," Conright said.

"It won't make no difference if we kicked in the door, snapped some photos and ran away – the old-fashioned way, like my daddy did it in the olden days. Shiiittt! Don't matter," Les confessed.

"But we're a class act. We got style. Fight the old fight in a new way. That's why videotape was invented. Let it do all the work. And it lasts a long time, like a bad memory," Conright said.

"True. What about something else my father used to do? Fliers," Les suggested.

"Fliers?" Conright said, somewhat puzzled.

"Yeah. Fliers that show you as Nazi and Klan Wizard, whiter than white. We get some brothers to distribute them, making it look like the mayor is paying people to defame you. We could even tell the brothers that the mayor's re-election fund is paying them. Turn the tables on that SOB. Make it look like he's the racist. People are expecting us to print up fliers showing blacks with big lips and kinky hair, holding spears and all the rest of it. So, it'll be interesting to see what the Press makes of the opposite happening and we blame it on Chenier," Les explained, looking proud of himself.

"Yeah. I like it," Conright said, as his smile widened across his face like a bomb flash exposing large white teeth.

"It's something you can take with you to the debate. I'll get Luther on it," Les said.

"Right. That and these," Conright said, pulling open a drawer of his desk, retrieving a manila envelope and tossing it on his desk.

"What's that?" Les said.

"Take a look," Conright said.

Les jumped up, opened the envelope and pulled out several 8x10 photos of the mayor's son buying drugs on a street corner.

"Holy shit! The photos!" Les said, smiling. "When did you get them?"

"A friend dropped them off last night. We got him red-handed," Conright said.

"Sure do. That kid's an asshole to buy drugs in the open when your dad's mayor. Good. Hit him at home. It's because of the mayor that this city is messed up with drugs and crime," Les said

"We'll put an end to that," Conright said, standing up. "When I'm elected, you'll be in charge of a special task force to rid the city of all drugs. I don't care if you have to arrest half the population to do it. But we will reclaim our city – street by street, house by house. We will wage a holy war. We will wash the shit off our streets. And no one can tell me it can't be done." Pointing to the photo of his parents, he continued, "My parents were immigrants. They had nothing. But they worked hard and built a life out of nothing, just like they built this house. And they brought me into this life and into this city. I owe them everything, and I owe this city, too. I'll be damned if I'll let this city succumb to the Evil living in the shadows and dealing drugs and committing crimes, and sins. I will wash this city clean if I have to break the levee and let the River sweep it all away. So help me God."

CHAPTER 12

The Bricks

"Drive to the mayor's office. We'll get some footage of the protestors and some interviews. I'm sure they're still out front," Ashley said.

"But we've got to repair the back windshield," Wyatt pointed out.

"I know. Right after City Hall. I want those interviews," Ashley said, stubbornly.

"I would think you would want to take a break for a minute, considering we were just shot at and everything. What are you trying to prove?" Wyatt asked.

"Listen to me, Walter!" Ashley said, commandingly.

"It's Wyatt! My name is Wyatt. Are you deliberately trying to piss me off? You've got a problem," Wyatt shouted.

"No. You do. Admit that you're prejudiced against uptowners. That's what this is about," Ashley declared.

"You're insane," Wyatt argued.

"Pull over!" Ashley demanded.

Wyatt pulled over to the curb on St. Charles Avenue near the Bultman Funeral Home.

"What?" Wyatt asked.

"I've been given an opportunity by Darryl to prove myself as a reporter of the news, the real news – not just fun places to go around town. And I'm taking Jennifer's place on the debate panel. I'm not going to let him down. But I'm doing it for myself, too. I'm doing this because I want respect as a reporter and as a person. And, yes, I do have something to prove. You may think everything has been easy for me because I come from a wealthy family. Well, you're right. Life has been easy for me. And I married a man from a wealthy family with a great future ahead of him. I was supposed to be a content uptown lady who knew her place in life and stayed in it – lunch with the ladies at Galatoire's, tea at the Windsor Court, dinner at Antoine's, sizeable servings of endless inane conversation about non-consequential topics and gossip for dessert, until death do I part, ashes to ashes, dust to dust, gone without a trace. But I wasn't so content after a while. I'm changing or growing or whatever you want to call it. And, of course, I'm concerned about the shootings; and I'll probably be sick about it tonight when I stop to think about it. But right now I don't want to think about it. I want to see what the mayor's up to. I want to cover him, Conright, last night's murder and today's shooting, and anything else we discover. All right?" Ashley determinedly said.

She looked at him sternly and extended her hand to shake, as if validating a contract. Wyatt understood her better now and realized she possessed the same zeal for newsgathering as he did. He looked at her pretty, perfect glistening oval face, her crimson lips, slightly parted, auburn hair falling over auburn eyes. Though they were different in many ways, he felt strongly attracted to her, especially now seated so close. He did not want to shake her hand; he wanted to kiss her. But he slowly raised his hand and slipped it into her soft palm, his index finger sliding over her thin wrist.

"Okay. Just remember my name," Wyatt said.

"I will . . ."

"Wyatt," Wyatt said.

"Wyatt," Ashley acknowledged.

Wyatt pulled away from the curb and noticed out of the corner of his right eye, Ashley lightly rubbing her palm over the seat cushion. He shook his head and continued down St. Charles, approaching Lee Circle. On his left was the Katz and Besthoff Drug Store's corporate headquarters, another New Orleans company recently sold to a national drugstore chain, another casualty of war in a city under siege. He rounded Lee Circle to Howard Avenue, drove up Howard to Loyola Avenue. He turned onto Loyola and got into the left lane as he passed the main post office and approached the rear of City Hall at Poydras and Loyola.

"There he goes," Ashley said as she noticed the mayor's black Cadillac limousine taking off up Poydras, across from the Superdome. "Follow him. I want to catch him off guard."

"He's not going to answer you," Wyatt said.

"We'll see," Ashley retorted.

Wyatt made a U-turn on Loyola in front of Civil District Court and then turned up Poydras.

"He's got his blinker on. Looks like he's heading down Claiborne," Wyatt said, narrowly missing a jaywalker.

"Watch it!" Ashley blurted. "Stay with him."

"I've got him," Wyatt said.

Wyatt sped up and turned onto Claiborne Avenue after the limo. A couple of blocks down on the right on Gravier street was the rear emergency entrance to Charity Hospital. Next to it was the Louisiana State University Medical School. Wyatt followed the limo across Canal Street. The NOPD car pound came into sight on the left under the expressway. On the right was the first block of the rear of the St. Louis Cemetery; white roofs and crosses on top its houses of the dead could be seen above its surrounding wall. If black was the color of death, white was the color of its internment. Scrawled on the brick wall was "Sooner Than You Think."

"Where are we?" Ashley asked. "This is kind of spooky."

"We're now in no-man's land," Wyatt said, looking left, then right.

"Lock the doors," Ashley said, beginning to feel the slither of snakes in her blood.

"How's that going to help? We've got no window in the back," Wyatt said.

"Just do it," Ashley commanded.

Wyatt pressed the door locks button. Clampdown.

"Feel safe now? You shouldn't," Wyatt cautioned.

Ashley saw black men and women on the sidewalk. Some made eye contact with her, making her feel uneasy and even frightened. Her skin tingled; her back stiffened. She felt like a foreigner in her own city. She didn't even know this part of town existed. On the cemetery's second brick wall were the words "MARIE LAVEAU LIVES HERE." On the cemetery's third brick wall in the third block on S. Claiborne were the words "COPS=CRIMINALS." Below these words and resting against the wall and on the ground were freshly cut flowers bunched together in a horizontal garden watered by tears; some wrapped in clear plastic, some held together by rubber bands and a small cross made of red carnations.

"That's odd to see flowers outside the cemetery wall," Ashley wondered aloud.

"That means someone was killed there. You've never seen that before?"

"No," Ashley replied.

"People place flowers on the site where someone was killed by a car or shot and killed, creating a garden of sorts, a garden like no other, and it never needs tending," Wyatt said. He then paused. "Looks like the mayor's turning on Orleans. Must be headed for Dooky's."

"Dooky's?" Ashley inquired.

"Yeah. You know Dooky's, don't you? Dooky Chase's restaurant."

"I guess I've heard of it," Ashley feigned.

"Best soul food in town," Wyatt added.

"You've been there?" she asked.

"No. But that's what everybody says. It's a favorite with blacks, especially black politicians and activists. White politicians go to Ruth's Chris Steak House a few blocks down on Orleans and S. Broad. But some black politicians go there, too. It's the place to see and be seen," Wyatt said.

"Yes. I know. I've been there many times," Ashley boastfully said.

"I don't doubt it," Wyatt said, with a smirk.

Wyatt turned left onto Orleans, right behind the mayor's limo. Ashley noticed an old tan two-story brick building on the corner.

Its ancient dark purple sign hanging over the doorway said, "Cohen's Formal Wear. Since 1928." Its large window-eyes had witnessed the history of that street corner for sixty-six years. However, its vision had recently been constricted by the addition of cataract-like iron bars, an indicator of the present time and the effect of an aging city.

Wyatt followed the mayor's limo up Orleans, past small wooden homes in disrepair, a church and a boarded-up movie theater. He crossed over North Galvez Street, and then spotted Dooky Chase's Restaurant up ahead on the right, past the red light at North Miro Street.

"There's Dooky's," Wyatt pointed out.

Dooky's was a brick building with long light green shutters, some a little crooked and needing paint. But it was the tradition of great soul food and friendship on the inside that counted. The mayor had been a steady customer for over forty years. His father first brought him there. His limo pulled up in front and the mayor got out and entered the restaurant's side door.

"I'll park over here," Wyatt said, as he passed the limo, made a U-turn and parked on the other side of the street, right next to the Lafitte Housing Project in this Treme neighborhood.

"What housing project is this?" Ashley said, alarmed at encountering another such place.

"It's Lafitte. We passed Iberville this morning when we were leaving the Quarter, over there on Basin. Iberville, the great French explorer from the 1600s, has a project named after him. I'm sure he would be pleased. Ha!" Wyatt jested.

"Oh. I didn't realize there were so many," Ashley admitted.

"You need to get out more. There's more to New Orleans than St. Charles Avenue," Wyatt said.

Ashley looked to her right and noticed several black men and women standing on the porch to one building of the project, and they noticed her.

"Maybe we shouldn't park here," she nervously said.

"You wanted to follow the mayor," Wyatt said, looking around.

"Hey!" a voice shouted from behind them.

They both looked around to see two young men looking through the broken window opening.

"You know you ain't got no window back here?" one young man observed.

"Yeah, we know. Thanks," Wyatt said.

"Can we get you anything? Cool beverage, crack, Special K, BTH?" the other asked.

The two men convulsed with laughter, and then one said, "What you all doing round here? Must be some serious shit 'bout to happen for you news people to be here."

"No. Nothing like that," Wyatt assured them.

"Let me ask you something," the young man said, as he stood next to Ashley's window. He wore shorts to his knees and held a tee shirt in his hand which he draped around the back of his neck as he tapped on the window. "Can you lower this so we can talk face to face?"

Ashley exchanged glances with Wyatt, and then slowly lowered her window. "Yes?"

The young man continued, "Thanks. Tell me, why is it the police will harass poor black folk but not go after the rich people who drive Mercedes and Rolls Royces, even though those people probably get their money illegally? Why don't you report on that? They'll hunt down brothers for doing small-time crimes or for nothing at all. Hunt 'em down like dogs. Rich white men go free every time. Must have something to do with the fact white men own everything, even this town. You see. Police work for them. You want to report the truth. You want a real story. Real news. You report that." Ashley's face was becoming very tight as the man continued to push his face forward and look straight into her eyes. "This 'Protect and Serve' stuff . . . that's pure bullshit. It's more like protect and serve whites. We black people have good memories. We remember all this . . . mistreatment . . . second class citizen shit . . . this slave culture. Revolution's coming. We remember. And you wonder why we not so fond of white folk. Like that white woman got shot in the Quarters last night. Everybody making a big stink over her cause she's white. Maybe she had it coming."

Startled by this, Ashley said, "Do you know anything about her murder?"

"Do you know anything about the little black girl shot dead in the crossfire last night right up here on Claiborne by the cemetery?" he angrily countered.

Ashley looked at Wyatt who shook his head and said, "I guess he's talking about those flowers we just saw."

"No. What happened?" Ashley asked.

"Cops and some thugs had it out with each other. Girl got caught in middle. Next thing you know, she dead. Nobody cares. Investigate that. Report on why no one cares when a black person is killed," he said, thrusting his hands deep into his pockets as he backed away.

"Wait. What do you know about the murder last night?" she shouted.

"He doesn't know anything. He's just running on at the mouth," Wyatt said.

An old black man, pushing a grocery basket piled high with his belongings stopped by Wyatt's window. He wore a dirty old Saints baseball-style cap atop his curly gray hair that matched his patchwork shrub-like beard growing around the deep crevices on his face. His shirt, pants and shoes were brown.

"Today, I'm tired," the old man said. "Some days are better than others. But I'm kind of tired today. On days like this I worry about my life coming to an end and who's going to bury me. I've been putting some extra quarters in a jar I got for my burial. You ever think about how long you've been on this earth and how many more years you got? I'm eighty myself. I don't think I have many more left. I get kind of scared. You ever get scared thinking about your life being over? One day you're walking around and talking and breathing, and the next day you're gone. But you just got to give up your worries to the Lord. He'll take care of you. In return, you got to do the Lord's work. I praise his holy name. Jesus Christ is my Lord and Savior. He's everybody's Savior. All you got to do is open your heart. Do you think you could spare a couple of quarters? One for some food and one for my burial."

"Sure," Wyatt said, digging into his jeans for some change. He handed two quarters to the old man.

"Thank you, son. I have a Blue Plate mayonnaise jar full of quarters in my basket. If you find me dead one day, would you take those quarters and see that I get a decent burial? We're all going to die. We're all suffering from the same disease," the man said.

"Yeah, sure," Wyatt said, though completely bewildered by the man's request.

"Thank you, son. Jesus knows who His true disciples are. I'll see you," the old man said and walked on, pushing his cart before him.

"Okay." Wyatt turned to Ashley and said, "That's the weirdest thing I've ever heard."

They heard a police siren behind them and quickly turned around to see a teenage boy run across Orleans Avenue with a blue and white police car in pursuit. The boy, wearing black shorts and a red tank top, ran down the wide walkway between two buildings of the housing project. But he was met by another police car coming down the wide walkway from within the project.

"Bring your camera," Ashley said, as they both jumped out of the car.

The two policemen had already exited their cars and had cornered the boy in the walkway as residents drew closer.

"Hands on the car! Spread your legs," one policeman commanded.

"Man, I ain't done nothing!" the teenager said.

"Why you running?" the other cop asked.

"'Cause you chasing me!" the teen exclaimed.

"Black men have to run from the police 'cause you'll arrest us for just being black," a man in the crowd shouted.

"Let that boy be," a woman added.

Wyatt was recording as they made their way through the crowd. He had the teenager's head and the back of one policeman in his viewfinder. A young man with a black pit bull moved into view.

"What's that under your shirt?" the cop said.

"Where?" the teenager said.

"Bulging under your shirt in your waistband," the cop said.

"That's a gun!" the other cop said.

"That's my dick! You want that, you homo pig?" The cop slammed the boy's head against the car. "Fuck you!" the teen shouted. The boy struggled to release himself from a choke-hold. The cop pulled out his Smith and Wesson automatic pistol, as the second cop assisted.

The shirtless young man, who moments before was talking to Ashley, snuck up from behind and kicked the second cop behind the neck, and then disappeared into the crowd. The cop lost his balance and fell backwards.

"On the ground! On the ground!" the first cop yelled, continuing to struggle with the teenager.

"Get that gun out my face!" the teenager loudly protested.

The cop slipped and fell to one knee, taking the teenager down with him. Then the gun fired. The teenager groaned and slithered free from his unlikely and forced embrace with the cop. The teen grabbed hold of Mother Earth, his eyes closing and his lips softly kissing blades of grass, as if to warmly welcome his return home.

As if to block the sun's view, clouds rolled in, shadows dissolved and a familiar afternoon rain mingled with sweat and tears dripping down faces of bystanders; and the familiar momentary silence surrounding tragedy rolled in like gas and occupied the air. The spectators put hands to noses and mouths, as if not wanting to breathe noxious fumes. The pit bull growled.

Both cops quickly rose. The cop who had been struggling with the teenager had dark blood stains on his light blue shirt.

"Stand back! Stand back!" the cop said, holstering his gun.

The other cop turned on his radio phone velcroed to his left shoulder and said, "Dispatch, I need an ambulance to the Lafitte Bricks, Orleans entrance."

Thunder-like static broke the silence when the dispatcher's reply came through the receiver, "On its way."

"You killed that boy!" someone in the crowd said.

The cop bent down, put his ear to the boy's chest and thought he heard a faint heartbeat. Relieved the boy was not dead, he stood and said to the crowd, "He's alive. Y'all just stand back. Ambulance is on its way."

"He didn't have no gun!" someone said.

"Show us the gun!" another voice shouted.

"That's the way it always is. Cops kill us for no reason. What's our crime? What's our crime?" a man on the right screamed.

"We black!" a man on the left replied. "That's our crime!"

'Hey, pig, take a look over there," a disembodied voice said. "TV camera crew got the whole thing on tape. You be in jail soon! How you gonna like that? Squeal like the pig you are!"

The two cops looked over to Ashley and Wyatt, who felt momentarily paralyzed by the cops' cold stare. Ashley faltered and didn't know what to say, as if the camera was turned on her.

An ambulance's siren was heard speeding down Claiborne, and then appeared on Orleans and drove up on the grassy walkway area as the crowd parted. Two paramedics jumped out. One opened the rear door and quickly slid out an aluminum stretcher like an ice tray. Wyatt zoomed in on the boy, as the other paramedic ripped off the boy's shirt and placed an oxygen mask over his face, and then taped a large gauze pad over the wound on his side. All eyes were searching for a gun in the boy's waistband but there wasn't one. Then they both raised him onto the stretcher and into the ambulance. In less than fifteen minutes the procedure, which they had obviously performed many times, was over and the ambulance was on its way down Orleans Avenue to Charity Hospital.

"Y'all stand back. I've got to seal the perimeter," one officer said.

"Officer," Ashley said, holding the microphone in front of her. "Would you care to comment on what happened here?"

"Nothing to say. Boy put up a struggle," he said.

"Where's the gun?" a man asked.

"Where's the gun?" another person added.

"Where's the fucking gun, mother fucker?" a man angrily yelled.

"Y'all stand back. There'll be an investigation," the cop assured them.

"We don't need no investigation. We know what happened. You shot that boy in cold blood," a bystander said.

The two officers ignored the comments and rolled out the yellow and black plastic "Crime Scene" tape, signifying the aftermath of Chaos, or, as the French Quarter Jesus would say, proof of Satan's visitation.

"Yeah! It's a crime scene all right . . . and you the criminals! Seal yourself inside, you mother fuckers!" a voice in the crowd erupted.

"Officers . . ." Ashley said.

"They'll be other police showing up here in a minute. Probably a Sergeant. You can get a comment from him," Wyatt urged Ashley.

"All right. I'll wait. But keep an eye open for the mayor coming out of the restaurant. I want his comment, too," she said.

A brick suddenly came hurling in, thrown by someone beyond the crowd. It hit the head of the officer who shot the teenager. He immediately fell to the ground, bleeding from the temple.

"Jesus! Did you see that?" Wyatt said, turning to Ashley.

"Oh, my God!" she exclaimed.

Someone else threw a bottle that shattered on the hard ground. One cop attended the other.

"Where's the gun?" members of the crowd yelled.

"Dispatch, officer down! We need backup in the Lafitte Bricks on Orleans. We've got a hostile crowd here," the officer loudly said, as he spoke into his receiver and looked around. "Jesus Christ, I feel like Custer out here! Get me some backup."

"Already on its way," the dispatcher said. "Hang loose."

"Hang loose!? They're getting ready to hang me!" the officer shouted.

More rocks were thrown, shattering two windows of the cops' cars. Six young black men attempted to roll over one of the cars by rocking it back and forth. But it was too large to overturn. More rocks were thrown. The officer shot his pistol into the air. He pulled the trigger three times in quick succession.

"If anyone throws anything else, I'll shoot him!" the officer said, as some of the crowd dispersed. He applied his handkerchief to the officer's head wound, which was bleeding badly.

A small boy threw a rock from the stairway-balcony of the apartment building nearest the officers. The officer raised his gun and took aim, then noticed the perpetrator was only a boy. They made eye contact, and then the boy ran indoors. Then the Pit Bull charged. After hearing its barks, the officer turned toward it, leveled his pistol at its head, and pulled the trigger eight times when the dog was only six feet from him. He had emptied his clip into the dog which was blown backwards several feet, as if a hurricane force wind had hit it. With one hand, the officer unlocked the empty clip and let it fall to the ground from inside the handle. Then he took another clip from his utility belt and shoved it up to the gun's handle, locking it in place. He pulled back on the barrel of the gun, automatically sliding a bullet into the chamber. With both hands on the pistol and still crouching by the downed officer, he leveled it at the crowd. He swung his arms and pistol around to the right in a sweeping motion like a human clock, then back around to the left.

"He's aiming right at us," someone in the crowd said.

"Us and the world," someone added.

People backed away. Everything was quiet, except for the rain drops hitting bags of garbage stacked on the curb.

Wyatt and Ashley had moved to the side of an apartment building where Wyatt continued to film.

"I can't believe the violence we've seen just since yesterday," Ashley commented.

"It's like this every day," Wyatt said.

"Yes, but must I witness all of it?" Ashley said.

"If you hang around these neighborhoods, you just might,"

Wyatt added.

"Look! There's the mayor," Ashley pointed out, looking across Orleans avenue to Dooky Chase's. "Come on!"

They crossed the street as the mayor was rushed to his limo by his aides who were well aware of what was happening only a few yards away. The mayor tried to get a second look but an aide pushed his head down into the limo.

"Mr. Mayor! Mr. Mayor!" Ashley shouted, as she reached the limo. "There's been a shooting and protests. What do you have to say?" She knocked on the tinted glass window, "Mr. Mayor!"

Wyatt filmed the mayor's limo as it sped away, and also caught more police cars speeding down Orleans Avenue to assist the officer in distress.

"Come on! Let's follow him," Ashley said.

They crossed Orleans again and jumped in their car. Wyatt made a quick U-turn as Ashley hung onto the door armrest. They followed the limo to North Broad where it made an illegal left turn in front of Ruth's Chris Steakhouse.

"You want a steak, to go?" Wyatt joked.

"Catch him!" she shouted.

Wyatt also made the illegal turn and continued the chase down N. Broad.

"He's heading back to City Hall," Wyatt said, as he ran a red light at N. Broad and Bienville, named after Iberville's brother, the founder of New Orleans in 1718.

"Can you take a short cut?" Ashley suggested.

"Yeah, I guess." The limo turned left on Canal Street. Wyatt continued speeding up N. Broad. "Hold on!" he shouted, as he turned left on Tulane Avenue.

When he reached Tulane at Claiborne Avenues, he spotted the limo crossing a few blocks ahead on Loyola Avenue. He raced up Claiborne to Poydras and quickly turned left. Ashley slid all the way over to very near Wyatt's side. She put her hand on his thigh to push herself back to her side. Wyatt looked down, and then looked up just in time to come to a screeching halt on Poydras near the

Superdome. Blocking the lane were two police cars with lights flashing. In the distance he saw the mayor exiting his limo near the rear of City Hall. Two aides looked in his direction. Another police car pulled up behind Wyatt who noticed it in the rear-view mirror as the officer got out.

"Oh, shit!" Wyatt said, as Ashley turned around to see.

The officer looked in the car and said, "You're reporters, aren't you?"

"Yes, I am," Ashley said, crouching down a little and looking up to see the officer through Wyatt's window.

"Where's the fire?" the officer said, with a smile. Then he looked at Wyatt and said, "License, please."

A see-what-you-got-me-into look rearranged Wyatt's face as he looked over at Ashley.

She quietly said, "Sorry," and turned her head away.

Wyatt reached for his wallet.

CHAPTER 13

Rewind

It was 4:30 P.M. when Wyatt and Ashley pulled into the rear parking garage of TV3.

"Let's go! It's almost 5 o'clock," Ashley said, hurrying out of the car and heading for the back door entrance to the studio.

"That damn ticket took twenty minutes. It'll probably cost $200," Wyatt said, taking his camera from the back seat.

"Don't worry about that. My father will have it fixed," Ashley said, proudly.

"Must be nice to have friends in high places," Wyatt said.

"It is. He's fixed a number of things for me and my friends," Ashley proudly said.

"Have him fix that window while he's at it," Wyatt said, laughingly.

She looked at him with a sideways glance and shook her head. They opened the door and walked down a short narrow hall, and then up a slim spiral staircase to the second floor of this French Quarter house, known as the Brulatour Mansion, built in 1816, having been made into a television station forty-five years ago. Space was limited in the French Quarter since all the buildings were connected and shared common walls; the buildings themselves were small. Every square foot of the TV3 building was occupied with desks, chairs, file cabinets, typewriters, computers, and narrow walkways that could be traversed in one step.

"Hi Bonnie," Ashley said, as she reached the top of the stairs. Bonnie, Darryl's forty-year-old secretary, was seated behind her desk in a small alcove outside Darryl's office. "Is Darryl in?"

"He's around," Bonnie said. "I think he's in editing."

"That's where we're headed," Ashley replied.

"Got some good stuff?" Bonnie inquired.

"Very good," Ashley said.

"Yeah. You could say that. We were shot at. Now I know how war cameramen feel," Wyatt said, shaking his head.

They walked hurriedly down the hall to the dimly lit editing room where they found Darryl holding a videocassette in one hand and a Hubig lemon pie in the other. He was talking to Weldon, a young black man who was the fastest film editor in the city. Ashley turned on the lights.

"Darryl, I got some great footage for the five o'clock," Ashley exclaimed.

"What do you mean 'I'?" Wyatt said, under his breath.

"What you got?" Darryl inquired.

"A shooting at the Lafitte projects. Kid shot and cop hit with a brick," Wyatt said, jumping in before Ashley and removing his videotape.

"Yes. I thought it would be a good idea to follow the mayor to Dooky's, you know, where all the black politicians congregate," Ashley said.

"Sure, I know Dooky's," Darryl quickly said. "Eat there whenever I can."

"That's when the cops cornered a kid across the street," Wyatt said. "Bad news."

"Dead?" Darryl wondered.

"No," Ashley said. "At least the cop said 'no'."

"Call Charity Hospital before air and find out. All right, Sparks," Darryl said to Weldon as he patted him on the back, "do your stuff. Make us a story. We'll open with it. Get ready, Ashley, you're on in less than twenty-five," he said, looking at his watch. "You can do this. I'll tell Jack and Jill and Space Command," he said, as he was about to leave the room.

"Wait, Darryl. I'm not sure what to say," Ashley nervously admitted.

"Just write a few sentences saying exactly what happened, and then we'll cut to tape. It's easy. You already did the hard part. Come on," Darryl said.

"There's one other thing . . . a stray bullet broke the rear window," Ashley said.

"Are both of you okay?" Darryl asked.

"Yeah. We're alright," Wyatt said, smiling at Ashley's quick thinking.

Darryl turned off the lights as they exited the editing room. Wyatt and Weldon sat in front of the editing console and began to view the tape. Flickering images of the day's news were reflected on the wall in the cave-like room, somewhat reminiscent of how primitive men illustrated the day's hunt on cave walls lighted by a flickering campfire, except today's hunt was not a bore or bison; it was a boy.

At 4:59 P.M. Ashley was seated at the left end of the news anchor desk, awaiting her cue from Jack. Jack Randall and Jill Uphills had just taken their seats after last minute makeup was applied to lessen the reflection of the bright lights. Ashley took a sip of water from a cup under the desktop. She was nervous about remembering exactly what to say. She looked over a piece of paper on which were a few sentences she had written with Darryl's help. She had occupied that same seat many times before, but as an entertainment reporter. She knew it was hardly reporting at all. Anyone could have done it after checking "Lagniappe," the entertainment guide, in every Friday's Times-Picayune newspaper. Now, something more was expected of her, something much more, and sitting next to two veteran news reporters, she felt anxious and insignificant. Could she pull this off, she wondered, without looking like the inexperienced reporter she really was? Her legs and buttocks were clenched together, her back stiff and straight. She forced a mild smile. She tried to relax herself but it was impossible as she saw the stage manager count down the final seconds on his fingers from five to one as the news program's techno-intro music began; then, when the news program's techno-intro music reached its crescendo, he pointed to Jack and Jill.

"Good evening. I'm Jack Randalls."

"And I'm Jill Uphills."

"We have breaking news with startling and graphic footage of a shooting involving two policemen and a young black man," Randalls said, with severe seriousness on his face.

"And it was all captured on film exclusively by one of our own TV3 cameramen," Uphills added. "The reporter on the scene was Ashley Tarleton. Ashley . . ."

Ashley's throat tightened and the pressure behind her eyes intensified as Jack and Jill turned her way. She felt a sudden sickening sensation in her stomach, as if someone had injected it. All eyes were on her. The overhead lights seemed more intense and hotter than ever before. Her voice cracked. She cleared her throat and spoke again.

"Excuse me. Yes, a black boy," Ashley said. She realized her political incorrectness. "An African-American teenager was shot by police only thirty minutes ago in the Lafitte housing development. I was there. I witnessed the whole event and we captured it on film."

Wyatt, standing behind the cameras, shook his head for not mentioning his name.

"Why was he shot? Was the young man violent?" Randalls asked.

"Not really," Ashley replied.

"What was he doing?" Uphills inquired with a steadfast look of synthetic concern.

"He was running from the police, but they caught up with him," Ashley said.

"In the Lafitte housing development?" Randalls repeated for unnecessary emphasis.

"Yes."

"Then what happened?" Randalls asked.

"They frisked him against a police car," Ashley said.

"How many policemen were involved?" Uphills questioned, jumping in quickly before Randalls had the chance to continue to upstage her.

"Two."

"Ashley, how did a simple frisking become a shooting?" Randalls said, taking command again.

"I'm not quite sure. It happened so quickly," Ashley admitted. "One policeman either saw a gun on the boy, or thought he saw one, and then things got out of control."

"Let's take a look at the exclusive videotape you brought in only moments ago. We want to warn viewers as to the graphic nature of this video," Randalls said.

The edited videotape was shown, taking only twenty seconds, and ended when the policeman repeatedly shot the attacking dog.

"Incredible footage, Ashley," Uphills said, shaking her head, affirmatively.

"We know the young man is at Charity Hospital. Do you know his condition?" Randalls wondered, trying to look like the real, probing TV journalist he really wasn't.

"He's in surgery," Ashley said, having no idea about his condition. She had forgotten to call the hospital. She had faked it and felt momentarily good about it; then, wished she hadn't.

"Is the boy's name being withheld until notification of his family?" Randalls asked.

She didn't know that either but said, "Yes, it's being withheld for that reason." Her whole body remained rigid. Her facial muscles were very stressed. Her skin felt tight and inflamed. But her oval face retained its placid veneer. "And we'll have an update for you on the boy's condition at ten."

"Good," Uphills said.

"We will definitely hear more about this story after further investigation," Randalls added in his manufactured authoritarian tone, as he delivered the standard end statement for all breaking news stories.

Ashley nodded her head.

"Good job, Ashley. Thanks," Randalls said.

The two newscasters then looked into Camera 1 as they introduced the next news item. Ashley relaxed her body. Her shoulders, which had arched near her neck, fell back to their natural position. She slid off the chair and walked around the cameras where she noticed Wyatt.

"Nice going," Wyatt said with a slight smile. "Your first hard news story."

"Yes. It was okay. I . . . I did alright," she said, averting her eyes from his, not wanting to admit failure on any level. "Well, I'm meeting Conright for dinner."

"Eating with the enemy," Wyatt said, to which he attached a sly smile.

"Something like that," Ashley said.

"Where?" Wyatt asked.

"Antoine's," Ashley replied.

"Nice. I'm eating in with my daughter and mother. Pizza," Wyatt said.

"That sounds nice," Ashley said.

"Well, you can't beat the company. You're always welcome to join us for after-dinner ice cream and a Disney movie," he said, half wishing she would join them.

"Maybe some other time. I'll see you tomorrow morning," she said, as she moved away from him. She stopped, turned and said, "Thanks for your help today."

"No problem," Wyatt said, as he watched shapely Ashley exit the studio.

His eyes were first directed to her bouncing auburn hair, and then to her slender waist and hips, and, finally, to her slim toned legs which he slowly followed down from her knees to her ankles, like a drop of water running down a tall glass. He looked at the cameraman next to him and grinned.

"Don't even think about it," the cameraman said. "Untouchable."

"Probably so," Wyatt said.

"Definitely so," the cameraman added.

Ashley thought about exiting the building down the front

staircase to avoid passing Darryl's office. She was somewhat embarrassed by her performance and didn't want to face him. But he had been kind to her and believed in her, so she walked into his office. His office was small. On its white walls were numerous 8x10 photos of Darryl shaking hands with renown newscasters and a couple of presidents. Photos with Tom Brokaw, Walter Cronkite and Eric Sevareid were his favorites from his twenty-five-year career.

"Sorry about tonight. Next time will be better," she nervously said.

Darryl, who was watching the newscast on a small TV, looked up and said, "Don't be so hard on yourself. You were fine. Besides, it was your first time reporting a news story." He took a big bite out of his Hubig lemon pie and smiled.

"Thanks. But I can and I will do better. And I won't let you down during the debate, either. I wanted to mention that, in case it was on your mind."

"I know. I trust in you," he said, as he took a sip from his coffee cup marked "THE BOSS."

"Thank you," she said, gratefully and still feeling a bit embarrassed.

"So, are you still having dinner with Conright?" he asked.

"Yes."

"Let me know how that went," Darryl said. "Remember to count the number of times he says 'off the record.' I suspect he'll try to impress you with his knowledge of the world and this city and people. But like any politician, he'll be vague and cover his tracks. But when he says 'off the record,' that will indicate what he's really thinking or the truth according to Conright."

"All right. I'll listen for it," Ashely said.

"I want you to see something," he said. As he turned his swivel chair to rise, his large stomach hit his partially pulled out desk drawer. "Oww! I need a bigger office or a smaller stomach." They walked down the hall to the editing room where Weldon sat in the dark, viewing a videotape, his face illuminated by the light of the day's tragic news. "This is Conright's latest spot," Darryl said, while inserting a videotape into a TV with a VCR built in. He turned on the TV and said, "Take a look." He pushed "PLAY."

Keiffer Conright, dressed in a black suit and dark tie with small white *fleur-de-lis* emblems on it, stood before a blue screen on which were projected photo images of the city's poorest neighborhoods, men being arrested, and mothers crying near deceased victims of murder. "Hello, I'm Keiffer Conright . . ."

"Booooo!" Weldon howled.

"The next mayor of New Orleans – with your help. Let's make Mayor Xavier Chenier the ex-mayor because he's left a black mark on the city . . ." Conright said.

"A black mark! Racist!" Weldon interrupted again. Ashley looked down at him momentarily.

"A mark of disgrace. Crime and drugs are everywhere . . . and so is murder. The Press is calling us 'The Big Sleazy,' instead of 'The Big Easy.' Tourism and convention bookings are down. Cancellations are up. Citizens, we cannot survive more Mayor "X" years," Conright continued.

"Mayor X! Jesus! This guy is too much," Weldon said, in disgust.

On the screen appeared a blow-up of a police report showing the mayor's son's name and information of his arrest on possession of illegal substance charges.

Conright continued, "We cannot rely on him any longer to control crime and drugs when he can't even control his own son who was recently arrested on drug charges."

"Oh, man, what a low blow. That's cold-blooded," Weldon said, shaking his head.

"Our city is dying," Conright asserted. I want to revive our beautiful city that is now buried in filth." The photo images on screen now turned into ones of happy faces and clean and prosperous neighborhoods. "I want to wash the filth from our streets, keep the lawbreakers in jail, attract new business, restore the city's grandeur, and put the 'new' back in New Orleans."

"Ohhh! You suck!" Weldon said.

"Please let me remove the black mark Mayor 'X' has left on the city," Conright implored.

"He said it again!" Weldon complained.

"It's our city and we want it back. Vote for me and I'll give you back your city. Join us at my headquarters on election night for a real victory celebration. Thank you and God bless," Conright concluded.

"Yeah, but remember . . . it's B.Y.O.W.S., Bring Your Own White Sheet," Weldon joked. "*He* should be arrested."

"Can he say that about the mayor's son?" Ashley inquired.

"Yeah. He's got the proof," Darryl said. "But I wanted you to see this because no matter what he tells you, he's not above anyone else. He'll sling the dirt, too."

"But you reported it when it happened," Ashley said.

"We aired the story but there's a difference. We aired it as a straight news story without comment. He's commenting on it in his ad and using it as a smear tactic. But it is true. And he paid for the spot, so we'll air it. Ask him about it during the debate. This tactic says something about the person who would use someone else's pain for his own gain. Conright will try to woo you with his powers of reason. Don't let him fool you," Darryl advised.

"I understand. Do you think he has any chance at all to win?" Ashley asked.

"Anything can happen. It depends on how many votes he can buy," Darryl said.

"Ain't it the truth!" Weldon said, in sad resignation.

CHAPTER 14

Diabolique

Ashley exited the building through the parking garage on Chartres Street. She checked her watch. It was nearly 6:00 o'clock. She had more than enough time to make a stop before going to Antoine's. She remembered the message on the audio cassette she took from Yvette Lenieu's apartment. Yvette's friends told her to meet them at The House of Blues last night. Maybe someone there might know something, she thought.

She crossed over Toulouse Street, by the abandoned Wildlife and Fisheries building, which stood castle-like and out of place among the typical side-by-side businesses and residences of the French Quarter. She wiped sweat from her forehead with a linen handkerchief purchased at Godchaux's upscale department store on Canal Street, and then looked at K-Paul's Louisiana Kitchen, where a long line of casually dressed people across the street waited to enter. She looked in the large plate windows of upscale Bacco Restaurant, wherein its well-dressed patrons seemed to be on public display as they silently laughed and toasted their own success. As she looked up Chartres street again, a man with a long full gray beard, round sunglasses, and dressed entirely in black, including a top hat, startled her and said, "Do you have the time?"

"What? No. I don't know." She looked down and noticed he was wearing two watches, with a watch fob dangling from his vest pocket. "You have a watch . . . or two . . . or three," Ashley pointed out.

"Do you know that we don't watch time go by; time watches us go by," the man said.

She ignored him, crossed the street and quickened her pace. She glanced at antiques through shop windows. She thought of how expensive each piece of fine porcelain or Queen Anne chair must be, but thought nothing of the history of the pieces or the history of the lives who once used those pieces.

"I'm cold," a voice from the shadows said. Ashley then noticed a small elderly woman emerge from a recessed doorway. The woman's face was gaunt, and the shadows that draped her face like black crepe, gave her a ghostly appearance. "I'm cold and I don't want to be alone. Will you stay with me?" she questioned, as her hand touched Ashley's hand. Ashley, who disliked being touched by anyone except her parents, instantly recoiled her hand. After walking a few steps, she turned around. The old woman, whose cold touch reminded her of her mother, was gone as if a fold in the night had enveloped her.

She walked up Chartres toward Bienville Street where the French Quarter Jesus with a new homeless disciple turned the corner. "Oh, no!" she mumbled, as she turned away.

"Hey! I need you," he said, running toward her. Catching up with her, he said, "I need you to broadcast the news that the giant, righteous hand of God will soon reach down from the sky to capture and crush every evil-doer in this city."

Furious that he was invading her privacy, Ashley turned and said, "Don't you have anything better to do with your life?"

The French Quarter Jesus, unshaven and sweaty, stared intensely into her eyes and said, "Don't you?"

They locked stares. She backed away and turned, realizing it was pointless to talk to him. She walked a few steps, and then looked back. He still stood there staring at her from beneath an old black 1900s' streetlight. The light reflected off his matted hair and sweaty face, giving the appearance that his face was on fire.

She turned left on Bienville and walked toward Decatur Street, when she realized the street was dark and she was alone. She quickened her pace down the narrow street, and then heard someone say, "You're just a bourgeois girl living in a bourgeois world." She turned around to see who spoke, thinking it was the French Quarter Jesus, but no one was there. It appeared as if the night itself had called to her. She felt a chill run down her spine, even though a warm wind blew back her hair.

"The weirdos in the Quarter!" she muttered.

She reached the well-populated part of Decatur Street nearer

Canal Street. She felt calmer walking among the many tourists on this part of Decatur that was considered a dangerous "No Man's Land" only a couple of years before. Drunks, foreign sailors and prostitutes waiting for their Johns in slow-moving cars had owned these first two blocks of Decatur off Canal Street. But the opening of the House of Blues brought new promise to the area.

Ashley walked by the line of people of various ages lined up to enter the House of Blues for the Bonnie Raitt performance. She walked up the alley entrance way, and then into the building. The concert hall was to the right, but Ashley turned left toward the bar and restaurant where the crowd was three-people thick in front of the bar. Drinks were passed overhead from the bar as outstretched hands passed tens and twenties back to the bartender. A short man jumped up and down, trying to get the bartender's attention. Heads and shoulders were twisting and turning as the men and women searched each other's faces for silent signals from inviting eyes.

"Excuse me. Can I get through here, please?" Ashley said in a raised voice to overcome the loud crowd noise, as she pushed her way to the bar.

The bartender recognized her from TV and immediately said, "Hey, Ashley, what can I get you?"

"Yes. I need some information," she said.

"That'll cost you," he said, with a piano-key smile across most of his small face.

"I'm looking . . ." she said, but was interrupted.

Someone's arm bumped her head. A ten-dollar bill seemingly floated next to her temple. The bartender grabbed it.

"Go ahead. I'm listening," he said.

"I'm looking for a friend or friends of the girl who was killed last night in front of Jackson Square." she said, as she held up Yvette's photo. "She was supposed to meet friends here last night."

"Wow! She's the one?" he asked.

"Yes," Ashley replied.

His smile evaporated as he said, "Right. I've seen her. I think that girl over there was with her a few times. Go ask her. I think

I'm right."

Ashley looked left and saw a woman in her early thirties sitting alone at a small table against the wall on which hung a photo of legendary blues guitarist Clarence 'Gatemouth' Brown. "Thanks," she said, and moved to the table.

"Hi. I'm Ashley Tarleton of TV3 News," she said, extending her hand.

"I'm Juliette," she said, shaking Ashley's hand. She was wearing a business suit. Her somber, pale white face with sad eyes made her look desperately out of place.

"Were you friends with Yvette Lenieu?" Ashley asked.

"Yes," Juliette said, combing back her straight raven black hair with her hand. "I know . . . I knew her. We were friends for several years and tomorrow I will be at her funeral. I never thought this violence would reach my own circle of friends. I thought it might be comforting to be around people tonight, so I came here."

"I was there last night, about twenty feet away," Ashely said.

"My God! You could have been shot," Juliette said, quite alarmed.

"Yes. I was lucky. I was definitely shook-up. My mind has been flashing back to that scene all day now," Ashley said, sitting down. "Did she have any enemies that you know of?"

"Why? Do you think she was murdered?" Juliette said, alarmed at such a thought.

"I don't know. But there exists the possibility," Ashley said.

"I don't know of anyone who would've wanted to kill her. She was so sweet and smart. And she would've been a terrific and loving mother," Juliette said.

"Was she pregnant?" Ashley asked.

"Yes. She found out last week. She was very happy," Juliette said, with a half- smile.

"I didn't know that. And I don't think her mother knew. I spoke with her this morning," Ashley said.

"No one knew except myself and a couple of other close

friends. She was nervous about telling her mother and father," Juliette admitted.

"Who's the father?" Ashley asked.

"She wouldn't say. She told me it was a secret she would never divulge. She probably would have told me eventually," Juliette said.

"You have no idea? Was she dating anyone?" Ashley inquired.

"No. Not that I know of," Juliette said. "I wanted to introduce her to a nice guy I know."

"She must have been dating someone. Did she meet anyone here recently?" Ashley asked.

"She would talk to guys here on occasion, like all of us," Juliette said. "She was very attractive. Men were drawn to her. But she never went home with one. She wouldn't do that. And I don't remember seeing any men at her apartment when I visited her, though once a man came to the door. I could hear his voice but couldn't see him. His voice sounded like that of an older man. She talked to him outside her door."

"How long?" Ashley asked.

"Only for a few minutes, and then he was gone. She said he was a friend of her father," Juliette said.

"Forgive me for saying, but it sounds like she had some kind of secret life going. How else could you explain all of this?" Ashley asked.

Juliette paused and said, "I can't explain it. I can't explain her life or her death. I thought it was a random shooting, but now you have me wondering." She suspiciously looked around at the large crowd of people.

"When I was in her apartment today, I heard another message on her machine besides yours. It was a man's voice asking her to meet him in front of Jackson Square," Ashley said.

"Oh, God!" Juliette said, putting her hand to her mouth and looking straight into Ashley's eyes.

"That message has me wondering, too. If you remember anything out of the ordinary, please call me," Ashley said, handing Juliette her card.

"All right," Juliette agreed, taking the card.

"This may sound strange, but you did know she was black, didn't you?" Ashley asked.

"Yes. That didn't make any difference to us," Juliette said.

"No. I'm not suggesting that it did. I'm wondering, though, did she date white or black men?" Ashley asked.

"I've only seen her with white men, though none lately," Juliette said.

"All right then, Juliette, thank you. Sorry to have bothered you at such a time," Ashley said, getting up from her chair.

"That's all right. It was a pleasure to meet you. If she was murdered, please help find who did it," Juliette said, with nervous concern.

"I will. I will find out who did this," Ashley said in parting, knowing that that statement was indeed wishful thinking.

To avoid dark side streets and sideshow attractions, Ashley decided to walk down Decatur Street to Jackson Square, then up St. Peter Street to Royal Street, and Royal to Antoine's on St. Louis Street. She knew these streets were well traveled, and that in crowds there was comfort.

As she moved closer to the Square, she noticed crowds on both sides of Decatur. On the right, just next to Café Du Monde, people sat on the steps leading to the Moonwalk on the River. They applauded a fire and sword juggler on the sidewalk stage below. Tune leaned against his lamppost and played "Swing Low, Sweet Chariot" on his saxophone. On the left, in front of the Square's gates was a silent crowd. Ashley could not see who the people were surrounding until she made her way past a few people. Individuals were moving up from the crowd to lay flowers at the place where Yvette had died the night before. Another horizontal garden was in full bloom in this season of sorrow. A large black wreath hung from one gate. Leaning against the gates were long- and short-stemmed white and crimson roses. Long yellow, white and pink gladiolas flowed below them onto the sidewalk, and a few white lilies were mixed among them with little white crosses populating the floral cape that cloaked the memory of another lost soul. The perfumed aroma of the flowers hung thick in the air with the heat and grief.

"She's still here. I can feel her presence," an older black woman said, who was dressed more like a gypsy in a peasant blouse, full skirt to the ground, and bandana tied around the top of her head.

The image of Yvette's bloody face and her dark doll's eyes was illuminated by the lightning in Ashley's mind, as if Yvette herself rose from beneath the flowers to ask for help in solving her own killing.

"You can?" Ashley asked.

"This city is haunted by many grievous spirits, but you know that, don't you?" the woman questioned.

Ashley looked into the brown eyes of this gypsy-voodoo-priestess-like lady, and then backed away from her. She turned and quickly moved up the paved walkway next to Jackson Square where the Tarot card readers sat behind folding tables lit by flickering candlelight. When she reached the end of the walkway at the opposite end of the Square, she noticed one young woman motioning to her friend to "Come see!" They ran up Pirates Alley between the Cabildo and St. Louis Cathedral. Thinking of a possible story, Ashley followed. She quickly passed the Faulkner House bookstore where William Faulkner lived for two years in a casket-sized room while writing his first novel. She hurried by other shops on the Alley until she reached its end with St. Anthony's Garden on her right. In the quiet garden behind St. Louis Cathedral were trees and a tall statue of Jesus Christ with its comforting arms open wide.

There, behind the garden where Royal Street – closed to traffic – meets Orleans Avenue, stood a six-foot tall earthly angel. A crowd had grown in front of it. A few tourists were busy taking photos of this motionless person dressed in a white flowing robe with large white-feathered wings attached to the back. Ashley could not distinguish if the person was male or female because the face was white, too. Everyone was quiet in the presence of this costumed angel, as if a heavenly angel had appeared to position itself at the intersection of Royal, Orleans and Heaven, in this quiet part of the French Quarter, shaded from the intense southern sun by trees and shielded from omnipresent evil by Jesus in His garden.

Then a woman about a block down Royal caught Ashley's eye. She was dressed in white and looked like someone from the 1800s. The woman then waved. Ashley turned around to see if anyone responded, but no one did. When she looked back again, the woman was gone. She felt compelled to find the woman, and walked down Royal. Perhaps this was because Yvette was on her mind.

Ashley walked quickly down Royal Street looking in shop windows for the young woman. She thought she saw the mystery lady inside a shop called Mystic Curios. She walked up the few steps and entered. She saw a young girl with black hair looking at a display of souvenirs. She was about to question the girl but realized she was not the woman because her hair was too short and she wore black jeans. Then Ashley noticed that the souvenirs for sale were rather odd ones. They were miniature white burial tombs in three sizes, exact replicas of those in New Orleans cemeteries. Each had a small cross standing alone on the roof above the Roman-Graeco-styled doorway.

Ashley looked at the Ozzy Osbourne-like man dressed in black leather pants and vest, sitting behind the counter. His arms and chest were tattooed with crosses and fiery images of hell.

"Do you sell many of these?" she asked.

"Sure. In fact, we often sell out, especially the small one. The artist who makes them can't make enough," he said, with a smile, though Ashley half-expected fire to shoot from his mouth.

"Very Goth," the girl said, with smiling black lips.

Ashley had no idea of what the girl meant, as she stared at the girl's ashen-white face with dark eyes. Ashley was taken by decorative tomb faceplates hanging on the wall in front of them. She couldn't understand the fascination with these tombs that were so plentifully used here, because the city was below sea level and often flooded by relentless rain. During the nineteenth century, thousands died due to yellow fever spread by murderous mosquitoes. And coffins often surfaced from their eternal resting places in the ground, temporarily interrupting eternity.

Ashley suddenly glimpsed through the shop window a black-haired woman in white, entering a business a block up, by the

Cathedral garden.

"There she is," Ashley softly said.

Ashley quickly jumped down the short three steps onto Royal Street. In seconds she stood before the doorway of The Bottom of the Cup Tea Room. She entered the arched fanlight doorway of the three-story, two-hundred-year old haunted building. The only person in the shop was the young woman dressed in black, sitting behind the counter at the left rear of the small room. To Ashley's immediate right, along the wall was a long multi-leveled glass shelf that displayed crystal balls, small statuettes of horses and hands, uniquely patterned voodoo dolls, a crystal skull, and other items. On the left side of the room, near the counter was a bookshelf containing books on vampires, ghosts, tarot cards, and psychic-related subjects. Next to the counter was a glass case displaying numerous decks of tarot cards of various types and origins.

"Can I help you with anything?" the young woman behind the counter said.

"Yes. I saw a young woman dressed in white enter this shop only moments ago. Where did she go?" Ashley inquired, a bit out of breath.

"Just now?" the young woman asked.

"Yes. A few seconds ago," Ashley said.

"No one came in here," the woman said, tilting her head left.

"You're mistaken. I clearly saw her," Ashley said.

"Are you sure it was this shop? Cause we're all connected. Each block looks like one big building, sort of," the young woman said.

"No, this shop," Ashley insisted.

"Let's take a look at the reading rooms," the woman said, as she walked a few steps from behind the counter to the psychic reading rooms a few steps away down a short hallway at the rear of the right side. She opened the curtains to each of the three narrow stalls connected by thin walls, each containing a small table and two chairs. "No. No one here," she said, as she parted the last curtain.

"I know I saw her," Ashley said, turning around. "My God, I

believe that's her." Ashley was looking at a small painting of a reclining young woman on the wall directly across from the reading rooms. The woman was beautiful, fair-skinned with black hair, wearing a long white nineteenth century dress, exposing slender arms and bare feet.

"Are you sure?" the young woman asked.

"I think so. Yes. Does she live here?" Ashley asked.

"Sort of," the young woman said, tilting her head again.

"What do you mean by that?" Ashley asked.

"She's Julie. She lived here in the time before the Civil War. The person you saw was her ghost," the woman said.

"Are you serious?" Ashley asked emphatically.

"Very," the woman said. "I saw her once myself. Julie was one-eighth black or an octoroon, as they were known."

Remembering what Wyatt told her that morning about black mistresses, Ashley asked, "Like a quadroon?"

"Yes, quadroon being one-quarter black blood. There was a lot of mixing of white and black blood in the city, but secretly, of course. A wealthy white businessman owned this house back then and took Julie as his mistress. It is said he met her at a Quadroon Ball, a block away on Orleans Avenue where the Bourbon Orleans Hotel is today. It has a beautiful ballroom dating back to before the Civil War. Anyway, the story goes that Julie wanted to marry the businessman but society forbade it, just as society frowns on it now. But you can imagine what it was like then. If a woman had a drop of black blood in her, she was considered black and ostracized by white society."

"What came of the affair?" Ashley asked.

"Death. Julie's," the young woman said. "Supposedly, one night after arguing about marriage, he told her he would marry her if she stood naked in the freezing rain on the rooftop to prove her love. He thought this would stop her requests because surely she wouldn't do it."

"But she did," Ashley said.

"Yes. They say he found her on the roof, frozen to death. On the coldest night of the year, she makes a naked appearance there. Other times, you'll see her in the white dress," the young woman said.

"As light as she was, she was still considered black," Ashley stated.

"Black and forbidden fruit. It's not much different today. Is it?" the woman confessed.

"I guess you're right. I don't see many inter-racial couples in New Orleans." Ashley paused and said, "Though I did meet one today. The woman was a light-skinned black and the mother of the girl killed on Decatur last night."

"Oh! Was she black?" the young woman said.

"Yes. But looks are sometimes deceiving," Ashley replied.

"Especially in New Orleans," the young woman said, smiling.

"True," Ashley said, turning around "Thank you for your time."

"Come back again. Julie is always around. Where else does she have to go?" the young woman asked.

"Maybe I will. Thanks," Ashley said.

Ashley exited the shop and stepped onto Royal Street. She turned around and looked up at the balconies, searching for Julie. But she saw no one. She thought the story of Julie was just a legend and untrue. Part of the Quarter's mystique, after all, was its ghost stories. She walked a block up Royal and felt the urge to look back again. But she didn't.

She continued up Royal, headed for Antoine's. She saw someone tall and green approaching her. It was a woman in a lime green dress, lime green shoes and purse, lime green stockings, with a lime green bouffant hairdo. When the woman got closer, Ashley could easily detect that the woman was a man.

"Nice outfit," the transvestite told her.

"Yours, too," Ashley said, in false compliment.

"Thanks. I'm the queen of the south, and I'm going to a funeral," the transvestite said, with a loud laugh that mocked death itself.

Ashley did not wish to engage in conversation, so she quickened her pace and crossed to the other side of Royal, past various antique shops. On display in one shop window was an original musical composition by nineteenth century composer and native New Orleanian, Louis Gottschalk.

An anonymous shout shot into the humid air from Bourbon Street one block over. "Come aboard my Crystal ship!" It was knocked down by the quickly multiplying rain drops that Ashley tried to evade by staying close to the wall after she rounded the corner of St. Louis Street.

Antoine's Restaurant occupied most of the middle of the block. Its name was written across the front of the restaurant in black letters twelve inches tall. The building had four stories: two arched windows on the top floor, and ornate Spanish-styled cast iron balconies on the next two floors with tall shuttered French windows to allow the breeze entry and the heat to escape. On the first floor two narrow doors with opaque glass marked the entrance, flanked by two sets of tall French fanlight windows on either side. The windows on the inside were draped entirely with cascading ruffles of white satin that muted the light of the brightly lit main dining room, giving a gaslight glowing appearance to the outside of Antoine's. Four large nineteenth century French Chateau lanterns, each with a small eagle adorning its top, softly illuminated the front of the restaurant, silently signaling to all passers-by that in New Orleans the past is perpetually present.

Ashley hurried by a few patrons in line in front of the restaurant and turned down an enclosed well-lit alley entrance a few steps away. The alley was once part of the coach entrance to the restaurant in the 1800s. In the twentieth century it became an alternative entrance way for those who frequented the restaurant often.

Ashley picked up the receiver of the phone next to a door at the alley's end. She heard a man's voice say, "Yes." Ashley simply stated her name to which the man's voice said, "Yes, Miss Tarleton. I'll be there at once." She hung up the phone and heard a voice from the alley entrance. She looked toward the street and saw a young woman looking oddly at her.

"Excuse me," the woman said. "Is this another entrance to

Antoine's?"

"Yes, but it's private," Ashley said, matter-of-factly.

"Oh," the woman said, disappointed that she was not privy to this private entrance of exclusivity and mystery. She looked like a child scorned.

The Tarleton family waiter, Henry, opened the door and said, "Good evening, Miss Tarleton. So good to see you again."

"Thank you, Henry," she said, entering.

"And how's your mother doing? I haven't seen her here in some time," Henry said.

"I'm afraid she's quite ill," Ashley said, feeling somewhat emotional as pressure momentarily rose behind her eyes. "Thank you for asking."

"I'm so sorry to hear that. It's been my privilege to serve your mother for thirty-five years. Please tell her our prayers are with her," Henry said.

"Thank you. I will," Ashley said.

"I trust your father's doing well," Henry said.

"Yes, he is," Ashley said.

"Good," Henry said. He led her to a table in the center of the Large Annex or "Red Room," so called because its walls were a muted Victorian red. Of the fifteen dining rooms Antoine's offered, it was the largest and the favorite of the local aristocrats because it was the place to see and be seen. Photos of celebrities, politicians and royalty decorated the walls. "Here we are, Miss Tarleton," he said, pulling out a curved cane back chair that would have easily fit the decor when the restaurant opened one-hundred and fifty-four years ago.

"Thank you," Ashley said, sitting down and placing her purse on the chair next to her.

"What would you like to drink?" Henry asked.

"An Old-Fashioned, please," she replied.

"All right. And I'll bring you some soufflé potatoes as well. I know you like those," Henry said.

"Yes. Thanks."

As Henry walked away, Ashley's view of this remarkably unique crowded dining room widened to reveal a room full of white faces, varying in age from eight to eighty. She immediately spotted people she knew, and, of course, all of whom came from affluent families. She smiled at each and nodded slightly in their direction. They returned in kind. Dining at Antoine's was a family tradition among the wealthy of the city and a private club of sorts for them. The same families dined regularly here throughout the year. Some families reserved the same private dining rooms at Christmas Eve. Antoine's was a real part of these families' histories and as familiar to them as their own houses. And the restaurant itself was family owned and operated since 1840 when Frenchman, Antoine Alciatore, opened it.

Ashley noticed a doctor, who was once her pediatrician, sitting nearby with his wife. She greeted them and was struck by how much they had aged. The doctor had been a handsome man with wavy black hair. Now, what was left of his hair was white and his square-jawed face had collapsed on both sides. The doctor's wife reminded Ashley of her own mother. The two elderly people took on the same pale gray, worn look of old age. The woman and Ashley's mother now looked like sisters, she thought. That thought of the relentless push of time made her feel anxious. She surveyed the Red Room and realized that she knew many of the older people there. She had watched them age over the years in Antoine's but wasn't aware of it until now. Dining at Antoine's was a pleasurable experience for her in many ways, even an educational one. She could have filled a photo album with all the snapshot memories she had collected from her years of encounters with family and friends at Antoine's; faces expressing the joy of the occasion and the reluctance to end it; and faces showing the scars of time, as if the relentless rain had carved them. Only Antoine's itself would not have aged.

Ashley caught sight of a good friend sitting near the room's entrance. Paige Hightower and her husband, James, dined at Antoine's at least twice a month. Paige, like Ashley, was a lifelong uptowner. They had attended the same schools, wore the same style of clothing, enjoyed the same interests, and even spoke and thought alike. They visited each other's homes often and had tea at the Windsor Court Hotel nearly every afternoon. The only major difference between them was that Paige was truly content as an uptown wife to a wealthy and powerful lawyer. She wanted to be protected, even insulated, from life's "annoyances." "King James," as she sometimes lovingly called her husband, did just that. Ashley, until recently, lived a similar life with a similar husband. But an awakening in her had occurred, inasmuch as she wanted to break free of her husband's control, break free of the person he wanted her to be and to turn over that role to one of numerous uptown actresses waiting in the wings. Her emotional separation started in the last year of their seven-year marriage when her husband's demands became more obsessive. He wanted her daily itinerary of places she was going and the people she planned to meet. He didn't want her to talk to the wives of rival lawyers, or to members of other uptown families who were rivals of his parents. She had to call him during certain times every day to "check in." He did not want her to have a job and was outraged when she became "Entertainment Reporter" because it meant crossing outside the boundaries of her role. He had become less of a husband and more of a correctional officer at a halfway house. She finally had enough when at a social function she was about to speak to one of her husband's friends and her husband silenced her with an icy stare. It was at that moment when she realized that the man she married had become a stranger to her. Any threads of an emotional bond were severed that night. The only thing she knew for sure about her husband, who she once thought was so charming, was that his Mardi Gras mask had come off, revealing the asshole he really was. The next day she called a divorce lawyer, a rival of her husband.

Paige and Ashley exchanged waves, and then Paige strolled over and said, "Hi stranger. Where have you been? Haven't seen you at the club or the Windsor lately."

"I know. I should have called you. I'm covering the election for the station. I just don't have time," Ashley said.

"Well, look at you! Super! Moving up!" Paige said, smoothing out her white blouse beneath her scarlet jacket. She hated wrinkles.

"I'm trying," Ashley replied.

"I'm proud of you. I could never do that. I wouldn't know where to begin," Paige said, smoothing out the wrinkles in the crisp white linen tablecloth at the edges of the round table.

"I'm learning," Ashley said.

"What are you doing sitting by your lonesome over here? Come join us," Paige said.

"I would, but I'm having dinner with Keiffer Conright," Ashley confided.

"Oh! Well now. Very good for you. Maybe you'll become a politician's wife, Mrs. Mayor," Paige said, with a sly smile.

"No. This is strictly business," Ashley said.

"Well, I hope he wins. It would be nice to have one of us in the mayor's office, if you know what I mean," Paige said, smiling. Ashley returned the smile but said nothing. "Well, let me get back to my husband. He hates to be left alone. Do call me so we can have lunch at the club. I want to hear all the behind-the-scenes details of this election. I hear tell the mayor's son has a drug problem," she said, rolling her hand across another wrinkle.

"I will, Paige. I promise," Ashley said.

"Yes. Do. Bye. And enjoy yourself tonight," Paige said, with a wink.

"I'll try."

As Paige returned to her table, she encountered Keiffer Conright entering the room.

"Hi there, Mr. Conright. Your dinner guest is waiting. And, by the way, I hope you win," Paige said, slightly tilting her head..

"Thank you . . ." Conright said, pausing.

"Paige. Paige Hightower. I'm a fan of yours."

"Thank you, Miss Hightower. I appreciate your support," Conright said.

Conright approached diners at other tables for a handshake as he made his way to Ashley. Some shook his hand but others ignored him. Some saw him as a fraudulent uptown want-to-be whose politics and reputation were considered embarrassing to the city. Others thought he did not deserve acknowledgment or respect he had not earned. And to others he was simply not quite their class.

"Hello, Ashley. I'm so glad you could join me tonight," Conright said, sitting down at their table. "I might add, you look lovely tonight."

"Thank you. And thank you for the invitation," Ashley said.

"My pleasure indeed."

Henry brought Ashley's drink and a basket of soufflé potatoes to the table and said, "Mr. Conright, it's a pleasure to serve you, sir."

"Thank you, Henry. Good to see you," Conright said.

"And good luck to you in the election," Henry offered.

"Thank you. Much appreciated."

"What can I get you to drink?" Henry asked.

"Whiskey sour, please."

"All right. I'll return shortly," Henry said.

As Henry walked away, his assistant, Jules, handed menus to Ashley and Conright. Then another young waiter brought warm bread and butter to the table. Still another waiter filled their water glasses.

As Ashley placed a soufflé potato, a large puffed hollow French fry, on her plate, she said, "I noticed that some people did not want to shake your hand. Does that bother you?"

"Not really. It's to be expected. I'm still an outsider to some. Plus others think I'm a Nazi," Conright said.

"Are you?" Ashley asked, while leaning over her plate to take a bite of the soufflé potato. "You're certainly the talk of the town."

"I see you're definitely not an entertainment reporter anymore. You get right to it, as you did this morning," he said, smiling and reaching for a soufflé potato.

"You brought it up," Ashley said.

"*Touché*. No. I am not a Nazi. But that claim makes good press, doesn't it?" he asked.

"Yes. But it's said of you for a reason. They say there's a photo of you in a Nazi uniform. And, supposedly, you sell Nazi literature from your home," Ashley said.

"Not true. If there was a photo, don't you think you would have seen it by now? And you're free to check my home for Nazi propaganda anytime you want," he said, looking deep into her eyes. "And if you find a copy of *Mein Kampf,* I will admit guilt as long as you allow me to read it to you in front of my fireplace."

"Really!" she said, as her eyes widened. "Does that line work with some women?"

"With all *frauleins,*" he said, laughingly.

"You make light of it," she said, sipping her Old Fashioned.

"Well, what should I do, Ashley? People take what I say to extremes because I have spoken my mind in the past about white and black America and our support of Israel. People should focus on how successfully I've run my business. That experience will be significant in running the city. Whether I have a photo of Hitler on my wall or if I sing "Happy Birthday" on April 20th, is of no consequence to the city," Conright stated.

She looked straight into his eyes and said, "But it is of consequence to blacks and Jews in the city. Wouldn't you agree?" She picked up another soufflé potato and sprinkled salt on it.

"No. Why would it be?"

"They think you have no sympathy for them, will treat them unfairly and arrest them in numbers . . . at least the blacks do. They already cry police brutality," she said.

"I don't care," Conright said. "I will arrest anyone who breaks the law – white, black, Jew, Christian, whomever. It just so happens that Orleans parish is over sixty percent black and so are most of the people who break our laws. The numbers reflect that. And the prisoners in jail prove it." Satisfied with his answer, he took a sip of his water. His eyes then slowly traveled down Ashley's neck and he touched her leg with his.

Noticing this, Ashley said, "Is April 20th really Hitler's birthday?"

"Yes."

"How do you know that?" she inquired.

"I read it somewhere. I'm a student of history," he said, sensing a trap.

Ashley thought twice about asking him if he was perhaps just a student of German history, but refrained. Henry returned with Conright's drink and gave them both menus. The menus were thin and beige, written entirely in French with an antique-looking photo of the restaurant on the cover.

"The usual, Ms Tarleton?" Henry inquired, referring to Ashley's favorite dish, "*Poulet Sauce Rochambeau.*"

After hesitating briefly, Ashley said, "Henry, I believe I'll just have the '*Salade Antoine*' tonight with Balsamic vinaigrette dressing, please, and an iced tea."

"Yes, ma'am," Henry said. "And you, Mr. Conright?"

"'*Pompano en Papillote*' and 'Oysters Rockefeller,'" Conright said.

"Very good sir," Henry said, and he walked away.

"Are you feeling all right?" Conright said, before sipping his drink.

"Well, I was an eye-witness to the drive-by shooting last night in front of Jackson Square," Ashley confessed.

"Were you? I didn't know," Conright said, alarmed.

"Yes. And I'm still a little shook up about it. I'm actually experiencing flashbacks. I never knew what that meant when war veterans spoke about it. Now I do," she said.

"I'm sorry to hear that. It will get better. And remember you can always call me if you need someone to talk to," he said, staring straight into her eyes. "It was because of the murder rate that I decided to have my press conference today on the courthouse steps in front of the hallowed halls of justice – and above the morgue. I want my city back, Ashley. Our city. The city we know and love. The city that your parents can only remember now because it's in ruins. Chenier can't control the city anymore. He can't even control his own son. He's out there buying drugs on the street. He's actually contributing to the problem."

"I saw your latest commercial showing videotape of the son.

Do you think that was perhaps cruel?" Ashley asked.

Feigning indignance, he said, "What's cruel is what the mayor has let happen to this city. What's cruel is allowing the many drug dependent citizens of New Orleans to continue their drug dependency financed by criminal activities that you report on every day. The mayor should imprison those people. But he won't because they're mostly black and his son is among them. Imprisonment is the only way to end this tragedy. And this town has seen too much tragedy lately. This is politics. This is how it's done. I speak the truth." Conright, pleased with himself, sat erect, stretched his arms before him, tilted his head and said softly and deliberately, "I speak the truth."

Ashley, recognizing this to be an obvious display of male ego, like a peacock fanning its bright tall feathers to attract a mate or a Klansman in full regalia, or standing on the courthouse steps to attract attention, said sarcastically, "And apparently you videotape it, too."

"Let me tell you something, off the record," Conright said. Ashley remembered Darryl telling her that Conright would use that phrase. "My man who videotaped the mayor's son buying drugs could have called the police on him. With that in mind he got off easy."

"You put the spotlight on that kid to attack his father. Do you really think he got off easy?" Ashley asked.

"I spotlighted the problem. And I will continue to do so. Seventy percent of all crimes are drug related. And I don't care who I embarrass. I'm going after everybody – dealers and users. I'll bring in the National Guard to police the streets. And that videotape was given to the Press," Conright said.

"Some business people don't want that. They say it will scare away tourists who might see the city under military law," Ashley noted.

"Tourists have already been scared away. Even conventions have been cancelled. I'll get both back. But it starts with an iron hand," Conright righteously said.

"I wish you luck," she said.

"Thank you," he replied.

Then all was quiet between them. Other diners, all friends and relatives to each other, ate and talked with ease. If there was a silence at any of the other tables, it was a comfortable, tensionless silence and not full of expectation. But Ashley's and Conright's dinner was fraught with nervous energy. Ashley wanted more information from him regarding his background and the mayor's race. She was beginning to feel uncomfortable due to some disapproving stares from fellow uptowners, and due to stares from Conright himself, fish-eyeing her slender figure.

Conright was prepared to give her information because he wanted a reporter as an ally. He thought Ashley was his best opportunity, being new to the job. And, because she was an uptowner, he saw her as a potential conduit to the uptown vote and status. He also wanted to impress her with his unique perspective on life, and hoped his charm might lead to a relationship, though uptowners rarely mixed with those outside their class. After all, the exclusivity of being a wealthy uptowner was their main draw. Her picture perfect, *Town-and-Country* beauty was extremely alluring. And though her hair was not Nordic blonde, he still wanted to be in that picture.

Trying to regenerate conversation, they interrupted each other.

"Congrats on you . . ." he said.

"Did you . . ." she said. "Oh, sorry. Go ahead."

"No. You speak," he insisted.

"No. Please," she courteously replied.

"I just wanted to congratulate you on your promotion," he said, looking at her beautiful brown eyes, then glimpsing her chest.

"Thank you," she said.

"You must be very proud," he continued.

"I am. Very," not explaining that her promotion was hastened by a colleague's never-ending, inconvenient pregnancy.

"I know you will be a fair and open-minded reporter, unlike others in the city," he said, referring to the recent articles about himself.

"I'll do my job the best I can," Ashley said.

"I'm sure you will. Just be truthful."

"That's a journalist's job, to search for the truth," she said.

"Right," he said. "And that's all I've ever asked of them or anybody, is to consider that my statements could be true – about any topic. People are so quick to condemn me that they are the prejudiced ones, not me."

Seeing a window of opportunity in his statement, she crawled through by saying, "Do you remember the little old lady who interrupted your speech this morning?"

"Yes," he said.

"Her name is Bella. She's a survivor of the Holocaust. I spoke to her after you hurriedly left. She says you deny the Holocaust ever happened and that all those people were killed," she said.

He took a sip of his drink, raised one finger and said, "Here's the truth about that. I don't deny that many people were interned in camps during World War II. Many different people were: Christians, socialists, communists, gypsies, homosexuals, and others. The Jews would have you believe they were the only ones. Did people die? Yes, they did. But my research tells me they died of disease and some were shot trying to escape and things like that. To say the Nazis deliberately killed them and incinerated them is a lie."

"What about the ovens? I've seen pictures . . ." she said, as he cut her off.

"How else would they dispose of all the diseased bodies?" Conright asked. "They probably did burn some to rid the place of disease and parasites. But the ovens were used to burn the waste and trash from all those people. All prisons have incinerators. It makes sense. But a deliberate campaign to kidnap, execute and incinerate? Come on! That's impossible. And let me give you a little lesson in history that will shed light on the truth. If a large number of prisoners of the Nazi state were Jews, it was only because the biggest threat to the Nationalist Socialist Party was the Communist Party. And the majority of Communist Party leaders in Germany then were Jews. So, indeed there was a Jewish-Communist conspiracy against the Reich. It makes sense that Hitler focused on the Jews, not as scapegoats, but as enemies. If communists tried to take over this country, what do you think the U.S. government would do?" Before Ashley had a chance to respond, Conright cut her off. "Jail them! All of them." Indeed, he does know German history, she thought. But is it the truth, or only his version of it? "There's a reason for everything," he continued. "But sometimes people don't want to hear it. Like my mother always said, 'The Truth hurts.' Often it does."

"But what about Bella?" Ashley asked.

"What do you mean?" he replied.

"She was an eyewitness. She was there. Her entire family was murdered at Auschwitz," Ashley stated.

"They may have died there. I don't think they were murdered. My research indicates . . ." Conright suggested.

"She was there. An eyewitness account should be at the head of all research on such a matter. Don't you think?" she said, feeling proud of her insightfulness.

"Ashley, you may have a point."

"I do have a point," Ashley said, with conviction.

He took a sip from his drink, leaned into her, looked straight into her eyes and said, "Let me tell you another truth. And this is strictly off the record. Jews have been soliciting sympathy for themselves with stories of the Holocaust for years now to get support and money for Israel. They'll say anything. All these stories of murder are lies and a means to an end."

"So, you're saying all Holocaust eyewitnesses are conspiring to promote Israel," Ashley submitted.

"I'm saying they're all mistaken about murder. And because Hitler waged the most devastating war in history, a myth sprang up on how he did it. The Jews use it to their advantage. Instead of letting the tragedy of that war go, they drag it through history with each passing year. They say six-million Jews were murdered. If they could, they would write it across the sky every day. You never hear them say anything about the twenty-million Russians killed in the war, soldiers and civilians." Ashley's eyes widened. "Or the many Christians killed. Millions of Germans died, too. It's been fifty years, but they won't let it be. They're dangerous to this country,"

Conright said.

"How so?" she said, lifting her glass.

"They are in control of the media. They're writers, publishers, directors, producers. There's a Jew in just about every TV show, looking for sympathy," he said.

"Maybe they're just trying harder to be accepted," she said.

"Oh, come on!" he exclaimed. "Their influence reaches high in our government and affects national policies. My God, is it any wonder that one of the most important positions in the country, the chairman of the Federal Reserve, is a Jew! And we're much too close to Israel in our friendship. That will cause problems for us in the Mideast. There may come a time when U.S. troops will be sent to defend Israel. If you had a son, would you want him to fight and die for Israel? Personally, I'm tired of hearing about the Holocaust."

Ashley thought of the Holocaust photos she looked at in the bookstore that morning. Pages of black and white, grotesque photos of people looking less human with each page now appeared in her mind, like looking through a photo album of torture, tragedy and lives engulfed by flames. She then thought of Bella's gentle face, tracked by tears and time, and said, "Bella isn't."

A waiter placed a plate of Oysters Rockefeller on the table in front of Conright. "Did you not order an appetizer, Ma'am?" the waiter asked.

"No, thank you," Ashley replied. "But I will take my salad now."

"Yes, Ma'am," the waiter said, as another assistant brought another basket of small loaves of French bread.

"And *Pouilly Fuise*," Conright requested.

"Yes sir."

"I don't think I want any," she said.

"Oh, have a glass with your salad. It might help calm your nerves," he said.

"True," she said.

"I see I'm getting some nasty stares from some of your uptown crowd," Conright joked.

"I noticed that," she said.

"Some may not like me, but I'm better for the city than Mayor Chenier. But I can be a likeable guy. I hope you like me," Conright said.

"Well, I'm trying to remain impartial," she said, dodging the statement. "I don't really know you or Mayor Chenier well enough to say I like either one of you."

"I hope you will give the opportunity to get to know one another better when you start dating again." Ashley felt anxious about this. Her fingers and toes clenched. "How long ago did you divorce your husband?"

"Within a year," she said.

"Things better now?" he asked.

"I think, overall things are better," she said.

Curious about this, he asked, "Do you mind me asking what the problem was?"

Somewhat shocked at such an invasion of her privacy, she said, "Yes! I do mind. But let's just say it became an unequal partnership and then no partnership at all."

"Fair enough. I apologize for intruding," Conright offered.

"That's okay," she said politely. But it really wasn't, she thought.

"May I say I think your husband was an idiot for being so unappreciative of such a lovely lady," he said, trying his best to charm her.

"Thanks. I feel the same. And it cost him," she said, feeling obliged to answer him though his intentions were quite conspicuous.

"Alimony?" he asked.

"No. I didn't want money. I have my own. I just wanted out of the marriage. It cost him the lifelong companionship of an irreplaceable woman. Something I think he's only now realizing," Ashley proudly proclaimed.

"Perhaps he'll be more considerate with other women now," Conright suggested.

"I doubt it," she said.

"Why?" he asked.

"Men don't change. They only say they will. Or, if they do change, it's usually for the worse," she said, looking straight into his eyes, meaning that he, too, was included in that assessment.

Laughing, he said, "You might be right about that."

"I know I'm right about that and many other things," she said, lifting her glass.

"Now you've peaked my curiosity. What other things?" he asked.

"I just mean that I possess a high degree of self-confidence about anything I attempt. My parents instilled that in me," Ashley said.

"Good. Hitler would love you," he said. Ashley laughed, but thought of Bella and was quickly quieted. "It was just a joke."

"I know. I suppose it's good to have a sense of humor about it, considering so many people really dislike you," she said.

"That's exactly why I have a sense of humor about it. Without it I would not have been able to handle your question about being a Nazi at the press conference and ask you to dinner the same night," Conright confessed.

She smiled and said, "I was just doing my job."

"Your salad, Miss Tarleton," the waiter said, placing a white plate with Antoine's logo and full of green leaves glistening with dressing. Another waiter brought a glass of iced tea.

"Thank you," she said, as she tore the tops off five sugar packets and poured them into the glass.

"You like a little tea with your sugar, I see," said Conright.

"You know we southerners like our tea sweet," she said.

Seeing an opportunity at sexual suggestiveness, Conright said with arched eyebrow, "What other sweet things do you like?"

How common, Ashley thought, and looked the other way.

A waiter arrived with Conright's dinner and a bottle of wine. He ripped open the brown bag in which the fish was cooked. He uncorked the bottle and poured a little in a wine glass. He offered it to Conright who tasted it and nodded. The waiter filled the glass, then Ashley's.

"Thanks," Conright said.

"Thank you," Ashley said.

Raising his glass in toast, he said, "Here's to you Ashley and your new job. May you find the truth and all that you are looking for."

Tapping his glass with hers, she said, "Thank you. I hope I do. And I wish you luck in the election."

"Thanks," he said, and they sipped their wine.

An assistant waiter, who was black, had just cleared a table behind theirs. He stumbled and fell near Conright's chair, splashing him with water and wine.

Upset, Conright said, "Boy, watch your step!" as he wiped his coat sleeve.

"You better watch your step," the young man said, as he picked up bits of glass.

"What was that!?" Conright angrily asked.

"I said you'd better watch your step here. There's glass by your chair," the young man said.

Not knowing if the waiter was telling the truth about his comment, Conright continued to look at the young man but said nothing. The waiter picked up all the glass, took a last look at Conright, and then left the room.

"I think that boy is a smart ass," Conright said.

"But you don't know that for sure," Ashley said.

"They're all like that, especially the young ones," he said. "Off the record, I think in large part they have created the state of emergency in this city. They kill each other every day over drugs or money or territory. They're violent and vulgar. Their music promotes both. They live in an upside-down world where bad is good, and doing time in prison is considered manly, and shooting someone or getting shot is a red badge of courage. And just in general, blacks are impossible to get along with. And they hate all white people."

"But maybe they think that about us, too," Ashley said.

"Perhaps, but not all whites hate blacks. I do, however, get the feeling that all blacks hate whites. I mean everything has got to be all about them, and how they were wronged by whitey. And they want to take it out on any white person. Remember the L.A. riots resulting from the Rodney King beating trial. The blacks went wild and started attacking any white person they saw, like that poor truck driver who was dragged from his truck and beaten," Conright said.

"But wasn't it a black man who saved him and brought him to the hospital?" she asked.

"I don't recall that," he said.

"I think so. I could be wrong but . . ." Ashley said.

Ignoring her comment, he said, "And they have a built-in excuse for not helping to make this country a better place because they feel the U.S. owes them. And no matter what they are given, it's never enough. Take the Confederate monuments, for example. Blacks are insistent on removing all Confederate monuments, especially General Robert E. Lee at Lee Circle. Our city is called historic New Orleans but they want to remove part of its history. They refuse to compromise by maybe removing a couple of monuments, or erecting new monuments to tell a more complete story of New Orleans during the Civil War. That is an intelligent approach. But, no, it must be their way or no way. As a white person and taxpayer, that stance offends me. Off the record, white people float this city financially, and commit more time and energy to community organizations, volunteer groups, Carnival krewes and so forth. Why, then, should the white populace be ignored entirely? I guarantee that the City Council, which is mostly black, will vote to remove the statues. This is a dangerous thing because where will it end? They, then, could vote to remove anything they want and ruin our beautiful city like Andrew Jackson's statue in Jackson Square. The mayor has purposefully divided the city. I call him Boss Chenier because he thinks whatever he says is right and is actually good for the city. What we have now in Orleans Parish is taxation without representation. That must stop. Mark my words, this is headed for the U.S. Fifth Circuit Court of Appeal."

Ashley was getting the information she desired through Conright's confessional. She spurred him on by asking, "What do you think of reparations to blacks because of slavery?"

"Don't get me started on that," he said, taking another bite of his dinner. "Reparations would be the worst thing the government could do. The door would slam shut forever on race relations. Blacks need to forgive and forget."

"But why not at least apologize?"

"Look, we both seek the truth, right?" Conright asked. "Here's the truth about that. Slavery turned out to be the best thing that ever happened to blacks because it led to the cushy life they now lead here. Take a look at Africa. I never heard of one African-American who wanted to return there to live. Have you? That country has been ruined by civil war and AIDS. That's where AIDS started. The truth is the white man has kept the black man alive. Without intervention from whites, the black man would be extinct by now by his own hand. Blacks bring on their own suffering themselves. They cannot as a people rise above. Whites have and do rise above," he said, finishing his fish.

"That sounds racist. Don't you see that?" she asked.

"It's the truth. Don't you see that? Most people don't. They don't like what they hear and blame the courageous person who had the guts to speak the truth," he said.

"But what you call the truth is not necessarily the truth. In large part it's your opinion," she said, placing her fork on her plate of half-eaten salad.

"It's truth because it is fact," he said "What I said about Africa is fact. Do you mean to tell me the USA is not a better country than Africa? Of course it is. I know I'm a better man than most because I know my capabilities and I know who I am. Are you not a better person than one of the crazies who walk the Quarter streets day and night? It's truth, Ashley."

"I'm not saying I'm better than anyone," Ashley said.

"I am asking you to admit that that is what you are thinking, though. We all think that way. It's what drives us. I am one of the few to admit it. It's the natural order. Some people are indeed better than others. It would be naive for someone to deny that," he said, leaning toward her.

"Maybe more talented in some respect," she admitted.

"I am asking you to admit that one person can be a better person than someone else in every respect, not just talented in math or something else. If you admit that, then take it a step further by saying a group of people can for specific reasons be better than another group. It's competition; it's struggle; it's nature; it's life; it's survival of the fittest. You've heard that term used before, haven't you?" he asked.

"Yes. I remember it from college. But you're applying it to people, especially whites and blacks," she observed. "And you're saying blacks are a very violent people who keep themselves down. But from what I remember from school, most wars were whites against whites. Doesn't that blow your theory?"

"It's part of the struggle and growing stronger as a result. People from all over the world have waged war. But what people have contributed more to the advancement of the human race?" he asked.

"You think it's the white man?" she asked.

"I know it is because history tells me so. We are smarter, more compassionate and have contributed more, and have fought to do so to be on top," he said, then smiled and leaned back.

"It sounds like it's all about conflict and control. And whoever is left standing is the winner, though only temporarily. And that it's anybody's game. It's all about who wears the chains and who has the key," she said confidently and feeling for sure that Conright was full of shit.

"Ah! But ask how did the owner of that key get it to begin with? I will concede that there is conflict all around us, but that there's an evil on the loose and in some people who promote conflict," Conright said.

Looking straight into his eyes, Ashley said, "Many people think you are that evil."

The lights to the Red Room were dimmed as one waiter cleared their table while another brought over a small pot of coffee, a ladle and two demitasse cups.

"This is a special treat for two special people. I would like you to try Antoine's own creation of spiced coffee. We call it '*Café Brulot Diabolique*,'" the waiter said. He then struck a match and lit the pot. Blue flames danced above the rim. Next, he dipped the ladle in the pot and poured flaming coffee in a circle on the tablecloth. He did it twice more. Ashley had seen this done there, but never at her table. Other patrons were looking at this fiery display. Perhaps Conright had ordered it for that reason, she thought. She noticed the blue flames reflected in his eyes. She wondered if the flames were from the display, or, were they always in his eyes, but only visible in darkness?

CHAPTER 15

Frankenstein Steps

Ashley thanked Conright for the dinner and declined his offer of an after-dinner drink at the Napoleon House, though it was one of her favorite places in the French Quarter. She didn't want to be seen out with him. She had viewed the dinner as more of a business dinner. She left Conright sitting alone at the table because she wanted everyone to see that she was not his date. She felt somewhat guilty for a few minutes until she remembered her father's saying, "Guilt is an executioner."

As she exited Antoine's onto St. Louis Street, she heard a clarinetist on Bourbon Street blow a rocket-like Benny Goodman jazz riff that parted the liquid night air and seemed to herald Ashley's appearance. She reached Jackson Square where a young man imitating Black Crowes' Chris Robinson, loudly sang "She Talks to Angels," dancing himself into a foot-stomping, soul singing, elevating musical frenzy, as his blues guitarist friend strummed on near the row of tarot card readers. Some young people applauded; some joined in; older observers gawked.

"Watch out, lady!" Ruthie the Duck Girl shouted as she skated toward Ashley, almost colliding with her.

Ashley quickly stepped nearer to the Le Petit Theatre and mumbled, "Weirdo."

She drove her BMW from the TV3 parking garage out of the Quarter, across Canal Street and up St. Charles Avenue. She knew she had to return the cassette tape she took from Yvette Lenieu's answering machine that morning. The police would definitely want to listen to it. She put the cassette in her player to listen to it one last time as she drove around Lee Circle. A raspy voice said, "Be at the Decatur Street entrance to Jackson Square. I'll pick you up and bring you to him." She rewound it and played it again. Just listening to it made her nauseous again. Who was the man connected to that voice and who was the man waiting to see Yvette, she wondered. Was it premeditated murder or coincidence that a drive-by shooting occurred at that location at that time? Just like any other city, drive-bys happened frequently here, too, she thought, but never in the French Quarter. She drove by a large lighted billboard that said, "Those Who Are Blind Are Those Who Do Not Want to See." But she didn't notice and drove on.

She turned down Nashville Avenue. She parked her car around the corner from Yvette's apartment house so as to not attract attention. The side street was narrow and dark. She left the keys in the car and the car door unlocked for a quick getaway. She grabbed the tape and walked behind trees, close to the house. There, covering one side of the steps to the house was another much smaller horizontal garden in memory of Yvette. She paused momentarily to breathe the scent of remembrance, and then entered and climbed the staircase slowly, quietly by stepping on the balls of her feet.

On the next floor her pace slowed even more, like creeping through a cemetery so as not to wake the dead. As she passed by the door of Yvette's strange neighbor, Ashley was so accustomed to having doors opened for her, literally and figuratively, that she hadn't even thought about the apartment being locked. She discovered it was when she turned the handle. "Damn it!" she whispered through clenched teeth. Then she noticed a window at the end of the short hall that was next to Yvette's balcony facing the backyard. Perhaps she could crawl through it and step onto the balcony. It was her only chance she had to replace that tape. She slowly opened the window inch by inch. She looked out and saw she would have to jump from one to the other. But as she lifted her leg, she heard the apartment door open. At first, she thought it was the neighbor. But it was Yvette's door, so she cautiously entered.

"Hello. Is anyone here? Anybody?" she inquired in a low tone.

She closed the door. A shaft of moonlight shone through the balcony's glass doors and slid across her face, softly illuminating the kitchen and living room. She looked around but didn't see anyone. She spotted the answering machine by the phone and the phonebook. She placed the tape into the machine. She was nervous and wanted to leave, but she also wanted to look for possible clues. She would not have this chance again. But even she was uncertain why she was driven to discover the truth about Yvette.

Feeling very uncomfortable about being in the home of a deceased stranger, she stood momentarily motionless as her eyes surveyed every corner of the quiet room. The mournful stillness increased the flow of her slow-drip anxiety. She looked at a family photo in a mahogany frame partly draped by a shadow, like a black funeral sash. Yvette's parents and she were locked arm in arm and smiling. Yvette favored her mother. Both were very attractive with long black hair and skin light enough to make crossing over from black to white quite easy, especially for Yvette.

She moved into the kitchen. A crystal vase stood on the countertop, bursting with pink and orange Gerbera daisies and Van-Gogh sunflowers. She looked through the windowpanes of the kitchen cabinets and saw stacks of yellow Fiestaware. A small vacation photo of Yvette and her parents was stuck to the white icebox door by a daisy magnet. She opened the icebox door. Inside was a large Kung's Dynasty takeout bag next to a bottle of white wine, grapes, cheese and homemade soup.

She moved into the bathroom next to the bedroom. A white towel, bearing the monogram "YL" was draped over the white shower curtain. She looked at herself in the mirrored door of the medicine chest and stopped before opening it. Perhaps, she thought, she should have more respect for the dead and leave that apartment immediately. She felt more anxious now. The flow had increased and her senses heightened. It was important, she thought, to stay for a few more minutes and search. So she closed the door on guilt and opened the chest door. She found toothpaste, a razor, deodorant and a pregnancy test box. So, indeed, Yvette's friend was right. Yvette was pregnant. But by whom, she wondered.

When she closed the door, she thought she saw the reflection of someone or something quickly move out of view behind her. "Oh, Jesus! Someone's in this apartment," she whispered. "Why didn't I leave when I had the chance? Why didn't I leave?" Her body shuddered.

Now she wanted to leave and quickly. She could see part of the front door from where she stood. She looked left, then right, and listened for any sound. Nothing. She felt pressure building in her head and settling behind her eyes. Then she bolted for the door. It was locked. She tried the small lever lock on the doorknob but it wouldn't release. She hit the door and said, "Let me out!" she looked behind her but saw no one, as she struggled with the knob. She now heard footsteps on the wooden staircase. She ran to the sliding glass door in the kitchen. But its lock, too, was stuck. The floodgates of her pressurized anxiety were now wide-open. Panic was flowing throughout her body, fueling her rapid heartbeat. The footsteps stopped outside the door and the doorknob turned. She ran to the bedroom and slid under the bed. The mystery person jimmied the lock until the door opened. She heard the person moving about the living room and kitchen. She thought for sure the person was a man because of his heavy footsteps. He was definitely looking for something, she thought. He was moving things around. He came into the bedroom and turned on the light. She saw two huge feet in big, black motorcycle boots, standing less than three feet from her. They moved about with the slowness of Frankenstein steps. He rummaged through drawers, and then opened the closet. She heard the sliding of coat hangers across the metal bar like a streetcar screeching to a halt. Then he left the room and entered the bathroom.

Ashley slid herself from beneath the bed and hurriedly tiptoed into the closet, thinking it was safer there now. She stood in the dark in between Yvette's suits, blouses and skirts. She smelled Yvette's scent and perfume on the clothes. She was surrounded by Yvette's life. The only thing missing was the life itself. Ashley was experiencing history in the making. But Yvette's apartment was a museum closed to the public. Death, as always, brought silence, and then noisy intruders searching through drawers, clothes and papers.

She could hear the intruder searching the bathroom, moving things on the glass shelves in the medicine chest. She ran her fingers down a linen suit and wondered who the man was and what he was looking for. Frankenstein suddenly became quiet. Then she heard his slow steps again moving her way. Through a thin crack in the closet door she saw the back of a tall, large man with a crew cut in a tee shirt and black jeans. He knelt down and looked under the bed, and then looked between the mattress and box spring. He stood up and stepped backwards, surveying the room. Ashley pushed her way deeper into Yvette's wardrobe, losing sight of him.

He lumbered into the living room when Ashley suddenly heard the sounds of pots and pans hitting the walls and floor. The door slammed shut and all was quiet again.

Ashley was petrified. She knew she had to run for the front door. She remembered something her father had said about visualizing her goals. Her goal right now was to stay alive. So, she visualized the rest of her life, after flying down that long wood staircase. She took a deep breath and ran through the dark apartment. What she didn't count on was stepping in a pot. "Oh, shit!" she said, as she lifted her leg and tried to pull it off, looking like a character in a comedy, spinning around while searching the darkness. She kicked the pot off and turned the doorknob but it was locked. "Oh, come on!" she exclaimed.

A gust of cold air rushed through the open sliding glass door toward Ashley who was looking in that direction. The wind seemed to be illuminated by the moonlight, as if it could be seen. Goosebumps popped up on Ashley's arms. She noticed the top of the answering machine was open and the cassette was missing. She stood against the door, uncertain as to what would appear next. The lamp on the small table where the family photo stood, turned itself on, spotlighting the photo. Then it turned itself off; then on again; then off again.

"If there's someone in this apartment trying to scare me, you've succeeded. I'm scared, alright. I'm sorry I intruded. I'm leaving now." She turned and tried the doorknob but it would not unlock. She hit the door and inexplicably said, "I'm wealthy. I don't have to take this!" Deciding to call her father, she grabbed for the phone. But it was thrown to the floor with the phonebook before she could touch it. She moved to the center of the room and nervously said, "I can't believe I'm about to ask this . . . but are you the ghost of Yvette Lenieu?" The lamp turned itself on again. Ashley put her hand to her mouth and said, "Oh, my God!"

The pages of the telephone book on the floor began to turn. Ashley watched with amazement, as if a driving force within the book was turning them, or a force without. Pages of the names of the city's residents cascaded one atop another in this book without plot or purpose, full of names specific, yet anonymous. Then the fluttering of pages stopped on pages 242 and 243. These were "C" pages, specifically, "CONNERLY-CONNOR" and "CONNOR-

CONSTANCE." Ashley bent down and quietly read the last names: Connerly, Coney, Congemi, Conino, Conkerton, Conley, Connell, Connelly, Conner. Her eyes jumped to page 243 as she continued to arrive at the front door of each of these people, then immediately leave. She read on: Conrad, Conrady, Conran, Conraney, then Conright.

"Conright, Keiffer A.," Ashley said. "Did Conright have something to do with your death?" The pages again began to turn rapidly forward to the pages containing "TANG-TARANTO" and "TARANTO-TASSIN." Her eyes scrolled down each column of names until she spied the Tarleton names. Hers was at the top of the list. Her parents' name was among the ten other Tarletons. "I think I understand. You want me to investigate Conright. That's it, isn't it? That's why you turned to his name, then mine." The pages tumbled backwards, stopping on Conright's page again, then quickly back to the page listing Ashley's name. "Yes, I understand. There's no doubt now that you're speaking directly to me to follow him. Did he have something to do with your death?" The pages turned back to the page containing Ashley's name, then forward to the Tarleton name. "I don't know if I can help you, but I'll try." She stood and wondered how does one say good-bye to a ghost, still partly disbelieving what had happened. She walked to the door, turned and said, "I'm sorry." Then the lamp turned itself off, and the door opened.

She walked out of the apartment and closed the door. She started toward the staircase when the nosy neighbor opened his door and stuck his crew cut head out like a cuckoo bird out of its clock.

"Oh, no," she whispered to herself and felt a pain across her stomach.

"Hi!" he exclaimed. "Back so soon! Did you forget something?"

"No," she said, looking down.

"Don't you want to interview me about Yvette?" he smilingly said, trying to entice her.

Ashley stopped, eyed him suspiciously and said, "Should I?"

"I may have seen something," he said.

"What do you mean?" she said, moving toward him.

"On occasion I would see a gentleman caller," he said.

Now standing in front of him, she said, "White or black?"

"Well, white, of course. There aren't too many uptown girls who would date a black man," he said, surprised by her question.

"Who did you see?" Could you identify any gentlemen callers?" she asked.

"Well . . . no . . . I didn't really see their faces," he said.

"Several men on different occasions?" she inquired.

"Yes. I suppose so," he said.

"Why are you telling me this? Do you think foul play was involved?" she said, noticing a small candlelit table with two place settings in his apartment

"I don't know. It's sad, though. Truthfully, I just wanted to talk to you. I would love it if you would dine with me," he said. "My name is Igor. Sometimes I think my name frightens people."

"No thanks," she said. Ashley thought about saying maybe it wasn't his name but himself. She wondered if he was dangerously weird and capable of committing a crime, like murder, or was he just a sad case. She was almost expecting a plastic love doll to float into view behind him as his dinner companion; instead, she realized it was probably loneliness. "Well, nice to meet you, Igor. Maybe we'll chat again," she said, moving away.

"Anytime. Just knock on my door," he said, hopefully.

"Apparently, I don't have to. You seem to know when I'm here," she observed.

"It's your heels. Any man can hear a woman's heels and takes notice," he said.

"Did you hear anyone else outside your apartment tonight?" she asked.

"No. But I was in the shower for a while. Why?" he asked.

"I was just curious. Goodnight," she said, and turned away.

"Goodnight. You're my favorite!" he said, and closed his door.

Ashley sidestepped the horizontal garden of flowers near the door and stayed close to the house as she made her way to her car. But she felt as though someone was watching her. She opened her car door, then turned around quickly. But no one was behind her. She got into her car, turned it around in a nearby driveway and turned onto Nashville Avenue. Looking in her rearview mirror, she noticed the headlights of a parked car come on, like a leopard opening its eyes in a dark forest. It then slowly approached her as she sat waiting at the red light on St. Charles Avenue and Nashville. It stopped a couple of car lengths behind her so she couldn't see the driver.

The light turned green. Wanting to check on her mother, she turned right onto St. Charles. The car behind her continued up Nashville. It was a 1973 Oldsmobile Ninety-Eight four-door sedan and longer than the width of many old houses in the city. She noticed that it was a light lemon-lime color with patches of primer on the right side, and it had a black vinyl roof. She wondered what an old car like that was doing parked in such a prestigious neighborhood. But she didn't let it worry her, as long as the driver wasn't behind her.

She drove down St. Charles a few blocks, and then made a U-turn, all the while thinking about her encounter with a possible ghost. She now wondered if perhaps the wind through the opened sliding door turned those pages. Maybe she talked to no one but herself. Her heightened nervousness of being in the apartment with a burglar could have caused her to think strangely. Her father always told her to think as long as she could before making any serious decisions in life. She wondered if that advice applied to the supernatural.

She pulled into the arched driveway of her parents' grand home. She noticed a soft light coming from her mother's room. On getting out of her car, she glanced at St. Charles Avenue and saw the Oldsmobile as long as a houseboat glide by. A chill ran down her spine. She hurried up the steps, unlocked the crystal door and entered her crystal palace. She looked through the window but saw no one on the Avenue. Could that have been the man in Yvette's apartment, she wondered. If it was, then he was now following her.

She thought she should talk to her father. She saw a light on in his study and entered. She saw him asleep in his large, regal leather chair. She decided not to wake him. He had been working. Papers, envelopes and a checkbook lay open on his desk. She removed his reading glasses and placed his arm, dangling over the side of the chair, on his lap. She loosened his striped tie and unbuttoned the collar button on his starched white oxford button-down shirt. As a child, she enjoyed running her hand inside the starched pockets of his just dry-cleaned oxfords to open them. She remembered how reassuring it was to hug him. He was such a loving father. Though he traveled a lot, he would always make it up to her when he returned. He would bring her toys from around the world and would tell her stories of those travels. He would take her and Mother to plays and the symphony and to all the expensive restaurants. She especially loved Delmonico's on St. Charles Avenue. He would always have the answer to any question she asked. He was the ideal to her. The reason she divorced her husband was, in part, related to the fact that he was not enough like her father. She always knew him to be strong, but gentle, strict but fair.

She saw now the imprint of old age on his handsome, square-jawed face. To her, he had always symbolized the very look of authority. Now, wrinkles and creases climbed on his face like vines beginning to cover a statue, as a natural subversion to any pretense of authority. She had begun to notice them a few years earlier. But the years were quickly passing now and were mercilessly replacing the youthful-looking man she always knew to be her father with this aging man in the penumbral time of his life who sat in the penumbral area between the desk lamp and the wall of books behind him. Some time in the not too distant future the shadows would overtake him completely. Ashley was beginning to realize that now, about both parents, though her father was still in good health. He was even quite vigorous for a man in his sixties. She needed his strength and support now, more than ever because of her divorce, and Mother's illness.

Ashley turned off the lamp and noticed her father's business checkbook was open, revealing six check stubs. The recipients of those checks were all identified on the stubs by initials only: "C.J.," "T.Z.," "K.C.," "A.T.," "L.T." and "Y.L." She noticed her father's small wall safe was open. Inside were a videotape, papers, cash and a handgun. At first, she thought it strange that a video would be there. But then she realized that he would often have detectives follow anyone who posed a threat to his business, for any reason, and have them videotaped as evidence. She was shocked to see the gun and didn't know he owned one. She closed the safe, kissed him on his forehead and walked upstairs to her mother's room.

Beverly, the nurse, was asleep in a large, gold brocade Queen Anne chair. A low glow from a Tiffany lamp illuminated a corner of the room, leaving her mother's bed mostly in shadow. She knelt by her mother's side to see if she was breathing. The gray duvet covering her mother rose slightly, fell and rose again. She felt comforted just to see her mother breathing. She didn't want to awaken her just to say hello. She wanted her mother to get as much sleep as possible. Sleep was as intermittent as the pain that woke her from it. She touched her mother's face and found it to be cold. She pulled the duvet up near her mother's neck. Her mother's face grimaced for a few moments. Ashley touched her mother's cold face, wishing she had healing hands to stop the pain. Pain and sadness had come to her crystal world. Perhaps childishly thinking that her family's wealth and position could isolate them from anything, including pain, she realized with each new day that her family and their mansion on St. Charles were not as exclusive as she had hoped. She wiped away a tear and whispered, "Get well, Mother. Don't leave us. Don't leave us." She looked at a photo on a nearby table of her and her mother ten years earlier. During those years her mother was disappearing and she hadn't noticed. Now the lines on her mother's face were like cracks across an old portrait of an elegant, beautiful woman, captured at her beauty's zenith but signed finally by time's own artist. It seemed the whole city was cursed and everyone in it would soon die; it was just a matter of how.

Ashley kissed her mother's forehead and walked to the doorway, looking back to watch the duvet rise and fall. She walked downstairs and checked on her father. She entered his study but he wasn't there. She turned around to leave the room and bumped into him.

"Oh! You scared me," she said, holding on to one arm.

"Sorry, sweetheart," her father said, placing his other arm around her shoulders.

"I didn't hear you. I noticed you were sleeping before I went up to visit Mother. I wanted to wake you up before I left," she said.

"You just missed me. I was in the kitchen. Is Mother sleeping?" he asked.

"Yes," she said.

"Good."

"Well, I'm going to go. I'll call Mother or stop by tomorrow." She gave her father a hug and a kiss on the cheek that seemed to quell some of the nervousness she was feeling about her mother and about the mystery man in his car who may have been following her. She was going to mention him to her father but decided not to. After all, she thought she was probably just imagining being followed. But she did think of something else to ask. "When did you decide to bring a gun into the house?"

"What do you mean?" he asked.

"In the safe," she said.

"Oh, of course," he said, as he moved to his desk, closed the checkbook, placed it in the safe and locked it. "Truthfully, I am concerned about all the crime and about someone breaking in here. I thought it best."

"It's just so unlike you," she remarked.

"The city is out of control," he said, walking toward her. "We need a new mayor."

"Don't tell me you're voting for Conright," she said, disbelievingly.

"No one else was man enough to step forward. He's all we have," he noted, resignedly.

"I had dinner with him tonight. I think he's a Nazi," she said.

"Why?" he asked.

"The accusations and some of the things he said tonight," she replied.

"Do not believe all the hype. The Jews and liberals in this town would have you believe he's a Klan member and a Nazi. He's neither. He just speaks his mind," he said.

"Do you believe him?" she asked.

"Some things I can't disbelieve because they're true," he said.

"What do you mean?"

"Jews control lots of money and blacks commit most of the crimes in the city," he pointed out. "At first that sounds racist, but when you stop to think about them, they're really true. Statistics, Ashley. Numbers are quite telling. I'm not worried about what he says. I just want him to stop the crime because it's bad for business."

"I suppose you're right, but . . ." she said.

"Sweetheart, I'm always right," he said, with a smile.

"But people have said that some organizations, maybe many, would cancel their conventions here, if he's elected," she said, with concern.

"A handful will cancel, initially. Those losses will impact the city much less than a continued rise in crime. Same goes for the City Council. They'll balk, at first, and then help him turn the city around. They'll have to and I'll help," he said.

"How well do you know him?" she asked.

"I met him at a function once. He's not the brightest guy around, but he's committed to action. And he's a Republican. I'm not voting for a Democrat. Never!" he sternly exclaimed.

"That's true," Ashley agreed, though a bit perplexed. But, then again, she thought why should she be? Conright was simply controversial. What political candidate isn't? Only allegations had been made against him without evidence to substantiate them, only innuendo. However, now that she had spoken to Conright face to face, she could not easily dismiss an unease she felt about him. "Well, Daddy, I'll trust your judgment. But there is something a little creepy about him."

"That's just because he's been slandered lately. When you judge a man, judge him on what he has said or done, not what others have said about him," her father said.

"Good advice, as always," she said, giving him a hug.

"As always," he said, laughingly.

"Well, let me get home and get some sleep. Another big day tomorrow. The mayoral debate's coming up on Saturday. I'm on the panel," she said, proudly but nervously.

"Don't be too hard on him," he said. "Remember, he's going to help the city and me. The other reporters will take turns ripping him apart. I only wish they would see the bad guy is Chenier because he's enriched his friends and impoverished the city in many ways and divided the city regarding the removal of Confederate monuments."

"Okay. Night. Tell Mother I'll talk to her tomorrow."

"Okay," he said.

She hugged him again to experience the reassurance only a hug from her father could provide. "Night, Daddy."

"Night, sweetheart. See you tomorrow."

"Okay."

She kept the top down on her BMW and drove away from the crystal world of Tarleton Manor onto stately St. Charles Avenue where what really separated travelers on the Avenue from those inside the magnificent homes that lined it, was not physical distance but wealth. The golden gates to this enchanted, unmapped world were well hidden and unreachable by most people. The lives of those inside the mansions were as mysterious as the history and depths of the River that paralleled the Avenue, not too far away. Each demanded respect from all passers-by, like ancient gods that sat in silence and never acknowledged their worshipers.

She looked in the rearview mirror and saw nothing but elderly oak trees hunched over the avenue, secluding its residents in a secret garden and sparing them the harsh sunlight that burned everyone else. She thought of her privileged past and wonderful parents without whom she could not live. She had been hidden away from all the problems of the outside world for thirty years, until now. Again, she thought of her mother fading into obscurity, nothingness and dark, silent eternity. The image of her mother in a coffin surfaced in her mind. She felt a heaviness in her head as she fought back tears. Her mother was on her mind nearly all the time now. She momentarily closed her eyes and ran her hand through her hair as if she could comb out the weighty web of sorrow that covered her brain. She opened her eyes to find she was headed for a solar white Porsche 928 parked on the Avenue. She hit the brakes in time to only tap the Porsche's rear bumper. She looked around and saw no one. But when she checked her rearview mirror, she saw a set of double headlights coming up the Avenue. She waited for the car to pass, but it didn't. She then realized the car was stopped in the middle of the Avenue. Possibly the driver was waiting for her to back away. Perhaps, however, the driver would report her if she didn't check for damage. So, she got out, inspected the bumpers, then looked at the driver and shook her head, indicating no damage. She got into her car and continued up the Avenue, noticing the other driver maintained the same distance but was moving. Apparently, everything was fine, she thought.

She turned right on Upperline, drove a block and a half, and then turned into her driveway. Another car also turned onto Upperline. She sat in her car and saw the old lemon-lime green Oldsmobile Ninety-Eight slowly drive by. Fear and trembling overcame her. She didn't know whether to return to her parents' house or not. She decided to take care of this herself and bolted from her car to her front door. She hurriedly rummaged through her purse for her keys before realizing they were still in the ignition. She ran to the car, yanked the keys from the steering column, and then paused to listen to the rumbling sound of the old Olds. The car had turned around and was heading back in her direction. She felt panic permeate her body. She ran to the porch, dropped her keys, knelt and grabbed them while checking over her shoulder. The car was not two houses away. Her hand shook as she shoved the key in the lock and turned. She was pushing so hard on the door, she stumbled inside when she opened it. She closed the door quickly and parted the curtain to see the car slowly roll by.

She was certain he was the intruder in Yvette's apartment and he knew she was there also. He now knew where she lived. She left her Gucci leather purse on the floor and went into the kitchen. She pulled out a drawer and took the largest knife from a cutlery set given to her for a wedding gift. She had not used any because she hated to cook, something that had always been done for her. The knife would now possibly be used for unintended game. She returned to the living room and peeked through her linen curtains. He had not returned, but she thought for sure he would. She kicked off her shoes, raised her legs beneath her chin and sat on her couch. One hand was clenched into a fist while the other held the huge stainless-steel knife. She waited, watched the door and listened for rattles, rumblings, and Frankenstein steps.

CHAPTER 16

Happy Birthday

Jacques "Jack" Poirier, nicknamed "Tune," sat naked playing his saxophone on a red, vinyl and aluminum chair at his red 1950s' Formica dinette table in the kitchen at the rear of his Creole Cottage house. A large turquoise-colored box fan sat in the middle of the narrow hallway that ran the length of the house. Its low rotational hum sounded like background bass to Tune's tenor blue notes that shot from his sax like a fresh air dispenser filling the one-hundred-fifty-year old house with the bittersweet scent of the blues. His neighbors didn't mind because they, too, understood the blues which hung in the air like the heat in this part of town whether Tune put those feelings into somber notes, or not.

He lived on Henriette Delille street between North Rampart street and North Claiborne avenue in the Treme neighborhood, situated across from the French Quarter. The street was named in honor of Henriette Delille, a Creole "free woman of color" (*gens de couleur de libres*) in New Orleans in the early 1800s, who entered into a civil union, or *placage*, agreement with a wealthy white planter, and who gave birth to two children who died at young ages. She then became a confirmed Catholic and founded an order of nuns, Sisters of the Holy Family, who cared for the sick, the enslaved, and the elderly. Claiborne Avenue was once tranquil with some grand homes and majestic oak trees standing tall up and down the median or "neutral ground," as it was known in New Orleans. Then came the elevated expressway in the 1960s which allowed New Orleanians to speed over the old city and break free of the time warp that kept New Orleans captive, lowering property value by paving paradise. And the rest of the world was free to rush in to gawk at the oddity on the Mississippi. African Americans populated the area, many working in the hotels and restaurants servicing the growing tourist trade. With time, criminals, like trash, collected around the freeway neighborhood, and streets grew mean. Shots were often heard and lives – often young – were silenced. Sometimes a bullet-ridden body would suddenly appear at night in the middle of a street; vendetta, vengeance, or drug deal gone bad or temporary insanity induced by heat and hopeless poverty. The residents here and in other high-crime areas downtown lived their lives as courageously as they could, looking out for one another and hoping each night would be a silent one. Whites could not fully understand living with such stress, and blacks could not fully explain it or escape it. It was survival.

It seemed everyone in the neighborhood knew someone who had been killed. The nearby cemeteries were visited regularly, just as they were when yellow fever claimed many lives in the summers of the nineteenth century. Tune's good friend, Shammy, who washed cars, was shot in the head when asked the time by a young man. Little did he know that he was about to announce the time of his own death. Tune's own brother, Clarence, a cabdriver who worked long hours, was shot in the back through the backseat by a customer with no destination. He was found slumped over the wheel of his cab on a side street near the Claiborne Avenue overpass. His brother's death took a toll on Tune. The two were very close. They were the only children of a single mother, Abby Poirier, whose grandfather had been born to a Louisiana sharecropper in the 1870s. Her father, Francois Poirier, was born in 1895 and moved to New Orleans twenty years later where he met and married Clara Torregano, a mixed-race house servant. They hoped for a good life there and eventually had two daughters – their "blessings." Their daughters, Abby and Matilda, inherited their mother's beautiful green eyes, their father's bright smile, and the enslavement of being poor in New Orleans. As kids, the girls did odd jobs for pennies and nickels. They stuck together. When they got older, Matilda married, but later Abby was struck and killed by a drunken driver as she stood at the bus stop early one dark morning on her way to work as a hotel housemaid. Their aunt Matilda took them in for a while, but gave them up for adoption because she could not afford to feed and school them on an assistant beautician's salary. Her husband refused to spend his hard-earned money on "your sister's kids," as he always referred to them.

The two brothers broke free of the Milne Home for Boys near

the lakefront one hot summer night in the early 1960s. They did odd jobs in the city for nickels and dimes, history repeating. They learned to tap dance on Bourbon Street and picked up sizeable tips. With nowhere to go they would often sit outside some of the jazz clubs listening most of the night to Dixieland jazz, jump-joint jazz and the blues. A black musician, a saxophonist named Slowride, befriended them and let them sleep on the floor of his small apartment sometimes. That's where Tune learned to blow the sax. Clarence was surprised how quickly Tune learned. But the musician was not. Slowride said, "Some young men are born to blow the blues. And, boy, you're one of them." Tune knew the blues. He and Clarence lived it from attending their young mother's funeral as children, to being cast out of their aunt's house, living in an orphanage, and then living on streets, and everywhere the signs "Whites Only." Tune knew the blues. Clarence got married first and had two kids. Tune played in a number of jazz bands but never made much money. He didn't get married until he was in his forties. A few years later his daughter, Keisha, was born. Then Shammy was murdered, and then his brother was murdered. Tune felt he had to leave town to make money in the music industry in Los Angeles to provide for his family. He also thought the city was killing everyone close to him, and he feared he might be next. But the hurtful sense of loss accompanied him to L.A. He made the wrong kind of friends and took the wrong kind of drugs. The music industry didn't hear or care about Tune's blues. He returned to New Orleans a broke, embittered man, staring poverty, obscurity and turning fifty-five straight in the face. But he knew he could make some small change playing his blues in the city that caused it, and it comforted him. He also knew a lot more money was needed to take care of his teenage daughter and to make her proud of him and to help his brother's children. His wife had divorced him. So, now he was afraid he would lose the one person he loved more than anyone, his daughter. Already heightened tension was heightening more. Pressure was building. He felt it in his head and behind his eyes. Sleep was infrequent but migraine headaches were not. Marijuana helped. But his pain was deep, deepened by the need to help his daughter, the need for money, and by the crimes he had recently committed to get the bloody money. He was expecting another call tonight. Deep down, mixed with all of this was the painful fear of losing his soul. The righteous words his mother often quoted from the Bible rose from his wellspring of memories. With eyes closed, he heard his mother's voice say, "Do unto others as you would have them do unto you. And don't be a sinner." But he could not heed those words now. He let his mother's voice and the meaning of those words sink again into the memory-sea, weighted and carried down by depressed, lead-lined blue notes.

The phone rang. Tune didn't hear it. It rang twice more, activating the answering machine which then caught Tune's attention. He heard a raspy male voice say, "Tune, we need your services again, my man. We want dirt on a wealthy businessman who lives on Diamond Drive on the lakefront. Every now and then he throws a kinky sex party for himself and a few fair maidens. He's having one tonight at midnight. We want you to videotape a few minutes of it. We know one of the girls. She'll leave a crack in the blinds in the room where the ritual is held. Check your mailbox for the camera and address. There's cash, too. Deposit the videotape in your mailbox and we'll double that amount. Watch yourself. That's rich white man's country by the lake. It's a dirty job but someone's got to do it. Right, my man? It's a dirty world and we're all unclean." The caller ended his message with laughter.

"Go to hell!" Tune said, in a low voice. He was depressed and thought about not going. But he needed the money, however unclean. He walked the length of the house to the front door. Still naked, he stepped down a few steps and retrieved a small box in a plastic bag from inside the black mailbox. The camera and five-hundred dollars were inside. He stepped back into his small, square living room with a crucifix above the front door; Christ in His agony was watching. Seeing and handling the five crisp one-hundred- dollar bills energized him and temporarily relieved the pressure in his head. He decided to do the job and rushed to get dressed. It was 8:00 p.m. As he dressed in black jeans, black tee shirt and black running shoes, he thought of how to pull off the job. To park his 1977 emerald green Cadillac Coupe De Ville, with Landau roof, on Diamond Drive would be too noticeable, he thought. But if he parked on Lakeshore Drive, the long winding road that separated Lake Ponchartrain from the huge homes across from it, someone might still see him and his license plate number. He decided on an amphibious assault. Underneath the house was a small mint green *piroque* and engine. He would park his car far away and row a few miles on Lake Pontchartrain to the point of embarkation where the wealthy reside just across Lakeshore Drive. Then he would run low and fast like a black cat across lawns and through hedges. On arrival he would film white people at play, and then quickly disappear into the blue-black night.

Tune tied the piroque to the top of the Cadillac, threw the small outboard motor in the trunk and headed south on North Claiborne, and then west on Elysian Fields Avenue which belied its name; there was nothing paradisiacal about this avenue. Small, old wooden houses lined this part of the avenue, largely populated by black families whose Elysian Fields were paved in concrete, poverty and pain. Their dreams were of escaping these Elysian Fields.

He continued up the avenue until it intersected Leon C. Simon Boulevard, where the homes on the lake side suddenly became palatial and ornate, as if, indeed, Elysium had appeared at the end of a lifelong journey. But Tune could not enter this realm. Those houses might have been constructed by people like him, but not for people like him. So, he veered right and drove down Hayne Boulevard to its end where he parked his car behind a cypress tree and large hedges wrapped in ravenous ivy spiraling up crooked branches on its idolatrous trek toward the sun. He put the motor in the piroque and dragged it down a path unnoticeable to anyone who had not walked down it before. But Tune knew this path. It was once the entrance to Lincoln Beach, part of the Lake Pontchartrain shore segregated for blacks only, during the years of open discrimination. He and his brother would often escape the orphanage's oppressive heat during the summer and hitchhike to the beach to swim and meet girls. Sometimes they would sleep on the beach all night, though they knew they would be harshly reprimanded when they returned to the orphanage. Finally, they didn't return at all. They were on their own and free to go anywhere that didn't say "Whites Only," and free to sleep on a segregated beach.

Tune clamped the motor to the rear of the boat, pushed it into the lake and jumped in. He started the motor, and then looked back at the ghosts of his past on the shore. He then looked off to the far distance toward the city where a halo-like glow marked either a city full of light and life, or a city on fire.

He started the engine and the boat slowly moved away from shore and into the darkness. A light wind wrapped around and cooled his warm face. He moved about one-hundred yards off shore. He passed a part of barren shore, then an industrial area where industry had failed and metal beams rusted. Farther down the shore, light could be seen coming from within expensive brick homes, standing tall like lighthouses for the rich. On the beach a few hundred yards away, Tune spotted the remains of the Pontchartrain Beach amusement park that was reserved for whites until the Civil Rights Act in the 1960s mandated amusement for all. Tune stared at the shore, shook his head slightly and then spit.

He continued up the shore. He could see the rooftops of more expensive homes removed from the shore behind a low levee. He cut the engine and let the tide push the piroque to the seawall. He slung his camera over his neck and stepped into the water, pulling the boat behind him. He crouched as he lifted it onto the thin grassy area, separating Lakeshore Drive from the lake. He sat quietly for a few minutes, surveying the land and getting his bearings straight, as he had learned to do so well in the Army. Caution was key. Lakeshore Drive was known as Lover's Lane for white kids. He didn't want to drive here because he knew his emerald green Cadillac might attract too much attention, not to mention his black skin. Police regularly patrolled the area. A running black man in this part of town would only arouse suspicion that he was running from a crime or running to commit one.

To his left he saw Mustang Sally and her boyfriend performing amorous acrobatics in her GT. A black Camaro with tinted windows was parked just beyond that. To his right were a young man and woman bent over a silver Mercedes SLK. Tune stayed down, remained vigilant and waited for the right moment to run across Lakeshore. An aqua-colored 1968 Cutlass convertible driven by a young white man rounded a wide turn. The sight of that car brought back memories of the late 1960s when he then envied that car and its white driver. He was still envious. The past, like the waters of the Mississippi, had returned again in the continuous circle of time. Everything was older but the same. He watched the car's long, thin, red taillights disappear into the darkness, only to illuminate the night farther down the road that Tune could not see.

Tune felt a tightening inside his head. He felt a wave of anxiety pour over his body and suddenly ran across Lakeshore Drive. Like a snake, he slid over the low levee on the other side. He was momentarily motionless, hoping he had not been seen. His camera had mud and grass hanging from it. Sweat ran down the sides of his face. He was in enemy territory, as he saw it. His stomach had tightened. His senses were heightened. He smelled the aroma of garbage riding a warm breeze circling the rear of a beautiful brick house ten yards away. His eyes were drawn to a neighbor's bedroom wall and ceiling where projected light images from a television created psychedelic suburban cave paintings. He then spied a cat on a sidewalk about twenty yards away to his left, leading into the heart of the neighborhood. And like the ancient Egyptians, Tune followed the cat.

His heart was beating rapidly like a man on the run. He wished now he hadn't taken this job. But it was work and he needed the money. The thought that finally spurred him on was again having to work for another supervisor who treated his employees like he owned them. There are two types of people, Tune thought, slaves and slave masters. And history was nothing but repetition. Tune wanted to break from the past. If he had to videotape people doing what they shouldn't or even if he had to place someone in harm's way, then he would do it to finance his freedom from a white man's world.

He jumped to his feet and started walking fast down a curving sidewalk. He was looking for Diamond Drive. He used to deliver flowers for a living and thought that street was nearby. But when he reached the corner, he realized he was lost. He looked left, then right. He felt pain and pressure in his head. He had to act quickly, so he walked hurriedly down another block. He gazed upward, looking for that blue Diamond Drive sign against the blue-black sky. But the street signs were made of other stones like Amethyst, Topaz, and Crystal. He couldn't stand under the streetlight very long. He moved into the familiar darkness. He looked around, and then spotted the cat again meandering down the sidewalk. He faithfully followed the cat to a large white brick house around the curve. Two cars were parked in the driveway. Six more were parked in front of the house that resembled a stately plantation home.

The cat walked up the driveway, turned its head back toward Tune, and then continued on. Tune followed low in the shadows. He then noticed a light come on in the neighbor's kitchen that partly shone on Tune and framed him like a Caravaggio painting in a penumbral area between light and darkness, wealth and poverty, tranquility and dread. Tune quickly crouched behind a new huge black Cadillac Fleetwood sedan docked in the carport. He heard someone moving around in that kitchen. Sweat rolled down his face as he looked around. His teeth were clenched and every muscle was stretched to the max. He couldn't wait any longer, so he bolted to the nearby redwood gate. As he pulled it open, the hinges squeaked loudly. He panicked and started back. But he heard footsteps again in the neighbor's house, so he continued through the gate, rapping the camera against it as he passed through. He shut the gate, looked through a gap between two of the boards and saw a woman's head pop into view. Her eyes, like searchlights, scanned the area, and then she withdrew.

Tune wiped a handful of sweat from his face and breathed deeply. A fog-like darkness shrouded the rear of the house. Tune crawled to the first window but the blinds were shut. He then moved to the sliding doors which offered a view of an old style 19th century brick kitchen and a hallway. But he couldn't see anyone. His pants legs were wet from the dew-laden grass. He crawled to another window where the blinds were down but open enough to see into the room which seemed to Tune to be a dimly lit den. He moved to another window on the side of the house where the curtains were parted on one window, revealing a study with a long mahogany table in the middle of the room. The room was lit by twelve candles. But tune wondered where were the people? Six cars were parked in front of the house and two in the driveway. They must be in the living room near the front entrance, he concluded. But videotaping that room would mean placing himself right in front of the house and clearly in harm's way. "No way," Tune whispered. "I ain't going back to the joint for this." He began to retrace his steps through the backyard. As he walked slowly past the sliding doors, he looked in and could not believe his eyes, which quickly widened like opened parachutes. He backed up and witnessed the strangest thing he had ever seen. He quickly turned on his camera. Walking barefoot down the hall were eight women of varying ages between twenty and fifty, all dressed in white negligees and white headbands, and all holding lit, flickering candles in candleholders. Two of the women walked on either side of a naked, aging, smiling man. They led him into the study. Tune scampered around the side of the house where he positioned himself at the window with an angular view.

In the study, the women placed their candles down on the floor, encircling the man and the table. They then let their negligees drop to the floor and stepped inside the ring of candlelight. His smiling eyes greeted theirs as they slowly walked around him. He was a child in the middle of a carousel of flesh. The ladies then moved in closer and placed their hands all over his body, rubbing his wrinkled and coarse skin, like flowers over sandpaper. The women then guided the man to the table and gently pushed him back onto it, so that the bottom half of his legs hung over the side. A white birthday candle magically appeared in the hand of the oldest woman, who knelt before the man.

"Jesus H. Christ!" Tune uttered, his hands nervously shaking the camera. "I knew white people were weird, but holy shit!" The women began to close in around the man and behind the kneeling woman, obscuring Tune's view somewhat. "Shit! Come on!" Tune whispered.

The kneeling woman dripped hot candle wax over his abdomen, and then over his groin and penis. Then they all began to sing.

"Happy Birthday to you. Happy Birthday to you. Happy Birthday, our master. Happy Birthday to you." All the women laughed and applauded.

"Insert the candle and light it. Then let's eat!" a younger woman said to the kneeling woman.

On hearing this, Tune's legs gave way and he fell to his knees, his face smashed against the windowpane. He landed on the cat that had quietly sneaked between his legs. The cat squealed a high-pitched meow and blew out of the yard, as if rocket-propelled. The women turned and looked at the window where they saw Tune looking in. The women screamed and ran from the room, leaving their perplexed master stretched out on the table, his legs dangling from one end.

Tune jumped up, ran around the rear of the house and banged into the gate, which he thought was unlocked. On opening the gate, the neighbor spotted him and ran screaming from her kitchen window observation tower. Tune ran down the driveway and into the street. He ran as if the plantation hounds that dogged his slave ancestors, were on his heels. He ran as if he was fleeing his childhood orphanage all over again. He ran as if he was a boy again and his aunt's husband was threatening to kill him and his brother again. He ran like the day he ran away from his wife and daughter, escaping all responsibilities by running to the comfort of anonymity in Los Angeles. And he ran because he was afraid. He feared what some blacks feared most – being chased by white men in a white neighborhood. Every cell in his body knew how to run; a knowledge that was memorized and passed from generation to generation, through years of experience and lessons learned of freedom lost. Tune knew how to run.

He ran through the darkness, away from the streetlights. He left his large footprints on perfectly manicured lawns. He hurdled shrubs and a black lawn jockey that almost took off his testicles. He was frightened by his own reflection in picture window frames. Dogs barked; lights came on. He sidestepped expensive and exotic cars, white men's toys. Finally, he was able to exit this jewel-encrusted neighborhood and made it to the levee.

He rested for fifteen seconds, took a look around, and then ran across Lakeshore Drive when no cars were coming. He dragged his pirogue from the shore wall steps into the lake, started the engine and glided out one-hundred yards. Only then did he look back to see several sets of car headlights pointing his way. He turned the throttle, turned right and headed into his familiar darkness, thoughts and heartbeat racing.

CHAPTER 17

More Dirty Deeds

Luther pulled into the deserted parking lot of Uptown Square Shopping Center where Broadway meets Leake Avenue, not far from Ashley's house in the Black Pearl.

He completely circled the mini-mall, looking for his connection who had not arrived. He slowed down his long, champagne-colored Chrysler LHS sedan, turned off his headlights and rolled to a stop a good distance from the mall itself, so he could see to the left and right of it. The mall was longer than it was wide. Sales were down and some stores within it had already gone out of business. Like a sickness, other merchants wondered if they were next to be infected. But Luther had money to trade for goods and services that were always in demand and even more popular as the infection worsened.

It was 3:00 a.m. and eighty degrees in the dead of night. Luther kept the car engine running to use the air conditioner. Heat filled the air like fire across the night sky. Lightning bugs floated by and moths circled the tall parking lamps in whirlpool patterns. Luther turned on the car radio and heard AC-DC playing "Dirty Deeds Done Dirt Cheap." He smiled, tapped his foot, sang along, farted and wallowed in his dark comfort.

A distant police siren screamed like someone crying for help. Luther didn't hear it. But he did notice headlights heading his way, entering the parking lot from Leake Avenue to his right. He clicked his lights from low beam to high beam, twice. A white 1972 Lincoln Continental Mark IV in showroom condition, slowly came to a stop next to the Chrysler. A tall black man dressed in a Hawaiian shirt, white slacks, white Panama hat and white boots stepped out. He looked into the Chrysler, spotted Luther and smiled.

Luther, a big man, took a few extra seconds and moves to

dislodge his large stomach wedged behind the steering wheel. "Oh!" he said, as he pushed free, planting two size eleven feet on the black top parking lot.

"Come on, Luther. I ain't got all night. Get your fat ass over here. Let's do this deal," the other man said in a Jamaican accent, laughing loudly.

"Screw you, Uncola man. And keep your voice down," Luther said.

"Hey, boy, I talk as loud as I want. That's the trouble with you white people. You're afraid of the night. We black folk own the night," the Jamaican said.

"You stole it. Who the hell wants to walk the streets with you black folk roaming around?" Luther questioned.

"Hey, man, pretty soon we steal the day, too," the Jamaican said.

"Go downtown. You already have. Where's the goods?" Luther said anxiously.

"Open sesame," the Jamaican said, while pulling the trunk release lever inside the driver's side dashboard.

The unique trunk, with its built-in wheel well to accommodate the spare tire, popped open. They walked around to look in. The black man opened a large, brown box to reveal hundreds of 8" x 10" leaflets. He handed one to Luther who began to laugh. Pictured in black and white were a crudely drawn black man hanging by a rope from an oak tree and twelve smiling white men. Beneath the drawing were the words, "Justice-Keiffer Conright Style."

"Oh, Jesus! This is beautiful," Luther said, farting as he spoke.

"I thought you'd like it, my man. Now all you have to do is have your boys put these in black folks' mailboxes around town to make it look like the mayor's boys are doing the dirty deed of slandering poor Mr. Conright as a racist! Now we both know he's not that, is he?" the Jamaican said, releasing an atomic blast laugh.

"Jesus Christ! Be quiet! My boys know what to do. They're waiting for me now," Luther said, wiping sweat from his face.

"Tell your boys to be careful. It's kind of dangerous for white boys to be roaming black neighborhoods in the middle of the night. And remember . . . we black men turn into werewolves with the full moon," the Jamaican said, pointing to the blazing white moon and exhaling a laugh just as large.

"Would you shut up," Luther said, farting again.

"Luther, I'll make a pact with you, man. I'll stop laughing, if you stop farting. Is that possible, man?" the Jamaican said, laughing loudly.

"Let me get my shit and get out of here," Luther said, picking up the box of leaflets.

The Jamaican placed his large hand on Luther's shoulder, dug in and said, "Got to give some shit to get some shit, man. You know the rules."

Luther turned his head and stared right into the Jamaican's dark eyes. The man was no longer laughing. Sweat rolled down his face and a few drops rolled off his chin. But the man stood unaffected and silent, like a gunfighter. Luther smiled to diffuse the situation and tasted his own salty sweat.

"Of course, my friend," Luther said.

The Jamaican loosened his grip as Luther dug deep into his underwear. He pulled up a roll of one-hundred-dollar bills moistened by his sweat and handed it to the black man.

"Oh, Jesus Christ, man! You couldn't have put this in your glove compartment? It's got your testicle sweat on it, man!" the Jamaican said, grimacing, as if with pain and tossing the roll from hand to hand.

"It shouldn't be that bad," Luther said, picking up the box of leaflets. "I've only got one testicle." He let loose a hearty laugh and a fart, and then threw the box in the trunk of his Chrysler. "Don't spend it all on drugs and bitches. I know you won't. Right?" he said, as he flopped down in the car, and then sped away up Broadway.

"Oh, you're disgusting! You white sweaty, one-testicle mother-farter, you! Son of a bitch!" The Jamaican opened his car door and threw the roll of cash in. "All you white people are disgusting! I'm going back to Jamaica and shoot me some tourists. Screw this place!"

He got into his Lincoln, revved the engine, and then laid rubber as he pulled away, leaving a smoky trail. He turned onto Leake Avenue and was gone in seconds.

Just across that road and over the levee was the River, rolling on as the only witness to this moment in time, to this meeting of small minds, as the long-living witness to the entire history of the city, and was all-seeing and all-knowing, like the strong brown god the poet said it was.

CHAPTER 18

Missing New Orleans

Jacques Daniel rushed around his small uptown bachelor's pad on Perrier Street, throwing Polo boxers, jeans, and an oxford shirt into his carry-on suitcase. His flight to Los Angeles was scheduled to leave New Orleans at 8:00 a.m. He checked the time on his Simpsons family wall clock. It was 7:20 a.m. "D'oh!" he cried. He thought he couldn't possibly make the flight. But he knew he had to try. He could stay in L.A. only one night to perform his comedy routine at "Clowns," a comedy club that featured open-mike night once a week for any and all unknown comedians brave enough to try and make the world laugh. He enjoyed his job as one of many assistant district attorneys for the city. But he had always kept hidden his secret ambition to be a comedian. He dreamt of national stardom and making a successful appearance on the *Tonight Show*. He told no one, but occasionally tried out jokes on co-workers just to get some kind of response. He usually told them to a couple of the secretaries, Cindy and Kathy, who always appreciated a good joke, even if somewhat lewd at times. But he would not tell them the truth about his visit to Los Angeles. He told them it was on business.

The phone rang. Jacques checked the caller ID and saw it was his mother calling. Though he was running late, he decided to answer the call. Leaving town without telling her would make her worry, and he was a good son.

"Hello, Mother," Jacques said.

"Yes, dear. You didn't come over last night. You said that you would. Is anything the matter?" she inquired.

'No. Nothing's the matter. I was working on a case. Listen, Mother, I'm on my way out. I'm going to Los Angeles for a day," Jacques said.

"Why?" she asked.

"I'm working on a case," he said, not wanting to tell her the truth because she would find it foolish and alarming. The last three generations of the family were lawyers and judges, not comedians. Three wooden bookcases stood tall against two of the dark green walls of his living room. Each shelf held heavy books on literature, art, history, science and especially the law, that marked man's quest toward the truth of his own existence. The works of Socrates and Plato supported Emerson and Thoreau; Reinhold Neibhaur leaned on St. Augustine; Tennessee Williams and Arthur Miller stood atop a horizontal Eugene O'Neil and Loraine Hansberry. On the shelf above, standing arm in arm, stood W.E.B. DuBois; Langston Hughes; James Baldwin; Eldridge Cleaver; H. Rap Brown; Malcolm X and Homer Plessy, forever locked in struggle with Judge John Ferguson. On the top shelf stood all the members of the Simpsons family, forever forged in plastic. Another bookcase held photos of his mother and father, aunt and uncle and grandmother and grandfather who wore his judge's robe.

"All right then. Come see me tomorrow," his mother requested.

"I will," Jacques replied.

"All right then. Have a safe trip and be careful," she said.

"I will. Bye."

"Good-bye, dear," she said.

He threw his razor, cologne and toothbrush in his carry-on. He was ready to roll, then realized he wasn't dressed. He slipped into a pair of khaki chinos, then into his penny loafers and white button-down shirt. He grabbed his suitcase and notebook, ran down the stairs and flew out the front door with SWAT-like force. He zipped down the path like the Road Runner being chased by Wile E. Coyote.

He jumped into the driver's seat of his VW bug convertible while tossing his bag into the backseat. He turned on the ignition and hit the gas pedal. With a mighty roar the VW sped away at thirty miles an hour, hitting the horn. "Beep, beep." He turned right at St. Charles Avenue where the traffic was confined to one lane and moving slowly. He turned on the radio to hear a traffic report on Lerner's talk radio.

"This is WORM, somewhere on your radio dial. We'll hear from Candy, our chopper girl, for the traffic report in just a couple of mementos," Lerner said. "Yesterday's trivia question was in the Jonny Quest cartoon series: who was Race Bannon's girlfriend? Race was the square-jawed, blonde bodyguard hunk who played opposite the intelligent but impotent Dr. Quest. Apparently, when Race wasn't watching Jonny and Hadji showering, he had a girlfriend. Go figure. She was the gender-jumping she-male whose name was Jade. Nobody knew the answer. You're all losers. So, I'll keep the hundred and spend it on a hooker I know with the same name. But wait! Don't feel bad. Here's something to cheer you up, New Orleans. There were four more murders. What's our total today, Ganja Bob?"

"Four-hundred nine," Bob said.

"Okay. So, let's try and break four-hundred ten by tonight! New Orleans, if any city can, you can! They don't call us the 'Murder Capital' for nothing. Okay. Listen to this . . . a little boy's sandals were found right next to the Mississippi River last night."

"New Orleanians, just refer to it as the River, not the Mississippi," Bob said.

"You're right. They were found next to the River," Lerner said, emphasizing the word. "The NOPD doesn't know what happened to the boy, but I can tell you. Obviously, the kid is fish food. Right? He must have been playing on the bank of the River, took his sandals off to play in the mud, then the River rose and grabbed him. He's history. But check this out. Somebody is still stealing stone angels from the graveyards. Ten or twelve have been taken, further proof that this is a strange, strange town. All right, here's today's trivia question regarding a 1960s' cartoon. What was the name of the cartoon where a lizard wizard sent a turtle back in time to become a knight, or an officer in the army or whatever other occupation he wanted, then had to rescue him each time? Come on losers. Let me hear from you. And I won't give you the station's number. If you're a fan, you'll know it."

"I know that!" Jacques said, as he was illegally passing a silver BMW 320i with a 'Tulane University' decal on the rear window. He swerved back into the lane, after almost colliding with the old, white horse-drawn 'Roman Chewing Candy' wagon parked to the side. "It's Tooter Turtle."

He checked his watch – 8:33, and then emitted a Homer-Simpson scream. "D'oh!" He then came to a stop at the Washington and St. Charles stoplight. Just ahead was a large, white Leidenheimer French bread truck, stalled in the only line of traffic. To the right were parked cars. Looking both ways, he checked the neutral ground for streetcars. None were in sight. Even after he passed the stalled truck, he continued on the streetcar tracks, beep-beeping anyone walking across the neutral ground. He could have returned to St. Charles after Louisiana Avenue where the avenue becomes two lanes, but he knew he would encounter a line of cars waiting to turn onto the Interstate 10 up ramp, underneath the overpass, just before Lee Circle. So, he continued down the neutral ground, just missing an ambulance wailing across the neutral ground on its way up Martin Luther King Boulevard. Two minutes later he reached the entrance ramp. Ignoring the red light itself, he turned left across oncoming traffic and made it up the ramp. He heard tires screeching and saw multiple sets of angry eyes in his rearview mirror. But he didn't care. He had twenty minutes to reach the airport.

He rose above the city and traveled as fast as his VW could go up the interstate, heading west, above ground. Below that was once a canal linking the River to Lake Pontchartrain, where in the 1830s many Irishmen dug feverishly for a dollar a day, not realizing some were digging their own graves. Thousands died of typhoid and yellow fever. The interstate pilings were grounded in mud, water, blood and bones, because some were buried where they fell.

He traveled up the Pontchartrain Expressway, passing the Superdome where 70,000 people cheered the Saints every football season. He then passed cemeteries on his right and left where those people and all the others would eventually end up, inhabiting necropolises with an expressway view of the living, blindly rushing to their deaths.

He then rounded the turn in the interstate that led into the suburb of Metairie, now heading north. He was flying as fast as a VW bug could fly. He feared a traffic jam, a common occurrence in this suburb, but it wasn't there. He sped by blocks of apartment complexes flanking the interstate, then took the airport exit which ran parallel to runways and finally brought him to the front of the airport and the familiar arched entrance to the airport terminal. He neared the parking garage and slowed down just enough to grab the ticket as the machine spit it out. He followed the ramp to the second floor and immediately found a parking place. Things were going his way.

"Yes! Thank you, Jesus!" he exclaimed. He checked his watch. "7:55! I can make it!"

He jumped out of the bug, grabbed his carry-on and walked past a new black Mercedes E300 sedan with its T-tag still taped to the rear window, parked right next to him.

Ticket in hand, he ran up the carpeted corridor connecting the garage to the terminal. He checked the arrivals and departures on the monitor near the Delta ticket counter. His flight came from Atlanta and was just arriving at Gate 20, Concourse D. He headed up the concourse. He held his notebook in one hand and placed his bag on the conveyor belt of the security station. He walked through the all-knowing security portal and watched his bag pass through the all-seeing security Cyclops. He jerked his bag off the conveyor and hurried up the corridor, circumnavigating teenagers who were slow-moving, as if they were Masters of Time.

He reached Gate 20 as passengers were disembarking. The waiting area was full of people trying hard not to look into each other's eyes and feeling very uncomfortable about it. He stood against a wall, opened his notebook, read a few of his jokes to himself and smiled. He particularly liked the Mardi Gras joke that New Orleans was the only city to give its population the day off just to get drunk. Killer, he thought.

Disembarking the plane was James Armstead, an old friend of Mayor Chenier. Both had participated in the Civil Rights movement in the sixties when they were college students. Both had become lawyers and continued to be active in social organizations within their communities, including doing *pro bono* work. Both had later become mayors of their hometowns. And both witnessed their cities consumed by crime that spread from neighborhood to neighborhood like fire. Finally, the fire of drug addiction reached the mayor himself. He was caught using cocaine while he was still in office. He was arrested and sentenced to a year in prison where he learned that Mayor Chenier was in a tough battle for re-election. On his release from prison, Armstead decided to visit the mayor, aid his campaign and revisit the past.

Sidestepping passengers embracing loved ones, Armstead began the trek up the concourse. A stream of travelers could be seen moving up and down the concourse, flowing like a river's current, like the very blood in their veins and arteries, ceaselessly flowing with new arrivals daily until the unseen, unknown force that started it all, stops it.

Armstead noticed an illuminated wall advertisement for the Chris Owens Club on Bourbon Street that featured Miss Owens in a shimmering bodice, exposing long, beautiful kicking legs, as if she was about to jump right out, her wild black hair draped around her aging but sexy face. He made a mental note to visit the club.

He then noticed another illuminated ad that featured the lobby of the Royal Orleans Hotel, bathed in a warm golden caramel inviting light. He knew then where he wanted to stay on his visit to New Orleans, the city he had briefly seen once before, thirty years ago when he and Mayor Xavier Chenier and others departed a Greyhound bus at the end of a long civil rights "Freedom Ride" originating in Washington, D.C. They were threatened and then beaten, as they traveled deep into the deep south. They were representatives of the black population and its struggle for enfranchisement, freedom and the American dream. They had participated in numerous rallies and marches in town.

He took the escalator down to the first level and then stood under the sign above the luggage carousel that flashed "Delta Flight 1968" in fiery red letters. The other passengers were arriving and took their places around the carousel, waiting for encased bits and pieces of their Eleanor-Rigby lives to magically appear from behind split, black rubber drapery, reminding them who they were.

Armstead caught sight of himself in chrome around the carousel. He saw a 5'9" fifty-two-year-old black man in a dark blue suit and white shirt who looked seemingly successful in life, but whose appearance belied the fact that he was just released from a half-way house and was trying to reconstruct his life. A closer look would have revealed the scars of time on his face and eyes weighted by regret. A small silver cross on a thin chain hung around his neck because he was strengthened by that most ironic tragedy: Goodness crucified.

Soon after the loud, annoying buzzer announced that baggage was on its way, his one black leather bag appeared. He grabbed it, showed the claim ticket to the porter and stepped through sliding doors into the heavy humid air, hot enough to singe hair. He felt like he was breathing in flames. He took a minute to adjust and orient himself, and then spotted a Yellow Cab. After tapping on the rear window, the driver hopped out and put his luggage in the trunk.

"Where you going?" said the driver, a black man dressed in a brightly colored bowling shirt with 'Acme Oyster House' printed on the back.

"The Royal Orleans," Armstead said.

"Nice hotel. One of the city's best," the driver said, as he opened the rear door.

"Thanks."

Armstead sat down on a warm black naugahyde seat as the driver closed the door and then jumped in the front seat. He adjusted his rearview mirror from which purple, green and gold Mardi Gras beads were hanging and then pulled away from the curb.

"Where you from?" the driver asked.

"Up north," Armstead replied.

"Ever been here before?" the driver inquired.

"Yes. A long time ago," he said.

"Why did you come back?" the driver asked, curiously.

"To visit an old friend and take care of unfinished business," Armstead said.

The driver eyed him suspiciously in the rearview mirror, wondering what business could go a long time unfinished. Hoping for a large gratuity, he decided to keep the conversation going, as he got on Interstate 10. "Hot enough for you?"

"I remember a heat of another kind when I was here. The heat of anger spewing like a volcano," Armstead said.

The driver again eyed him suspiciously, wondering what that could possibly mean, and then asked, "Now what does that mean, if you don't mind me asking? First you mentioned unfinished business and now anger spewing . . . . What is all that? You got me a little worried here . . . if you don't mind me asking." He continued to watch the road and the rearview mirror.

"Don't worry, my brother. I'm a peaceful man," Armstead assured. "Last time I was here was in the 60s, during the Civil Rights movement. I was on a Freedom Ride on a Greyhound bus from Washington to New Orleans, and we took hell every mile of the way. Every time we stopped we were accosted. It got very ugly. Some people on the bus were seriously injured. If you had seen the faces of those white people waiting for us, you'd know what I mean. Anger burns inside, then explodes. It can be a motivator for change, but it can be a killer, too."

"Oh, all right," the driver said, feeling relieved. "I see where you're coming from. I've seen photos of that era. You're one brave brother to get on that bus. I think I would have gotten on a plane instead." They shared their laughter, the wine of life. "Well, you ain't got to worry this time. It ain't like that no more."

"You sure?" he said, with a crooked smile.

"I'm not saying whites and blacks here are the best of friends, but we get along. It's a friendly atmosphere. There's a lot of crossover," the driver remarked.

"Posing as white?" Armstead asked.

"Yeah. *Café au lait.* You know what that means?" the driver said, eyeing the rearview mirror.

"Yes. I know what that means," he said, laughingly.

"More of that than you might think," the driver admitted.

"I'm not surprised. If you can't beat them, join them, some people would say," Armstead confessed. "Not me, though. I am a man who's comfortable in his own skin."

"Yeah, you right," the driver said.

The cab did sixty mph down the interstate, passing businesses and many apartment blocks all along the way. The road curved as the parish boundaries changed from Jefferson Parish to Orleans

Parish. The change was indistinguishable to out of towners, except for the ominous appearance of cemeteries on either side. On the right side was Lakeshore cemetery for the wealthy with white, gray, brown and black marble monuments to the dead. It was a racetrack long ago. No doubt some people, who once visited this site to place a bet on their favorite ponies, returned for their eternal rest, having lost their final wager. Across the interstate was Greenwood cemetery for less fortunate souls. It, too, was a necropolis, with some graves above ground in the Spanish tradition, but less fine and ornate. As in life, in death these people were segregated from the very wealthy across the road, as if their wealth would buy them special treatment. Arrogance was alive even in death. But through death's wide door, all were granted free admittance, but no exit. All the wealth of the world could not buy favor because Death, the Great Equalizer, was deaf, dumb and blind, and in need of nothing except patrons for its sustenance. The only foe that could kill Death was religion and its promise of resurrection and eternal life.

Armstead noticed one woman kneeling before a small elevated vault with her hands in a prayerful pose in submission to God. As she cast her appeals toward heaven, three birds flew into the brilliant blue sky and beyond the low-hanging clouds.

They continued down I-10 or, as this stretch leading to downtown was known, the Pontchartrain Expressway. After passing the silvery spaceship-like new-gladiatorial-games Superdome, he noticed to his right the onion-shaped golden dome of St. John the Baptist Church rising above the expressway. Beyond that he noticed a makeshift banner hanging high from an old building that said, "Only the blood of Christ can put out this fire." The cab rolled right and exited at St. Charles Avenue, and then turned left, heading toward Canal Street and the French Quarter.

"You know the Royal Orleans used to be the St. Louis Hotel in the 1800s. And before the Civil War slaves were auctioned there," the driver said.

"Really," Armstead said.

"Absolutely. There used to be a dome on the building, and under that dome the slaves were auctioned," the driver informed.

"Is that right?" Armstead asked.

"Yeah. I've seen photos. They had long blocks of wood all around the circular floor area. The slaves stood in chains on those blocks. I've seen receipts, too. One I saw was for $1,800," the driver said. "They used to sell our folk all around the city, even on street corners."

"My mother always claimed we were descendants of a slave, James Armistead. He spelled his name a little differently from ours. But she could prove it. He served in the Revolutionary War. For that, he was given his freedom."

"Right on," the driver said.

As they drove around the circular Robert E. Lee monument, Armstead looked up at Lee's statue atop a tall Doric column and said, "The price of a man."

The driver turned right on Howard, then left on Camp Street, crossed over Poydras and continued through the Central Business District. He crossed over Canal Street and into the French Quarter where the streets, like the history, atmosphere and attitudes, changed. Camp Street now narrowed and became Chartres Street. On the right was the mammoth monolith Marriot Hotel facing Canal Street and looming large over the Quarter's short buildings behind it. On the left were barrooms that were once residences or reputable businesses, but which now offered passers-by the company of a woman or two, sitting suggestively on stools near the doorways.

The cab continued down Chartres with the steeple of St. Louis Cathedral in sight. He turned left onto St. Louis Street and stopped in front of the Royal Orleans.

"Here we are," the driver said, hopping out of the cab. He opened the passenger door and said, "This is the main entrance. Just walk straight up the stairs inside to the front desk. Let me get your bag." The driver opened the trunk as Armstead got out of the cab. He looked up at the impressive six-story building. Its front occupied the entire block. Elegant, cast iron balconies overlooked the street. Characteristically southern fanlight windows adorned the top of every tall window on the first floor, as well as the main entrance. "Here you go," the driver said, placing the bag down.

"Okay. Thanks," Armstead said, handing the driver a twenty-dollar bill. "Keep the change."

"Thanks. Enjoy your stay."

The uniformed bellman opened the door. Armstead walked up a few steps into a wide foyer area where the front desk was located to the right.

"Yes, sir, may I help you?" the assistant manager said.

"Good morning. I need a room," Armstead said.

"Just yourself?" the assistant asked.

"Yes," Armstead said.

"We have a number of categories from which to choose," the assistant said.

"Something nice but not too expensive," Armstead requested.

"All right. I can give you a deluxe room beautifully appointed with French and Creole accent," the assistant said.

"French and Creole. Sounds interesting," he said, and handed the man a credit card.

"I'll get a bellman for you," the assistant said.

"That's okay," Armstead said. I'll carry my own bag. This hotel was once the St. Louis Hotel. Is that right?"

"Yes, sir. It was in the nineteenth and early twentieth centuries," the assistant said.

"The driver told me slaves were auctioned here," Armstead said.

"Yes," the assistant admitted. "Unfortunately, they were, as did happen in other places in the Quarter at the time. The St. Louis Hotel once had a rotunda in the middle and slaves were auctioned there. But that was a very long time ago. And, of course, the present owners had nothing to do with that. But it is part of the history of the St. Louis Hotel. There's a large painting of the St. Louis; just to the right of that are the elevators."

"Okay. Thanks."

Armstead picked up his suitcase and moved to the nearby elevators. There, on the wall in front of him, was the large painting of the St. Louis Hotel with its golden dome. It was a beautiful hotel, he thought, and slavery such an ugly institution. He wondered if, for whatever reason, a beautiful creation became affected by an ugliness, no matter how large or small, would that beautiful creation still be beautiful, or would it lose its beauty for all time like a scar on a beautiful woman's face, or slavery and the memory of its presence embedded in the South? Could it ever be accepted or ignored or forgiven, he wondered?

He looked left, toward the Rib Room restaurant and then walked to the elevator in the middle. He got off on the fourth floor and walked down the hall to his room, as a bellman came around the corner with a newspaper in hand.

"Can I buy that from you?" Armstead asked.

"Well, it's for another guest, but you can have this one. I'll get another," the bellman said.

"Thanks," Armstead said, handing the bellman one dollar.

He entered his room and placed his bag and his paper on the bed. The room was nicely appointed with *fleur-de-lis* patterned golden drapes, solid oak furniture, a painting of the French Market on Decatur street and one of the St. Louis Cathedral and Jackson Square. He looked out the window which overlooked the hotel's entrance on St. Louis Street. He unpacked his bag, putting several shirts in the dresser drawer and pants on hangers. He then washed his hands and face. While looking into the mirror, he ran his finger through gray hairs on his temples and said, "Not yet. I'm not done yet. There's more fight left in me." He walked to the bed and picked up the *Times-Picayune* newspaper. The front-page story was the new murder toll: 409 – an all-time record. The latest victim was a tourist who strayed too far from the herd and was jumped near the River. Another person was stabbed but not killed in the French Quarter late the night before. He told police that his assailant took all his money and then said, "Here's something to remember me by." The assailant then stabbed the man in the back. "No mercy," Armstead softly said. Elsewhere on the front page was a photo of a large mound of trash due to the continuing garbage strike. There was also mention of the upcoming televised debate between Xavier Chenier and Keiffer Conright later that night, to be held at the WONO-TV3 studio in the Quarter. "Good for you, Xavier. Give him hell." Armstead then determined that he would watch the debate in his room or a nearby bar, and then meet his old friend when he exited the TV studio and offer any help he could give to Xavier's re-election.

The hotel brochure mentioned a rooftop observation deck, so Armstead took the elevator to the rooftop pool where several men and women were sipping daiquiris and soaking up the sun on a beautiful but hot day. He then climbed a short flight of stairs to the observation deck. As soon as he stepped onto the deck, he witnessed New Orleans in all its grandeur. He looked north toward the Central Business District and its business towers, though not many. The Crescent City Connection bridge to the city's west bank caught his eye. He did not know the city had a west bank region. He then turned to his left and saw a huge cargo ship coming up the River to dock at one of the many wharves. There was the crescent or bend in the River that gave the city the nickname "Crescent City." He made a slight turn and once again the east bank was now in view. He was looking south at the French Quarter where the St. Louis Cathedral with its tall steeple dominated the old world, original city landscape. This was New Orleans, the city of fame and fable, he thought – the city of Mardi Gras, Bourbon Street and letting loose – the one- time Queen of the South whose regalia had long since faded but whose legend and history lives on, kept alive by the constant flow of curious tourists, by the River itself and by the grace of God who was in the minds of the city planners in the early 1700s because St. Louis Cathedral was the centerpiece of civility in this clearing called "New Orleans." He then turned a few degrees to the left and looked out over flat eastern New Orleans, having no tall buildings or major landmarks, except for the high rise, roller coaster bridge over a canal which was part of Interstate 10.

At the top of that interstate bridge was a white Chevy Suburban heading into town. Inside were four white men of the American Nazi Party and their two German Shepherd dogs, Mannlicher and Carcano, who were restlessly jumping from seat to seat and occasionally barking.

"Mannlicher. Carcano. Settle down!" the driver said.

The driver, who called himself *"Untesturmfuhrer,"* after the German military tradition in WWII though his real name was Ted, was the oldest of the American Bund at forty. The other three were in their twenties and had an all-American appearance to them. The driver, however, looked more like Adolph Hitler, complete with a narrow black moustache, dark eyes, short black hair and a *blitzkrieg* temper. They were dressed casually, but their Nazi uniforms were in their luggage, along with their handguns.

One of the Hitler youth opened a window for some fresh air. The two dogs immediately stuck their heads out the window and barked at black motorists.

"Close that window! You're attracting too much attention to us!" Ted said angrily.

Like a good soldier, he did as ordered. He then whispered to the Waffen SS tattooed young man next to him, "We got to find him a fraulein in New Orleans. He needs to get laid."

"I heard that!" Ted said. The others also heard and laughed, and the dogs barked. "You are a disgrace to the cause. There will be no fraternizing with the opposite sex. We're here to do battle in the name of 'White Power,' if Keiffer Conright likes it or not. Now, behave! What would the Fuhrer think?"

"We're sorry," the men said in unison; then they giggled.

"I'll turn this Tiger around right now! I mean it!" Ted exclaimed.

Silence and sour faces filled the SUV. The tension was as thick as their skulls.

They continued up I-10 and became lost. Ted decided to get off the interstate and exited at Causeway Blvd. He pulled into an Exxon station and asked directions to a cheap motel, though he hated asking directions to anywhere. He then drove down Causeway to Airline Highway, the famed US Highway 61. Not far down Airline, on the left were several cheap and cheap-looking motels. He pulled into the Travel Inn where the twenty rooms were arranged in a vice-grip pattern. He told the men to muzzle the dogs and walked inside.

"Yes, sir, can I help you?" the greasy clerk said, looking like a character in a 1950s B movie with skin and hair bathed in cooking oil.

"Yeah. I need a room for a few nights," Ted said.

"All right. Did you want the Jimmy Swaggart suite?" the clerk asked.

"Swaggart suite?" Ted inquired.

"Yeah. You know . . . where the preacher man himself was caught messing with a prostitute," the clerk said.

"Right. Did that happen here?" Ted asked.

"Yeah. Lots of people come here now. It's a tourist attraction. There's money in sin," the clerk admitted.

"You're right about that. Sure. I'll take it. And let me have one of those newspapers, too," Ted said.

"Okay. You owe me $25.50. Room 7, straight ahead," the clerk said.

Ted paid the dipstick clerk and drove a few feet ahead to the room.

"Okay, boys, this is it," Ted said.

They all fell out of the SUV, grabbed their luggage and the ice chest and moved inside. The room had two beds and some cheap particle board furniture.

"I got a bed," one of the young men said and jumped on it, followed by both dogs and two others, making it look like a Nazi trampoline jamboree.

"Now wait! Two to a bed and the dogs on the floor," Ted ordered. "Pop some Heines while I take a look at the police reports, so we'll know where to bash some heads."

CHAPTER 19

The Signs Are Everywhere

Later that day in the French Quarter, signs from angry residents and shop owners protesting high crime in the area were visible hanging from Decatur Street balconies in and around Jackson Square. Fifty merchants, residents and reporters from local, national and international news agencies were present to record this unusual press conference regarding out-of-control crime. Tourists gathered also, wondering what was going on. Amid tap dancing boys and sidewalk artists, Jerry Couvillion of the Merchants Association stood poised to speak in the exact spot where Yvette Lenieu was killed three days earlier. But menacing dark clouds finally collided and a river of rain fell quickly, forcing everyone to run for shelter into the gift shops of the Pontabla buildings and Decatur Street shops. Some ran to the Café du Monde across Decatur and watched what the Mother of Loneliness, Blanche Dubois, called the rain, "a little piece of eternity," fall to the ground.

Everyone ran, except one. Jesus was within the crowd and now stood alone, the rain mixing with his own tears.

"The signs are everywhere, people. Don't you see the signs?" Jesus shouted, while pointing to the sky. "The news is not good — murder every day, drugs everywhere, young girls becoming harlots, despair like black clouds hangs over us always. Why? Because we have forgotten God! His tears fall on us every day because we pray to false idols and disregard His covenant with us, His children. We are all children of God. Accept that you have sinned and release your prayers toward heaven. God is Love. God is Compassion. God is Forgiveness." Jesus fell to his knees, clasped his hands together and said, "Oh, Father, forgive them for they know not what they do. Forgive them. Forgive them." All eyes were focused on Jesus, as the rain lightened up. Tourists could not believe their eyes as Jesus took a pen knife from his pants, lifted his shirt and cut into his side. Blood mixed with rain streamed down his right side. "My blood for your sins," Jesus cried. A policeman, who was nearby for the press conference, ran to Jesus. He brought Jesus to his feet, though he fought the officer. "I am not a criminal!" Jesus shouted. "I am not a criminal! When will you learn? I am the Light!" The officer handcuffed Jesus and forced him into a police car. Jesus looked through the rear window at the shocked people who were beginning to leave their shelter. Tears rolled down the face of Jesus, forever doomed to constant sorrow and the burden of perfect wisdom.

Jerry Couvillion was again the center of attention, having retaken his place in front of the gates of Jackson Square. Framed by two tall battered banana plants with leaves shot away, a rotund Couvillion with sprouts of white hair on an otherwise red head, addressed the crowd. Ashley and Wyatt joined the ranks as he was about to speak.

"Well, that was a dramatic opening," Couvillion said. "Don't worry about him. He'll be back on the streets soon. Thank you all for coming out today, despite the rain. And like the rain in our city, our crime problem is also predictable. There are lots of both every single day. You see from the signs we posted all around here that we, the merchants and residents of the Quarter, are sick and tired of the rising crime problem." Wyatt and the other cameramen made sure to shoot the signs and audience reaction. "I was just told the mayor's office has been made aware of these signs. And the mayor is not happy. Well, guess what mayor, we are not happy either! We are determined to make the problem in the Quarter known to all. We want our visitors to live to return to our fair city. Recently, a young lady was killed right on this same spot where I am standing. Yesterday afternoon in broad daylight, a tourist was shot and killed a few blocks from here. The killer told her and her boyfriend to lie down on the sidewalk and she refused. He killed her for defending herself. Do you realize what news tourists are taking home with them now? It's not good news! The city already has a bad and unfair reputation as 'Sin City,' even though the truth about our city is that it is family-oriented and deeply religious. Visitors refuse to believe that. And the crime in the city today only supports everyone's misconception about New Orleans. It's as if we're luring people here just to rob and kill them. I'm sure we are all tired of that misconception. We have news reporters from across the country and around the world here, and I want all of you to know the truth about our city. The signs you see are there to pressure the mayor because we're tired of it. These signs are the signs of our times. These signs are the truth . . . the awful truth."

"Are you trying to embarrass the mayor?" one person shouted.

"I'm not trying to embarrass him," Couvillion continued. "But . . . he must take action. Our city is dying! And it needs immediate care. There's no city like our city in the entire country. That's why everyone who visits here loves it so much. In Jackson Square behind me, in 1803 the French handed over New Orleans and the Louisiana territory to the United States. What do you think our forefathers would say about the sad state of affairs here today? What would the residents at that time say about their city, our city today, our city full of bullet holes? They left us a truly beautiful, unique city. They wouldn't recognize it today. They wouldn't want to visit and they certainly wouldn't want to live here."

"So why are you here today? What are you going to do?" Ashley asked.

"We're here today to say that our crime problem is far worse than any of you could imagine. We're here to announce this to the world, so the mayor will come down from his tower at City Hall and face the people. This city belongs to us. And we want it back, even if it means calling in the National Guard. Let's take it to the mayor right now," Couvillion said, wiping sweat off his face. "He won't come to us, so we're going to him. Follow us to City Hall!"

A policeman took Couvillion aside and said, "You don't have a permit to march to City Hall. You're not going anywhere."

"Take a good look around you. The whole world is watching," Couvillion said, motioning toward the cameras and reporters from all over the world. "You really want to stop me? You and I have known each other for twenty years, John. We both know that the city we grew up loving, is dying day-by-day. The city our parents gave us is all but gone. I'm angry and I'm mad enough to admit that I'm frightened too. And I want the mayor to assume responsibility for this, instead of evading it."

The policeman looked around to see many eyes, human and electronic, staring straight at him. His skin tightened, his blood pressure rose and his mouth turned dry. With resignation weighted with lead, he said, "You're right. I'm angry, too. Go ahead. But I'm going to catch hell for this."

"Thanks, John." Addressing the crowd, he said, "Listen up! We're going to City Hall. Follow me!"

Couvillion, the other business owners, concerned citizens and some members of the press proceeded up Decatur Street toward Canal Street. Other reporters jumped into their cars or vans, deciding instead to meet everyone at City Hall.

"What do we want?" Couvillion shouted.

"Peace," the crowd replied.

"When do we want it?" Couvillion continued.

"Now!" the crowd resounded.

Ashley and Wyatt ran to their TV3 Chevy inside the station's garage.

"Tell me if anybody's coming," Wyatt said, as he put his camera in the trunk.

Looking up Chartres Street, she said, "Come on! Come on! You've got it." He backed out and she jumped in, "Take a left on Royal."

"You want to follow them?" Wyatt asked.

"We'll park at Canal where we can get a shot of them marching. Then we'll make it to City Hall and shoot them arriving," Ashley said.

"All right. Sounds good," Wyatt said, as he turned onto Royal from St. Peter. "Oh, look who it is." He motioned to the right sidewalk where a man dressed in a white shirt with a drawstring collar and white puffy sleeves, black pants and black shoes with large silver buckles on them, stood looking at a rolled parchment paper map. He then looked up and down the street and at buildings as if looking for an address.

"Who is that?" Ashley inquired.

"That's Clyde Bienvenu. But everyone calls him 'Bienville.'

He's a mental case. He thinks he's Bienville."

"Who's Bienville?" Ashley asked.

"You don't know your New Orleans history. Jean-Baptiste Le Moyne de Bienville. He and his brother, Pierre, founded the city in the early 1700s. This guy walks around like he's laying out the city. He thinks it's his city. Look at the way he's dressed," Wyatt said.

"That's really weird," she said.

"Only in New Orleans," he added, shaking his head.

Wyatt sped ahead, leaving Bienvenu to explore this territory but unable to map his own mind. Wyatt drove past the Royal Orleans Hotel and proceeded past the abandoned but beautiful Beaux - Arts building on the left that once housed Louisiana's Supreme Court and Brennan's Restaurant on the right. In the next block were The Monteleone Hotel and antique shops. He rolled up to the corner of Royal and Canal streets, and illegally parked. They ran to the neutral ground on Canal and walked down a block.

"I hear them," Ashley said.

"Me, too," Wyatt added.

Like an approaching army, the chanting and footsteps were heard before the crowd was seen. Suddenly, the crowd rounded the corner by the Customs House onto Canal. Cars stopped short, horns blew, but the crowd of about fifty people continued on its way up the main drag that separated the French Quarter from the central business district. Most of the city's history had been lived out on Canal Street. Businesses on it had come and gone, like the citizens themselves, and only three remained from Wyatt's and Ashley's childhoods, Adler's Jewelers, Rubenstein's men's clothing store and Maison Blanche department store.

Wyatt brought his camera closer, then zoomed in on Couvillion and the marchers, and then zoomed out to include the amazed onlookers. Some applauded as the marchers continued to shout, "What do we want? Peace! When do we want it? Now!"

"Got it?" Ashley asked. Wyatt nodded affirmatively. "Okay. Let's go."

They made it back to their car at Royal and Canal and were able to pull away across Canal where Royal turned into St. Charles

Avenue.

"Oh, look! Rubenstein's has a sale," he said, as he smiled, while motioning to the left corner men's store, knowing he could not afford any clothing there, even at sale prices.

Ashley looked back through the rear window and caught a glimpse of the beautiful one-hundred-year-old white Maison Blanche department store building that was rumored to be for sale. She looked to the right and saw the one-hundred-forty-year-old D.H. Holmes Department Store that had already been sold to an out-of-state retailer. She sat straight again and noticed a boarded up store to the left and the vacated one-hundred-year-old Kolb's Restaurant to her right. She realized that Couvillion was right – the city is becoming unrecognizable to those who grew up here. There were missing pieces elsewhere in the city, too. Maybe the New Orleans she knew and loved was dying. Then she thought of her mother. She retrieved her portable phone and called her.

After a couple of rings, Beverly, the nurse, answered, "Hello. The Tarleton residence."

"Hi Beverly. It's Ashley."

"Hello, Miss Ashley."

"I just called to check on my mother."

"Oh, she's doing fine. She's sleeping," Beverly said.

"Have you noticed any change in her condition?" Ashley nervously inquired.

"No. I'd say it was about the same," Beverly said.

"Okay. Let me know if there's a change. You have my portable phone . . ." Ashley said.

"Yes. Yes. Listen, darling, I'm right here with her. If anything happens, you'll be the first one I call," Beverly assured.

"Thanks Beverly. We're lucky to have you."

"That's all right, baby. I'll take care of Mama," Beverly said, reassuringly.

"Okay. Bye."

"Everything okay?" Wyatt inquired.

"Yes," Ashley said, placing her portable phone in her purse. "I just had an eerie premonition. It's okay."

Wyatt turned right onto Poydras street in the middle of the CBD, and then right again onto Loyola five blocks down. There, on the left, was City Hall, a plain unassuming rectangular building. Police were on the plaza and steps in front, anticipating the crowd. Wyatt pulled up at a parking meter. They both jumped out.

"If we position the camera here on the sidewalk next to City Hall, we can get a good long shot when they reach the library and get some good close shots when they arrive," Ashley recommended.

"Yeah, I know," Wyatt replied, stiffly.

"Is the mayor in his office?" Ashley inquired from an officer.

"No," the policeman coldly said.

"I think I hear them," Wyatt said.

"Is that them?" Ashley asked. "Sounds like a siren."

Suddenly, a siren's shrill sound harkened the arrival of an ambulance as it rounded the corner of Tulane and Loyola avenues, and then took a sharp right onto the well-traveled, blood-stained Gravier street one block in front of City Hall across Duncan Plaza, on its way to Charity Hospital's Emergency Room, a block down.

"Not a nice way to start a day," Wyatt said, shaking his head. "That's the sound of a city dying."

"Wait. I can hear them now," Ashley said, looking down Loyola toward Tulane.

"They must be coming off Canal," Wyatt speculated. "They should hit the library in a minute."

A minute later Couvillion and his now sizeable crowd, having picked up recruits along the way, appeared at Canal and Elk's Place, and then moved to Loyola and Tulane, next to the public library.

"There they are," Ashley noted.

"Got 'em," Wyatt affirmed, looking in his viewfinder while wiping sweat off his face.

The battle cry of this aggressive but non-violent army still remained. "What do we want? Peace! When do we want it? Now!" as they marched down Loyola Avenue, stopping traffic and pedestrians all along the way. The group passed the Supreme Court of Louisiana on its right and the Holiday Inn on its left and stopped in the middle of Perdido Street, directly in front of City Hall where twenty policemen stood. Some members of the group were covered in sweat; some passed around bottles of water; others sat down on the short granite wall and grassy knoll, forming holes in the crowd, as if by cannonball fire.

"We're here to see the mayor," Couvillion said, now wearing a sweatband around his head with "Peace Now" printed on it.

"Not possible," one policeman said.

"This is our city. And he is our mayor." Looking up to the eighth floor where the mayor's office was recently relocated from the second floor because of eggs and insults having been thrown at him, Couvillion said, "We elected you. We pay your salary. You work for us! If you want to remain as mayor, come down and earn your pay. Come down and face the people of New Orleans. Mayor Chenier, come down! Mayor Chenier, come down!"

Couvillion continued the refrain as the crowd joined in, shouting upward, as if reversed thunder shot up at the man in the clouds.

Mayor Chenier looked down on the crowd from his office, safely out of reach, but not out of earshot. "They hate me," he said to Byron Boussier, the chief of police, standing next to him.

"I don't think they hate you," the chief said. "But you're definitely on their shit list."

"And you're right behind me," the mayor added, smiling and rolling a tall iced tea glass over his forehead.

"That's true," the chief said, wiping sweat off his neck with a handkerchief. "But you have to win their vote. I don't.

"And I could lose this election," the mayor conceded.

"If the turnout is low, you might. We have to make sure that doesn't happen," the chief said.

"Organize vans and buses to bring people to their voting

places. And get more people registered. If we can get some of these young people to vote instead of smoking crack, we could get sixty percent of the vote," the mayor said.

"Sure. All we have to do is offer free crack at every polling place, cause that's the only way we'll get most of them to vote," the chief said.

"That's probably the awful truth," the mayor said.

"I'll do my best," the chief added.

"You need to do a lot better than your best," the mayor said.

"How so?" the chief asked.

"When's the last time you arrested someone?" the mayor said, somewhat angrily. "I want to see at least one arrest every day. I want to see that person walk down the 'Walk of Shame' where the news people videotape the criminals on their way to New Orleans Central Lockup. I want to see that every night. I don't care who you arrest. But for Christ's sake, arrest somebody daily. It looks like nothing works in this town. Hell, the air conditioner in my office doesn't even work. Garbage is piling up everywhere, and so are bodies. I really can't blame those people down there. I really can't," he said, briefly closing his eyes in regret. "There's one thing I can do right now. I can do the unexpected. I can go down there."

"Good luck," the chief said.

"Oh, you're coming, too. Let's go," the mayor said.

"Oh, Lordy," the chief softly said.

As the mayor and chief got off the elevator on the first floor, the reverberating sound of the crowd's continuous chant became a frightening force in and of itself. They felt like ancient gladiators entering an arena. When they walked through the doors toward the crowd on Perdido Street, the chanting stopped. The mayor wiped away sweat rolling down his face, as he walked to the edge of the elevated walkway leading from the building to the steps. He cautiously looked out over the deep multi-racial crowd which extended from the street onto the grassy, tree-covered knoll behind it, where some took refuge from the sun.

"Good morning. It's good to see you all," the mayor said, nervously and unconvincingly.

"Oh yeah! I bet!" someone in the crowd said.

Ignoring the comment, the mayor continued, "I'm here to address your concerns."

"We're dying in record numbers. Can you address that?" another person yelled.

"Mr. Mayor, we're angry and frightened," Couvillion said, taking a few steps toward the steps. "And our businesses are suffering."

"Get him," Ashley said to Wyatt.

"I know," Wyatt said.

The news cameramen jostled for positions as they zoomed in on Couvillion.

"We want answers," Couvillion continued.

"Yeah! Like, when will the killings stop?" another man said.

"I can't answer that. I wish I could. But I can tell you in all sincerity we are doing all we can to . . ." the mayor said, trying to continue.

Before he could finish, another man shouted, "That's not enough!"

"Mr. Mayor," Ashley asked, "What is your plan?"

Wyatt zoomed in on the mayor's face while Ashley held her audio cassette recorder high.

"He has no plan. This guy is clueless!" a shop owner shouted.

Angered by the comments, the mayor raised his voice and said, "I came down here to speak with you, so let me speak." he paused. "Police Chief Boussier and I intend to hire one-hundred and fifty young recruits for the force and place them in high crime areas."

"But the entire city is a high crime area. We need help now. We suggest you bring in the National Guard," Couvillion said.

Others agreed by saying, "Yes! Now!"

"If we brought in the Guard, people would stop coming here altogether," the mayor said. Would you visit a city where the Guard was patrolling the streets? The State Police may help on some weekends. If we work together in neighborhood watch programs, we can stop much of the crime. My new program is called 'Eyes Wide Open.' The chief will deputize some citizens to patrol the streets in cars and on foot. These citizens will be paid. Not much. But they will be paid. Once this program is implemented, we should see results. I'll talk more about this during tonight's debate."

One shop owner turned to another and said, "Is this guy a moron, or what? 'Eyes Wide Open,' what kind of bullshit is that? It's more like 'Mind Completely Empty.' The city is hemorrhaging and he comes up with a 'program.' I'm voting for the Nazi. This guy has got to go." He then yelled to the mayor, "You're an idiot!"

A woman dressed in black suddenly moved through the crowd, made her way to the front, passed Couvillion and walked up the steps. She then approached the mayor and slapped his face. The crowd gasped. The mayor did not know what to do.

Ashley turned to Wyatt and said, "It's Mrs. Lenieu, the mother of the girl killed."

Wyatt zoomed in and said, "I got her."

"You killed my daughter, Yvette, two nights ago," Mrs. Lenieu said. "You killed her as if you fired the gun yourself. You've lost control of this city. Why don't you just admit it and resign. People die violent deaths every night in this city. There's someone alive out there now who won't be by tomorrow. I buried my child this morning. My flesh and blood is gone forever. And that's a scar on my heart that will never heal. Never."

Mrs. Lenieu began to cry. Mr. Lenieu walked up to his wife, put his arm around her, and led her away through the crowd, which parted to allow this somber and silent, slow-moving two-person parade to pass.

"Sorry, Mayor," the chief said.

"Yes, so am I. I'm very, very sorry," the mayor said. Looking like a defeated soldier, the mayor turned and walked slowly into City Hall.

"Incredible footage," Wyatt said.

"We've got to get back to the station," Ashley said.

The crowd slowly dispersed as lightning cracked the sky with a thunderous boom, setting off all the car alarms around City Hall and down Gravier street to Charity Hospital.

CHAPTER 20

Master Plan

At Conright's headquarters, his assistant, Guy, was eating Charles Chips potato chips from a huge round tin, and drinking Lowenbrau beer from a huge round stein, with his feet propped up on the desk. He let loose a lion-like roaring belch as he watched the tape of Mr. Ginsweet's ceremonial sex party involving the six almost virgins. The sound was turned down so he could listen to the Lerner show on the radio.

David Lerner announced, "I just got word that Mayor Chenier was slapped outside City Hall by the mother of that girl who was killed the other night in the Quarter. He was addressing angry business owners when it happened. I don't blame her. I would have socked him, too. The guy is useless. That happened today just after the cops arrested Jesus for disturbing the peace, trying to save us from hell and damnation., There's the thanks he gets. And listen to this . . . I'm reading from today's newspaper stating that stone-carved angels are still being stolen from local cemeteries. What idiot is doing that? And how is he getting away with it? How does a person remove those heavy statues without being noticed? Now here's another story that just blew me away. A mother killed her son last night; motive unknown. What the hell is happening in this city? Jesus is hauled off to jail, angels stolen, the mayor slapped, and a mother kills her own flesh and blood. But wait! There's more. A cop was arrested for having a woman killed because she complained about his brutality. I know you've all heard about that. Where is human decency? Can anybody end this insanity? Watch out, people! This city is cursed. This city is going up in flames and headed straight to hell. In response to all this madness, a mid-city neighborhood is having a 'Night Out Against Crime' block party to show solidarity. All I can say is, if you go, make sure not to talk to the police, and bring a gun."

Keiffer Conright walked into the room, loosened his paisley tie and said, "Turn that Jew bastard off!"

"He's funny," Guy said.

"He's hypercritical of me and all Aryan men. He can go to hell! I'd like to send him there myself. And get your feet off my desk!" Conright demanded.

"He just said the mayor was slapped today by Yvette Lenieu's mother," Guy said, turning off the radio.

"Did he? Good. Let him take the blame. I'll be sure to mention that at the debate tonight. Get the human candleholder on the phone." Pointing to the screen, Conright said, as he watched the tape of Joseph Ginsweet's birthday party. "Look at that fat bastard, corrupting the women of New Orleans with his debauchery."

Guy picked up the phone receiver, dialed the number and said, "It's ringing. He just picked up." He handed the phone to Conright.

"Hey, shoeshine boy," Conright said, referring to the first job Joseph Ginsweet ever had. "How do you like your X-rated video? You're a star!"

"Conright," Ginsweet said, angrily. "Don't you know I have many men in my employ who would love to beat the shit out of you for this?"

"Sure. But they couldn't reach me before I aired this video," Conright said.

"You asshole! No TV station would air this," Ginsweet angrily said.

"Not by itself," Conright confessed. "But if I blanket the city with copies, Joseph and his Magical Candle will be newsworthy. I don't think you'd want that, Mr. Titan of Industry. So don't threaten me! I want you to stand on the neutral ground between Pontchartrain Boulevard and West End, and raise my sign high, for all your rich friends to see. And I want to see you at the Lee Circle rally. Help me get elected any way possible. I'll be looking for ideas from you to do that. You don't want to be remembered as the man with a candle in his dick, do you? I want your whole family out there, or your naked birthday party goes public!" Conright slammed the phone down. "That fat fuck! He thinks he can do anything and get away with it. He made his millions by stealing from this town. Time to atone. What's that old saying? 'What you do will come back to you.'"

"Yeah. That's right."

"What did you find on that Jew, Rothman?" Conright said, while drinking from his tall iced-tea glass and wiping away sweat from his temples.

"Nothing on him. But his wife is having an affair," Guy said.

"Good. Get that on tape," Conright said.

"She may have spent some time in DePaul's," Guy said.

"A psychiatric hospital. Find more. Time is running out," Conright said.

"I do have some photos you'll like," Guy said.

"Of whom?" Conright asked.

"The mayor's son," Guy said, tossing a manila envelope on Conright's desk.

"Oh! These are golden," Conright said, sliding out several 8 X 10 color photos of the mayor's son exchanging cash for drugs. His smile widened as he looked at all the photos.

"I thought you'd like them," Guy said, finishing his beer.

"You thought right. Imagine the look on the mayor's face tonight when I show these at the debate," Conright said.

"A Kodak moment," Guy said, with a Joker-like smile.

"He can't even keep his own son off drugs, so we can forget about him helping the city get straight. That's just what I'll tell them," Conright said, smiling.

"And don't forget this," Guy said, handing Conright the racist leaflet that was placed in mailboxes throughout the city, looking like the mayor designed it to slander Conright.

"No. I definitely won't forget this. I'm going to make him look like the destroyer he is. He and his cronies have sucked all the life out of this city. It's payback time. So, Mr. Mayor, what you do will come back to you. Tonight, I'm going to lynch that black bastard.

And I'll use his own rope," Conright said.

Conright taped the leaflet to the paneled wall and smiled.

253

CHAPTER 21

Do Me a Favor

"Happy birthday to you. Happy birthday to you. Happy birthday, dear Daddy, happy birthday to you. Blow out the candles, Daddy," said Keisha, Tune's thirteen-year-old daughter. Tune leaned in and in one breath blew out the three candles on the red and white birthday cake. "Yeah," Keisha said, giving him a kiss.

"Happy birthday, Jack," Eva, his ex-wife said, sitting across the red 1950s-style kitchen table.

"Thank you. Thank you both. I'm glad you came over to my little house, such as it is. This is a big surprise. I wish I could have cleaned up first," he said, looking at the dishes in the sink.

"Oh, Daddy!" Keisha said, hugging his neck. "Time for your gift." Eva handed her a rectangular box which she handed to her father. "I hope you like it."

"I know I'll like it. What is it?" he said, his eyes shifting upward. He ripped off the blue paper and white box and opened the box to reveal a black silk, pull-over shirt. "Oh, Lord, this is beautiful." He stood up and took off his tee shirt, revealing the stretched scar of a bullet wound on his right side. He pulled the shirt over his head. "I love it! This is me."

The wrapping paper and tissue paper wrapped around the shirt both suddenly blew into the air, floating on a powerful gust of wind from the old large box fan sitting in the kitchen window; though, seemingly, they could have been propelled by the energetic luminescence of Keisha's joyful face.

"I'm so glad. They had another color, but this one looked better," Keisha said.

"It's beautiful. Thank you, sweetheart," he said, hugging her.

"Happy fifty-fifth," Eva said.

"Thanks," he said, looking into Eva's beautiful eyes and wishing things had turned out differently between them. She had stood by him many years as he pursued a career in music, his passion. Keisha was not even ten years old when she divorced him, after he refused to get a full-time job. He then left for Los Angeles. But the people he met there were mostly into hustling, not music. And now, so was he. He had to do anything he could to help Keisha achieve a better life than he had. Fathering Keisha was the best thing he had ever done. He wanted her to remember him as a good father, after he was gone.

The phone in the bedroom rang. Tune walked into the bedroom and answered it. "Hello."

"How's it going, Tune?" a raspy-voiced man said.

"I'll call you back. My daughter is here," Tune said.

"This is more important," the man said.

"Hey, man. You watch what you say!" Tune shot back.

"It seems an overly eager assistant district attorney by the name of Jacques Daniel is in Los Angeles. He can only be there for one reason: the hit men."

"No, man. He couldn't know."

"What other reason would he be there for? I got this from a good source. He must know something. Call your boys out there. Tell them he's on United Flight 777. He's a light-skinned Creole black who walks with a limp. They can't miss him. Tell them to tail him and hit him tonight. Make it look like a robbery. That won't be hard, will it, Tune? They did a 'bang up' job the other night, didn't they?" the man said, laughingly.

"Listen, I want nothing to do with this no more. Find yourself some other brother. I'm done, man!" Tune exclaimed.

"You're in deep already, boy," the man said.

"Don't call me boy!" Tune loudly said.

Keisha looked into the bedroom, wondering what was going on.

"You're in it, so shut up! You wouldn't want anything to happen to that little girl of yours, would you? Think about that!"

Tune turned around and saw Keisha. "Get this done or you'll be attending her funeral before the weekend."

The man ended the conversation. Tune hung up his phone as Keisha backed up into the kitchen. He sat on the edge of his bed and stared at his picture of Jesus on the wall. Tune wished Jesus could step out of that photo, place his healing hands on him and take away his sins and the sins of the world and grant him peace. He felt like Jesus must have felt – a man resigned to his tragic fate. He opened the dresser drawer, grabbed a handkerchief and wiped away sweat from his face. Underneath his underwear, in the drawer, was the life insurance policy he had recently purchased with Keisha as his beneficiary.

He walked into the kitchen

"Is everything okay, Daddy?" Keisha inquired.

"Yeah. Everything's okay," Tune reassured.

She hugged him and said, "Good."

He raised her off the floor a few inches and said, "Baby, there is nothing I wouldn't do for you. Nothing."

CHAPTER 22

Neighbors Against Crime

"Go down Canal Street to the cemeteries and turn right," Ashley said to Wyatt, as he drove down a street in mid-city.

"That will just lead us to City Park Avenue. They're not going to close off City Park Avenue for this thing. It would back up traffic," Wyatt explained.

"I'm sure Darryl said the 'Neighbors Against Crime' event was on City Park Avenue," Ashley insisted.

"We'll see," he said, as he continued up Canal Street past old homes and businesses. This residential area of Canal Street did not equal the grandeur of St. Charles Avenue, but some stately homes did stand on this main thoroughfare from the River to Lake Pontchartrain a few miles away. Meant to be a canal, it never realized its intended purpose and instead became another ghostly oddity in the history of New Orleans.

They pulled up to the intersection of Canal Street and City Park Avenue with Greenwood Cemetery straight ahead.

"Take a right," Ashley said.

"Well, that makes sense, since it doesn't look like anyone is partying in the cemetery. Party over . . . out of time," Wyatt said.

After Wyatt turned onto City Park Avenue, Ashley said, "There they are."

Two blocks away was a crowd of people in the middle of City Park Avenue, separating City Park on the left from a residential neighborhood.

"I'll be damned. They did close City Park Avenue," Wyatt said in amazement. "We'll have to park in Delgado." He turned into the parking lot of Delgado Community College which faced City Park Avenue and was only two blocks from the event. As Wyatt got out of the car, he noticed Holt Cemetery down a short road next to the College.

"There just ain't no getting away from the dead in this city," Wyatt said, chillingly.

He grabbed his camera from the trunk as Ashley retrieved her micro-cassette recorder and notebook. They crossed Orleans Avenue where a policeman stood routing traffic around and away from the crowd. They walked down about two blocks to N. Murat Street at the edge of the event, which took up the block to N. Alexander Street at the entranceway to City Park and Tavern on the Green to the right. The aroma of barbecue and Cajun sausage filled the air. A large sign stood above a makeshift stage that read, "Neighbors Against Crime." Usually, this area of town did not experience much crime. However, this year all areas throughout the city had been infected, and people were outraged and fearful to leave their homes at night.

"Why don't you get a wide shot while I find someone to interview?" Ashley directed.

"Yeah, I know how it's done," Wyatt retorted.

Ashley moved through the crowd, scanning faces for an expressive one to tape. People were eating, laughing and conversing with one another and with cops. The crowd was mixed black and white, and everyone was getting along well. Ashley noticed a white man off to her left, standing alone, staring at her. His hair was a bit long and he had a slight beard. He wore gray jeans, a white shirt and black harness boots. She felt a bit nervous but knew that that feeling was part of her profession. She then bumped into a lady who smiled, but appeared wounded emotionally. Ashley then noticed the tee shirt the woman wore which had a large photo of a smiling young man. On the shirt was written, "Tyrone Washington, 1974-1994, Rest in Peace." Ashley realized the shirt was a tribute to the deceased young man and that the tee shirt served as a portable gravestone and visual reminder of the raging fire of crime consuming New Orleans.

"Was he a victim of violence?" Ashley asked.

"Yes, an innocent victim," the woman said.

"I'm Ashley Tarleton from TV-3 News," she said, shaking the

woman's hand. "How did he die?"

The woman closed her eyes for a moment to transport her to that terrible scene that would now always be a part of her mind's landscape. Opening them she said, "He was leaving out a little grocery store in our neighborhood when shooting broke out between two young men. One of the shooters grabbed my son and used him as a shield. My son was shot in the head by the other gunman. He died at Charity Hospital. I have cried a lifetime of tears, but now I'm angry. I want the mayor to open his eyes and admit that New Orleans is dying. A mother somewhere in this city will grieve tomorrow for her son she will lose tonight. Just as sure as we're standing here, young men will die tonight in this city and across the country, due to violent crime and drugs. Even though pushers are killed, another one always takes his place like a weed. They keep coming back to push their poison. The gunfight that took my son's life was between two pushers. I damn them to hell. One day they will stand and be judged by the Almighty. Knowing that helps me through my days. Without the love from Almighty God we would all perish from the sadness."

Ashley noticed out of the corner of her right eye that Wyatt had been taping the entire interview.

"Is it okay to use . . ." Ashley said.

"To put me on TV? Yes. I want people and the mayor and especially the man who shot my boy, to see this. I want everyone to remember my baby's face," she said, looking at her chest and running her hand over the photo, as if stroking her son's face.

"I will. Thank you," Ashley said, as she wrote down the woman's name.

She motioned to Wyatt to follow her through the crowd. As they moved forward slowly, people turned around, curious about her and Wyatt. Ashley noticed that many people wore tee shirts with enlarged photos of their young loved ones on the front. These shirts all commemorated deceased young black men and women, obviously taken from them by violence. She felt nervous as she walked, as if walking solemnly through a graveyard where the dead stared back: Tiffany Broussard, RIP, 1973-1994. "We will never forget you;" Gerald Washington, RIP, 1975-1994, "You are always with us. Love, Mama;" Terrence 'T-bone' Jackson, RIP, 1970-1994,

"Our beloved is in Heaven with angels now." She was in the midst of pain and despair so dark and deep, she found it difficult to relate to it or understand it easily. The news was all around her and it was grim. But she knew she had to attempt an understanding because that was part of her job and should be part of her purpose as a compassionate person. Still, she felt terribly out of place.

Reverend Abraham Paternostro stepped onto the small stage and approached the microphone. The stage shook a bit due to the size of the man. He was well over two-hundred pounds with a large, round smiling face.

"How ya'll doing this glorious afternoon? Good?" the Reverend asked. The crowd responded affirmatively. "I know our lives are filled with uncertainty. There are many things we are unsure of. That's why we are here today. We want each other's company. We want somebody to hold onto in this grievous time. Our minds are filled with doubt. There is so much we don't know about life. There is a limit to what we can understand and make sense of. And, Lord, we need you to show us the way. But there's one thing we are certain about. One thing we know for sure is that it is a glorious day in Heaven, each and every day."

"Amen," the crowd returned.

"I want those of you who have lost loved ones to console yourselves with that knowledge. Will you do that for me?" the Reverend asked.

"Yes," the crowd replied.

"Because every day in God's Kingdom is a glorious day. And for all of you who are suffering for the loss of your loved ones, know that they are suffering no longer. Every day with God is a beautiful day. There are no drug pushers. There are no rapists or murderers. There are no guns or knives or criminals in Heaven. We know where they went, don't we? Don't we?" the Reverend again asked.

"That's right! We know," the crowd offered.

"Praise Jesus! Your loved ones are suffering no longer. And you will see your loved ones again. Oh, praise Jesus! You will see them again! That is the Lord's promise. When you say your prayers tonight before going to sleep, I want you to say the name of your dearly departed. I want you to say it three times out loud and then add, 'I will see you again. I will see you again.' Will you say that tonight and each and every night?" the Reverend asked, exciting the crowd.

"Yes. I will. I will . . ." said people in the crowd.

"I know you're hurting. I can see it. I see the many beautiful faces on the shirts you wear today in their memories. And I know you're hurting. But if you believe . . ." the Reverend said, pointing to the sky. "If you believe in God Almighty and the risen Jesus Christ, you can conquer death."

"Praise Jesus!" the crowd responded.

"Death is just a transition from this troubled life to paradise. It is not the end. It is the beginning. And you will see your loved ones again! Believe! There is no death! Believe!" the Reverend shouted.

"Amen. Amen. I believe," people in the crowd replied in unison.

Ashley looked all around her as Wyatt videotaped the Reverend and the crowd. She saw bright eyes and smiles, though they were weighted by heavy pain.

"We want this killing to end. And it will, if we make it happen. I know many of you are mad at the mayor," the Reverend pointed out.

"That's right," some said.

"But we must forgive the mayor for his inability to stop the crime," the Reverend continued. "And we must help win re-election and help him to end the bloodshed. The mayor is weak but his opponent is the devil. I know we can do this through Jesus Christ. We must all be apostles and take active part in spreading His Good Word to our young people. And we must all register to vote. School buses will be used to take you to City Hall to register. Call my office for locations and times. Now, the mayor has plans for the city and policemen to put an end to it all. And we need to talk to our City Council members to make sure the money is there to initiate these plans. But it will be through Jesus Christ that victory will be won." The crowd applauded. "We don't need no voodoo or hoodoo like some people are taking part in at Marie Laveau's tomb. We need Jesus. Jesus!"

The crowd applauded again.

Ashley turned to Wyatt and said, "What's that about? Where is Marie Laveau's tomb?"

"It's in St. Louis Cemetery, Number One, on Basin," Wyatt said.

"We've got to get over there," Ashley said, motioning to Wyatt to follow her, though she felt guilty leaving these people and their suffering behind to cover other suffering elsewhere. But wasn't that the nature of news, she thought. As they were nearing the edge of the crowd, she noticed the unkempt man in jeans and boots quickly stare at her, and then turn away. Ashley and Wyatt ran across Orleans Avenue and back to Delgado's parking lot. Wyatt opened the trunk and laid down his camera. As they backed out, Ashley saw an old lime green 1970s' Oldsmobile 98 sedan with spots of gray primer that looked familiar. "Where is this place again?" Ashley asked, rubbing her fingers with antibacterial gel from a tiny plastic bottle.

"I can't believe you don't know St. Louis Cemetery, Number One. It's by the project. We pass it all the time," Wyatt said.

"That's not a safe place," Ashley said.

"If you go with a group, it's okay," Wyatt said.

They sped down Canal Street running red lights at Jefferson Davis and again at Broad. The traffic was heavy as they neared downtown. Wyatt turned left at Crozat Street, next to Krauss's department store that was out of business, another longtime New Orleans landmark lost to time. He turned right onto Iberville, then left onto Basin. He drove down a few blocks, then parked the car a short block away from NOPD 1st District.

"You hear that?" Wyatt said, grabbing his camera.

"What?" Ashley responded, as two cars sped past them.

"Drums. Listen," Wyatt said.

"I think I can hear something, faintly," Ashley said.

"Come on. It's right over here," Wyatt urged. "Got your tape recorder?"

"Yes."

They ran across Basin and through the iron entranceway with an iron cross on top. A beautiful bronze plaque in the shape of a tomb informing tourists of the higher, heavenly, holy purpose of this graveyard read, "St. Louis Cemetery No. 1 Established 1789. Welcome to this holy place. This Catholic cemetery is the last resting place of the souls of the faithful departed awaiting reunion with their souls at resurrection on the last day." A much smaller slate plaque attached low on one entrance column reminded tourists that they themselves were still very much alive here on this earth and that if they wanted to remain so, walking in front of tombs rather than lying in one, they should heed its advice which was, "Visitors are welcome, but enter these premises at their own risk." Ashley stopped Wyatt and pointed to the sign.

"Don't worry about that. Come on," Wyatt said, touching her back to urge her on.

They could hear voices from somewhere in the cemetery. They walked down several rows of tombs, like small homes facing each other in this city of the dead. They passed white tombs; a black tomb; a stone tomb; a sinking tomb; open tombs; and the tomb of Homer Plessy who fought against racial discrimination and found equality in this cemetery interred next to many aristocratic whites who would never have taken the seat beside him on a train. They passed statues of weeping women, praying women and a woman holding a child. Then they saw a small crowd standing before the six-foot tall white tomb of Marie Lareau, Voodoo priestess. The tomb bore the name of Marie's husband's family, Glapion. Wyatt began filming immediately. Ashley turned on her cassette recorder while feeling tense, anxious and a bit nauseated. She noticed no other TV crews were present which spurred her on.

Ten white tourists, holding cameras, guide maps and wiping sweat from their faces, stood on either side of a black female practitioner of Voodoo, dressed in a multi-colored long dress, a white blouse and wearing a turban headdress. She held a Papa Legba Voodoo doll in the shape of a cross. The doll had a head with two circular eyes and was dressed in black cloth with red ribbon crisscrossing its chest. The doll was stuffed with moss that hung out of its arms and base. She placed the doll at the base of the tomb.

The priestess said, "We place this voodoo doll of Papa Legba at Marie Laveau's tomb to seek his help to open the gates of the spirit world and to ask that Marie Laveau cross over to our world — the world of the flesh — and intercede to stop the senseless violence and bloodshed that stain our city. Work your powers, Marie Laveau, voodoo priestess, and cleanse our city of sin." She reached into her dress pocket, pulled out a handful of kernels of corn, a few sticks of taffy and a small bottle of rum and placed them all at the base. "Papa Legba, we have brought you nourishment for your journey." She lit two candles — one white and one black in eight-inch glass cylinders and placed them at the tomb. From a woven bag she took a small sack of herbs tied with string. "We place this Gris-Gris bag at the altar to bring positive energy to this place." She fished a piece of folded black cloth out of her pocket which she opened, revealing a gold embroidered *fleur-de-lis* symbol at its center. She laid it at the tomb's base. Next to it she placed a copy of the Times-Picayune newspaper. She removed the page containing the death notices, folded it and placed it at the center of the makeshift altar. "Remember those who died violent deaths — so many, so young." She placed a small crystal skull at the back and said, "We pray to our ancestors for help in this terrible time in our city and to watch over us." She then placed a six-inch statue of the Virgin Mary in blue and white robes, next to the skull. She sprinkled holy water from a small bottle and said, "Our Lady, bless this altar." She closed her eyes briefly and stood reverently for a minute. She reopened her eyes and said, "Marie Laveau. Marie Laveau. Marie Laveau," as she made three "X" marks on the tomb with a black rock. She turned around three times and knocked three times on the tomb, while the wide-eyed tourists were nearly climbing over each other to get a photo. "Papa Legba, help Marie Laveau to cross over from the spirit world to our world. Lead her here where she can use her powers to heal our city." Ashley was somewhat frightened by this and stood behind Wyatt, knowing, however, that she would need to interview the voodoo priestess after the ceremony. Then Ashley almost jumped out of her shoes when the Chicken Man appeared, as if magically, holding a python snake like a long thick glistening ribbon, over his arms. He handed it to the priestess who wrapped it over her shoulders and the back of her neck. "The snake symbolizes wisdom," the Voodoo priestess said. "And we pray for wisdom. We pray for guidance from Marie Laveau and our ancestors. Voodoo is a religion. It is a positive force, not a worship of Satan. Voodoo rejects all that is evil." The priestess began walking back and forth and in a circle before the tomb. "Voodoo is life. If you believe in voodoo, there is no death. The spirit lives on. Life continues. We, still trapped in our bodies, ask Marie Laveau and all spirits to intercede on our behalf and stop this violence; stop this negative energy that burns another part of our city, our soul, each day making it burnt beyond recognition; stop this fire and save our city. I feel the spirits. I see the spirits rising to protect us." She began twirling. "Do you feel the spirits, people? Do you see them? Look around you. They are all around you." Ashley, Wyatt and the tourists nervously turned around. "Look there," the priestess said, as she pointed to the side of the tomb. "Marie Laveau!"

"Oh, my God! I saw her," one tourist exclaimed.

"Where?" her husband said.

"She was like a shadow by the side of the tomb," the woman said.

"I think I saw her, too," another tourist said. "She had some kind of bandana around her head and a long dress."

The priestess began to twirl faster and faster, then fell to the ground, letting the snake loose to slide among the tourists. The Chicken Man helped her up.

"Awww!" the tourists shouted, and ran in all directions.

"Come on, Wyatt!" Ashley shouted.

But Wyatt had been knocked down onto his back. The snake headed right for him. His camera caught the mighty python slither right between his legs and over his stomach. Frightened, Ashley also fell down and watched the snake quickly slide out of sight, as if it, too, had been frightened by Marie Laveau. She got to her feet and helped Wyatt with his camera. They then began rapidly walking away.

With the help of the Chicken Man, the priestess stood up and said, "It's Marie Laveau! It really is Marie Laveau! Jesus, save me!" She ran past Wyatt and Ashley, leaving the Chicken Man laughing at the tomb.

CHAPTER 23

Ecce Panis Angelorum

As Wyatt pulled into the TV-3 garage, Ashley checked her watch.

"Jesus! It's 5:20! I've got to write my intro," Ashley said.

"I'll get this to editing," Wyatt said, removing his camera from the trunk.

"Okay."

Ashley ran up the spiral staircase to the second floor. "Where's Darryl?" she said to the secretary behind her desk.

"I think he's in the studio," the secretary said.

"Okay. Thanks." She then rushed down to the other end of the hall and opened the doors to the studio. She spotted Darryl, talking to a cameraman. "Darryl, Wyatt is in editing with today's footage. I can use the protest at the mayor's office with this afternoon's stories about 'Neighbors Against Crime' and a voodoo ceremony to ward off evil spirits and Marie Laveau. The ceremony turned out to be a disaster. The snake got loose. Tourists ran away."

"Well, don't use that footage," Darryl said.

"Why?" Ashley asked.

"Because it would take away from the seriousness of the subject," Darryl said. "And it would reinforce the 'Crazy New Orleans' image too many people have about us. So, drop the Voodoo footage and close with 'Neighbors Against Crime.' Cut it to three minutes."

"All right." Ashley entered the editing room on the opposite side of the hall. "Wyatt, lose the voodoo stuff," Ashley said, sticking her head inside the door. "Darryl doesn't want it."

"Are you sure?" he said.

"Yes. And cut it to three minutes," Ashley said.

"Okay," Wyatt said, looking over the shoulder of Weldon.

Ashley ran half-way down the hall and turned on to a short hall that led to a desk by a window overlooking Chartres Street. She looked at her watch. The time was 5:30. She felt fatigued and stressed. Her heart was racing. She sat down and wondered if she had taken on too much responsibility. She whispered to herself while tapping a pen against paper, "I'll start off with the rising crime rate, and then go right to the French Quarter merchants' walk to City Hall. I'll transition to 'Neighbors Against Crime' by showing the deadly results and the victims' relatives."

An intense bright light shone through the window and warmed the right side of her face. She looked up and noticed a white dove on the windowsill. The bird tapped on the window with its beak. As Ashley rose to leave, the bird flew a few feet away from the window, and then quickly dove down to the sidewalk. Ashley looked out of the window and saw a little girl with long blonde hair, wearing a white, sleeveless summer dress and no shoes, standing in the street. The girl smiled and beckoned Ashley to follow her by waving her hand.

Ashley opened the window and said, "Are you waving to me?" The girl nodded, yes. "Are you sure you want me? Who are you?" The girl continued to smile and walked a few steps toward St. Louis Cathedral.

"Ashley!" Cato, the floor manager, shouted down the hallway.

Ashley turned and said, "Yes."

"It's almost six! You're up!" he said, as if sounding an alarm.

"Okay. Sorry. I'm coming," Ashley said.

Ashley looked for the girl again, but she had disappeared. She ran down the hall. When she entered the studio, Cato said, "Is your copy on the teleprompter?"

"Oh, no! I didn't have time," she said, shaking her head.

"Get up there and say something," he said. "This is very unprofessional, Ashley. You'll have to do much better than this. Learn to manage your time. This business is all about deadlines!"

"I'm so sorry," Ashley said.

She took a seat at the end of the news desk, feeling rejected, punished and angry from Cato's rebuke. She silently reviewed her notes, as the floor manager counted down the seconds until air time.

"Good evening. I'm Jack Randalls. Jill Uphills is off tonight. Well, the rising anger over crime in the city finally came to a boil today when French Quarter merchants marched to City Hall and demanded to speak to the mayor. This all happened only hours after five people were found shot to death in a house near the Quarter. Our own Ashley Tarleton was there at City Hall when the protesting merchants arrived." Turning to Ashley, he continued, "Ashley, what was the scene like there today and was anything accomplished?"

Ashley's mouth was dry when she tried to speak. A wave of fear rolled through her body, causing a slight trembling in her hands. Clearing her throat, Ashley whispered, "Jack, the scene today . . ." she paused to clear her throat again, and then resumed in her normal voice. "Excuse me. The scene today at City Hall was both loud and somber. A large number of French Quarter merchants and many irate citizens converged on City Hall and noisily demanded to speak with the mayor who finally appeared to address the issue of crime in the Quarter. However, he was cut short after being slapped in the face by the mother of the young woman who was gunned down in front of Jackson's Square just a few days ago."   The videotape of the incident was shown, as well as the interview from "Neighbors Against Crime." After three minutes, the clip ended. Feeling proud but nervous, Ashley said, "As you just saw, I interviewed several people from the 'Neighbors Against Crime' street gathering this afternoon to show a few of the parents, spouses, friends and relatives who have experienced firsthand the real tragedy of losing someone to murder. Those people are coping as best they can. And gathering together with people they know is a much-needed connection. They, too, want the mayor to know that they are suffering, and they want an end to crime now."

"The mayor was obviously very stunned, having been slapped in the face," Randalls said.

"Yes. It was an embarrassing moment. The crowd was shocked into silence," Ashley said.

"And what about those tee shirts with the victims' photos on them?" Randalls asked.

"Yes, those shirts are being printed within twenty-four hours of a victim's death. As the tee shirt shops in the French Quarter suffer because fewer tourists are coming to town, a new tee shirt industry is thriving in various parts of the city. It's a souvenir of a different kind; one you wouldn't want to own," Ashley said, in a serious tone of voice.

"Tragic. Thank you, Ashley. Good job. And we'll see you shortly as a panelist for the mayoral election debate," Randalls said.

"Yes."

"Great. We're looking forward to it." Randalls then turned to his camera and said, "In other news . . ."

Ashley relaxed in the chair, feeling weak. She could barely muster the strength to get up. Her entire body felt like one overtaxed muscle. She felt a little nauseous as she stepped away from the desk. She shook her head a little, as if trying to cast away the thoughts of doubt orbiting her mind.

She walked into Darryl's office and said, "I'm sorry. I can do better. I will do better."

Eating an Oreo, Darryl said, "Relax, you did great. It's baptism under fire. We all go through it. You gave a nice intro and you answered his questions well. What more could you do?"

"I'm surprised words even came out of my mouth at all," Ashley said.

"Don't talk down about yourself. Here, have an Oreo. Get yourself a bottle of water and take a break," he said, offering a glass jar shaped like the Superdome and full of Oreos.

"No thank you. My stomach is tied in knots. But I think I will get a bottle of water and review those questions," Ashley said.

"Good. We'll see you on the set in forty minutes," he said, looking at his watch.

"Okay."

Ashley went downstairs and bought a bottle of Kentwood water from the vending machine. She walked through the garage and stepped onto the Chartres Street sidewalk. Sipping her water, she walked down a block, nearer to St. Louis Cathedral, looking for the little girl in a white dress. Seeing no one but tourists and a young man with a guitar imitating Bob Dylan, she continued a few steps farther, as a warm wind blew up her dress and swirled around her body, neck and head, like gentle fingertips. She was starting to relax a little while sidestepping camera-carrying, Hurricane-holding, tote-bag-toting, wide-eyed tourists. She looked left before crossing Toulouse Street. When she looked straight ahead again, she saw the girl standing under an arch of the Cabildo, a block away. The girl smiled and beckoned Ashley to follow, as she moved toward St. Louis Cathedral.

"Wait!" Ashley shouted. People on the street looked at her and in the direction she was moving, wondering to whom she was shouting. "Stop," Ashley cried, as she picked up speed.

The girl ran to the entrance of the Cathedral, looked back at Ashley, and then disappeared inside.

Ashley's heartbeat quickened. Who was this child, she wondered? Who was this child?

Ashley tossed her bottle in an overflowing trash can and speedily walked toward the Cathedral which had always been at the center of the city from the very beginning, symbolizing the mind of God and the eternal fight against Evil.

When she reached the Cathedral, she opened the large heavy door, wondering how the little girl managed it and walked into a quiet, holy sanctuary in the middle of what some people called "Sin City." The back of the Cathedral, full of coming-and-going whispering tourists, was dimly lit. But the long nave was wide and bright, lit by chandeliers hanging above either side of the center aisle. Paintings of Christ, Mary, Joseph and the Apostles adorned the ceiling. A large mural depicting Saint Louis,

13th century King of France, trumpeting the Seventh Crusade, was on the rear wall, directly above the altar. On the cornice between were the words, *"SUM VIA, ET VERITAS, ET VITA."* Below those words was the altar framed within a Greek architectural setting, using three Corinthian columns on either side of the baroque 1852 golden altar centerpiece. The Holy Eucharist was at its center within a sunburst pattern, flanked by angels and cherubs. Above them was a dove, representing the Holy Spirit, wings spread wide. The words *"ECCE PANIS ANGELORUM"* were written above the centerpiece.

Ashley saw the girl kneeling at the altar, so she walked down the long aisle and knelt beside her.

"Who are you and why aren't you wearing shoes?" she inquired.

"Shhh!" the girl said. "I'm praying."

After waiting a few seconds, Ashley said, "What are you praying for?"

Still looking straight at the centerpiece, she replied, "For the people of this city. They're dying and only the Word of God can save them."

Not knowing what to think of this, Ashley asked, "Where are your mother and father?"

"My father is in heaven," the girl said.

"Where is your mother?" Ashley asked. The girl giggled. "Is she alive?" The girl smiled. "Where do you live?"

"I live with a friend. I want to take you to meet him. It's very important."

"A friend," Ashley said, somewhat alarmed. "I can't go now. I've got to race back to the studio for a debate."

"Oh! But this is the most important thing you could ever do," the girl declared.

The girl got up and walked toward a side altar. Ashley followed and watched the girl light a candle in a small, round, red glass holder.

"Who is that candle for?" Ashley inquired.

"For the people of this city," the girl said.

She then lit another candle, prompting Ashley to ask, "Who is that candle for?"

"For everybody everywhere," the girl said, with a smile.

Ashley looked at this angelic, beautiful little girl and was amazed at her profundity. She checked her watch again. It was after six o'clock.

"I'm sorry but I've got to get back to work. I'm needed," Ashley said.

"I understand, but this is God's work," the girl informed.

"I'll look for you tomorrow. Okay?" Ashley asked.

The girl shook her head affirmatively and said, "It's important that I introduce you to my friend. He has good news."

"Okay. I've got to run. I think you should go home now. It's getting dark. Take care," Ashley said.

The girl gestured for Ashley to come close, and then said, "Don't be frightened."

"I'm not frightened," Ashley said, looking straight into the girl's azure eyes.

"Yes, you are," the girl replied, looking straight into Ashley's eyes.

Ashley just stared in wonder at the girl, and then walked down the aisle. When she reached the end of the aisle, she looked back to see that the girl was nowhere in sight.

CHAPTER 24

Beating Hearts

The sign above the opened French doors of the two-story building at Bourbon and Bienville Streets read, "Jean Lafitte's, Old Absinthe House, Since 1807."

Wyatt walked in the opened French doors to the dimly lit bar and stepped up to the copper-topped wooden bar where thousands of people, some famous, had been served over the years. Marble fountains behind the bar were once used in the preparation of Absinthe, a now illegal narcotic-like drink that, no doubt, aided in attracting people from around the world and further promoting the city's "why-don't we-get-drunk-and-screw" image. Hanging from the ceiling's cypress beams were football jerseys, helmets of famous players and antique chandeliers. Covering the walls were the business cards from thousands of visitors, giving the walls a paper mosaic look and reminding all patrons of the bar's famous motto, "Everyone you have known or ever will know, eventually ends up at The Old Absinthe House." And on the wall behind the cash register were more than one-hundred dollar bills left by patrons who wanted to make sure they could pay for a drink the next time they visited.

"What can I get you, Wyatt?" Josie, the tall, attractive bartender wearing a New Orleans Saints cap, asked.

"Hey, Josie, give me a Blackened Voodoo and a bowl of popcorn," Wyatt said.

"You got it," she said, as she opened the cooler and popped the top off the Dixie beer. She placed it on the bar with a bowl of popcorn.

"Thanks," Wyatt said.

Wyatt surveyed the patrons who included about a dozen journalists, some foreign, and a dozen or so tourists. The journalists were there to watch the debate on the two televisions above the bar. Keiffer Conright had become international news because of his possible neo-Nazi and Ku Klux Klan ties. Wyatt knew, though, that some reporters wanted to make New Orleans and its people look ridiculous and dumb, reflecting the prejudice some northerners still maintained about the south.

The time was nearing 6:30pm, the start of the debate. Wyatt adjusted the jeans around his boots, lit a cigarette, and looked out the two narrow French doors only ten feet away that opened onto Bienville Street where cars were moving slowly through the crowd at Bourbon Street, which bore the endless passing parade of every type of person on the planet, step by step, each and all anonymous, unaware of each other, unaware of themselves, unaware of their histories, unaware of their futures, unaware of their beating hearts and the life and the light within them.

"Hey, sweetie," a drunken journalist from New York said to Josie, "What's your name again?"

"Josie," she said, with a pissed-off grin.

"Josie. I like that," the journalist from New York said to another journalist from Massachusetts, sitting next to him. "Guess what mine is?"

"Pain-in-the-ass Pete?" Josie replied, with a smile.

The journalist from New York let loose a loud pig-squeal laugh that caused the beer he was holding to spill all over his white button-down shirt.

"Now, I like a girl with a sense of humor. You'd do well in New York City, unlike other people in this town who are just dumb-asses, slow Confederate dumb-asses." The man then released a Bikini Island-after-the-blast belch that shook the walls. "*Pardonne.* You see, I can speak French. How come no one here speaks French? New Orleans is French, isn't it?" the journalist asked.

"You're about three-hundred years too late," Wyatt said, annoyed.

"What can I get you?" Josie said.

"I want an Absinthe drink. I want to taste that," the journalist said.

"Yeah. I want to try that, too," his friend said.

"They don't make Absinthe anymore," Josie said.

"What's this Absinthe House Frappe crap on the list?" the journalist asked.

"That's made with Herbsaint. Try it," Josie suggested.

"I'm not trying some fruity drink," the journalist said.

"They got enough fruity drinks and fruity men in this city," his friend said, laughingly.

"Why don't they make it?" the journalist asked.

"It's illegal. It has a narcotic effect, causing hallucinations, among other things," she replied.

"That's what the people in this town need – hallucinations, just to escape this shit hole of a town for a while. Everyone's so poor and dirty here; you'd think they stopped making running water, too," the journalist said, while belching.

"You couldn't clean the filth in New York with the Atlantic Ocean," Wyatt replied.

The journalist looked at Wyatt, and then said to his friend, "Look here, Cajun cowboy can actually put words together in sentence form. Did your paw teach you how to talk when you were out catching crawfish and shrimp and alligator? Swamp delicacies. You backwoods rebel."

The two men roared with laughter.

Wyatt stood up and took a step toward the men, but Josie stepped in.

"That's enough!" she said, then called to Jim, an ex-football player who was tending bar on the other side. "Jim! Over here."

Jim walked over and said, "Any trouble here?"

"No," the two journalists said. "We were just having some fun in your great city. You know what they say here, '*Le Bons Temp Rouler.*' We're doing fine."

Wyatt moved down the bar a few stools. Josie and Jim

exchanged glances and shook their heads.

"Can you turn up the sound, Josie? It's starting," Wyatt requested.

"Sure," she said, standing on her toes to reach the volume control.

On the Sony thirty-two-inch screen appeared the TV-3 studio, showing the mayor Xavier Chenier at the left podium and Keiffer Conright at the right. Seated behind a long table were the three panelists: Joe Schiro, longtime AM radio talk show host; Cozy Dufrense, one of the first female reporters for the Times newspaper, and Ashley Tarleton, nervously reviewing her notes. The moderator, Toni Fullilove, was seated behind another smaller table.

"Welcome everyone to our only debate between mayoral candidates, incumbent mayor Xavier Chenier and businessman, Keiffer Conright, for this runoff election," Fullilove said. "We wish there had been more debates, but the candidates are very busy, of course, and we welcome and thank them for their time. And welcome to our three panelists: Joe Schiro, Cozy Dufrense and Ashley Tarleton. The rules are simple. The panelists will ask questions and each candidate will have three minutes to respond, as well as a ninety-second rebuttal. At the end of the debate each candidate will have two minutes for final statements. Let's begin with Mr. Schiro."

"Age before beauty. I understand," said Schiro, laughingly. "Mayor Chenier, with the upsurge in all crime and with the current number of murders in our city at 409 and more each day, giving the city the dubious title of the nation's 'Murder Capital,' how do you plan to combat crime, especially murder, and do you have plans in place now?"

Conright chuckled and shook his head.

"Things will change dramatically if the City Council approves the extra funding for the police department," the mayor said, running his hand over his green, black and red tie. "Our city needs more police on the street and we need to pay them more. A policeman on the job for roughly five years only makes about $23,000. Recruits make even less. How can we attract new police officers if we don't pay them well? They'll go to Memphis, Boston or Portland, all of which pay police in the $35,000 to $45,000 range. These new officers will be significant in stopping drug trafficking, which will reduce the murder rate because every three out of four murders are drug related. With a greater police presence on the street, combined with neighborhood crime watch programs, crime, especially murder, will be greatly curtailed. To implement higher salaries and reforms would take about $100 million dollars. We can get the job done. Top priority would be the arrest of not just the local pushers, but also the traffickers and importers of drugs. We will all experience a hopeful coming together, a commitment, and a reaffirmation to life in our city."

"Mr. Conright, would you like to respond?" Fullilove asked.

"Yes, thank you," Conright said, as he pushed back his blue-striped seersucker suit coat and put his hands in his pockets. "Well, of course, the mayor is dreaming. I doubt seriously if the City Council will allocate $100 million dollars for the police when the city's total budget is under $500 million dollars. It's just too much money. What we must do is keep the criminals behind bars. Crimes are largely committed by recidivists, people who are in and out of the system regularly. This happens because witnesses to these crimes are intimidated or, more often now, are shot to death, allowing the criminal to go free. We need a much better witness protection program. The police department itself is corrupt. Morale is low. It needs to be swept clean of dirty cops who sell their badges to drug dealers. Just last month six officers were arrested for guarding a warehouse used to store cocaine. It was a huge operation that would not have been broken up if the FBI had not gotten involved. We're being investigated by the federal government because of widespread thievery and corruption. Not two weeks ago a cop was arrested for arranging a hit on a woman who complained about his brutality when he arrested a young man. The woman was murdered! We have killer cops on our streets! I also put the blame on the Orleans Parish Criminal Court judges who often issue reduced bonds, so murderers go free. It's a revolving door at our courthouse on the corner of Tulane and South Broad. It's a joke. Someone recently placed a large sign there which said, 'Caution: Prisoner Crosswalk.' And the D.A.'s office refuses cases weekly. What's wrong with this picture?" Conright adjusted his red paisley tie, looked over at the mayor and said, "They say New Orleans is the 'City That Care Forgot'. I think it's the city that the mayor forgot. How can he ignore the ambulances every day rushing to Charity Hospital? This city is on fire, with new fires raging every night. It's getting to the point where New Orleans is being burned beyond recognition. Where does it all stop? Bring in the National Guard to put out the fires and stop new ones. The presence of the Guard on the streets of our fair city will let the criminals know that we mean business. The only thing the criminals respond to is force. And we'd better show some. This mayor is a coward! And he's lost control of the city. And someone will die tonight due to violent crime. Arrest somebody, Mayor! Arrest someone!"

"We arrest people every day," the mayor angrily shouted.

"Then you let them go," Conright blasted.

"Gentlemen, please, stop the accusations and shouting," Miss Fullilove said. "Miss Dufrense, your questions please."

"Thank you. Mr. Conright, if you become mayor, what would you do to improve the city's economy and create new jobs?" Miss Dufrense asked.

"That's a good question," Conright said, eyeing his notes. "The first thing I would do is create a Master Plan for the city . . ."

"You mean Massa's plan," the mayor whispered.

"From what I can see, the mayor does not have one," Conright said. "It would be a sort of blueprint for the city's future and it would include specific goals to achieve. Every major city has one and ours would be subject to review by the City Planning Commission. In this, the city's 276th year of its founding, certainly such a plan is needed for both our immediate future and for long-term goals. These goals would definitely improve the quality of life for our citizenry. The future is diversity, so we must diversify. We must make New Orleans more attractive to big business owners from out of state. We do that by securing the crime problem and offering tax incentives. By ridding our city of crime, we will attract more tourists and conventions. The word is out across the country that New Orleans is not the place to visit. Several conventions have already cancelled. A tourist was just murdered not long ago while walking back to his hotel near the Central Business District. *Newsweek, Time, 60 Minutes* and *A&E Investigates* have all dumped on the city. We must stop the trafficking of drugs. We must win back tourists and businesses through the media and our public relations campaigns. Also, I believe we should look into gaming. Perhaps a big time casino would help. More specifically, I will propose over $100 million dollars in public works improvements. You have my word that all professional services contracts will not be given to friends of mine, unlike the mayor's cronyism."

"You're lying!" the mayor interjected. "Show me the evidence."

"You know who, Mayor. The whole city knows. I'll reveal all names when I take office. You and your friends on the payroll also took many trips to Vegas," Conright said.

"That's a lie! Your friends go to KKK rallies and bund meetings," the mayor exclaimed.

"Prove it!" Conright said. "That's all hearsay."

"Gentlemen, please, let's keep an orderly debate here," Fullilove implored.

"But wait a minute. I want to respond to this accusation," the mayor said. "I have not used my position to put money in the pockets of friends. I am not unethical. My opponent mentioned millions in public works because I stated that to the press more than a month ago. He's mimicking me to sound more mayoral. I'm aware of the media's portrayal of our city. We're hurting now but I will work with the City Council for more police funding. Things will change. I need more time. My opponent said one must diversify. I know that. We all know that. The irony of his comment is that he cannot accept diversity in our population here. This city is comprised of many ethnicities. How can a far right and far too white man relate to our diverse cultures – African American, Vietnamese, Hispanics and others? The fact is he cannot. And I firmly believe he has very strong ties to white hate groups. For that reason alone, he cannot be mayor of a racially mixed city which is sixty percent African-American."

"Prove it! Prove I have ties to white hate groups," Conright said.

"I"m working on it," the mayor said.

"There is no proof. We cannot allow a man who harbors prejudice against whites, run this city," Conright added.

"That's insane," the mayor said, with raised voice.

Conright straightened his tie and said, "You recently proposed to the City Council the removal of all Confederate monuments in our city, even the iconic statue of General Robert E. Lee at Lee Circle that has stood there since its commemoration in 1884. If the City Council agrees to remove our historic monuments, which I believe it will since it is predominantly black, then I contend that whites in Orleans Parish are the newly oppressed. You made this a political and personal issue. You even told the press you were tired of living in the shadows of those monuments. You are supposed to represent all of the people. Instead, you divided the city along a color line. You betrayed all the white people in this city. They are the very people who pay a ton in taxes, organize community and volunteer groups, keep the carnival krewes going and maintain the city as they always have. And you betrayed them for political gain. You have knowingly embraced an organization of rabble-rousers whose fascist refrain is 'Take 'em down!' These people want to rename half the streets in the city. They even want Tulane University to change its name due to the fact a few of its benefactors in the 1800s were Confederate sympathizers. That was more than a hundred years ago. That line of reasoning could apply to anything historical: the Roman ruins should come down because slavery was a mainstay of their society; or Mercedes Benz, BMW, Michelin Tire Company, Hugo Boss Clothier and others, should be destroyed because they contributed to the Nazi cause in World War II. Where does it end?"

"The Confederacy was an inhumane form of government that enslaved people who look like me and sixty percent of our city's population. I will not have Lee, Beauregard, Davis and the White League monuments occupy central spaces of honor in our city. They are symbols of racism, oppression, and white supremacy," Chenier said.

"Not anymore, if they ever were. They are simply historic artifacts that mark a time in our city's history. Only fascists raze history to the ground. Preservationists resurrect it and learn from it. And where would we get the money to remove four Confederate statues?" Conright asked.

"Private donations," the mayor declared.

"That wouldn't be enough. You'll have to use city funds," Conright pointed out. And that would be misappropriation of funds and malfeasance in office. And you think statues are the problem in a city where young black men are killing young black men and innocents in the crossfire, where heroin overdoses have doubled, and poverty is everywhere like a plague, and the city streets are like those in third world countries, and the NOPD is horribly understaffed. You are insane. I will insist the federal government investigate you and the City Council. You're all a bunch of racists."

"Don't you dare use that vile word to describe me!" Chenier angrily said.

"Gentlemen, please . . . " Fullilove said, trying to regain order.

"You held debates in Council chambers for citizens to speak on the issue. I contend you have perverted the democratic process under the pretense of debate because the majority of Council members are blacks. It's obvious what the vote will be. There's no debate. It's a sham. It's a kangaroo court. The removal of these great relics and works of art proves you are the racist because you are embracing only blacks and not caring for whites who built this city and maintain it still. You, Xavier, are the racist!" Conright shouted.

"That's just downright crazy," the mayor said, thoroughly flabbergasted.

"Is it?" Conright asked. "Then why didn't you propose a compromise of some sort, like take down two of the monuments and keep the two most important, Beauregard and Lee? Or you could have proposed adding monuments along Howard Avenue leading to Lee Circle and the Confederate War Museum right around the block. Right now they're history but, if removed, they will be lost to history. This thoughtful and considerate compromise would have shown your appreciation for the white population which overwhelmingly supports keeping the monuments. And you knew that. Instead, you've created a division between whites and blacks that has reignited a new Civil War of sorts. And let me tell you something, Boss Chenier, whites carry this city financially through their tax dollars; and you know that, too!"

"I proposed the monuments' removal because they are symbols of oppression, and I wanted to create a 'more perfect union,'" the mayor declared.

"You're not a smart man because the proposal had the opposite effect. What we have here, ladies and gentlemen, is a movement afoot to remove history from historic New Orleans, a movement to remove white man's history and put a statue of a black man where General Robert E. Lee now stands. You want to make whites suffer because you're vindictive and vengeful, and then you want to twist that knife. What we have here is the shaming of the old south, the shaming of the new south and the shaming of whites. You, Xavier, are a liar, a con man, an opportunist and a Democratic party sycophant. Tell you what, mayor, there won't be any monuments built to honor you," Conright boasted.

"Gentlemen, please," Miss Fullilove said, trying to intercede.

"Conright, you have lost what little mind you had," the mayor said, indignantly.

"No, Chenier. Wasn't it with your blessing that a group of black radicals called for the removal of white men's names from twenty-nine public schools to be renamed after black men of little or no consequence? And what was the name of that group? The African Liberation League! Liberation from what?" Conright vehemently asked.

"From the continued remembrance of white oppression. Those names renamed were Confederates," the mayor said.

"I do believe George Washington was one of those names. Not a Confederate," Conright said.

"This is outrageous! Moderator, stop this diatribe and ask another question," the mayor demanded.

"You are servicing the one segment of the population, albeit the largest segment, that contributes little to the city in any way and commits most of the crime," Conright observed. "Young black thugs roam the streets committing crimes at will and you are more concerned about appeasing the very people who are ruining the city by removing Confederate monuments, and by so doing disrespecting and ignoring the white population which is pleading before the City Council not to raze history to the ground but resurrect it and learn from it."

"You racist son-of-a-bitch! You just lost the election with your racist comments," the mayor said, incensed.

"I stand for all people by speaking the truth. You hide from it on the eighth floor of City Hall and in full view of the Emergency Room of Charity Hospital where all the victims of violent crime end up, day after day, victim after victim, because you're too ignorant and impotent to stop it. You're a coward," Conright exclaimed.

"Gentlemen, please," Fullilove said.

"You know nothing about being mayor. The mayor of this city must maintain excellent race relations. He's anti-black in every way. He said he would stop supporting minority contractors. He'll set race relations back a hundred years," Mayor Chenier shot back.

"Minority set asides are prejudicial to whites, not good for business and un-American," Conright said.

"Gentlemen, please," Fullilove said, trying to regain order.

"You're buying votes at $60 each. And you're handing out these racist leaflets, trying to make voters think that I created and distributed them to make you look bad," the mayor said, holding up a leaflet of a lynched black man. "You don't need anyone's help to make you look bad."

"I know nothing of those. As far as I know, you distributed them," Conright said.

"Gentlemen," Fullilove again interjected. "We must press on." Finally, both men fell silent. "Thank you. Miss Tarleton, it's your turn."

Ashley felt a wave of anxiety rush over her body, like water, chilling her to the bone. Inexplicably, she smelled the sweet scent of lilies which made her think of a funeral parlor where she saw her mother in a casket. When she began to speak her voice momentarily cracked, causing everyone in the room to look her way. She had committed the one cardinal rule of journalism: never show emotion.

"Holy shit! She's gone south," Wyatt said, sitting on his stool in the Old Absinthe House where all went silent, wondering about her.

After a long, *The-Day-The-Earth-Stood-Still* silence, Ashley regained her composure and, though embarrassed, asked a question that just popped into her head and was not on the list Darryl had given her.

"Mr. Conright, are you a Nazi and do you sell Nazi books from your home?" Ashley asked.

"Right on, sister," the mayor said.

"And is it true you celebrate Adolph Hitler's birthday and deny that the Holocaust ever happened? And have you ever used the 'N' word?" she concluded.

Another much shorter silence descended on everyone in the studio and The Old Absinthe House.

"What ridiculous questions. You're obviously trying to make the slanderous accusations about me plausible," Conright said. "Wild rumor and speculation are not a journalist's stock and trade. You must have graduated from the Acme School of Journalism," Conright said in defense. "I'll simply say 'no' to all of those inciting questions and add that people were not murdered in labor camps in Germany and Poland. They were held because they were Communists and those who died, died of typhus. Let us not forget that it was a world war and prisoners were held for a long time. I wish to address the topics at hand. I will return to the most tragic problem our city faces — illegal drugs on our streets and the many murders resultant to their use. The mayor does not have a plan for stopping drug trafficking. The mayor can't do a thing to stop the drugs and drug-related crimes. He wants to remove statues, yet he cannot remove drug dealers. The mayor can't even stop his own son from buying and using drugs, so how can he stop anyone else?" Holding up a large photo, he pointed to a young man buying drugs from a drug dealer on the street. "Take a good look. This is the mayor's son committing a crime. Take a good look, New Orleans."

Again, an Ice-Age silence descended on the studio, The Old Absinthe House and the city. The mayor walked to Conright and took the photo. He rubbed his thumb over the image of his son, stared at the photo, and then let it drop to the floor. He turned and walked out of the studio with the weight of a great sadness slowing his pace. His assistants followed.

After a few moments, Fullilove said, "Well, this debate has ended. I want to thank. . . "

"No. No. No. No. No," Conright fired. "Though our highly ineffectual, cowardly mayor exited hurriedly and did not deliver his closing remarks, I demand time to deliver mine."

"All right, Mr. Conright. You have ninety seconds," Fullilove said.

"Thank you," Conright said. "To the citizens of New Orleans, I want to say I am on your side. Whoever you are, black or white, I am with you. My character has been slandered, maligned, vilified by a weak mayor who readily employs vilification of people and even bronze and granite Confederate monuments for the sake of political gain. You have been had by a self-centered, ignorant, immature, impotent, ineffective opportunistic mayor who is more concerned about gaining national acclaim and position of prominence in a Democratic president's administration than he is concerned about stopping crime and ending poverty in his own city. That is why he insists on removing historical Confederate monuments – just for the attention. Any thoughtful person knows this. In so doing, he has pitted whites against blacks. Doesn't it make sense to take care of the city's real problems instead of creating a fictitious one? Don't believe him and don't believe in him. The real problems facing our city are murders, rapes, robberies, drugs, potholes so large and deep they are more like craters found in third world countries, and, of course, the city's drainage system. It is absolutely reprehensible that while the mayor is giving grand speeches nationwide, the city is flooding due to incapacitated pumps and turbines, and clogged catch basins of which the city has nearly 70,000. And poor blacks were affected more than any others, losing property, businesses and homes, not once, but twice within two weeks. Now I ask the black population of Orleans Parish, do you really want to re-elect this incompetent fool who has just used you to promote himself and has aspirations for national office? Citizens of New Orleans, the monuments are simply historical markers, artifacts and works of art from a time that once was. We must concentrate on the present and bringing all of us together, not segregating and shaming whites and preservationists. Shame on Mayor Chenier for doing that. Author and activist, Jane Jacobs, said, 'Cities have the capability of providing something for everybody, only because, and only when, they are created by everybody.' I agree. Citizens, you don't need a dirty, corrupt politician like Chenier. You need a man of the people, a statesman. You need me. I am a man of my word. You can believe that. And you can count on me to protect the rights of all citizens of New Orleans and to protect our American Heritage. Thank you, good night and God bless."

"Thank you, Mr. Conright, for your time," Jack Randalls said. "And thanks to our panelists, Mr. Schiro, Ms. Dufrense and Ms. Tarleton. Thanks to everyone at TV-3 for the use of its studio and to everyone watching. Goodnight."

Keiffer Conright thanked everyone, and then said to Ashley, "Shame on you. You should know better."

"So should you," she quickly added and walked away, leaving Conright sweating under the hot, bright lights, which blinded him as he tried to get a good look at Ashley's shapely figure.

Ashley stopped by Darryl's office and said, "I'm sorry Darryl. I let you down again."

"Are you okay? What happened?" he said, while eating candy corn.

"My mother is very ill and the doctor doesn't really know why. I thought of her as I was about to speak. And then when I did, the only thing I could think of was Conright's Nazi past he claims he doesn't have. You saw my interview with Bella a few days ago who is a Holocaust survivor. It angers me that he claims there was no Holocaust. I guess I goofed. Sorry," Ashley confessed.

"It wasn't really bad. You asked the questions everyone wants to know. Can I still count on you?" Darryl asked.

"Yes. Don't worry. I get a little emotional at times these days. But you can count on me," Ashley said.

"You know Conright is speaking tomorrow at Lee Circle at 10

o'clock," Darryl said.

"Yes."

"I need you to cover that live," Darryl said.

"Yes. I'll be there," Ashley said.

"Go home and get some rest. If there's anything I can do to help with your mother, just let me know," Darryl offered.

"Thanks. I will."

He held up the jar of candy corn and said, "Candy corn?" Ashley smiled and said, "No thanks. I'm good."

"Okay. I'll see you tomorrow," Ashley said.

"Yes. Tomorrow. Thanks," she said.

Ashley walked to the end of the hall, went in the ladies' restroom, sat down in a stall and called her mother.

"Hello. Tarleton residence," Beverly, the nurse said.

"Hi, Beverly. How's Mother doing?" Ashley asked.

"Hi, baby. Good. She ate most of her dinner and fell fast asleep," Beverly said.

"She isn't in any pain, is she?" Ashley asked.

"Not now. No. Sometimes I see her face wretch up. That's when I ask if she wants her pain medication. But that hasn't happened today," Beverly said.

"Good. I'm heading to my house now. I'm going to try and get some sleep, but call me if she is in pain and I'll be right there," Ashley said.

"Okay. Sure will, baby. Get some rest," Beverly said.

"Okay. And, Beverly, thank you for all you do for us. We appreciate your care and kindness," Ashley said.

"Thank you so much. I'm pleased to help in any way," Beverly said.

"Thanks. Goodnight," Ashely said.

"Night to you, too," Beverly added.

Ashley closed her portable phone, closed her eyes, cupped her face in her hand, lowered her head between her legs and cried. She felt cold and fearful, as if she had seen a ghost.

Inside The Old Absinthe House bar, patrons were still talking about the debate. Wyatt was finishing his third Dixie while the New York journalist he butted heads with earlier was finishing his seventh.

"Just like I said, they're all dumb asses down here in KKK country," the drunken journalist loudly proclaimed. "You got a mayor who cannot govern his city and a Nazi Klansman as an alternative. Holy shit! Get me out of this city that is oppressive in every way possible, from its heat to the assholes who live here. Yeah, assholes on parade right here," he said, as he took a long drink of is beer.

"I see only one asshole here and it's you," Wyatt said, defiantly. "Go back to New York and all its filth. You're not welcome here."

The journalist slammed his beer bottle down onto the bar and said, "Listen to me, you rebel asshole! We're civilized in New York City. We read books! We attend plays! We discuss the great questions and problems of today. We are cultured. You know what culture is to you? Sucking crawfish heads and telling stories about the bayous and alligators. You people would be even more backwards without our help. This is third world country down here. The north brought civilization to the south and saved your sorry asses. Don't tell me anything about New York City. That city is a palace compared to this shithole! People care about New York. No one cares about this city. The only reason I'm here is to cover this Tales-from-the-Crypt election. Just like I said, assholes on parade, including you!"

"Screw you!" Wyatt shouted. "And what a fine representation of New York City you are. Are all New Yorkers like you – drunk, disorderly and fucked out of their minds? Down here our pace is slower because we appreciate good living and good people. You people are so conceited and full of self-importance that you think the world should genuflect before you. Here the common man can live a good life. Like Huey Long said, 'Every man a King!'"

"Yeah. And every king is an asshole in this city," the journalist replied, while laughing heartily. "You people are so stupid. You can't comprehend your own stupidity. And you, you Confederate bastard, you can go to hell with all your Confederate heroes and flags and your 'Hell No, I Ain't Forgettin' license plates. Jesus! What a bunch of assholes!"

Wyatt jumped to his feet and threw the remainder of his beer in the man's face. The journalist threw his glass at Wyatt and tried to rise from his chair but couldn't. Wyatt grabbed the man's collar in one hand and hit him with the other. He then pulled the man from his seat. Big Jim then jumped over the bar to break up the fight. At that moment a black sedan stopped on Bienville Street, next to the open French doors. The rear window on the driver's side slowly lowered. The barrel of an AK47 jumped out like a snake and its handler clicked the trigger, spraying the inside and the outside of the bar with finger-sized bullets. Everyone inside hit the floor as glass broke and business cards flew off the wall. Pedestrians at Bienville and Bourbon also hit the ground, as the car sped across Bourbon, moving toward Rampart Street.

A very busy and noisy part of Bourbon had become silent for a few minutes. The flashing lights and neon ignorantly pulsed to attract the crowd that was face down and one foot tall.

Slowly, people rose to their feet and checked themselves for blood stains. Police sirens, like a slap to the face, awoke the stunned crowd.

A paramedic shouted, "Who's hurt?"

But no one answered.

A policeman entered The Old Absinthe House and said, "Is anyone hurt?"

"No. No one here," Josie said.

"Was the shooter on foot?" the policeman asked.

"No," Wyatt said. "He was in a black four-door."

"Yeah," Josie said. "Then they took off down Bienville."

The policeman walked around the area, asking, "Is anyone injured? Can I help anyone?"

Wyatt helped the New York journalist to his feet and asked, "Are you all right?"

"Yeah, I'm fine. Thanks. That scared the hell out of me. Listen

. . . what I said before . . . forget it. I apologize," the journalist said.

"Me, too," Wyatt said.

"Let me buy you a drink. I'll be right back. I think I soiled my pants," the journalist said.

"Okay," Wyatt said.

The man headed toward the restroom, shaking his pant legs.

Wyatt stepped to the door and watched the policeman talking to people. Wyatt thought the policeman looked like a concerned parent trying to maintain order and quell fear among his children. Then Wyatt thought of his daughter at home and how much he wanted to see her now. He left the bar and quickly walked toward his car.

CHAPTER 25

Nazis' Night Out

The young Nazis, Earl, Herman and Ralph, were having trouble sorting through their orders from Burger King.

"There's a fish sandwich in here, but nobody ordered fish," Earl said, disgustingly.

"Then don't eat it, stupid. Just throw it away. We've got enough hamburgers in this bag to feed the entire SS," Ralph shot back.

"Who sat on my cap?" Herman said, pointing to his khaki cap with a skull and crossbones symbol tacked just above the visor.

"Don't leave your cap on a chair, Hermy," said Ralph.

"Don't call me Hermy. I want to be known as Heinrech," Herman said.

"Sure, Heine. Anything you say," Ralph said, laughingly.

The neo-Nazis were half-naked and tossed hamburgers and clothes at each other like college boys on spring break. The motel room was a mess with khaki Nazi uniforms, black combat boots, suitcases and bags of food strewn across the beds and floor of the small room at the Travel Inn on Airline Highway. An 8x10 inch, framed photo of Adolph Hitler in khaki uniform stood on the dresser. And the two German Shepherds, Mannlicher and Carcano, were pacing and barking.

"I've got it," Ted, their elder leader, said, walking through the door with the Times Picayune newspaper in hand. He opened to the police reports. "Here's something we need to take care of." The young men gathered around him. "Take a look. See what the report says? A young white woman was out last night, got lost and ended up in this area where drugs are sold. They pulled her out of her car and beat her. The cops were patrolling the area and saw her on the street. The only reason she's alive is because they got her to the hospital in time and stopped the bleeding. They did this to a white woman! They're going to pay for this."

"Where was it?" Ralph asked.

Reading the report again, Ted said, "On South Galvez near the Lafitte housing project. Yeah, always near a housing project."

"It's *blitzkrieg* time," Herman said.

"Grab your burgers and get the dogs. It's head-banging time. We'll show them how it will be when they mess with white people. White power!" Ted said.

"White power!" the others shouted.

"Tonight, we can wear our uniforms. Tomorrow at the Robert E. Lee statue we can't," Ted said.

They hurriedly dressed and stood in front of the photo of Hitler and shouted, "*Seig heil! Seig heil! Seig heil!*"

They all climbed into the SUV. They were giddy about the violence to come. Mannlicher and Carcano couldn't sit still and kept jumping over the seats.

"Everybody got your whacking sticks?" Ted inquired.

"Yeah," they all replied, holding up lead weights wrapped in leather.

"Let's roll!" Ted commanded.

Ted pulled halfway out of the parking lot when Herman said, "Wait! I forgot my milkshake."

Ted pulled up to the room again. Herman got out by climbing over the other men.

Then Ralph said, "Get the fries, too!"

The Nazis sat in the white SUV-Nazi-mobile waiting on a milkshake and fries. But minutes later they were headed down Airline Highway, US Highway 61.

Herman placed the milkshake between his legs and opened a map of New Orleans. "We're going the right way, it appears," he said, following Airline Highway on the map with his index finger. "It looks like this road will turn into Tulane Avenue up ahead."

"It better turn into something up ahead because there's nothing out here," Ted said, looking up and down the dimly lit Highway 61 which was once the main highway in the state before Interstate-10 was built in the 1960s, leaving 61 to languish in the past, lined with old courtyard motels, adjacent railroad tracks and postcard memories of a brighter time.

The SUV topped an overpass and on the other side was the continuation of Airline Highway, now within the city limits and known as Tulane Avenue.

"It looks like civilization suddenly," Earl said, as the SUV stopped at the traffic light at the corner of Carrollton and Tulane.

"Maybe ancient civilization," Ted said. "Check out these old buildings," he continued, as they rolled down the brightly lit Avenue with the old one- and two-story buildings on either side.

Several old motels came into view on their right side. Two women, one white and one black, stood on a nearby corner and eyed the SUV as it rolled by.

"Let's offer them a lift, at least the white girl," Herman offered.

"You don't want to mess that. No telling what's crawling around inside that *fraulein*," Ted added.

"Jesus, Herman, she looks like a lumpy mattress. You'll sleep with anything," Earl said.

"Yes. The Fuhrer teaches to propagate the Aryan race," Herman responded.

"Yeah," Ralph said, "she looks more alien than Aryan."

They all laughed.

"Okay. *Achtung!*" shouted Ted, as they crossed over Jefferson Davis Parkway. "Get your minds right. We are about to do battle. We are the U.S. Waffen S.S., Death's Head Unit. Fight bravely, as always. Where the hell is Galvez street?"

"Not too far," Herman said. "Stay on Tulane," he said, looking at the map. "South Broad should be the next major intersection."

As they approached South Broad, the dirty granite Criminal District Courthouse appeared on that corner, looking more like an ancient castle than a courthouse. A lone black man stood on its steps to justice.

Several black women stood at the bus stop. Many more black men singly walked the sidewalks and crosswalks of this intersection and others like it in the city, perpetually on the move toward a dream unfulfilled.

"Lock your doors, *Kameraden*. We have entered the valley of death," Ted said.

The SUV continued down, passing the Dixie Brewing Company and numerous small one-two-and-three-story businesses, scarred and stained with age and by a succession of owners.

"There's Galvez. Take a left and see what streets come up," Earl said.

"But the sign says 'No Left Turn,'" Herman hurriedly said.

"Oh, shut up! We're Nazis. We can turn wherever we want," Earl said.

They slowly cruised up Galvez Street, which looked much the same as Tulane, but less traveled. They crossed over Canal Street and into the Treme neighborhood, and then crossed over streets that began in the French Quarter – Iberville, Bienville, Conti – stopping at St. Louis. Not far ahead was the menacing Lafitte Housing Project dimly lit and far-reaching into a darkening interior.

"This is it. This is where the woman was dragged from her car and beaten," Herman said.

"Let's see them pull that shit on us," Ralph said, defiantly.

"We won't give them the chance," Ted assuredly advised.

"What do we do now?" Earl asked

"We wait. Someone will show up soon. This corner must belong to some person or gang for drugs." The dogs became restless and started barking. "Quiet the dogs," Ted ordered.

Herman fed the dogs pieces of hamburger and fries.

"This has got to be the heart of darkness in this city. You'd think these people would find some other way to live," Herman said.

"They probably want to, but this may be all they can do for

now," Ralph said. "Everyone in the SUV looked at him as if he had said Adolph Hitler was gay. "What? I'm just saying . . ."

"What the hell, man! Are you one of us or not?" Earl asked.

"No. I meant . . .," Ralph said, trying to explain his comment.

"Shut up. Here they come. Keep the dogs quiet," Ted demanded.

Everyone sat quietly and looked out the tinted windows to their right where three young black men wearing dead man tee shirts, three-quarter shorts, bandanas and ball caps emerged from the darkness down St. Louis Street. They walked up to the SUV and checked it out.

"Hermy, crack your window. Wait until I say '*blitzkrieg!*' to jump out. Tell them you're looking for drugs," Ted ordered.

Hermy rolled the window down a crack and said, "Hey man, where can I get some blow?"

Trying to look into the SUV, the man in the middle said, "I got the blow, if you got the dough."

"I got the money. Don't worry about that," Herman said.

"If I don't see it in three seconds, I'm gone. One . . . two . . .," the young man said.

"Do you know who attacked that white woman last night?" Herman asked.

"What kind of shit you trying to pull?" the dealer said, pulling out a 9mm Ruger from his waistband.

"Why don't you try taking me now, you bitch!" Herman shouted.

"*Blitzkrieg!*" Ted shouted.

The Nazis exploded out of the SUV with the two dogs, one of which immediately bit into one dealer's arm, causing him to fall on his knees. A side door slammed into the head of the dealer who had been speaking, knocking him flat on his back. Ted kicked the gun out of his hand, saying, "If you ever attack a white person again, you die." The Nazi hit the young man so hard that the bandana flew off his head with a gold tooth from his mouth. Dark red blood covered his mouth and face. He then kicked the Nazi in the groin, causing the Nazi to go down like a falling tree. But Herman blindsided the man with a kick to the head, spewing more blood from his mouth and knocking him unconscious.

The third drug dealer was being furiously tossed around by the other Nazis who screamed, "White power! Don't you ever touch a white woman again, boy! You got that, boy? Save your violence for your bitches! We don't care if you kill each other." When one Nazi slipped and lost his hold, the dealer cut lose. But Mannlicher was on his leg and pulled him down, dragging him back.

Ted found the cocaine on the unconscious dealer and poured some of it on the young man's face. The remainder he threw up in the air where it mixed with lamplight and fell like a gentle snow on a bloody scene not likely to appear on a souvenir postcard of New Orleans nightlife.

"That's how we solve the crime problem," Ted said.

Moans were heard as the Nazis retreated into the SUV. Mannlicher and Carcano were heard barking as the SUV sped away down Galvez.

CHAPTER 26

The Past is Present

Mayor Chenier, holding a Chivas on the rocks in his hand, stood looking out the window of his eighth-floor office in City Hall. He had come straight to his office after the disastrous debate, wanting to hide and ponder the possibility that he could lose the election if enough people didn't vote and Conright paid enough people to vote for him. It didn't seem possible at first, but now he had his doubts. He realized that far too many people hated him and others were indifferent toward him. He felt as if he didn't have a friend in the entire city. How could this have happened to him, he wondered, as another ambulance with pulsating lights and shrieking siren rounded the corner on its speedy approach to the Emergency Room of Charity Hospital.

"My God!" he whispered. "Will this ever end?"

His heavy breath hit the glass where he saw his reflection – a tired, frightened, gray-haired man, a failure at fifty-five, most of his life over.

His assistant knocked on the door, then opened it saying, "There's someone to see you, mayor."

"I told you no visitors," Mayor Chenier said.

"I know, but he said he's an old friend," the assistant said. "He showed me a picture of the two of you during a civil rights rally."

The assistant opened the door wider to reveal James Armstead standing in the hall.

"Good God Almighty," Chenier said, as he approached Armstead and Armstead approached him. After giving him a big hug, the mayor said, "You look good, my brother."

"For an ex-con," Armstead said.

"When did you get out?" Chenier asked.

"Two weeks ago. You made Time Magazine and I thought, I've got to go down to New Orleans to help my friend win this election," Armstead said.

"I could use your help. I just might lose this thing," Chenier conceded.

"No. No. Think positive," Armstead reassured.

"Take off your coat. Have a seat. How about a drink?" Chenier asked.

Armstead took off his blue pinstripe suit coat and hung it on the back of a chair as he sat down and said, "No. No more of that poison or anything else. I was going to come over here tomorrow. But I was watching the debate in my hotel room. When it ended, I thought I could catch you at the station. When I arrived, your limo was pulling off, so I caught a cab and followed you."

"Everyone's following me, cameras at the ready. They're trying to create a scene for a sensational photo of an angry, old man unfit for public office," Chenier said, sitting down in his big leather chair behind his desk. "It eats away at my stomach. It makes me angry, then sad, then tired," he said, pouring a little Pepto Bismol in a small glass.

"I know that feeling," Armstead added.

"Yeah. I'm sure you do. That was sneaky the way they got you," Chenier said.

"Sneaky. Tricky. Underhanded," Armstead said. "They set up a sting and brother did I get stung! Caught red-handed with my hand in the cookie jar. But, listen, I can only blame myself. I slept with a crack whore. But I don't kid myself. I was a crack whore, too. I can't blame everything on that girl, Xav, I did twelve months in prison. I lost my house, public office and reputation. The most tragic part was losing my wife. My most grievous fault."

"Was it twenty years?" Chenier asked.

"We were married twenty-five years," Armstead said. "And I don't blame her for leaving. It was just as shameful to her as it was to me. I hurt her deeply and I'll never forgive myself for that, Xav. She is the last truly righteous person I've ever known, other than Martin himself. But what I did broke her heart. She cried for days.

And I had strayed from the flock before, several times. Seeing me on TV in handcuffs was the last straw. And, Xav, I'll tell you that night in jail I cried, too. I worshiped the golden calf. I strayed from the path of righteousness. I betrayed my wife, and Martin and the Movement, too. Martin always told us to stay on that path and keep our eyes on the prize. And I am sorry to say I was blinded by that golden calf."

"But you've repented and paid the price. We all have our moments of weakness. That's part of living and being human," Chenier said, drinking from his glass. "Still, I know what you mean. We've both fallen. No one respects or believes in me. *Time* and *Newsweek* have been here, along with *60 Minutes* and *A&E Investigates*. I'm the mayor who can't govern his own city. City Hall is the jail and I'm the prisoner. And just like Conright said, I can't even stop my own son from doing drugs," he said, then pausing to pick up a framed photo of his son. "Conright showing that photo tonight . . . . That was a low blow. That was like a knife in my heart. Conright is a low-life, white power, Nazi, KKK son-of-a-bitch. And everybody knows it. But tonight he was right. I just don't know how to save my city or my son. It's like watching flood waters rise all around me. And I'm powerless to stop it," he said, rubbing his thumb over the photo of his son, and then putting it back on his desk.

"But there was a time when we were giants," Armstead said, pointing to the photos on the wall behind Chenier. "There was a time when we could do anything. Together."

"Yeah, we were giants once," Chenier said, turning around in his chair to look at the photos. "These photos mark the path to the mountaintop."

"That's right," Armstead said.

"Look at us here," Chenier said, pointing to one photo showing the two marching with a crowd of black civil rights protestors. "The march to Montgomery."

"1965," Armstead said, bowing his head slightly in remembrance.

"How brave we were," Chenier said.

"We were Davids in the land of Goliath." Armstead said.

"Yeah. And Goliath beat the hell out of us in that first march," Chenier said.

"I still have my red badge of courage," Armstead said, running his finger over a scar on his forehead.

"Got mine, too," Chenier said, pointing to a scar on his chin. "We were scared and hit hard, but I felt so much stronger when Martin later joined us."

"Yes."

"And, my God, on that third march, no one could stop us. No one could stop us," Chenier said, with a righteous smile.

"We must have been 20,000 strong by the time we reached Montgomery four days later," Armstead said.

"Sleeping in those fields at night wasn't fun," Chenier said, grinning.

"No"

"But it was worth it. We got what we wanted. We got that Voting Rights Act, my brother," Chenier said, proudly.

"Yes, we did. When I saw President Johnson sign that document, I had tears rolling down my face," Armstead admitted.

"Me, too. Me, too," Chenier agreed.

"The power of peace," Armstead proclaimed.

"Just like Martin taught us," Chenier said.

"That's right. Just like Martin taught us," Armstead said, smiling and shaking his head.

"Look at Martin here," Chenier said, taking down another old black and white photo of a huge crowd standing in front of the Lincoln Memorial in Washington, where Martin Luther King, Jr. addressed a crowd of two-hundred fifty thousand people. "August 28, 1963 . . ."

"The March on Washington," Armstead said, touching the photo. "I can hear Martin now, speaking those words that rang out like church bells."

"Yes. Our finest hour. The power of the truth," Chenier said.

"It was only thirty years ago, but it seems like a hundred. We were so young and strong . . . so full of promise . . . the promise of . . .," Armstead recalled.

"Dreams," Chenier added. "We are heroes in our dreams. Making them come true is a whole other thing," he said, sipping his drink. "It's almost like Martin taught us how to dream. And to dream big. And if Martin was here, he would tell us to dream big again."

"Yes," Armstead said.

"Because now we're living a nightmare," Chenier said. "And we can't blame everything on the white man. Some of our young men are just out of control with that gangster bullshit . . . killing, killing, killing. It's all about them and no one else. No reverence for life. It's time to show them where we came from . . . and the power of a peaceful demonstration."

"I'm with you," Armstead said.

"I want us to be remembered as the peaceful warriors we were, not as the failures we've become . . . not as failures. Conright is holding a rally at Lee Circle tomorrow. I think we should gather as many people as possible and march from here and meet them," Chenier suggested.

"Yes. Let's do that. Let's march!" Armstead agreed.

"And we'll think of Martin and the Cause every step of the way. It will only take a few minutes to walk over there – a short walk, thirty years in the making," Chenier said, smiling.

"We'll make Martin proud again. I know he's looking down on us," Armstead said.

"Yes. I'm sure he is. It's so very good to see you again, my brother," Chenier said.

"Same here. We were lost, but now we're found," Armstead said.

"Yes. Now we're found. I can feel the power again and see Martin's beautiful smile," Chenier said, raising his hand toward heaven.

CHAPTER 27

Spirit in the Night

Ashley pulled into her driveway at 9:00 p.m. She grabbed her purse and got out of the BMW. She engaged the car alarm and then looked in her purse for her house key. She had forgotten to turn on any lights before leaving, including the porch light, and found it difficult to see under the cloud-encased moon. She finally found the key and attempted to insert it in the lock. But she suddenly heard a noise like the clanking of a gate in the wind. She turned around but could see nothing unusual, though she felt like she was being watched. The shaking branches on nearby nervous trees and bushes seemed to warn her. The warm wind wrapped around her neck and whispered, "Watch out!"

Her second try was a success. She opened the door, hurriedly walked in and turned on the lights. She then peered through the blinds, searching her small yard and the street beyond the fence, as was her custom.

She walked down the hall, looking behind her half of the way. She entered the bedroom where a framed poster entitled "Monet's Garden at Giverny" hung on the forest green wall. She threw her suit coat and purse on the white bedspread and kicked off her periwinkle pumps. She unbuttoned the top button of her blouse when she noticed the drawers to her mahogany dresser were open. Her closet door was also open. A shockwave rippled throughout her body. Her fingers felt tingly and cold. Someone's here, she thought.

She moved slowly out of the bedroom and into the hall, turning left, then right. She walked into her immaculate, white kitchen and started toward the phone hanging on the opposite wall. She suddenly heard slow, Frankenstein steps coming from the small second bedroom she used as an office. Her heart began to pound even faster. She lunged for the phone and dialed 911.

"I'm calling the police," she said, loudly. She grabbed a steak knife and said, "Whoever you are, I've got a gun!"

The steps quickened, seemingly heading right for her. But the man turned and bolted through the front door.

Ashley looked down the hall, but could only see the back of the man. Not thinking, she dropped the phone and ran after him. She saw him hop over the fence and run down the street. When she reached the street, he was gone. She stood in her stocking feet in the middle of the street with a knife in her hand, looking for a phantom in the night. She then saw a long sedan cross Benjamin Street at the next block. She ran to the corner but could only see the tail lights, each one standing vertically and divided by a center chrome piece.

Feeling very fatigued, she returned to her house, looking around outside for other strangers and for neighbors who may have seemed puzzled by her behavior. Noticing none, she closed the front door and headed straight for her office. The drawers of her file cabinet were open and the papers disheveled within. Some papers were on the floor. The papers on her mahogany desk were in disarray. What was he looking for, she wondered. But nothing seemed to be missing, except her feeling of security. She felt fearful, anxious, violated and angry. Someone had broken in and touched her things. And that pissed her off. Adrenalin was pumping through her veins, stoking her heart like oxygen to a fire.

A few minutes later, she heard a knock at the door. A new wave of fear overcame her. She slowly, quietly walked to the front door and peeked out the curtain. She was relieved to see a police car, though she hadn't reached the police on the phone. Maybe a neighbor did see her in the street and called the police department, she thought.

"Hello," Ashley quietly said, opening the door to the officer dressed in dark pants and a dark tee shirt with the imprinted badge of the NOPD over the heart.

"Yes, Ma'am, did you place a 911 call from this residence?" the officer asked.

"Yes, but I didn't get a chance to speak with anyone," Ashley said.

"Well, it's police procedure to investigate any 911 call when there's no response from the caller," the office said.

"I see."

"So, is there anything wrong? Why did you place the call?" the officer asked.

"There was an intruder here. He ran out of the house when I phoned. I ran after him," Ashley said.

"Don't do that! We advise against pursuit or engaging the perpetrator in any way. Give him what he wants and run away, if possible. Are you hurt?" the officer asked.

"No. He didn't harm me," Ashley said.

"Do you wish to file a police report? Many victims do not file reports in cases such as this one, where nothing was taken and no one was hurt," the officer said.

"Really?" she asked, totally perplexed.

"They don't want their names or addresses in the newspaper. They don't want to be associated with crimes of any sort," the officer said.

"That's strange," she replied.

"There's such a thing as a copycat crime, like the one tonight at the Old Absinthe House bar," he said.

"Oh, no! Someone I work with was there tonight to watch the debate," she said.

"No one was hurt," he said. "But we believe it was young men copying the recent shooting in front of Jackson's Square, just for a thrill. A young woman was killed in that shooting."

"I know. I was there. Have there been any leads in that case?" she asked.

"No. Not yet. We don't know if it was murder or a random shooting. The department is still investigating," he said.

"What do you think?" she asked.

"Murder. The gunfire was concentrated on her. Tonight's shooting . . . the bullets hit the ceiling. That's a copycat. So, do you want a police report for tonight?" he said, twisting his head and bending his neck down.

"Well . . . I guess not. Like you said, nothing was taken. But I'm really not sure," she said.

"You can let it go this time. But be on the lookout for him. And get your locks changed. This lock here is worthless," he said, pointing to the lock on the front door. "All a thief needs is something stiff to stick in between the door and the frame. It'll pop right open." A police dispatcher's voice was suddenly heard summoning the officer to another crime scene. "That's me. If there's nothing else I can do for you, I'll hit the street."

"No. I suppose that's it. Thanks for coming out," she said.

"Okay. Don't hesitate to call again if you need me. I'm Officer Gungeri. Anthony Gungeri. It was a pleasure to meet you, Miss"

"Tarleton. Ashley Tarleton."

"Mrs.?" He inquired.

"Miss," she said.

"I'll make sure to patrol this area more often. And if you ever need someone to talk to, just call me. I'll be right over," he said, backing up while looking a little too long into her eyes.

"Okay," Ashley said, breaking eye contact.

The officer turned around, walked to his car and slid behind the steering wheel. He then spoke police-speak involving a series of numbers into his walkie-talkie, hit the accelerator and shot into the night, chasing down the ignorant but illusive enemies of the people.

Still thinking about the officer's advice and parting stare, Ashley stood in her doorway. Was he trying to hit on her while pretending to "protect and serve," she wondered. Was no one to be trusted? Was no one honest and sincere?

She looked up and saw a mist rising in the heavy, humid air, rising like a spirit in the night. An overwhelming feeling of loneliness overcame her. She had always liked her neighborhood because it was quiet. Now, the quiet made her nervous. She needed to call someone who could calm her down, someone who could be trusted with her frightened heart. She locked her door, returned to the kitchen and picked up the phone which was still hanging to the floor. She dialed her parents' house to speak with the one person who was always strong when she needed strength, her father.

CHAPTER 28

Killer

It was eight o'clock at night in Los Angeles when Jacques Daniel parked his rented Cadillac on Sunset Boulevard, a few blocks down from the Comedy College. It was open-mic night. Jacques had flown all the way from New Orleans to participate and live his dream of becoming a stand-up comedian. If he did well on the comedy circuit, it could lead to a TV sitcom and that would be gold.

Jacques took a look up and down Sunset and was amazed that he was actually standing on the "Strip." He looked into the windows of the chic shops and restaurants, thinking how expensive everything must be. He noticed beautiful foreign sports cars gliding down the road like mercury. He smiled at groups of coolly clothed young ladies looking for excitement as they laughed all the way down the boulevard. He realized he was a bit out of place in his preppy clothing, very un-LA. The night air was cool and crisp, unlike the heat and humidity of home. He was excited and glad he made the trip, if only for one day. But he didn't notice the black Oldsmobile SUV with tinted windows that had followed him and parked one block down from his car.

He felt a little nervous as he came near the club. He was about to walk in the front door when he noticed three young men pacing up and down an alley next to the building.

Walking up to one, he said, "Hey, is this where I sign up for open-mic?"

"Yeah. Inside," the young man said, puffing on a cigarette and pointing to the side door.

These would-be comedians looked as depressed and nervous as the criminals he represented as an assistant district attorney. Where's the comedy, he wondered.

Once inside, he made his way to a dimly lit hallway behind the stage where a man with glasses, wearing a black tee shirt with a frowning smiley face on it, sat at a small square table.

"Hi. I'm Jacques Daniel I want to sign up for a few minutes tonight. Is that all right?"

"Are you funny?" the man asked.

"Well, some people say . . ."

"We'll see," the man interrupted. "Print your name," he said, pointing to a legal pad with four names on it. "You're up after the next three. You get ten minutes. We reserve the right to pull the plug on you at any time."

"Okay. Any talent scouts out there?"

"Probably," he said.

"Thanks," Jacques said.

After printing his name, he moved to a point near the stage where he could see the first comedian now performing and most of the audience, which numbered about thirty in the club that could seat one-hundred fifty.

"You know what really gets to me? You know what really bugs me?' the comedian asked. "When I'm in the drive-thru at the bank and the moron in front of me decides to take out a loan. Doesn't it bug you when the person in front of you takes a long time to do his transaction? The line to the left of you is moving okay and the line to the right is moving. But your line is not moving at all. It's like time has come to a complete standstill. You feel your blood pressure rising and your stomach turning. You're clutching the steering wheel so hard, you're about to break it in two. And the lines on either side of you are moving right along. Except now, it looks like the people are pointing at you and laughing. They're holding up their fingers in a 'L' sign for 'Loser.' and your head is about to explode. But then that weird Jetsons' tube returns to the driver in front of you, making it appear that the wait is over, but noooo, the idiot forgot to sign his name on the check. So, he sends it back down the tube. And you start to weep because you can't take it anymore. Doesn't that bug you? Here's my solution. In a perfect world we all get four minutes to finish our transactions. After that, the guy behind you can legally push you out of the way.

Imagine pushing the car ahead of you into the street with your car. Imagine that."

"That's not funny!" a man from the audience yelled.

"What do you mean? It's hilarious!" the nervous comedian said, fidgeting with his hair.

Jacques turned away and walked outside, feeling bad for the comic and worrying that the same thing would happen to him. The group of young men now waiting in the alley, had grown to ten. Most were smoking and looked morose. Some exchanged words with others. Some looked over their notes. The scene had the look and feel of gladiators being called to the arena, one by one, to do or die.

"Mark. Is there a Mark Stone here?" the man with the frowning smiley face tee shirt asked, looking out the doorway into the alley.

"Yeah. Right here," a young man said, stamping out his cigarette and following the man inside.

The young comic, wearing a distressed "Smiley Face" tee shirt and who had just finished his routine, exited the side door with his head held down.

"How was it up there?" one guy asked.

"Bring a gun. Shoot them or yourself, but you'll need it either way," the dejected comic warned as he passed through the crowd toward Sunset Boulevard, the road to stardom at one end, or oblivion at the other.

That somber advice mainlined the man with an injection of fear that stopped them all in their tracks for a minute or two.

"Jesus," Jacques uttered under his breath.

"I'm leaving," one of the comics ahead of Jacques said.

"Yeah. Me, too," his friend said, as they both exited the alley.

"Oh, shit! That makes me next," Jacques nervously murmured. Jacques began reading over his notes. Sweat broke out on his forehead and palms. He began pacing, circling and fingering his hair. A mushroom cloud of smoke rose from the alley, making him choke. He then heard boos from the audience. "Oh, shit! They're hostile," Jacques said.

"Yeah. As Dangerfield would say, 'rough crowd, rough crowd,'" another comic said.

The booed comic hit the door on his way out, shaking his head all the way through the crowd and saying, "You've got to be nuts to do this for a living."

"Jonathan," the man at the door shouted.

"He died," a comic said.

"No Jonathan? What about Steven?" the man asked.

"Suicide . . . just now . . . in the street. Call a cleanup crew," the same comic said.

"What about Jac, Jacques, Shack?" the man at the door shouted.

"Jacques. Right here," Jacques said, and vaulted through the doorway.

"Follow me behind the curtain. You'll enter from the other side, after I announce you. And watch your step," the man advised.

"Okay," Jacques said. Jacques felt his heart pounding and mouth suddenly felt dry. "Can I get some water first?"

"No. What city are you from?" the man asked.

"New Orleans."

"All right. Stand here," the man said, pointing to a spot next to the curtain. He then walked on stage and said, "You didn't like the last guy, but how could you not like someone from Sin City itself, New Orleans? And this is his real name, Jack Daniels." He motioned for Jacques to come on stage while the crowd laughed.

Jacques walked onto the stage, thanked the man and took his place at the microphone. How can I be dripping wet but my mouth is so dry, he thought.

"Hey, everybody out there. I can't see everyone. I didn't count on these lights being so bright," Jacques said, shading eyes for a moment.

"You'll get no sympathy from us," said a patron in the rear.

"Oh! Okay," Jacques said. "Thanks for your support." He decided to go right into his jokes. He felt nauseous and his vision was blurred, but he decided to stick it out. "You've got to love New Orleans . . ."

"Not really," the heckler in the back said.

"What I mean is New Orleans is like no other city. It's the only city in the U.S. that shuts down for a day on Mardi Gras so everybody can get drunk," he said laughingly. "Now that's a town!"

"You're wrong," the heckler said, "Chicago and New York both do it on Saint Paddy's Day."

"Yeah. But I'm talking about the whole town. It's great! And the women show their breasts for a string of worthless beads. But the women who do that are usually grotesque and probably reveal themselves at work and on the way home; so, it's no big thrill to most men." Laughing, Jacques added, "Know what I mean?"

"No. We don't," someone else in the audience said.

Jacque's throat tightened and his head throbbed. He was sweating like a sinner in a confessional. But he continued, saying, "And we have drive-thru daiquiri shops back home. Can you believe it? It's a drunkard's dream."

"Your observational humor sucks!" the heckler shouted.

"What about those alien abduction stories?" Jacques said, hurriedly trying to change the subject matter while noticing Mr. Frowny Face fidgeting by the edge of the stage. "Why is it the aliens always come for those people in the middle of the night when they're in a semi-psychotic state? Why can't the aliens show up where someone works at lunchtime and say something like, 'Hey, bub, before we make a science project out of you and probe you from top to bottom, we'd like to take you to Wendy's for lunch. It's the least we can do. What do you say?'"

The man in the frowning smiley face tee shirt suddenly bolted onto the stage and loudly announced, as he commandeered the microphone, "What do you say, everybody? Give Jack a nice round of applause. He's all the way from New Orleans. Give me a minute and I'll bring you a fresh comedian."

He ushered Jacques off stage as the audience offered a

minimalist's version of applause. He was led out the side door with the ringing of the next comedian's name in his ear, as well as the smell of onions and beer from Mr. Frowney Face's breath.

Sunset Boulevard was straight ahead, but he had to walk that walk of shame through all the young comics staring at him. He pushed forward through the smoke, trying not to make eye contact.

"Let him pass, boys. Dead man walking," someone joked.

"Like John Belushi said, 'My advice to you is to start drinking heavily,'" another said.

"The Hollywood sign is not too far, if you want to throw yourself off," quipped another.

Jacques crushed his notes in his hand and threw the wad in a trash can as he emerged onto Sunset. The fresh air felt good as he strolled back to his car. Though down, he attempted to meet two ladies walking his way. Maybe wild sex with strange women would cheer him up. But it was not to be, so he kept walking. When he reached the car, he looked at his watch and realized he had to pick up his pace to make it to the airport on time for his flight. After all, he had to be at work the next day. He eased the pain by telling himself that he did what he wanted to do and was glad for that. And he enjoyed working in the DA's office. But he would work on his act and try again in New Orleans, if only a comedy club would open there.

He unlocked his rental car, sat down and checked his map, trying to get a lock on the airport's location. He drove down the boulevard a couple of blocks, looking at street signs, but not noticing the Oldsmobile SUV behind him. Seated inside were two men wearing sunglasses and dressed in black. One wore a black and silver LA Raiders jacket.

It seemed the boulevard became darker as Jacques drove farther east. He then heard a booming bass sound behind him. He looked in the mirror and noticed the two occupants of the Oldsmobile pointing at him. He wasn't sure what expressway entrance to take, so he took a right onto a down ramp which took him to a darker area, just the opposite of what he expected. With Sunset Boulevard long behind him, he didn't know where he was. When he looked in the mirror again, there was the Oldsmobile. He decided to circle back toward Sunset, but he didn't come upon a "U-Turn" sign anywhere. He felt he was being pushed farther away, toward a LA vortex that swallowed lost souls. Then the SUV bumped him. His eyes widened in the mirror and his heartbeat accelerated, realizing he had more serious problems than just not finding the airport. And the SUV bumped him again.

Instead of racing away, farther into unknown territory, he decided to confront the men. After all, he thought, he was involved in law enforcement. He pulled over and so did the SUV. He stepped out and walked to the rear of his car. He stood there with his arms folded, looking at two black men who were smiling. Jacques motioned with his fingers for them to come out and talk. The two men looked at each other, laughed and pointed fingers at Jacques. Finally, they exited the SUV and walked up to Jacques.

"Hey, boy, don't you know you were speeding?" said the man in the Raider's jacket.

"I wasn't speeding . . . you bumped my car. You could have caused me to run off the road," Jacques said, angrily.

"Don't yell at me, boy!" the other man said. "What are you doing in Los Angeles, New Orleans boy?"

"How do you know where I'm from? And who the hell are you to ask me what I'm doing here?" Jacques asked.

"We own this town," the man in the Raider's jacket said. "You're out here to get evidence on us for that girl's death, aren't you?"

"What girl?" Jacques asked.

"You know . . . the girl shot dead in the Quarter," the man said.

"I'm not out here for that. A prosecutor hasn't even been assigned to that crime yet," Jacques said.

"Bullshit!" the other man said. "Why else would you be out here?"

"That's my business," Jacques said. "I don't know how you got information about me, but I'm going to find out. I'm an assistant district attorney for the City of New Orleans, and . . ."

"Yeah. We know," both men said, as they each pulled out 9mm handguns from the back of their waistbands and fired multiple shots at Jacques who fell to the ground, bleeding profusely from the chest.

The two men got back into the Oldsmobile SUV and speedily drove off. Their night's work had been completed in only a few minutes. They were then free to celebrate the murder of Jacques Daniels, son to a proud and loving mother and father. He was an honest, hardworking young man who dared to dream, they would say of him at his funeral, after his parents would come to Los Angeles to identify him and take his body home. They would all ask, "Why? Why had God taken him so young?" And they would all be sad and perplexed when his coffin was lowered into the ground in the cemetery where two granite angels would keep watch over his grave every day. Friends and relatives would walk up to his parents and tell them how sorry they were and that he would be missed. Then the mother and father would leave in a black limousine, though not wanting to leave their son alone in his grave, and never knowing why their son was killed. But after all had gone, Jacques' spirit would rise from the grave and join the thousands of lost souls circling the planet. His spirit would then descend, appear next to each of his killers and persistently whisper while they slept, the word, "Murderer."

CHAPTER 29

We Shall Overcome

"Those of you not registered to vote, please follow the people getting off the bus now into City Hall. Members of my staff will show you to the designated area for registration," Mayor Chenier said, as he addressed a small crowd of blacks and whites on the lawn in front of City Hall, while pointing to the yellow school bus parked on Loyola Avenue, as fifty people exited. "I want to thank those of you who showed up this morning to march with us to Lee Circle," the mayor told the crowd, as James Armstead and Reverend Paternostro stood behind him, applauding. "You are much needed and so is your courage. Reverend, would you offer a blessing before we begin?" the mayor asked, moving away from the microphone.

The Reverend, dressed in a black suit and gold shirt and tie, approached the microphone and said, "Thank all of you for coming this morning. This march is for freedom and against oppression. This march is for hope. Please join hands. Father, give us strength and courage this day and every day to stand tall in the face of evil and prejudice, and to defiantly stand our ground when confronted by some people in this city who want to live by old rules and do not wish to embrace a hopeful future for all people of this great old city. Lord, give us strength. Sweet Jesus, we ask that you march with us. We know that you will. And thank you, Lord, for all you have given us. Amen. Let us begin our short walk by reminding ourselves and others of our long history and fight for freedom. Join with me now and sing: *We shall overcome, we shall overcome, we shall overcome some day.*" The Reverend continued to sing as they all began their march onto Loyola Avenue. "Oh, deep in my heart, I do believe, we shall overcome some day."

Wyatt had just finished the last few pieces of his waffle while sitting at the counter inside the Camellia Grill at the corner of

South Carrollton and St. Charles Avenue. The Grill had always been Wyatt's favorite place to eat and it stayed open unto 2:00 a.m. For forty years this little grill with its plantation styled entrance provided good eating to all the regulars and visitors, too.

"I'll see you later, Mr. Harry," Wyatt said to longtime counter waiter and New Orleans character, Mr. Harry, as he was finishing his chocolate freeze. "I'm off to film Conright at Lee's Circle." Two black waiters and a black cook looked at him.

"Oh, grand!" Mr. Harry said. "That Nazi! Tell him the war is over."

"Will do," Wyatt replied, leaving a couple of dollars on the counter.

"Yeah. And tell him something for me," the black cook said.

"Watch it now, Theodore," Mr. Harry said, as everyone started laughing.

"See ya," Wyatt said.

Wyatt then paid the cashier, walked outside, and got in his TV-3 white Chevrolet sedan. He adjusted his seatbelt, revved the engine, and turned left onto St. Charles Avenue while tuning into David Lerner's radio show. He turned up the volume and checked his watch.

"Life is cheap in this city!" Lerner announced. "The city continues its record-breaking year, for the most people gunned down, knifed, strangled, bludgeoned, run over, burned alive and any other way you can kill a human being. I'm talking murder! It's now. 414. Who will be the lucky one tonight? Maybe me, maybe you. Come on, New Orleans, you can do it. You can top that number. Give it that old 'can do' effort. The whole world is watching. New Orleans can do. Pathetic! This city is run by hoodlums and everybody knows it. You can't walk the streets without the risk of being shot. There's garbage piling up everywhere. And look at your choices for mayor – a Nazi and a mayor on the take who promises more welfare checks and Section 8 housing if you vote for him. Pathetic! This city deserves what it gets. Can't trust the mayor or the judges, who let criminals out of jail and who are, in effect, criminals themselves. And the police? Forget about it. They're gunslingers, too. Listen to this New

Orleans. Guess who killed two innocent people and a police officer last night? Are you ready? Another cop! I kid you not. An off-duty female police officer walked into a Vietnamese restaurant on Chef Menteur Highway, where she sometimes works as essentially a security guard after working her regular police hours, and shot and killed another police officer who was there last night, also working extra hours which is called working a 'detail.' She then killed two members of the Vietnamese family who were working in the restaurant. She then took a large sum of money and left, only to return to the scene of the crime dressed in her police uniform and acting like she was responding to the murder call. But one family member hid in the freezer and saw her. Unbelievable! May she rot and die in jail. That bitch! What a sad state of affairs. And you can really tell this city is condemned to hell and damnation because last night Jesus himself was murdered. The guy called the French Quarter Jesus was found beaten to death on Ursuline Street, just off Decatur. The cops suspect Dennis Mena, known as 'Dennis the Menace' because he likes to beat up homeless guys in the Quarter. Friends, this is not a good omen. But wait, there's more. As it turns out, New Orleanians are murdered even if they're not in the city. Last night New Orleans assistant district attorney, Jacques Daniels, was found shot to death on a freeway off ramp in Los Angeles. A passing motorist saw him talking to two black men just before he was shot. They sped away in a black SUV."

"Oh shit! Jack!" Wyatt exclaimed, as he passed the Bultman Funeral Home, heading toward Lee Circle. "Jesus Christ!"

"Yeah. Can you believe it?" Lerner commented. "Let me tell you something, my friends. This city is cursed. Call it voodoo . . . hoodoo . . . or whatever you want to call it. This city and its citizens have a hex on them. There's no doubt about it. This city is a city of sin and despair like no other city I've known. And someone is still stealing concrete angels from the cemeteries. Incredible! Not even the dead can rest in peace in this town. And people criticize me for knocking their town. They say I'm from out of town and should keep my mouth shut. Some call me a damn Yankee! The Civil War has not ended. It rages on in the minds of many people across the south. I say get over it. Accept some constructive criticism. Like, why is there a Lee Circle in this city? That's offensive to some people, like the Confederate flag. And then you got a moron like Keiffer Conright actually holding a rally at Lee Circle right now. And he is the Republican candidate for mayor. Come on! How divisive can you get? Maybe this city deserves the voodoo spell cast over it. Maybe we should summon Marie Laveau from the other side, as they say, to stop this city from total ruin. I don't know. Just a thought. And the Mississippi rolls through this town, snatching lives, too. Last night a child's shoes were found on the bank of the River. He strayed away from his mother and apparently got caught in the River's undertow. All right. It's 10:00 a.m. Do you know where your conscience is? We'll be right back after these capitalist messages. Watch your back, New Orleans. Stay tuned."

As Wyatt approached Lee Circle, a roundabout in the middle of St. Charles Avenue where General Robert E. Lee stood defiantly atop a tall Doric column, he searched for a place to park and looked for Ashley's car. He checked across the street in front of the K&B Plaza, a square concrete office building where the old, public library, inspired by ancient Rome's *Tempio di Marte Ultore*, once stood from 1909 - 1959. No openings there, he thought. Then he quickly spied a space big enough for two small cars right on the corner in front of an old three-storied, slightly crooked wooden building that was standing when the statue of General Lee was commemorated in 1884, and that had survived the wrecking ball and the sweep of time.

As Wyatt backed into the space, he hit another car – Ashley's. She had tried to steal the space hurriedly, not realizing Wyatt was driving the other car.

"Hey!" Wyatt shouted, looking out of his window.

"Sorry!" Ashley said, backing out. "Take it!"

Wyatt then successfully parked. Ashley, seeing no other spaces, parked her BMW vertically in the small space behind Wyatt's car.

"Nice job," Wyatt said, walking to Ashley's car.

"Don't tell my father. See any cops?" Ashley asked.

"Yeah," Wyatt said, positioning his camera on his shoulder. "Right there."

Wyatt motioned toward the Robert E. Lee monument. Scattered around St. Charles Avenue where it circled the monument, were a half-dozen policemen. Standing in front of the monument, and as defiant as General Lee himself, high atop the column, was Keiffer Conright, facing reporters on Howard Avenue where the mayor would soon appear. With Conright were his two Hulk-like bodyguards. Also nearby were the four Nazis, dressed in civilian clothes which hid their Swastika and skull and crossbones tattoos. Their shaved heads reflected the hot sunlight, as they frolicked with Mannlicher and Carcano, imagining they were guests of the Fuhrer on the terrace at Berchtesgaden in the early 1940s. Soon the cocaine-snorting, call-girl-enthusiast Dr. Goodnight was present to lend feigned support, lest his wicked and debauched habits be revealed. Also present on the periphery was businessman and pervert, Mr. Ginsweet, wearing a black parka, black jeans and black Ray-Ban aviator sunglasses, to obscure his identity.

"Jesus! It's a media blitz," Ashley remarked, as she surveyed the area packed with reporters from the other three local TV stations, as well as from other U.S. and foreign TV stations. "There are more people here than his last press conference at the courthouse."

"Yeah. That's because they expect some serious violence to go down today," Wyatt said.

"You think they'll get violent?" Ashley asked.

"You can count on it. He's got his goon squad with him. Watch yourself. But there's something else." He looked straight into her eyes. "You know my friend at the DA's office, Jacques Daniels? He was murdered last night in Los Angeles." A look of horror slowly spread over Ashley's face, as she slowly digested this news and thought of her own attack. "So really watch yourself," Wyatt warned.

"Was it robbery?" Ashley asked.

"No. Two men murdered him in cold blood. Obviously, those men tracked him down. He knew or had something they wanted. One of his cases may have had an L.A. connection. Maybe that girl who was killed outside Jackson Square. So, I'd back off that investigation, if I were you," Wyatt said.

"Why would her death be connected to L.A., though?" Ashley asked.

"I don't know. But we don't have time to talk about it now," Wyatt said.

"Right. Let's go," Ashley said, as they walked toward the monument and pushed through the crowd. "Mr. Conright, why would you have your press conference here at Lee Circle?" But a foreign reporter elbowed her left temple, causing her to stop. "Hey! Watch out!" she cried.

"Mr. Conright, the mayor and others are marching here now. What will you do when they arrive?" an out-of-state reporter asked.

"Stand my ground," Conright replied, taking off his suit jacket and rolling up the sleeves of his white button-down collar shirt.

"What does that mean?" the reporter added.

"What do you think?" Conright quipped.

"Mr. Conright," Ashley said, "why choose the Robert E. Lee monument?"

But Ashley's voice was overpowered by a reporter from a Slavic country bellowing his question with a thick accent, asking, "What will be your first order of business, if elected?"

"You mean when elected," Conright joked. "The first thing I'll do is round up all the criminals and ship them to your country." Conright laughed, though no one else did.

"Mr. Conright, why did you choose the Robert E. Lee monument today?" the German reporter next to Ashley asked.

Ashley blurted out, "Son-of-a-bitch! That was my question. How impolite. Isn't there journalism etiquette wherever you are from?"

"Well, I'll tell you . . ." Conright began.

Ashley decided to jump in by saying, "Considering that Robert E. Lee was a Confederate general during the Civil War and considering black citizens find this monument offensive and divisive."

"Good point, Miss Tarleton. I can see you're still trying to stir things up," Conright replied.

"So are you," she added. "Some say in a very racist way. And what's your connection to Yvette Lenieu, the woman murdered in front of Jackson Square?"

"No connection," Conright said. "But if it's racist to love the city of my birth and want a brighter future for its citizens, then I'm a racist. If it's racist to want to imprison those who are committing the serious crimes in this city, regardless of their color, then I'm a racist. If it's racist to want to walk the streets of my city at any hour of the day or night without fear of being accosted or even murdered, then I'm a racist. If it's racist to protect and defend my American heritage, then I'm a racist. Standing here at the base of this magnificent monument to a great general in American history is a privilege. I am honored to stand in his shadow. Some people must understand that General Lee and the Confederate flag are of our culture and history. Do we tear down and burn monuments and flags and books regarding our American heritage just because some people are not true patriots? Where would it stop? I pledge to clean up this town in more ways than one and return it to its previous glory days . . ."

"When the black man knew his place," a black man said, jokingly.

Conright continued, "When we could all enjoy the city and all it had to offer, and we did not have to watch our backs every minute of every day. There once was a New Orleans where we could shop with our parents on Canal Street that was clean and was lined with special shops and department stores, instead of tee shirt shops and tennis shoe stores and pawn shops there now. There once was a New Orleans where parents could let their children play outside without looking left and right and all around for suspicious characters and flying bullets. There once was a New Orleans where young graduates could plan a bright future, instead of having to move away the day after they receive their college diplomas to find good jobs. There once was a New Orleans that attracted business, tourists, families and praise. Today our city attracts ridicule and warnings. Ladies and gentlemen, we all want our city back. Isn't that right? We want our city back. Say it with me. We want our city back! We want our city back!" People in the crowd began to chant with him. "We want our city back! We want our city back! And look there." He pointed up Howard Avenue to the mayor and his friends marching toward him. "There's the man who's too weak to do anything about our city's problems."

"Do you know Yvette Lenieu?" Ashley shouted.

The mayor and his supporters were seen two-hundred yards away, making the turn from Loyola Avenue onto Howard. Locked arm in arm in front were the mayor, Reverend Paternostro, James Armstead and the spirit of Martin Luther King, Jr. Memories of the Movement and the winds of change propelled the crowd forward, as they sang.

We shall overcome
We shall over come
We shall overcome some day

Oh, deep in my heart
I do believe
We shall overcome some day
We'll walk hand in hand
We'll walk hand in hand
We'll walk hand in hand some day

Oh, deep in my heart
I do believe
We shall overcome some day

We shall all be free
We shall all be free
We shall all be free some day

Oh, deep in my heart
I do believe
We shall over come some day

Donald Patrick O'Callahan

We are not afraid
We are not afraid
We are not afraid some day

Oh, deep in my heart
I do believe
We shall overcome some day

We are not alone
We are not alone
We are not alone some day

Oh, deep in my heart
I do believe
We shall overcome some day

We shall overcome
We shall overcome
We shall overcome some day

As the group marched toward Lee Circle, all cameramen swung around to get their best shots. They trained their cameras on what seemed to be a scene from the 1960s with the marchers stepping out of a time portal, but still facing the same foe. As they drew closer, the marchers began singing John Lennon's "Power to the People," lifting their fists high.

Their song and their steps grew louder, like an army approaching Armageddon. Even Conright felt a nervousness in his veins. Mannlicher and Carcano began barking fiercely and had to be restrained by the undercover Nazis.

Dr. Goodnight saw the opportunity to slip away and took it. Noticing the doctor's exit, Ginsweet followed suit and ran down Camp street into the confines of the Central Business District, where perversity was tolerated, if it was profitable. Reporters and cameramen parted like the Biblical Red Sea to allow the marchers to step in about ten feet in front of Conright and stop.

"We are here today to take a stand against you and all people like you who jeopardize the freedom of all people of color, and who wish to spread hatred and contempt for your fellow human beings," the mayor declared.

"That's right!" someone in the crowd behind him said.

"We are here to say 'no' to bigotry. We are here to say 'no' to hatred. We are here to say 'no' to racism. And we are here to say 'no' to you and your Nazi friends," the mayor said.

"Tell it like it is, brother," another person in the crowd said.

"You'd better watch what you say and who you accuse of being Nazis," Conright fired back.

"You're KKK, too," the Reverend shouted.

"There are four skinheads and two German Shepherds right over there. Yet you say you're not Nazis," Armstead added.

"I want all you reporters to note who is doing the name calling here. I want to see that in the news tonight. This is slander," Conright insisted. "There are no photos or recordings of me that show any connection to hate groups. I've said that many times before. This is slander! Reporters take note! This is nothing but a smokescreen to divert your attention away from the mayor's many failures."

"We are here to . . ." the mayor continued.

"That we know, mayor. You've come down from your ebony tower for the first time in years to pretend like you're interested in the city. We're not buying it, Mayor X. And after the election, you'll be just another part of this city's history," Conright said.

"The fact of the matter is that every black man, woman and child have been, continue to be and will always be part of New Orleans history. We helped to build and populate this city. We built businesses and made the city's economy strong. We are executives and hourly workers. We run the transit system. We deliver the mail. We serve the food. We clean the tables. We make the beds," the mayor said.

"Yes, and you do them all badly," Conright said.

"And we run City Hall!" the mayor defiantly said.

"Praise Jesus!" the Reverend said, as applause broke out.

"And we are buried in numbers in every cemetery across the city and in unmarked graves too numerous to count," the mayor declared. "We are flesh and blood. And we are ghosts that roam these streets. And we are spirits that fly over this city every minute of every hour of every day. We are black and we are proud. We are the future and we are now. We are the soul of this city. This city will always be predominantly black. And you, Mr. Conright, had better get used to it. Put away your Confederate flag and Nazi paraphernalia, and join the union because we are this city and we are America. And we ain't going nowhere, my man."

The marchers applauded loudly. The two dogs, Mannlicher and Carcano, began barking ferociously. Two plain clothes Nazis restrained the dogs by tightening their choke chains.

"Get it straight! Get it straight!" one marcher shouted.

"Praise God Almighty who is looking down on you, Keiffer Conright, and He doesn't like what He sees," the Reverend said.

"I know He doesn't like what He sees because He sees an ineffectual mayor who is letting this city's citizens die painful and needless deaths every day. Do the right thing, mayor. Resign," Conright said.

"You mean do the white thing," the Reverend added.

"That's just like you, Reverend, to play the race card. That's all you do is to take part in rallies and stir it up. I want everybody here to see what the Reverend is doing. I'm trying to make a stand here for all New Orleanians but the blacks are trying to incite a riot," Conright replied.

"You reveal yourself in the language you use," Armstead said. "You said 'all New Orleanians' but you referred to these good people as 'the blacks' as if they are not New Orleanians, but rather some sub-people who live here too."

"Oh, that's ridiculous! You're fabricating fault where there is none. You're trying to be uppity by sounding like some pseudo-intellectual," Conright countered.

The crowd gasped. Some said, "Uppity?"

"Let me tell you something, Conright," the mayor angrily answered. "No one here is pretending to be someone he or she isn't. We are all hardworking, God-fearing people who have come out today to take a stand against you and all you represent in front of all these cameras and people from the press. We have made our point. You will not occupy this city like some conquering KKK army and chase all the black people away just so you can raise your rebel flag and say 'Hell No! I ain't forgetting!' like the license plate on the front of your car. It's not going to happen, not now, not ever. We've accomplished what we came here to do and now we'll go. And get those German Shepherds out of my face before I kill one of those sons-of-bitches. You'd love to let those dogs loose and turn on the fire hoses. That's your American Heritage you're so proud of."

"And I am proud of my American Heritage," Conright said

"If you're proud of that, you are undoubtedly a racist! Let's go everybody. This man is insane and so is anyone who votes for him," the mayor said, turning away.

"Walk away, mayor, like you've always done. You're turning your back on the real issue of corruption in your administration, of crime and murder, and the endless flow of drugs in this city. I'm sure there's a drug sale going on in that crowd of people you brought with you. You people just have to have your drugs, no matter what," Conright asserted.

"You people? We know what you mean by that, you racist son-of-a-bitch," the Reverend shouted. "You can kiss my . . ."

A lump of hardened tar hurled by an unseen hand came twirling and tumbling down from space, slicing through the heat and humidity, and landing hard on the Reverend's sweaty brow, knocking him to the ground, causing bleeding over his entire face.

"Jesus Christ!" the mayor said, kneeling to help the Reverend. "Somebody call an ambulance!"

The crowd was astonished by the sight. Wyatt brought his

camera in close, followed by other cameramen jockeying their way forward. Then one of the German Shepherds broke loose, or was let loose, forcing the crowd to recede. The barking dog came within six inches of the mayor's face. Enraged, the mayor grabbed his gold Cross pen from his top pocket and jammed it into the dog's chest. The dog let out a piercing squeal as it fell to the ground, bleeding and gasping for air. There was a moment or two of silence. As the mayor raised his bloody hand, the photographers feasted. And then all hell broke loose.

"Bastard!" shouted a Nazi, as he jumped on the mayor and began to pummel the mayor's face with his swastika-tattooed fists.

Armstead immediately slid his arms underneath the Nazi's arms, locked his fingers behind the Nazi's head, pulled him off the mayor and slammed his face down on the street. Another Nazi then jumped on top of Armstead, while the remaining German Shepherd shot into the crowd like a watery blast from a fire hose, forcing many to flee and knocking down Wyatt in the process. It was the 1960s all over again.

"Are you okay?" Ashley asked, as she helped him up.

"Yeah. I'm good. I got to get that shot," he said, pointing toward Conright running toward his white BMW.

"Mr. Conright!" Ashley shouted, as she ran after him while Wyatt trained his camera on the chase.

As the police moved in to quell the violence, two shots rang out. Everyone hit the ground, either falling flat down or crouching. After a minute or so of chilling silence that only a loud violent noise can bring, heads began to rise and eyes opened to survey the damage.

Ashley, crouching, looked over at Wyatt who was flat on his back and not moving. His camera was near his side. She ran to him, crying out, "Wyatt! Wyatt!" When she knelt by him, she looked for blood but found none. She then noticed a rounded impression on the side of the camera. A bullet had ricocheted off the camera. It must have caused him to fall and hit his head, she thought. Lifting up his head, she said, "Wyatt, are you all right?" She shook his head slightly and again said, "Wyatt, are you okay?" She felt a rising anxiety and her heartbeat quickened.

Wyatt suddenly opened his eyes and sprang up, saying, "What happened?"

"Shots were fired. You must have fallen and hit your head. It looks like one hit the camera," Ashley said, quite alarmed.

He took a quick look and said, "It doesn't look damaged. Is anyone hurt?" They surveyed the area and noticed two policemen were administering first aid to one demonstrator who was bleeding while two other policemen were subduing and handcuffing one Nazi who apparently fired the shots. "Come on. Let's get this," he said, picking up his camera.

As Wyatt videotaped the Nazi being handcuffed, the other German Shepherd went wild. It backed itself onto the steps of the Robert E. Lee monument, and barked like it was disembarkation time at Auschwitz. No one could get near the dog. Finally, a cop got as close as he could, took aim, and shot the dog in its head. The battle for Lee Circle was over. Sunlight struck the statue of General Lee, revealing a seemingly sad face, as if realizing the Civil War he ended by surrendering, was actually still being waged. He stood tall, hoping people would commemorate the Lee who grew to hate war, and not to commemorate a lost cause.

Ashley couldn't believe what she had just witnessed. She stood stunned, in silence for a few moments, wiping sweat from her forehead, and then finally, she looked over at Wyatt who shook his head affirmatively.

"You don't have to ask. I got it all, even with a wounded camera. I got to get this back to the station," Wyatt said.

"I need to speak to a cop first," she said. "Come on." Walking up to a police officer near the Reverend, she said, "Officer, would you like to comment on what just happened?"

The officer went on to describe the details of the bloody violence – who was hurt, who was arrested. While listening to him, Ashley realized that, like all news events and like life itself, the witnesses could recount what happened, but could not explain why it happened. She suddenly felt a sadness overcome her like a shadow descending. Then she felt a chill run down her spine.

"Wyatt, move on the tape and tell Darryl I'll be in shortly," Ashley said.

"Where are you going?" Wyatt asked.

"There's something I've got to do. An emergency . . . I'll be there later," Ashley said.

She turned around and quickly walked toward her BMW, sticking out onto the Avenue.

CHAPTER 30

Reflection

In her car, Ashley took another look at the scene around Lee Circle, as she crossed over St. Charles Avenue. She looked again in her rearview mirror and saw paramedics loading the Reverend into an ambulance. As she drove farther away, all she saw in the mirror was General Lee floating in mid-air against a red-hot blue sky.

While steering with her left hand, she tunneled with her right hand into her embroidered purse that she bought in Vienna and retrieved her anti-bacterial gel which she spread between her fingers, thinking perhaps that would sanitize the scenes she just witnessed. As she continued driving, disturbing images from her encounter with the intruder the night before flashed across her mind, causing sweating and an accelerated heartbeat, and adrenalin to rush into her bloodstream, like snakes into a river. She pulled over in front of the Pontchartrain Hotel, a place where many uptowners frequented for receptions and late-night drinks – a place she knew well.

She looked at her hands because her fingertips felt numb. Her peripheral vision darkened, as she saw spots before her eyes. She began to hyperventilate. And then the snakes reached her brain, sunk their fangs deep and released their venom, making her feel like she was dying. Her hands shaking, she thought she was having a heart attack. She wondered if she should drive herself to the Baptist Hospital on Napoleon Avenue. She felt so extremely strange, like she was moving under water, and drowning.

"Miss Tarleton. Miss Tarleton," a tall black man in a doorman's uniform said, tapping on the window. "Are you okay?"

Ashley looked up and saw the man inquiring about her was Ronald, the doorman whom she had known for years.

Lowering the window, she said, "I think I'm OK. I just felt

strange for a minute. Thank you, Ronald."

"Okay. Just making sure. Can I get you anything?" he asked.

"No thank you," she said.

Ronald's concern and friendly familiar smile were like a shining light that she swam toward to reach the surface again. As she watched Ronald return to the hotel, she felt the nervousness subside significantly.

With no visible signs of illness or injury, she slowly reentered the single line of traffic on St. Charles Avenue. She looked at herself in the rearview mirror and checked for blood or discoloring on her face, but found nothing. She knew something strange had happened to her. But like the policemen she had just interviewed, she couldn't explain why. It was strange, she thought, that at age thirty, she should experience panic. Why, she wondered? A gun, she thought ironically, might calm her down. It had reached that point in her city and in her life where self-defense was necessary.

She turned left on Napoleon, a wide grand avenue with beautiful big homes, many of which were now sectioned into apartments and doctors' offices.

She turned right on Magazine Street which ran between and parallel to the River and St. Charles Avenue. It was the shopping district for all uptowners. Unique restaurants, coffee houses, antique shops, cool clothing stores, bars, bakeries, candy stores, bicycle shops, hobby shops, used furniture stores, galleries, eclectic home furnishing shops, food stores and others opened their doors every morning to welcome the unique mix of people who populated the uptown area. She knew this street well. She and her mother had shopped here all of her life. She loved the specialty of the street because it reflected her own.

Ashley made her way up Magazine, which ran straight through Audubon Park, splitting the park in two. The park was a serene sanctuary that was a living memory of what the landscape was like before eternity was interrupted my man and measurement.

When it reached the levee at the River, Magazine made a sharp right turn and its name changed to Leake Avenue, marking the underbelly of uptown.

As Ashley slowed to make the turn, she noticed an unsavory

character standing on the corner. He smiled at her as she looked over and said in a Strother-Martin-Confederate- Soldier-Deserter's voice, "Hi, missy! How you doing? You know you still owe me," he said, as he pointed to his leg.

Ashley did not recognize the homeless man she had accidentally tapped on the leg with her car a few nights before in the French Quarter. Frightened by his approach, she hit the gas pedal and sped around the corner onto the two-lane road. She took the corner so fast that she veered into the lane of oncoming traffic, nearly hitting a silver Infiniti sedan. She looked in the rearview mirror as she returned to her lane. She didn't see the man. She was now more committed to get a gun, she felt, as she passed Uptown Square shopping center on her right, only a few blocks from her home on Lowerline, which ended at the center's parking lot.

She continued up Leake and drove into Jefferson Parish where Leake turned into River Road. She remembered a story a reporter did at the station that mentioned a gun shop near Shrewsbury Road and Jefferson Highway. Gun sales there were reported to be suspiciously high. But it was the only gun shop of which she knew, and it was close.

She drove up River Road, passing the rear of Ochsner Hospital, and then she spotted Shrewsbury where she turned right, next to the River Shack, an old bar recently refurbished. Driving up Shrewsbury, she passed the Jefferson Parish Waterworks on the left and small houses on the right in this suburban area that was once wide-open pasture land. When she reached the stoplight at Jefferson Highway, she turned right, not knowing exactly where to go. After passing St. Agnes Church on the right, she spotted Elliot's Gun Shop on the right. The door's brown color was lighter around the edges, becoming increasingly dark toward the center, which was almost black.

She parked in between a black 1981 Oldsmobile Cutlass with tinted glass and sixteen-inch rims and a New Orleans blue and white police car. She stepped out of her car and walked into a Tenth Avenue Freeze-Out, involving a young black man who had just left the shop with one-hundred rounds of ammunition and a cop walking out with a bulletproof vest. She saw herself in the reflective lenses of the young man's mirrored sunglasses.

"I'm watching you," the cop said to the young man.

"Yeah. I'm watching you, too. You better look out, Miss Uptown white lady," he said to Ashley. "You might get caught in the crossfire."

"And if she does, it'll be because you started shooting," the cop said.

"Yeah, in self-defense," the young man quickly replied, as he got into his Oldsmobile and speedily pulled out with the cop close behind.

After struggling with the weight of the door, she finally managed to swing it open, as if it was the final gate to a lost treasure. She stepped onto a concrete floor and saw guns on all four walls that were probably estimated at a small fortune. Even the ceiling had four assault rifles hanging from it. Then she noticed that every wall was actually a giant mirror, giving the effect that each wall was an endless row of guns, vanishing deep into gun hell. There was also a mannequin wearing a bulletproof vest, camouflage uniforms, camping equipment, radios, walkie-talkies, canned goods, and paperbacks on survival and the coming apocalypse.

Behind the glass counter, wearing a NRA tee shirt, was a wiry, greasy, sticky, spidery man in his forties, who gave the shop an X-rated feel and look. She got the feeling she should watch where she stepped. She realized she was in the belly of the beast, the stomach of Satan, churning and turning twenty-four hours a day just to excrete guns. Above the mirror behind him was a sign, "Guns Don't Kill People. People Do."

"What can I do you for?" the man asked, looking over Ashley, head to toe, as he put down his shrimp po-boy sandwich on the butcher paper and wiped his hands on an oily rag.

"I'm interested in buying a gun," she said, noticing that one of his ears was smaller than the other.

"For yourself?" he asked.

"Yes," she said.

"You don't feel safe?" he asked.

"Yes. You could say that," she said.

"I know how you feel. Nobody feels safe in the city anymore. Did you see today's paper? Two more murders last night. And you can be sure we'll see more tonight. People are killed for the change in their pockets. It's like every night is a new fire to put out. So, you got to fight fire with firepower." As he looked into his case, he said, "How did you find out about me?"

"I saw a news story reporting your extremely high sales in firearms," she said.

"A sign of the times," he replied.

"Really?" she asked.

"Especially with women. A lot of women these days are feeling the need. About half my customers now are women. I shit you not." Noticing her reaction to that comment, he said, "Sorry. I got to remember to watch my language. Take a look at this," he said, as he took a long AK-47 assault rifle from the case. It has a wooden stock and a curved magazine. "AK-47 assault rifle. Russian made. Holds thirty rounds. Serious firepower."

"I don't need that," she said.

"I know. I'm just showing you what's on the streets today. The police have their hands full, fighting crazy assholes with these. Sorry if my language offends you. Go ahead and touch it. It's heavy," he said.

"I'd rather not," she said.

"I understand," he said. "But you got to know about guns to use them. You got to sleep with them, so-to-speak. In fact, many women do sleep with their guns under their pillows. I'm serious. Here's another favorite of the brothers." He placed a Tec-9 on the counter. It was short, black and lean with a long narrow clip. "Wouldn't think this would do much damage, but it does. Holds up to fifty rounds. 9mm. Semi-automatic. But it's easy and quick to make into an automatic. Used a lot in drive-bys. Not too accurate though. The police are out-gunned. They may win a battle here and there, but they're losing the war."

"And you're selling to both sides?" Ashley said, looking straight into his eyes.

"I'm a businessman," he said, with a sly smile.

"What's all that firepower over there? Are you in the business of war, too?" she said, pointing to another case.

"Those are from World War II." He picked up two guns to show her. "They're German," he said, holding a submachine gun with pistol grip. "This is a MP 40. Also a 9mm. Holds thirty-two rounds."

"Nazis used this?" Ashley asked.

"Yeah. Mostly platoon and squad leaders. Not really infantrymen like you see in the movies," he said, feeling proud of himself for his knowledge of munitions.

Ashley thought of Bella's family being herded onto cattle cars at the train station by German soldiers pointing this weapon at them. "Is this authentic?" she asked.

"You betcha," he said. "Collectors love this stuff."

"Is there a big market in New Orleans?" she asked.

"More than you think," he replied.

"Have you sold any to Keiffer Conright?" she asked.

"Sorry. I don't sell and tell. That wouldn't be nice," he said, with a smile.

"Do you have more of these?" she asked.

"Yeah. And I've got the mother of all German handheld weapons right over there," he said, pointing to a long, narrow rocket launcher in the corner that had a large egg-shaped warhead. "It's a *panzerfaust.*' It means 'armor fist,' or "tank fist.' Anti-tank weapon. The Allies and Soviets caught hell from these," he said, smiling and showing his stained teeth.

"And you don't feel guilty?" Ashley asked.

"We won the war, didn't we? Wait. I've got the mother of all machine guns." He opened a small utility closet and pulled out a large .50 caliber black machine gun. "I call this 'barely legal.' You could start a war with this. How would you like to put this on the hood of your car? You could make a tank." His eyes were fixed on hers, and then moved down to her chest. "It's got a forty-one-inch barrel with scope. Overall, it's fifty-seven inches. Comes with this attached bipod stand. My father fought in Nam. He said he used to position a .50 cal like this on a hilltop outside a village at night. He'd fire right into the little kitchen area every time the peasants would try to fix food. Just to scare them, you know."

Ashley realized that this sad man was trying to impress her the only way he knew how. This was his little world that smelled of shrimp, metal, and overcompensation.

"Fascinating," she feigned, "but do you have something small for me?"

"Sure. I'm sorry." He reached into the glass case and pulled out a Walther PPK and a Lady Smith .38 caliber snub nose. "If you like a sleek look, but a smaller caliber, there's the German PPK, .22 caliber, like the one James Bond used. Or a good old American made Smith & Wesson .36LS. It's the Lady Smith, .38 caliber snub nose, 5 shot. Stainless steel. Got easy to hold rosewood grips. It's been around forever. Good gun. The ladies like it a lot. Go ahead and hold it. Don't be afraid of it. To know your gun is to love your gun. It is your own personal savior."

"That's ridiculous," Ashley proclaimed.

"Your survival might depend on it some day," he warned.

She slid her fingers around the grip and tried to lift the gun, but she didn't use enough force, so it fell to the glass countertop.

"Sorry," she said.

"That's all right. Take a firm grip," he said, as Ashley made another attempt. "Now just pull it up to eye level and aim. Aim at the mannequin over there. Don't be afraid. Use two hands. Like this."

The man put his hands around hers and positioned her fingers correctly. On the inside, Ashley was screaming that he put his smelly, greasy hands on hers.

"I got it!" she exclaimed, moving away from his reach. "Fingers around grip and trigger. Arms stretched out. I've seen this on TV."

The door opened and a man in a jean jacket and baseball cap took a step inside. Ashley immediately pointed the gun at him.

"Jesus!" the man said, backing out of the door hurriedly.

"Sorry! I'm sorry," she said, lowering the gun.

"You better give that back to me, Tex. You're kind of dangerous, even if the gun isn't loaded. Tell you what . . . I'll take you behind the levee right now and we'll fire off a few pops," he suggested.

"No. Not necessary," she said, handing him the gun. "I'll take it."

"You'll need some bullets," he said.

"I'll take those, too," she said, pulling out her American Express card.

"Okay. I'll ring you up. But you really need lessons," he added.

"Don't we all," Ashley slyly said.

She walked outside and noticed the man in the baseball cap standing off to the side of the building.

"I'm very sorry," she shouted. "Reflex." The man rushed inside before she backed out.

She retrieved a small squeeze bottle of anti-bacterial liquid soap. She rubbed it all over her hands and fingers. She noticed that a piece of butcher paper was stuck to her shoe. She threw it out the window. She took the gun out of its box and saw her warped reflection on the steel. She felt a sadness overwhelm her and a tightness climb her back and wrap around her neck like a vine. She wondered if her daily routine from this point on would include carrying a gun. She wondered if her city would remain under clouds of sadness and ignorance to be forgotten and dismantled, its timber and bricks used to build a different city, or would it self-destruct, to be unearthed and studied years from now when anthropologists would say, "This is how they lived and died in New Orleans in 1994. Let's study their primitive ways."

She thought also about her future and if she had one here. Then she thought about her mother's eventual death. The vine around her throat tightened. She felt an ache in her stomach. Her intuition told her to get to her mother's house immediately. She put the gun in its box and placed it on the floor. As she started her car, she could smell smoke and fire in the air and, in the distance, she heard a scream of Munch-like proportions.

CHAPTER 31

Dream

Ashley drove down River Road and down Oak Street where River Road and Leake Avenue intersected. A tall, dusty whirlwind caught her eye on the corner, across the street, as she came to a stop. A small, wooden sign with the word "PRAY" written on it, leaning against a building, could be seen vibrating and then was sucked up into the air by the force of the wind to carry its message to another city.

Oak Street was a two-way narrow street made more so due to cars parked on both sides. F. W. Woolworth Company, and many other specialty shops, made their homes here in the past. But since the late 1970s it had largely become a forgotten shopping district. A few small restaurants and live music clubs had moved in, attracting a young late-night crowd which didn't rise with the insistent sun, but rather was repelled from it, like Dracula feasting on the comforting warm, thick, liquid night.

She drove a few blocks to South Carrollton Avenue where she made a right turn. A streetcar was running parallel to her on the neutral ground. Its familiar humming sound and steel wheels on steel rails made her look up at the passengers looking down at her, only thirty feet away.

She passed small businesses, houses, an apartment building, a bar and the Camellia Grill where she and friends had spent many good times eating the specialty of large round waffles under a lake of syrup with a chocolate freeze drink while listening to Mr. Harry, the longtime waiter, tell his amusing anecdotes to cheer his patrons.

She turned left onto St. Charles Avenue where South Carrollton ended. She drove past Lowerline Street on which she lived. At this end of St. Charles, apartments were mixed with homes less ornate, though still appealing.

Ashley was now speeding and felt an urgency to see her mother. She got behind a slow moving Mercedes sedan and blew the horn. But the elderly, blue-haired uptown matron blew back and continued her slow pace through the warm, windy, humid air. So Ashley illegally passed her in the right lane and quickly reached Audubon Park on the right, across St. Charles from Tulane and Loyola Universities. The homes grew stately past these landmarks. As she was nearing her parents' home, she felt her nervousness rising. She knew something was wrong. Then, one and a half blocks from her parents' home on the left, she saw an ambulance exiting the driveway, red lights flashing. She got right behind the ambulance and could see her mother on the stretcher with Beverly sitting next to her, holding her hand. A paramedic was administering oxygen.

Ashley tried to get Beverly's attention by standing up in her car, but Beverly didn't notice her. She followed the ambulance a few blocks. When it turned left onto Napoleon Avenue and ran the red light, she ran it, too. Her long auburn hair blew wildly in the wind, as she raced behind the ambulance, and then ran the light at Freret Street and the one at Magnolia, too, nearly hitting crossing pedestrians in front of the large red brick Baptist Hospital that was built in the 1920s and took up one square block.

The ambulance turned left on Clara Street and up the ramp on the side to the ER entrance. Ashley was right behind. Ashley quickly exited her car and rushed to the ambulance just as the paramedics were lifting her mother onto a gurney. Ashley felt the need to touch her mother, as if touching her might transfer some magical healing powers from one who was well to one who was sick. So she clasped her mother's hand in hers. Her mother opened her eyes, as if she knew Ashley's touch, and smiled. Her eyes quickly closed as the paramedics rushed her through the sliding doors, through the waiting area and down a short hallway. Ashley stood at the edge of the hall and the waiting room and watched her mother being rolled into a room. Tears came, her stomach churned, and she felt snakes slithering within her veins.

"Why don't you come sit down, baby," Beverly said, pointing to a nearby row of cushioned chairs. They sat down and Beverly continued, "I tried calling you at work and your mobile phone, too. They said you were on an assignment."

"I was. Where's my father?" Ashley asked.

"I tried calling him, too," Beverly said. "But his secretary said she didn't know. He was home this morning. In fact, he fixed your mother her breakfast."

Ashley looked around the quiet, clean waiting room. There were two other occupants, both white, nervously paging through magazines.

"Beverly, I'm out of my mind with worry. One of these days she'll go into the ER and not come out. This could be that day," Ashley said, as snakes entered her bloodstream again.

"Don't say that. Dr. Yodl is a good doctor. He comes from a long line of doctors in his family. They been in New Orleans over a hundred years. If anyone can find out what's wrong with your mama, he can. And he will," Beverly said, reassuringly.

"I hope you're right, Beverly. Thank you," Ashley said.

"I know I'm right. She's going to be okay. I'm positive. I got a way with these things. Beverly knows. It comes in handy when you got kids," she said, with a big smile.

The sliding doors opened and a white teenage girl, wearing her gray Ursuline Academy uniform, hopped in on one leg and helped by her father saying, "It's just a sprained ankle. It'll be fine."

"I'm going to call father's office again," Ashley said.

As she got up, she saw her father walk through the sliding doors and she walked into his opened arms. She felt relief and comfort as she rested her head on his starched shirt over his broad chest and felt his strong arms around her torso. She could also feel the warm air from his nostrils on the top of her head at the same time a rush of warm air came streaming in through the opened sliding doors and under her skirt. His Ralph Lauren cologne filled her nostrils. And she heard his steady heartbeat. Ever since she was a little girl, she never felt more secure than in her father's arms. She cried on his shoulders.

"Everything will be fine. Has the doctor spoken with you yet?" her father said, as they walked toward a row of chairs.

"No," she said, sitting down.

"He'll take care of her. Don't worry," he said, putting his arm around her shoulder and kissing the top of her head.

"Beverly said you fixed breakfast for her. How was she then?" Ashley asked.

"She was fine. A little drowsy from her medications. They often cause nausea," he said.

"That's true. And she was nauseous. But she was also pale and complained of difficulty breathing and dizziness. So, I became alarmed," Beverly said.

"You did the right thing, Beverly," Tarleton said.

"Yes, you did," echoed Ashley. "Thanks."

"She'll be fine," Beverly assured.

"I hope so," Ashley said, nervously, feeling the weight of uncertainty and resignation. "I hope so." She slid back in her chair, leaned her head back and drove her fingers through her hair like two large combs. She then began massaging her scalp.

"You look really tired. Were you able to get any sleep at all last night?" her father asked.

"Not much," Ashley replied.

"I arranged for an officer to patrol your neighborhood after your call," her father said.

"Good. Thank you," Ashley said.

"I pulled some strings. They'll be there tonight, too. But I would rather you slept at the house tonight," her father said.

"No. I'll be okay," Ashley said.

"I figured you would say that," her father said.

"You know me well," she said.

"Well, I am your father. I still think you should pull back on the reporting. It's a nasty trade. Come work for me," her father said.

"I've got to pull my own weight and find my own way," Ashley said.

"You can still do that and work for me," he said.

"I like what I'm doing," she said.

"Do you? Driving over here I heard about Lee Circle. I was extremely worried about you. And you liked being in the middle of that mess with those people? Stay out of it. You're going to get hurt," he said.

"I can take care of myself," she said.

"Shots were fired today, Ashley. That kind of violence you can't see coming until it's too late. It's a different New Orleans now than the one you grew up in. You should know that by now," her father said, forcefully.

"I do know. But it's still my city. And I've got a job to do. Thank you for your concern and your love." She hugged him and stood up. "I've got to call Darryl and let him know where I am."

She walked to her car, reached inside, grabbed the phone from the console and punched in Darryl's number. As she told him about her mother's condition, she noticed two red ants approaching each other on the concrete. One carried a large cookie crumb, high in its jaws. The two met and clashed, locked in each other's grip, rolling like a tiny red ball on the cement battlefield. About a minute later they separated. The owner picked up its crumb and continued on its way. The other ant crookedly limped away in the opposite direction, toward obsurity.

After informing Darryl that her return to the station was dependent on her mother's progress, Ashley re-entered the waiting room, sat next to her father and rested her head on his shoulder. Having lost sleep the night before, she quickly gained entrance to a dreamscape where she saw her mother and herself as a young girl, riding in a green Jaguar sedan, her mother driving and wearing a fine wool cobalt blue suit, passing beautiful homes under towering oaks as they glided down the avenue, and then around Lee Circle, heading into the CBD where her father's office was located in the Hibernia Bank building across the street from the parking garage her mother always used. They would ride the golden Otis elevator to the seventh floor to visit him, she hugging him, and then slipping her hand inside his starched shirt pocket to unseal it. They would then walk to Baronne Street a block away to visit the dark cavernous nave of the 137-year-old Jesuit Church. She remembered holding her mother's hand and walking on a cushiony wooden floor, overhearing many monologues to God, whispered in hopeful earnestness by petitioners in need of immediate deliverance. Her mother would drop coins in the slot of an iron box at the base of an iron rack that held one-hundred candles in small red glass holders. She would then take a slender white stick, catch a fire from one candle and baptize another with the flame. After saying a prayer, they would exit the church, cross the street and enter Leo Miller Jewelry, where her mother bought her emeralds and diamonds. With her hand firmly clasped in her mother's, they pushed onto Canal Street, the widest street in the country and named for a canal that was never dug.

Canal's sidewalks were full of shoppers scurrying from one store to another, like Maison Blanche, Godchaux's, Kreegers, purple-ribboned Russell Stover, Rubenstein's, Krauss, Imperial and F.W. Woolworth. Sometimes they would meet a friend of her mother's under the clock suspended above the entrance to D.H. Holmes department store, just before eating lunch in its restaurant. After lunch, they would cross to Maison Blanche's department store by using the side entrances on Dauphine. Ashley always thought of it as a secret passage from one department store to the other, bypassing the crowd on Canal Street. And she knew many of the salespeople by their first names. Being with her mother was an adventure and fun. Now those stores and that time were history; the buildings were still there but occupied by hotel chains and tee shirt shops. Strangers had moved in.

Then Ashley dreamt of a dark figure standing near her mother's bed as she lay ill and sleeping. Ashley's heart began to race and she woke up in a panic, gasping for air. When she opened her eyes, she saw a man in a dark suit talking to a doctor. She walked toward them and realized it was her father, who had put on his navy suit coat, talking to Dr. Yodl. Her heartbeat quickened as she approached them. She feared bad news.

"How's mother, Doctor Yodl?" she anxiously inquired, as her father placed his arm around her shoulders.

"I was just telling your father that she's resting. She vomited twice and that seems to have helped. We pumped her stomach to flush its remains. It may have been a bad reaction to something she ate. What did she have today?" the doctor asked.

"I think it was grits. I'll ask Beverly," Mr. Tarleton said.

"But Beverly said you prepared breakfast," Ashley said, puzzled.

"No. She was eating when I checked in on her. I fixed breakfast for myself," he said.

"Well, I want to do some tests, including blood work and an electrocardiogram. We must keep in mind that she has a slight heart murmur and Mitral Valve Prolapse. If she ingested something that perhaps she was allergic to, that would definitely be injurious to her health. If all goes well, she can go home tomorrow, or more likely the next day," the doctor said.

"Oh, that's good news," Ashley said, relieved. Her heartbeat was slowing, as if it, too, was listening. "Can we see her?"

"Sure, for a few minutes," the doctor said.

They walked down the hall and entered the room where Mrs. Tarleton was lying, her right arm hooked to an intravenous feeding tube. To reassure herself that her mother was still breathing, Ashley watched her mother's chest rise and fall. Then she cupped her hand inside her mother's. Her mother opened her eyes and a thin smile appeared on her gaunt face. Her mother's frailty sent a shiver down Ashley's spine.

"Are you okay?" Ashley asked.

Her mother nodded once. Ashley could see she was too weak to respond to any questioning.

"We'll let you rest," Mr. Tarleton said.

"We'll be back later. Dr. Yodl will do some tests. You'll be back home soon. I promise. Beverly will stay with you," Ashley said.

They left the room, Ashley wiping away tears. Her father put his arm around Ashley and said, "Come on now. She'll be fine."

"What's wrong with her? It's like she's in limbo between life and death every day. They still don't know what is really wrong with her. She's suffering all the time," Ashley said, visibly upset.

"The doctor will find what's wrong. I'm confident of that," her father said.

They met Beverly in the waiting room.

"How's Miss Tarleton?" Beverly said.

"She's weak, but doing a little better," Mr. Tarleton said. "You'll stay with her, won't you, Beverly? I've got to get back to the office."

"Sure, I will. I won't budge," Beverly said, reassuringly.

"I'll call you," he said, as he kissed Ashley on the cheek and exited through the sliding doors.

"Beverly, are you sure my father fixed breakfast for my mother?" Ashley asked.

"Sure, I'm sure. He insisted. He brought it to her on a good silver tray. Why?" Beverly asked.

"The doctor said it may have been something she ate," Ashley said.

"I can't see how. We've been using those grits all week," Beverly said.

"Okay. Thanks, Beverly. I'll be at the station, then I'll be back," Ashley said.

"I'll be here," Beverly said.

"Thanks."

Ashley exited, got into her BMW, drove down the ramp and turned right onto Clara, a one-way street. An approaching driver blew his horn. She realized her mistake but kept going, turning right onto Napoleon Avenue and left onto St. Charles. Down the Avenue she glided, running a red light or two while thinking of the past, the present, and frightful future. She was nauseous and tasted fear.

CHAPTER 32

Deliver Us From Evil

After Ashley filed her report on the five o'clock news, she stopped by Darryl's office.

"You did a good job, considering all that happened to you today. How's your mother?" Darryl asked, sitting behind his desk, eating Elmer's caramel popcorn and drinking a Big Shot cream soda.

"She's in stable condition. The doctor's doing tests. I'm heading back there now. It's got me all twisted inside that they can't find what's wrong with her. Have you heard about the Reverend's condition?" Ashley asked.

"He's in Charity. He'll pull through. Want some popcorn?" Darryl asked, extending a bag of Elmer's caramel popcorn.

"No thanks," Ashley said.

"Election's Saturday. Ready?" he asked.

"Ready," she said. "Even though I'm worried about mother, I am definitely ready."

"I believe you. Get some real angry faces and some real joyful ones. We can't use any in between. Not good TV," Darryl admitted.

"I understand. We will deliver," Ashley said, but feeling nervous that she wouldn't.

"I want you and Wyatt at Conright's headquarters," Darryl said.

"Okay."

"Try to piss him off again, like you did in the debate. I want that reaction shot. Say something like the City Council won't work with him; we'll lose tourists; he's a Nazi," Darryl said, laughingly.

"Give me some good TV!"

"Will do," Ashley said, as she noticed the time on the Felix-the-Cat-with-the ticking-tail clock on the wall. "Let me go. Got to visit mother."

"Right. My prayers are with her," Darryl said.

"Thanks."

"You're sure you're okay? You look tired," he said.

She was about to mention the burglar she encountered the night before, but decided against it. Darryl might see it as another psychological distraction and might shake his confidence in her, she thought. She knew he had misgivings about her assignments already. She didn't want to overburden him.

"I'm fine. I can manage. See you tomorrow," Ashley said.

"Okay. Get some rest," Darryl suggested.

"I will," she said, with a smile, knowing it was impossible. Then she said, "Have you seen Wyatt? I want to talk to him about Saturday."

"He left already. He had to go pick up his daughter at school in Old Metairie," Darryl said. "How are you two getting along?" Darryl asked.

"Okay. We've had our differences. But we're good," she said.

"He's a good guy. He's been doing this for about ten years. He's sort of an investigative reporter in his own right. He can furnish you some leads. He knows a lot of people. All cameramen do," he said.

"All right. Good night," she said.

"See ya," he said.

She exited the station through the rear garage, dodged a pile of garbage and walked toward her car in the parking lot across Chartres Street. She then heard a whimpering sound from behind her. She turned around to see the weathered face of a tall, slender, sad Modigliani-looking woman and a young boy about eight years old. Over the boy's whimpering and with her hands on his shoulders, she said, "Can you help us please?"

"No. I don't have anything to give. Sorry," Ashley said and turned away.

But the child's whimpering, obviously motivated by hunger and poverty, reverberated in her mind. Only a few steps from her car, she decided to return and help the woman. When she turned around and retraced her steps, she found no one. She looked up and down Chartres but they had vanished. However, she could still hear the boy's cries as if he stood right in front of her.

She then looked to her right again down Chartres and there, a few yards from the St. Louis Cathedral, was the little girl in the white dress and bare feet she encountered the day before. She walked toward the girl and could see she was crying.

"Why are you crying?" Ashley asked.

"My friend is dead," the girl said, wiping her eyes.

"I'm sorry. How did he die?" Ashley asked.

"He was beaten to death by Satan," the girl said.

"Satan?" Ashley asked.

"Yes. He has taken human form. His name is Dennis," the girl said.

"Human form? Do you mean Dennis Mena, the young man called Dennis the Menace?" Ashley asked.

"Yes. Satan," the girl said.

"Watch out!" Ruthie the Duck Girl screamed, as she rounded the corner on her skates, nearly hitting Ashley.

Ashley jumped out of the way. After a few moments, she looked around to see the girl entering St. Louis Cathedral. She followed.

She entered the rear of the Cathedral which was dark and full of tourists whispering and seemingly afraid to venture into the nave.

Ashley bumped into several elderly ladies wearing tee shirts from the Busy Bee Crochet Club of Pennsylvania and asked, "Did you see a little girl come in here alone? She was barefoot."

They looked at each other and one said, "No. No little girl."

"Are you sure? She came through these doors a minute ago," Ashley said.

Another said, "No. We didn't see any little girl," as each looked at one another.

Ashley moved slowly toward the gift shop where most tourists were congregating. She bumped into a middle-aged couple whose faces appeared to float from the darkness into a soft light, Caravaggio-like.

"Have you seen a little girl by herself here?" Ashley asked.

"No," they said in unison, and submerged beneath the darkness.

Ashley then began walking up the center aisle, looking in all the pews. She thought she heard a girl's voice near the altar, so she walked to the first pew but didn't see the girl. As she approached a woman in prayer, the woman suddenly stood up.

"Do you know what it means to suffer?" the woman asked Ashley, while staring at the large crucifix behind the altar. "Can you imagine that dark day on Golgotha and how he suffered for us? Agony. He was in agony – for us!"

Ashley saw pain and compassion in the woman's naked face. The woman's eyes were transfixed on the crucified Christ, Lamb of God, who suffered to take away the sins of this world without end. Ashley knew that the woman's belief in the invisible was real. The woman had reached a place in her journey that Ashley had yet to reach.

Ashley thought she again heard a child's voice near the right aisle. She investigated the noise but found only more agony in a row of paintings along the way depicting Christ crowned with thorns and his humiliation on the *Via Dolorosa*.

Ashley stepped into a web of humid air as she left the cathedral. An early evening shower had just ended. Buildings sweated rain drops, as life returned to Jackson Square. The Tarot card readers were setting up their tables again, with a candle on each one. Ruthie the Duck Girl rolled past on her roller skates with beer in hand, as her duck tried to keep up. The fish-eyed elderly woman appeared around the corner, constantly walking her path to nowhere, looking like Blanche Dubois in her later years, burned and driven mad by the heat and by the Stanleys of the world. A resident of the Pontalba Apartments looked down from his balcony on the tranquil scene of lovers kissing, tourists taking photos, a Dylan impersonator singing, "The vagabond who's rapping at your door is wearing the clothes that you once wore," and the surrounding lights beneath a frail veil of repentance that would soon collapse to the weight of the ways of the flesh.

Two young women holding lilies crossed her path. She stopped and wondered where they were going and why. She turned and saw a middle-aged man and woman carrying carnations and gladiolas, as they rounded the corner at St. Peter Street. They walked in front of the Cabildo, St. Louis Cathedral and Presbytere, and in the direction of the two female flower bearers and then down St. Ann between Jackson Square and the Pontalba Apartments and shops. And now, very curious, Ashley followed the flowers down Decatur Street past Progress Grocery, muffalatta-heaven Central Grocery, Santa's Workshop, a coffeehouse which was once a "head shop" called "Nectar" in the 1970s, restaurants, bars, antique shops, retro-avant-garde clothing stores, and other specialty shops. Across the street was the fresh produce market itself, now over one-hundred years old. She looked behind her and saw three men carrying white mums. She let them pass her on Decatur and then noticed a mournful crowd of people blocking the sidewalk and spilling out onto the street a few blocks down. When the slow, sorrowful parade reached that point, the flower bearers before her laid their flowers on the sidewalk of the Louisiana Pizza Kitchen where five workers had been murdered the night before, execution-style with bullets to the back of their heads, and left in the freezer.

Ashley burrowed through the crowd of people of all ages and ethnicities, emerging to discover yet another all-too-common horizontal garden of beautiful rainbow-colored flowers leaning next to the closed French doors and fanning out onto the sidewalk like a velvet cape. She looked around her and saw somber faces, some people resting their heads on shoulders. Strangers had bonded with each other in an hour that would otherwise have taken weeks, months or years. She had stepped through the membrane of grief where whimpering and tears hung in the air like clouds and rain.

"I can see them," an elderly lady said, her face thin and

wrinkled.

"Who?" Ashley said.

"The spirits of the murder victims. I can see them. They're near the flowers, reading the condolence cards. And they're crying, too," the lady said.

"You're psychic, then?" Ashley asked.

"Yes, since I was a little girl. I didn't know how to handle it then. It was frightening. As I got older, I realized I possessed what some people call a 'sixth sense.' It's just something that I live with. It's part of who I am. I use my gift to help the victims, if I can," the lady said.

"What do you know about these victims?" Ashley asked.

"Only what I see and sense. I feel some of them here understand what happened to them," she said. "But I sense one or two don't. They're standing here like they're mourners and not victims. There are many more ghosts in New Orleans now. Victims. They roam the halls of these buildings and walk these streets, not really knowing what happened to them. Many have been traumatized. And they're in pain. A lot of pain. We're all like that in a way."

"How do you mean?" Ashley asked.

"We live our lives not really knowing much about anything, not even about ourselves. And then time runs out, sooner for some than others. And it's over. It's sad. Most never see the end coming. We're all blind," the lady said, like a somber alarm.

"I can't take any more of this," a young woman to their right said. "It's every day. I can't take it," she cried, as her boyfriend comforted her.

A teenaged girl wearing a black shawl walked to the edge of the horizontal garden, lit a candle, let some wax drip onto a small tin ashtray from the Café du Monde, positioned the candle on the ashtray and placed it on the sidewalk. She then lit other small candles from it and passed them out to mourners. An older woman helped her. Soon the somber scene was aglow with candlelight as night fell.

Ashley stood among the mourners and ghosts and watched

candle flames flicker as a warm wind splintered and passed through the crowd like purple ribbons.

Some people openly wept, some consoled others, and some prayed.

Our Father who art in Heaven,

Hallowed be Thy Name.

Thy Kingdom come,

Thy will be done,

On Earth as in Heaven.

Give us this day our daily bread,

And forgive us our trespasses,

As we forgive those who trespass against us.

And lead us not into temptation,

But deliver us from evil.

Amen.

The psychic closed her eyes. The heavens cried.

CHAPTER 33

Friend

When Ashley reached her car, she let out a sigh because she had again left her top down. Though afternoon or evening rain fell almost every day during the summer and well into September, she often did not remember to put her top up. She retrieved a towel from her trunk and wiped off her blue leather seats. As she turned around to get into her car, she thought she saw a man looking at her from the street. When she looked again, she saw no one. She thought possibly that the homeless man she saw earlier was following her. She didn't see anyone as she exited the corner parking lot and headed up Decatur across Canal and down to Poydras where she turned left onto St. Charles Avenue, looking in her rearview mirror all the way.

It was a little after 8:00 p.m. when she rounded Lee Circle on her return to Baptist Hospital. She drove slowly under the Avenue's cavernous canopy of old oak trees which blocked not only severe southern sunlight but also soft illuminating moonlight, making a nighttime drive on the Avenue a dark journey.

Ashley checked her rearview mirror again and noticed a large car with four headlights that seemed to slow down when she did. She tapped her brake pedal, making the monstrous car slow down. Her fingers tingled and tightened around the steering wheel. Her adrenalin spigot began to drip. She glanced at the gun on the floor.

She stopped at the Felicity Street red light and checked her mirror. The sedan slowly came to a stop two car lengths behind her. She saw two figures on the front seat, aglow in red light from her brake lights. She wondered if it was that car that had followed her from Yvette's apartment and drove down her street.

The light turned green and she slowly accelerated up the avenue. The car followed. She checked her mirror again as she passed Smith's Records and the Pontchartrain Hotel. She tapped her brakes and the car slowed down. She saw the passenger point at her. Snakes, she feared, were stirring.

She continued up St. Charles and stopped at the red light at Louisiana Avenue. Even though there was room for the car to pass on her right, it stayed several car lengths behind her. And now she thought she saw the passenger handling a metallic object, perhaps a gun, she thought. She punched in her father's number on her car phone, but he didn't answer.

When the light turned green, she drove a couple of blocks, and then pulled over to let the car pass. But the car stopped in the middle of the avenue about three car lengths behind her. Horns blew. Ashley wrapped her sweaty hand around the rosewood gun handle, lowered her window and peeked out. Now she was certain that was the car that followed her home. She knew the snakes were loose. Her stomach was in knots and she felt movement in her urinary tract. With trembling hands, she lifted the gun to her side, as a streetcar hummed and glided past.

The car made a sudden turn onto the streetcar tracks, continuing up and parallel to Ashley, who was pointing the gun at the men.

"Why are you following me?" Ashley shouted.

"Have you lost your mind? Put down that gun. We're not following you. We're trying to get away from you," the passenger shouted back.

"Why?" Ashley asked.

"Because you're a shitty driver. You're dangerous. Stay off the road. You're nuts!" the passenger shouted.

The car turned onto the Avenue again and sped away.

Ashley realized it was her driving that sparked the incident. She wasn't being followed at all.

Sweating and fatigued, she dropped the gun in the box on the floor and rested her head against the steering wheel. The words of one mourner at the restaurant haunted her. "I can't take it anymore," reverberated in her head. The stresses of living in fear, her job and her mother's mystery illness were taking their toll on her. She thought only of her mother now. She had to make it to the hospital before visiting hours were over. The people in the cars passing by looked at her as if she was a crazy person. She covered the left side of her face with her hand and looked straight ahead. Baptist Hospital on Napoleon Avenue was only a few blocks away. The only thing on her mind now was to get to her mother.

When she accelerated onto the Avenue again, she didn't check her mirrors until she heard the screeching sound of tires grinding to a halt and then a loud thud.

She hit the brakes, stuck her head out of the window and saw a 1970s' bronze-colored Buick Electra 225 smashed against an iron lamp post, its plastic silver grill on the streetcar tracks. Then she heard a baby crying. The passenger door opened and a black woman in her thirties, wearing a New Orleans Saints tee shirt, stepped out, holding the crying toddler.

"Didn't you see us coming!?" the woman shouted.

"What do you mean? I was just . . ." Ashley said, nervously, still in her car.

"You was just what? You pulled out right in front of us," the woman said.

"I didn't cause this," Ashley said, remembering her father's advice to never accept blame for anything.

"You most certainly did. My husband swerved to miss you. And it's lucky he did or else all of us would have been seriously injured. I got to get my baby to Charity for x-rays. I think he hit his head. Come on let's go," she said, moving toward Ashley's car. "Hector, stay here and wait for the police," she ordered, as Hector looked through the windshield.

"You can call an ambulance," Ashley suggested.

"I'm not waiting on an ambulance. I'll be here all night. They're busy picking up gunshot victims every night. If you don't take me, I'm taking you. I'll take that sports car of yours. I got to get my son to Charity Hospital," the woman demanded.

Ashley thought for a minute. She didn't want to cause a scene between a white and black and end up on the news. If she didn't accept blame, like her father always taught, she'd be okay.

"Get in," Ashley said.

"You know you got a gun on the floor here," the woman said, getting in the passenger seat, cradling her baby.

"Yes. Just push it aside," Ashley said.

"I don't blame you. You need one to live in this city. We got three," the woman admitted.

Ashley made a U-turn on St. Charles Avenue and headed toward Lee Circle. She felt exceedingly uncomfortable. Every muscle was stretched. She straightened up in her seat, focusing one eye on the road and the other on the woman and child. She didn't think she caused the accident. And she always followed her father's advice to never accept blame for anything.

"I'm not sure which way to go," Ashley confided.

"Just keep going straight until you reach Lee Circle, then take a left toward the bus station," the woman instructed.

"I don't know where that is," Ashley confessed.

"I'll show you," the woman said. Then she comforted her son by saying, "Come on. Come on. It'll be alright, sugar." She kissed his forehead. "Mama's here."

Ashley picked up the car phone and dialed Baptist Hospital.

"Mrs. Tarleton's room, please," Ashley said. "Beverly, how's mother?"

"She's fine. Resting. Where are you?" Beverly asked.

"I'm in my car. There was an accident. I'm driving a lady and her baby to Charity," Ashley said.

"Oh, Lord! Is the baby hurt?" Beverly inquired.

"I don't think so. I'll tell you more later," Ashley said.

"Okay. Well, don't worry about your mother. I'll be here," Beverly said.

"Thank you, Beverly. You're heaven-sent," Ashley said.

"Oh, I know that. But tell my kids, will you?" Beverly asked, laughingly.

"I will. And I'll be there within the hour," Ashley said.

"Okay. We'll be here," Beverly assured.

"All right. Bye, bye."

Ashley replaced the phone.

"Turn left here," the woman said, as they reached Lee Circle.

"On Howard?" Ashley asked.

"I don't know the name. But I know it leads to the bus station. See it up ahead?" the woman pointed out.

"Oh, you mean the train station," Ashley said, spying the 1930s building straight ahead. "My mother always takes the train. She prefers it."

"It doesn't matter what I prefer. I got to take Greyhound to my sisters in Mississippi. I have no choice. Take a right up here at the light." Ashley turned right onto Loyola Avenue, across the street from the terminal. "Get in your left lane. Turn left on Gravier," the woman directed, as they passed City Hall and approached Charity's rear emergency entrance.

She drove up the ramp at Charity Hospital's emergency room entrance as an ambulance was leaving. She got out and opened the passenger's door. The woman handed her the child so she could get out more easily. Ashley looked at the boy who had calmed down considerably during the ride. She felt a little strange holding a black child, like she did a few days before in the St. Thomas housing project when Alicia held on to her. Her knowledge about black people and her familiarity of how they lived was almost like meeting foreigners for the first time. She was uncomfortable and she didn't quite know why. She looked into the child's beautiful brown eyes and hoped he was okay, and that she wasn't the cause of any harm.

She handed the baby back to the woman. As she followed the woman through the sliding doors, she seemingly entered a portal to another world. The waiting room was packed with poor people, men, women and children of every color. Their faces were long and drawn. Their eyes were full of worry, doubt, fear and tears. Some sat bent over with heads in their hands. Others stood like mourners at a grave site. Most of the people had relatives or friends undergoing emergency treatment due to violence or drug overdose. These people were some of society's oppressed and forgotten. If Jesus was alive and visited this city, Charity Hospital is the first place he would come.

During her observation of the people in the waiting room area, Ashley realized she was being observed by those same people. She was well dressed in a tailored suit. Her hair was pulled back with a tortoise shell headband and she looked like she stepped from a page in *Town and Country* magazine. She was a suspicious character and knew she should leave.

Suddenly she heard voices and sounds of a struggle coming from the room at the end of the nearby hallway down which were other rooms where the most serious medical emergency patients were treated, initiating a lot of activity in that area. Ashley saw glimpses of a young woman being held down by doctors and nurses who were attempting to administer a sedative. She was cursing the staff as her arms and legs went flailing, left and right, up and down.

A doctor in green scrubs stepped out from a curtained area down the hall and walked up to a woman sitting down. When she saw him, she stood up and moved slowly toward him. She wore a "sunrise-sunset" tee shirt with a large photo of her teenage daughter on it.

"How's my boy?" she asked with tears in her eyes and clutching her chest.

"Mrs. Evangeline, we did all we could. He's gone. I'm terribly sorry. The wounds were large and severe. He lost a lot of blood," the doctor said.

"Jesus! No, Jesus!" the woman said falling to her knees, weighted by grief. A family member comforted her. "First my girl. Now my boy. Lay your healing hands on my boy, Jesus. Raise my boy!"

An ambulance siren was heard outside the sliding doors, loudly heralding the approach of another fallen New Orleanian. The sliding doors opened behind Ashley as a paramedic pushed a gurney through them. Ashley turned to see a blood-soaked bandage around the head of Alicia, the young girl she met in the St. Thomas housing project who wanted to be her friend. Ashley was close enough to see the girl open one eye, smile at Ashley and whisper the word, "friend." Ashley felt a wave of fear and adrenalin rush through her body. Then Alicia's mother rushed in behind the gurney, as the girl was taken down the hall and behind a curtain.

"My God, what happened" Ashley asked, wiping away tears.

"She got caught in the crossfire. She was on the porch when they started shooting," Betty Johnson said, also wiping away tears from a face full of pain.

"Who?" Ashley asked.

"Her brother, Mark, and his thug friends had it out with their enemies in the yard in front of my apartment," Betty said. "I'm afraid she's going to die. You can't stop those boys. They're all involved with guns and drugs. I can't take no more of this. My baby's dying."

"No, she won't. They'll save her. This ER is one of the best in the country. A reporter at my TV station did a story on Charity. Come here and sit down. I'll get you some water," Ashley said, as she brought Betty to a couch.

A paramedic stepped through the sliding doors and said, "Who owns that BMW convertible? Get it off the ramp. It's for ambulances only!"

Ashley ran to her car and started it. Her mind was now occupied with racing thoughts. She felt an adrenalin rush more powerful than earlier in the day. The snakes were loose. Alicia's bandaged face flashed across her mind. She kept hearing the word "friend." Tears rolled down her face. She hit the steering wheel with her fist several times. She unconsciously pushed her foot down on the pedal, revving the engine higher. She inadvertently hit the automatic shifter and the car raced down the ramp. Alarmed, she turned the steering wheel hard, making a sharp U-turn on Gravier, a one-way street. She tried to regain control but steered the car across the rolling lawn in front of City Hall, and then down to the sidewalk and onto Loyola Avenue. It appeared the car was driving her, as she took a left on Howard Avenue and blew the light at Lee Circle. But now as she headed up St. Charles, she knew she had to find Mark in the St. Thomas housing project. She personally wanted to bring him to Charity.

Driven by fury, Ashley sped up the Avenue until traffic came to a halt. She looked out of the window and saw the flashing lights of a tow truck up ahead a few blocks. She quickly realized the tow truck was removing the wrecked Buick from the accident scene that she had caused. She turned left, just missing a streetcar rolling on the neutral ground, and shot across the other side of the avenue toward the River. After passing large, stately homes on both sides, she turned right onto Prytania Street. She drove to Washington Avenue and looked right, noticing Commander's Palace on one side of the street and Lafayette Cemetery on the other. This was very familiar territory to her. Brunch at Commander's was a longstanding tradition in her family. She blew the light and turned left, headed toward the River again. The houses became less stately and, in her mind, the people more suspect.

She tried to remember the streets Wyatt used earlier in the week, as she traveled deeper into the forbidden zone. But that was impossible in the dark. She kept driving until she finally came to a dimly lit St. Thomas street sign and rounded that corner like a roller coaster, narrowly missing an emerald green Pontiac. Reason wrapped in fear told her not to do this. But her heart told her she had to do it – for a friend.

She saw the housing project ahead down the narrow street, looking like complete darkness at then end of a tunnel. She thought the street ran straight into the complex, but it didn't. She hit the curb at sixty mph and flew onto the gravel walkway. Her head hit her convertible's canvas top which caused it to unlock and spring backward halfway. She fell back into her blue leather seat and tried to regain control of this "Toad's Wild Ride" she was on, resembling a half-crazed white woman blowing the horn as she drove among apartment buildings in an impoverished neighborhood, looking for a heavily-armed young black man.

"Mark!" she screamed several times, as she neared the desolate, wasteland-like area called "The Big Valley."

Men, women and children, dressed and undressed, looked out windows and opened doors to see the strangest sight they had ever seen: a seemingly half-crazed white woman in her BMW blowing the horn and screaming the name Mark as she drove zigzaggedly among the apartment buildings of this stunningly impoverished neighborhood, finally reaching "The Big Valley," where she and Wyatt recently encountered the gang of youths. Although she had stopped her car, her heart was racing. She was now feeling the full impact of where she was and serious jeopardy regarding her very life. She was nauseous. Every muscle was taut. Her skin was tight and tingling. She was sweating which formed a large wet spot on the back of her blouse, yet she felt cold.

She shouted his name and blew the horn repeatedly until she heard a low voice from within the dark abandoned apartment building.

"He ain't here. Get out. You're in a combat zone," the disembodied voice said.

"That's bullshit! I know he's in there. Come out. I've got to talk to you now," she said with fake bravado. After a few moments of silence, Mark walked forward but remained mostly in the shadows. She could see his dark figure, dressed in a black skull stretch cap, black tee shirt, baggy black jeans, sunglasses and a large gold cross hanging from his neck. "Get in the car!"

"Don't order me around, you rich white bitch!" he said, angrily, still standing in that penumbral area, moonlight reflecting off his cross. She blew the horn again as she reached for her gun and lowered it to her side. "Cut that shit out!" he ordered, running down the stairs, pulling out his 9mm black semi-automatic pistol and pointing at her head. "You want to attract every thug in the city?"

Ashley then raised her gun and placed the barrel on his left cheek. Shocked, Mark looked cross-eyed down at the gun.

"Didn't expect that, did you?" she said, her hand shaking. "Do you want to make the news tonight? 'Gang leader killed by rich, white bitch'."

A "freeze out" ensued, each staring into each other's eyes. Ashley's blood pressure was rising. She felt pressure behind her eyes and her right arm felt like lead. Then Mark lowered his gun.

"You are fucking crazy! You know that? Do you realize where you are? You gonna get us both killed. What the fuck you want from me? And put that fucking gun away, girl, before you kill someone – like me!" Mark demanded.

"Get in the car, bitch!" Ashley said, lowering her arm and putting the gun on the floorboard under her legs.

"I'm not going anywhere with you. I'm in the middle of a war here," Mark said.

"Drop your gun and get in the fucking car now!" she shouted, only realizing she used the vulgarity after saying it.

"No one drops his gun around here, woman. We're warriors. Now what's this about?" Mark asked.

"Your sister. Get in the car!" Ashley shouted.

"My sister? What's wrong?" Mark asked.

Gunfire was heard. Mark quickly jumped over the door into the passenger's seat, and accidentally dropped his gun on the ground.

"Hang on!" Ashley exclaimed.

Ashley floored it as Mark hung over the door reaching for his gun.

"Wait a minute, bitch!" Mark shouted.

Ashley continued to speed away. More shots were heard as they rounded an apartment building in the complex. Mark reached under Ashley's legs and grabbed her gun.

"Hey! Give me my gun," she said, as she made another sharp turn.

Mark pointed the gun at the apartment building and pulled the trigger several times.

"This fucking thing ain't even loaded!" Mark said.

He then threw it on the floor and crouched low in his seat, leaving Ashley to find her way out. She made another sharp turn and spun out in wet mud. She was surrounded by drab, identical third-world-like apartment buildings.

"Which way?" she questioned. Her heart was racing and she was sweating through her clothes and down her face.

Mark lifted his lead and looked around.

"Take a left at that one," he said, pointing to a nearby building.

Shots were fired again. Mark retreated to his hole. Two bullets hit Ashley's car on the right rear wheel well.

"Jesus! My car!" Ashley said.

"You're lucky it wasn't your head. Hit it," Mark shouted.

The BMW spit mud as she floored it to escape. She drove sideways a few feet, then finally rounded the building. She spotted a side street and drove speedily toward it, hitting the concrete curb, which loosened the front bumper so that it became unattached on one side and hung low. She narrowly missed hitting parked cars as she sped toward St. Charles Avenue, blowing through stop signs along the way. She wasn't sure where she was but she could see cars moving in both directions on the Avenue in the distance. The Avenue was her true light at the end of this tunnel.

"Where are we now?" Mark asked, raising his head to window level.

"Near St. Charles," Ashley said.

"What happened to my sister?" he asked, as he sat down.

"She got shot tonight," Ashley said.

"Shot? By who?" Mark asked.

"You! She has your bullet in her head," she said, turning onto St. Charles.

"I didn't shoot my own sister," Mark insisted.

"She was playing on the porch and got caught in your crossfire," Ashley said.

"I didn't ...," Mark said, hesitating a bit.

"It's your fucking bullet in her," she said, looking at him and making the car swerve. "If it's not yours, it's your friends' or enemies'. You're all the same. Don't you get it, stupid? You buy guns with drug money, then shoot innocent people in the war you wage to protect your turf. It's all blood money from constant pain and suffering you cause. Then you sell people drugs to ease the pain. You hook them, then you kill them. It's a circle of grief. Open your eyes!"

Ashley lost control of the car again, causing it to swerve left onto the neutral ground where several people were waiting for the streetcar, forcing the people to scatter and shout.

"Hey, call the police. She kidnapped me!" Mark sshouted to

the pedestrians while standing in the car. Then speaking to Ashley, he said, "It ain't my fault. You people don't give a shit about us killing each other, so don't act like you do, especially when you got fucking Robert E. Lee guarding your city," he said, pointing up to Robert E. Lee atop the column in the center of Lee Circle. As Mark spoke, Ashley made a hard, left turn at Lee Circle, causing him to nearly fall out of the car. "Jesus Christ! You trying to kill me?" Mark said, as he hung onto the visor and windshield.

"Stop blaming me!" Ashley insisted.

"I'm not blaming you," he replied.

"Stop blaming white people for your sick way of life," she said, now driving up Howard Avenue.

Suddenly flashing lights atop a NOPD cruiser appeared in Ashley's rearview mirror. But Ashley had no intentions of stopping. She blew past the red lights at Girod, Poydras and Perdido which ran right in front of City Hall. She then blew the light at Gravier, turning left and speeding up that street and onto the ramp on the right, leading to Charity's emergency room. She bumped an ambulance in front of her when she stopped, and her bumper fell off. The cop car pulled up. Ashley and Mark ran inside with the policeman close behind.

Ashley led Mark down the busy hallway crisscrossed by doctors and nurses. Ashley found the room where Alicia was being treated by three doctors and two nurses trying to stop the large wound on the right side of her head that impacted her eye. Bloody bandages were on the floor and hanging on the rim of the trash basket. Ashley glimpsed the girl's pain and suffering and her fight for life through openings between arms and bodies constantly in motion.

Ashley pulled Mark close and said, "Look at her! Look at your sister fighting for her life. That's your bullet in her. Look and never forget what you see."

Mark stood stunned. Then suddenly the doctors and nurses wheeled the gurney from the room.

"Watch out, sir," one doctor said to Mark. "Please return to the waiting room."

"That's my sister. Can you save her eye?" Mark asked.

"We're trying to save her life. We'll do all we can to save her eye. But it was crushed by the bullet that lodged in her temple. We're going to the OR now. Clear the way, please," the doctor said.

Mark touched Alicia's hand as they wheeled her by. Alicia's eyes were closed, so she didn't see the look of grave concern or the tears on his face.

Mark knelt before his mother and said, "I'm sorry, Mama. I'm sorry. I'm sorry. I'm sorry."

CHAPTER 34

The Fatherlode

Wyatt followed Keiffer Conright, who was riding with George Tarleton and the young Nazis in their white Chevrolet Suburban as they drove up Airline Highway, and then into New Orleans International Airport. They drove through the passenger pickup lane, turned right toward the rental car drop-off area, and kept going toward a small hangar near the rear of the property. Wyatt knew he had to complete the circle and return to Airline Highway or he would surely be seen.

Wyatt parked near the Rodeway Inn across Airline. He took his camera from the trunk and crossed the highway. He walked around the fence perimeter, realizing it was too high to climb. He continued walking until he, literally, stumbled on a hole in the ground that a dog had dug under the fence. He deepened the hole with his pocket knife and hands, and then bent back the fence and slid through.

He picked up his camera, scraped wet mud from his jeans and ran commando-like across the field to a side door in the hangar. He peeked in and saw the Suburban, but the occupants were against the inside wall and out of his line of sight. He moved to the far end of the hangar to secure a better view. He looked behind him for a guard but saw no one. He laid down on the mud like a sniper and positioned his camera like a rifle. Whatever they were waiting for, he was going to film. He wanted to find out what Conright was up to as much as anyone and everyone else. He, too, was after the truth as much as any TV reporter with whom he had ever worked. He had always thought of himself as part of an investigative team. After all, he had been a TV cameraman for ten years. He knew his craft and he, too, knew a lot of people and had leads to follow. He especially wanted Ashley to know this, too. Her arrogant demeanor bothered him. And, like many people, he had something to prove.

As a small, private jet rolled into the hangar at the opposite end, everyone standing by the left wall stepped into Wyatt's view. Conright, Mr. Tarleton, Ted and the young neo-Nazis were all dressed in black and wearing red and black swastika armbands. The jet slowly rolled to a stop near the men. The engine turbines wound down. After a few moments, the captain opened the door and lowered a short narrow staircase. Conright's ninety-three-year-old father, Gustav Von Richtoff, descended the stairs with the help of the captain. Everyone gave him the Nazi salute by raising their right arms high and shouting "Heil Hitler!" Von Richtoff exchanged the greeting and then hugged his son.

"Holy shit!" Wyatt whispered. "The Fatherlode!"

It was a Nazi family reunion. All that was missing was a chorus of *Deutschland Uber Alles*. And Wyatt captured it all on videotape for the whole city to see: proof that Conright was a Nazi, proud of his German ancestry and its darker side of Nazism and his allegiance to the memory of a megalomaniacal dead man, Adolph Hitler and all the blood-soaked evil for which he stood, an evil that had murdered millions and swallowed families whole, like Bella Blum's.

Gustav Von Richtoff, who had been a sixteen-year-old soldier in the German Army in 1917, had come to the United States at the end of World War I after assuming the identity of a fallen U.S. soldier. He settled in New Orleans and due to the extreme prejudice against Germans after the war, he changed his name to Conright so he could find employment and later married a young German girl, Elle, in the 1930s. They both missed the Fatherland. And when Germany began World War II by invading Poland on September 1, 1939, Gustav felt the need to serve his country again. However, Elle was pregnant with Keiffer when he returned to Germany. He vowed to send money and call for them after the war. Once in Germany, he joined the *Wehrmacht* and requested service in the 2nd Waffen-SS Panzer Division, *Das Reich*, the elite division of the German Army. His request was granted and he served in one of that Division's units, the 4th SS Panzer Grenadier Regiment, *Der Fuhrer*, commanded by *SS-Sturmbannfuhrer* Adolph Diekmann. The unit was notorious for committing atrocities, like *Oradvous Zur Glade*, where 643 villagers in southwest France were shot or burned alive. Gustav machine gunned the nave of the church where 247 women and 205 children were herded; then, he threw in the first torch. It was June 10, 1944, only four days after D-Day on June 6.

The war soon ended and members of the Waffen SS became wanted criminals by the Allies. Gustav fled to Austria where he stayed with a friend who contacted the ODESSA, the secret organization to facilitate the escape of SS members. An ODESSA member arranged transportation and contacts to Rome where he was helped by a priest of German descent who felt compelled to help Germans escape the Communists and the Allies. He was given false papers and passage on a ship from Genoa to Argentina where Nazis were welcomed. He later secured a position in Juan Peron's government as an immigration advisor which allowed him to aid more ex-Nazis to enter Argentina. After Elle died, his father finally contacted Keiffer who visited as often as he could, but his father couldn't visit the USA in fear of being imprisoned for crimes against humanity he committed during the war. However, he gave lots of money to his son to establish him as a businessman in New Orleans and to purchase real estate. But he felt the need to be present for the election and the possibility of his son gaining public office. Even at his age, he could still be jailed because he had never paid for his crimes. But it was a chance he was willing to take for his only son, having felt guilty for not being able to spend more time with him over the years, something he always regretted.

Wyatt then heard Frankenstein steps behind him. As he turned his head to see who was behind him, he felt a motorcycle boot pressing down on the right side of his head, pushing his head hard into the mud until he tasted dirt. The man bent over to grab the camera, loosening his hold on Wyatt who then gripped the man's boot like a claw and flipped him. Wyatt was then face to face with the man he recognized as Conright's bodyguard who looked more Neanderthal than Nazi. The man's right fist came hurdling through space like a meteor heading for Wyatt's head. Wyatt jumped up, grabbed the camera, and ran across the field like a man on fire, as the man fired several shots at him, one bullet nicking the camera.

When he reached the fence, he shoved the camera through the hole and burrowed under the fence, ripping his shirt sleeve. He threw the camera over his shoulder like a weapon, ran across Airline Highway, tossed the camera on the backseat, jumped in and floored it. He peeled out and headed down Airline toward the city.

His hands gripped the wheel, like two vises-grips. It was all that kept him from shaking right out of the car. In his ten years as cameraman, he had never been shot at. But in the last few days he had been shot at twice. He thought of his daughter at home with his mother. All he wanted to do now was be with them. Then he saw a huge, old sedan in his rearview mirror. Neanderthal was behind the wheel, looking coldly at him through dark, hateful, ignorant eyes.

The man dropped his Frankenstein boot on the accelerator of his 1973 lime green Olds Ninety-Eight sedan, bumping Wyatt's wimpy Chevy with the huge chrome bumper on the Olds.

"Jesus!" Wyatt shouted, looking back and forth in the mirror between Airline ahead of him and the primitive life form behind him. "This guy's serious!" He ran the light at Williams Boulevard, weaving in and out of traffic and pursued relentlessly by Frankenmobile. He punched in Ashley's car phone number.

Ashley had just sat down in her car on the emergency entrance ramp at Charity Hospital. She was feeling a bit weak, having given blood for Alicia an hour earlier. The phone's ring startled her. Thinking the call was from Beverly, she quickly answered it.

"Beverly, what's wrong?" Ashley asked, nervously.

"It's Wyatt."

"Wyatt. Where are you?"

"I'm being chased by a circus freak on Airline Highway," he said.

"What are you talking about?" she asked.

"I followed Conright and the Hitler youth to a hangar in the rear of the airport where they met an old man on a private jet. They were all wearing Nazi uniforms. And I've got it all on tape. This is the proof we've been looking for. Now Conright's bodyguard is chasing me. He shot at me and rammed my car. This asshole is trying to kill me!" Wyatt exclaimed.

"My God! Take a side street and try to lose him. I'm on my way," Ashley said.

"Oh shit!" Wyatt shouted, as the mad man appeared in the right lane and smashed into the right side of the Chevy, trying to force Wyatt into oncoming traffic.

When the two cars collided, the impact knocked the phone from Wyatt's hand to the floor on the passenger's side.

"Wyatt!" Ashley screamed, as she drove up Gravier to Claiborne and left onto Tulane Avenue, headed directly for Airline.

Wyatt jumped the curb, narrowly escaping a collision with an oncoming SUV and drove down a side street to escape. He drove a couple of blocks, straining his eyes to read street signs, but the streets were dimly lit. Ashley was still shouting his name, so he pulled over, reached down and found the phone.

"I'm here," Wyatt confirmed.

"Where's 'here'?" Ashley asked.

"I'm not sure. He forced me off Airline. I'm about two blocks off. Where are you?" Wyatt asked.

"I'm by the courthouse. Listen, pull over and turn off your engine. Wait it out a few minutes. He may just go away," Ashley suggested.

"I doubt it. But I'll give it a shot," he said.

"Okay. Stay on the phone with me. Duck down." Wyatt parked in front of a small white wooden frame house and turned off the engine. "Did you do it? Are you ducking down?" she asked.

"Yeah. I'm ducking," Wyatt said, looking in his side view mirror.

"See anything?" she asked.

"No. Nothing. It's very quiet back here," he said. "Wait! I just saw a long car pass about a block and a half away."

"Was it him?" she asked.

"I don't know. Too far away. Where are you now?" he asked.

"Carrollton and Tulane," she said.

"Well, I can't wait here," he said. "I'm going to make a break for it. Meet me at the Johnson Street post office. I'll leave my car there and ride back with you."

"Johnson Street?" she asked.

"Yeah. It's a block off Airline and Severn," he said.

"I'm an uptowner. I'm not sure where that is," she confessed.

"It's just after the Causeway Boulevard overpass. It's flanked by two gas stations. Take a right on Severn, then your first left. That's the post office," he said.

"All right. I guess I can fine it," she said.

"You'll have to. I need to ditch my car with its giant TV-3 logo emblazoned on the side. It's like a bull's eye. All right. I'm heading out," he said.

"Okay."

Wyatt pulled out and could see Severn Avenue about three blocks away. He stopped at the next intersection and looked around. As he entered the intersection, the headlights of an old, long sedan parked behind two others on the street came on like spotlights and the driver revved the engine. Wyatt looked left to see that the car now headed straight for him. It was Conright's bodyguard behind the wheel of his U-boat on wheels.

Wyatt gunned the Chevy and avoided impact with his door. But the Olds still caught the backdoor, with a loud slap, like a gunshot, spinning the Chevy around and sending two hubcaps rolling down the middle of the wet moonlit street, like two dogs on the prowl.

"Wyatt! What's happening?" Ashley shouted over the phone.

But the phone had been thrown from his hand behind the seat. He looked over his shoulder and saw that the Olds had stalled on the lawn of a house across the street. Wyatt hit the pedal but the car wouldn't move. He smelled burning rubber. He looked out the window and realized his left rear fender was now crushed and pressing on the tire. He jumped out and used his hands to remove the fender from the wheel. He could hear the man trying to restart the Olds. His hands slipped off the fender and fell back violently. He tried again. Finally, he pulled it out enough to get going.

He jumped in, drove to Severn Avenue, turned right and sped down to Johnson Street. He turned into the post office parking lot where he picked up the phone and said, "Ashley, you still there?"

"Yes. What was that sound?" she asked.

"He smashed the side of the car," he said.

"I thought you lost him," she said.

"I did – for five minutes. I'm at the post office," he said.

"I'm coming up the underpass. I can see the gas stations," she said.

"Hurry!" Wyatt looked left up Severn and saw the Olds. "Oh shit!"

"What?" Ashley excitedly asked.

'He's heading right for me. Hurry up!" Wyatt shouted.

Ashley had just turned right on Severn and could see the Olds heading for her. She looked to the left and saw Wyatt next to his car waving at her. She turned sharply in front of the Olds and pulled up next to Wyatt, and so did the bodyguard, blocking their exit.

Franken-Nazi got out of the Olds and said, "You're in a lot of trouble."

Ashley got out of her car and said, "You're out of your mind. You tried to kill him. And I recognize that car now. You've been following me. And I bet you were the one who broke into my house and Yvette's apartment. I know you were," recognizing his raspy voice. "You're definitely the one. You set her up!"

"I don't know what you're talking about. Give me the tape," the bodyguard said.

Ashley retrieved her gun from her car and pointed it at the man.

"Ashley, put that away," Wyatt said.

"You better put that away, little girl, or I'm going to call the cops," the bodyguard said.

"You call the cops! You're the one who should be arrested," Ashley replied.

"You can't prove a thing. No witnesses. But that tape proves you videotaped a private function on private property. You broke the law. Give me the tape," Frankenman said. He moved forward toward the Chevy. Ashley cocked her gun. "You gonna kill me? I'm not threatening you. I'm unarmed. Shoot me and you'll spend the rest of your life in prison. Nice, soft uptown girls like you won't last very long there. And who's going to take care of your mommy, as sick as she is."

Ashley's eyes widened as adrenalin streaked through her body. She knew for sure now that this was the man who had been following her, and was involved in some way with Yvette's murder.

"You better stop following me and stay away from my mother. I know people in this city. And I'm a member of the Press," Ashley insisted.

The bodyguard laughed and said, "And that makes you important?" He paused and then shouted, "Give me the tape!"

Realizing this man, who towered over them was serious and had no intention of leaving empty handed, Wyatt opened the backdoor of his car.

"What are you doing?" Ashley questioned.

"I'm giving him the tape," Wyatt said.

"No!" Ashley shouted.

"Yes. Look at him. He's a nut. And he's huge. He could take your gun, kill both of us and no one would ever know. He's right. There are no witnesses to any of this," Wyatt said.

"I'll tell my father. He'll get this guy," Ashley said.

Wyatt took the tape from his camera, handed it to the man, as he wiped sweat from his face and then stepped back beside Ashley. The man quietly got into the long Olds and slowly drove up Johnson Street, the engine's valves loudly tapping his retreat.

"It was the only thing I could do," Wyatt said.

"Get in the car," Ashley responded, walking to the driver's side of the BMW and opening the door.

"Why?" he said, complying.

"Because that son-of-a-bitch has been following me. I'm sure he broke into my house," she said.

"When did that happen?" he asked.

"Last night. He could be linked to Yvette's death. And you saw

Nazis tonight. We know it's all true. The rest of the evidence is obviously in Conright's house. Where else could it be? So that's where we're going. Chances are, he's not home yet. That guy headed toward the airport," Ashley observed.

Ashley got on Causeway Boulevard and headed toward Lake Pontchartrain.

"Wait a minute. You're talking about breaking and entering. That's illegal, Ashley. That's crazy," he said.

"How did you get that video tonight? You broke the law," she said.

"That's a little different. That's a lot different," he countered.

"They're Nazis. And I'm sure I saw that car outside Yvette's apartment. Conright is mixed up in Yvette's murder some way. I'm convinced of it," she said.

She got on Interstate-10, and headed south.

"Why are you so sure?" he asked.

"Let's just say I got help from beyond the grave," she said.

"Oh, that's ridiculous. We're both going to get thrown in jail," he said.

"I returned to Yvette's apartment alone that same day we were there. I sensed her presence. Suddenly the phone book opened and the pages started turning by themselves. First they stopped on Conright's page, then on mine. It's obvious to me now that Yvette's spirit or ghost or whatever was pointing to Conright as her murderer and she wanted me to expose him. That's why she turned the page to my listing," Ashley deduced. Wyatt shook his head in disbelief. "You don't believe in ghosts?"

"No! And when did you start believing?" Wyatt asked.

"I'm not saying I'm a true believer. But I've seen and felt things in the last week that really make me wonder. Something's going on. I just don't know what it is," she said.

"It's probably just you. That's how it always is. It's all in the mind," he said.

"Don't be so sure," Ashley said. Ashley exited at Canal Boulevard and headed toward the lake. She turned right on a side street and continued for two blocks. She saw Conright's plain white, Bavarian style, two-story house on the corner. She passed it, drove down to the next corner, turned around and parked across the street from the rear entrance. "That's it," Ashley said, nodding toward the house.

"It's kind of unassuming," Wyatt said, lowering his head to look through Ashley's window, his face touching her right shoulder as Ashley tried to lean farther back. "I expected more."

"That's probably what his ex-wife said," she said, laughing. "It's all part of his propaganda to hide his forked tail."

"This is not a good idea, Ashley. Seriously. Let's get out of here. Let the police handle it. They can get a search warrant," he said.

"That would take a lot of convincing. I'm sure he has friends in the NOPD and DA's office. The truth is inside that house. I've got to go in there," she said.

"How you going to get in? Don't expect a ghost to open the door for you," he said.

"That's not funny," she said.

"Stay close to the windows. I'll flash the lights if I see anyone coming. And thanks for helping me tonight," he said, touching her right hand and leaning toward her. He felt an urge to kiss her. Her flawless skin glistened, as beads of sweat rolled down her temples. Half her face was bathed in moonlight. Her auburn hair looked like silk flowing down her face and neck. A smell of sweet, steamy perfume permeated the moist air between them. Her eyes were hypnotizing. He could hear himself breathe and hoped she would pull herself closer to him.

"I'm glad you're okay," she said, clenching his hand. A pause ensued during which Wyatt thought Ashley might kiss him. She moved toward him. He felt the sweep of her hair on his face and smelled her sweet perfume. Wyatt stuck out his chin and pursed his lips, but Ashley moved to his left, reached into the glove compartment and pulled out a screwdriver. "I'll need this."

She got out of the car and hurried across the street, leaving Wyatt to whisper to himself, "At least she didn't cover herself in hand sanitizer. Maybe I'm making progress."

Expecting a dog in the yard, Ashley rattled the wooden gate. She waited, then entered the yard and walked up the short concrete stairs to the backdoor where Wyatt could now see her over the fence.

She looked through the large windowpane of the wooden door. She could see into the dimly lit kitchen and into the hall and dining room beyond. She tapped on the door. There was no movement of any kind. She looked around and before she had the chance to lift the screwdriver to the lock, the door swung open.

She slowly entered the kitchen, cautiously looking around like a mouse looking and listening for a cat. She noticed the kitchen was clean with everything in its place and had a refreshing scent. The windowed oak cabinets revealed glasses and bowls with painted figures of *frauleins* dancing in pastures below snow-capped mountains. Beer steins as tall as encyclopedias stood in another cabinet. Above the cabinets was a row of small paintings of alpine chalets in idyllic settings and flower boxes below each window.

She walked around a round oak table, with a red and white checkered tablecloth and chairs, to look out the window. She spotted Wyatt in the car but no sign of trouble. But she knew she had to hurry. Her blood pressure was rising as her muscles tightened.

She moved through the short hall into the dining room occupied by a large rectangular oak table and six black wooden chairs with periwinkle blue cornflowers painted on the tops. Against a wall was a large wooden china cabinet full of Hummel figurines of children in apple trees, riding wooden horses, standing with an angel and carrying the black-red-gold striped flag of Germany. Also filling the case were German beer glasses and beer steins of all types and sizes, including tulip-stemmed glasses with crests and a glass boot with the German flag and eagle, a tall stein with a medieval forest scene depicting a mounted knight rescuing a maiden, and two horn steins, one with an elk and one with the German eagle, wings wide open.

She moved across the hall into the living room which had the appearance of an alpine lodge. She saw more Hummels on tables, the letters "KC" carved into the center of the large oak cornice and eagles everywhere – carved into the cornice, porcelain statues and a large crystal carving of an eagle soaring over mountaintops above the fireplace at the far wall. A cherry wood cuckoo clock hung on the front wall between two windows.

She returned to the hall and ran upstairs, knowing she had to get out of that house soon and frustrated over finding absolutely nothing incriminating but a love of German culture. She was very curious about who Conright was and how he lived. And she could see now that he was very ordinary and very neat.

At the top of the stairs, she spotted three small bedrooms and a bathroom. The first bedroom was very small with a poker table and chairs ready for use with cards, chips and beer steins on it. She quickly checked the closet which held more chairs.

She moved to the next bedroom which was larger and contained a bed with a headboard that again reflected the chalet motif. Above it was the flag of Germany tacked to the wall. On the white bedspread over the pillow sat a traditional German Tyrolean hat with a double-braided Bavarian green rope around it and flying eagle pin on the side which held in place an Edelweiss brush with feather. On the cherry wood dresser were old photos from the 1930s of Conright's parents and other photos of Conright growing up alone with his mother, including one of Conright wearing traditional German Lederhosen standing next to his mother wearing a traditional green dirndl dress with tulip embroidery, with white blouse and white linen apron. The room was awaiting Conright's father who planned to stay for the election and perhaps for good.

She then entered the master bedroom where Conright dreamt of masters and slaves, as he lay in his huge antique mahogany bed with a headboard befitting a king. Atop the mahogany dresser was a long piece of laced linen. At both ends of the dresser were family photos – one of his parents on their wedding day and at the opposite end, one oval photograph of his father in his military uniform from World War I. She looked through the drawers and found only clothes. He wore briefs; she thought boxers for sure. She found a silver ring adorned with two stag teeth and an old silver pocket watch which she opened, revealing an inscription inside the cover, "To my unborn son: I fight for you, Mama and Deutschland. I will return. Love Papa. 1939." Perhaps that would have been a sweet sentiment to anyone else, but Ashley now knew about Germany in the 1930s and '40s and what exactly went on there. She knew of the evil for which he had fought.

She went into the sparkling white bathroom and checked the medicine chest. Among typical items like toothpaste and shaving creme, she found a bottle of Xanax and ulcer medication, proving to her that even men who profess certainty in all they do, are not certain in all they do and they know it.

She heard a noise at the backdoor. She moved to the stairs where she heard it again. She froze. A shot of adrenalin burst within her body like a supernova. She looked straight forward through a window in the opposite wall. She saw a soft white light flashing like a beacon or warning. She rushed to the window and looked down to see Wyatt flashing the BMW's headlights on and off. Someone was in the house.

She quickly crept down the stairs and looked down the hall. She could see movement in the kitchen. Then she heard Frankenstein steps and bolted for Conright's office down a short hall to her left. A desk fit for a Fuhrer occupied a large part of the room. Ashley wanted to hide behind it, but heard more steps, panicked and ran for the closet. She quietly closed the door and moved to the rear, pressing against the wall. Then Frankenstein entered the room.

Again, the snakes were loose. A few drops of urine leaked onto her underwear. She felt a heaviness and tightness in her chest. She had a throbbing headache. Her thoughts and heart were racing. What had she gotten herself into, she thought. She realized this was an incredibly stupid thing to do. Was she so arrogant to think she was indestructible? She knew this ignorant giant was about to discover her and kill her. Then the paneled wall she was leaning against opened and she stepped through into a smaller closet. She closed the panel and waited. She stood in darkness, listening to her thumping heart.

Fuhrer's little helper ripped open the exterior closet door, fully expecting to find someone. He knew someone was in the house because the backdoor was open. He turned on the light but did not push open the rear panel. He then turned off the light, closed the door and left the room.

Ashley felt the wall for a light switch but couldn't find one. But then her head hit a chain hanging from the ceiling. She pulled it, turning on a naked light bulb that shined a light on the dark recesses of Keiffer Conright's mind. Wooden shelves lined the narrow wooden chamber. Against the far wall was a Nazi flag of Adolph Hitler's Third Reich, red field with black Swastika symbol in a white circle – the flag of a tyrannical and murderous government. On the shelves were framed photos of Hitler saluting the crowds, his straight black hair covering his black, bestial brain. One photo showed Hitler standing, placed before a black background, belying his true vicious character. Then she found a photo of Conright's father. But in this one he was not wearing his WWI uniform. He was wearing his WWII gray *Waffen SS* uniform with *Wolfsangel* insignia on his M43 *Panzer* field cap and uniform. And he was standing next to the corpses of Jews in striped prison uniforms. Ashley recognized photos like this from the ones she and Wyatt saw in books at the Maple Street Bookshop.

She moved down the shelves and noticed two Nazi daggers, a Luger pistol and a German infantryman's helmet. Then she saw a metal statue of a fierce gold-plated eagle with tight wings, standing on a silver-plated world. Next to that and in between another photo of Hitler was what she came for: a framed photo of Conright in a black Nazi uniform with red swastika armband and arm raised high in salute like his master. Ashley's eyes widened as she grabbed the photo and one behind it of a group of neo-Nazis with Conright in the middle.

She heard Conright's bodyguard again, this time on the stairs. She waited for him to reach the second floor before attempting her getaway. She looked on another shelf full of more Nazi memorabilia and saw two videotapes in black plastic cases. She grabbed them, pushed through the panel door, exited the closet, moved quietly through the office and into the hall. She looked up the staircase and onto the landing, but didn't see him. As she rounded the corner, she heard from above, "Halt!"

Adrenalin shot throughout her body and propelled her forward. She ran down the hall and to the kitchen door. But it was now locked. She looked back at Frankenstein who was now at the base of the stairs, as she fumbled with the lock. She thought her eyes were about to burst and her brain felt like it was on fire. She turned the deadbolt but then noticed the round handle needed a key to turn. She saw the key on the counter and dropped the tapes and photos, breaking the glass on one. She scooped up the key and looked back at the bodyguard who seemed to occupy the entire hall, width and height. As he entered the kitchen, Ashley jammed the key in the lock, turned it, opened the door and kicked the photos and tapes outside down the steps.

"Wyatt!" she screamed.

Wyatt had already jumped from the car and was approaching the gate. As Ashley picked up the photos and tapes, the bodyguard burst through the door. She could see the fire in his eyes, as red as that Nazi flag. This was the brute force of ignorance at its lowest.

"Watch out behind you!" Wyatt shouted back, as he opened the gate.

Then Ashley felt the vice-like grip of the bodyguard's thick, moist hand around the back of her neck. He picked her up by the neck and threw her down, causing her to hit her head and scrape her face on the concrete stairs. He grabbed her collar and began dragging her into the house.

Wyatt ran up the stairs and punched the man in the back of the head, stunning him enough to loosen his grip on Ashley who slid down the steps and gathered the photos and tapes. Wyatt helped Ashley but lost his footing and fell. It was then the bodyguard caught up with Wyatt, pulled him up and hit him in his stomach twice, knocking him to his knees. Wyatt, holding his stomach, looked up at the grinning face of a lumbering fool whose tragic lot in life was always to be someone else's servant.

"Looks like it's just me and you, dago! You're gonna bleed," the bodyguard said, as he lifted his boot to kick Wyatt.

But then the man felt the pointed kick to his crotch of a vengeful high-heeled uptown girl. As he fell to his knees, Wyatt could now see Ashley standing behind the man.

"Let's go!" Ashley exclaimed, helping him to his feet.

They stumbled and ran to the car. As they pulled off, Wyatt saw the bodyguard trying to sit up while shouting obscenities, so Wyatt shot him the bird.

CHAPTER 35

Crooked Cross

Ashley and Wyatt headed to his house, driving up Metairie Road which was once a trail used by Native Americans to transport their trade goods to town from this area a few miles away. Now, this real estate was very valuable and lined with expensive homes and quaint shops. It was thought of as a suburban uptown neighborhood, though there were still many houses off the road itself that were small, wooden and built after World War II. Wyatt lived in one with his mother and daughter.

Ashley turned right on North Labarre Road and drove down five blocks. She then turned into a narrow driveway next to a white wooden shotgun double house with a stucco front. A white 1984 Chevrolet Impala was parked down the driveway, near the old wooden garage. Behind it was a dark teal-colored Camaro with a black hard top.

"This is it," Wyatt said. "You'd better clean up inside. You're still bleeding. And thanks for saving my ass back there. I owe you."

"No. I owe you for coming to my rescue. I guess I pushed this too far," Ashley said.

"Not if he had anything to do with the death of Yvette, you didn't," Wyatt said.

It was midnight as Wyatt put the key in the windowed door. He opened it to reveal a small modest living room decorated in a colonial motif with a long pine coffee table and skirts around the legs of the heavily cushioned couch and chairs. The pine end table was decorated with a doily and several photos of Wyatt's mother and his daughter, Andie. A TV and VCR in a pine cabinet stood across the room. Adjoining the room near the kitchen was a small dining room with an etch-a-sketch and doll on the rectangular table. A stack of children's books stood in the corner. "The bathroom's through the hallway on the left."

"Okay," Ashley said, as she made her way through the dining room, and then into the hallway.

As she passed a small bedroom, she heard the door open.

"Hi," a child's voice said.

Ashley turned around and saw Wyatt's daughter, Andie, in her pink-footed pajamas, standing in the doorway. She was a beautiful little girl with a perfect oval face, pink cheeks, and long black hair.

"Hi," Ashley replied, totally caught off guard.

"Are you my daddy's girlfriend?" Andie inquired.

"Oh . . . no . . . not at all. I work with your daddy, and I had a little accident. He brought me here to clean up, that's all," Ashley replied, hoping that answered the question.

"I'll get you a face cloth. Follow me," Andie said.

Andie led Ashley into the small black-and-white-tiled bathroom that was straight out of the 1940s.

"Thank you," Ashley said, after taking the washcloth Andie had gotten from the tall, thin linen closet.

"You're welcome." Andie watched Ashley intently, as she washed her face. "You're very pretty."

"Thank you. You're very pretty, too," Ashley said.

"That's what everyone says," Andie confessed.

"Well, everyone is right," Ashley said, as she dried her face and hands, and knelt down. "Why are you up so late?"

"I couldn't sleep. I worry about my daddy because he's not home at night. Sometimes he is, but most of the time he's not, and it's dangerous in the city. I hear him talk about it to my Gram," Andie said, as she expressed her fear.

"Yes. It is dangerous in the city, but he can take care of himself very well. He's a good man," Ashley said.

"He's a good dad and I love him. I don't want anything to happen to him," Andie said.

'Nothing will happen. Don't worry. And he loves you very

much, too. And he's home now, so you can go back to sleep and dream sweet dreams. Okay?" Ashley reassured.

"Okay. Will you come to my tea party Saturday?" Andie asked.

"Sure. Where?" Ashley asked.

"In the backyard where it's sunny," Andie said.

"Okay. Save me a place," Ashley said, looking longingly at Andie and feeling as never before her maternal instinct.

"Okay," Andie said, with a beautiful smile.

Wyatt walked up and said, "You should be in bed." He then knelt down and hugged her.

"I was waiting for you. I woke up and I couldn't go back to sleep," Andie said.

Ashley was touched by this genuine display of emotion from Wyatt. There was more to Wyatt than she knew, she thought, as she moved into the living room and sat down on the couch. A pizza box from Mark Twain's Pizza Landing lay on the coffee table in front of her. She noticed more family photos on tables and shelves that were full of figurines, but only a few books. Most showed Wyatt with his gray-haired mother and daughter. One was by itself in the center of a shelf. It was a photo of a good-looking man with black and gray hair. It was framed in black and obviously a photo of remembrance, Ashley thought; surely, it was his father. This home was not like Ashley's crystal world, but was rich in love and memories.

She picked up one of Conright's videotapes and inserted it into the VCR beneath the television in a brown wooden cabinet across from the couch. She then pressed "PLAY" on the remote control. Immediately, a night rally appeared at Nuremberg, Germany, 1938, in the stadium housing thousands of people watching a torchlight procession by men in black SS uniforms, carrying red banners, bearing the black swastika – the crooked cross, *hakenkreuz*. And then Adolph Hitler, the crooked redeemer, approached the podium and the crowd's roar quieted, but swelled again when the man in black shouted *"Deutschland uber alles!"*

Ashley was disturbed by this scene, but also puzzled as to why anyone would admire such an angry, vile man. He continued his rant, stomping his foot and raising his fist against the night sky, as if threatening the stars with arrogant rage.

Wyatt walked in and sat next to Ashley.

"Is she okay?" Ashley asked.

"Yeah. She just worries about me. My job is more stressful than people might think. In many ways," Wyatt said.

Ashley looked at Wyatt and realized she had been too hard on him in the past. She hadn't thought about the demands of his job on his family. She hadn't thought too much at all about Wyatt himself. She just thought of him as an appendage.

"She'll be okay," she said, patting him on the shoulder. "Especially when all of this is over."

"Until the next big story. There's always something popping up or blowing up in this business because you're dealing with human behavior which ain't too pretty much of the time. Case in point – this guy," he said, pointing to Hitler on the TV screen. "Or Conright or his bodyguard and on and on. They're everywhere. But I like being a cameraman because I capture their bad behavior on video and expose them. And so it goes – world without end."

Loud *"Sieg Heil!"* salutes to the Fuhrer were heard from the television, as Germans from not so long ago ignorantly cheered a primitive evil as old as time itself.

"Is this what the world is really all about?" Ashley asked, looking at the screen.

Andie's voice was heard calling her father.

"Okay," Wyatt said. "She's what the world is all about. I'll be right back."

Wyatt exited the room. Ashley picked up the remote and fast forwarded, using the "SEARCH" button. She witnessed the tragedy of World War II go by: gray and green armies advancing over once peaceful idyllic terrain, guns exploding, buildings falling, corpses strewn everywhere. Whole cities were turned into smoking ruins. And then scenes from the death camps rolled by: the frail bodies in striped prisoners' uniforms, gaunt faces with hollow eyes; prisoners tortured, whipped to death, shot point blank; children recipients of medical experiments, crippled by surgery, sewn together, blackened skins, crowds of people herded naked into gas chambers and close-ups of crematoria smokestacks.

Ashley wiped tears from her eyes and knew that Conright knew the truth of the horrors of World War II and the Holocaust. And, therefore, like Bella Blum stated, he was an accomplice to mass murder by continually forcibly denying the murders ever occurred. The tape ended but the Nazi legacy continued, Ashley realized.

Wyatt returned and said, "What did I miss?" Noticing Ashley's sadness, he added, "Something pretty bad, I guess."

"Very."

"Well, let's see what's on this one," he said, putting the second tape into the VCR. "Probably more of the same."

But instead of seeing Nazis on parade, they saw two middle-aged men sitting on a couch in a nondescript living room of a small apartment. Their suit coats were draped over the back of the couch. The men chatted in low tones, drank Heineken beer from tall pilsner glasses and smoked cigars.

"That's Conright. And I'm sure the other guy was at the airport tonight with Conright. I'm positive of it. He . . ." Wyatt said.

"He's my father," Ashley interrupted.

"Your father!" Wyatt said, astonished. "What's your father doing associating with Conright. Everybody knows Conright is a shady character, aside from being a Nazi."

"I'm not sure why," Ashley said.

That reason became apparent to both as Yvette Lenieu appeared on screen and sauntered into the room from a bedroom on the left. She had shed the preppy clothing she wore the night she was murdered for a long white negligee. Her raven black hair fell to her chest and curled at her breasts. She was a very beautiful young woman with a beautiful form. She could pass for white but was actually Creole, a mixture of black, French and Spanish blood. Yvette felt she had to associate with and please wealthy men to make a name for herself in the white male-dominated New Orleans society, much like the young quadroon, one-fourth black women, did in ante-bellum New Orleans when they gathered at Quadroon

Balls in the French Quarter, to be chosen by wealthy men as their mistresses. Conright and Tarleton lustfully eyed Yvette as she paraded around the room and then sat on the couch between them. She playfully kissed them. As she unbuttoned Conright's shirt, Tarleton moved his hands up and down her thighs. Then she knelt on the floor, pulled down Conright's pants and performed oral sex. Tarleton eagerly slid out of his pants and knelt down behind her.

"That's enough!" Ashley exclaimed. "Stop it! Stop it! Stop it!" Ashley insisted, as she buried her face in her hands. Wyatt stopped the tape and looked downward. He didn't know what to do. He had no idea of what to say in response to such a sight. It was a silence unlike either had ever experienced, weighted by disgust and despair, especially knowing how Yvette died. After a few moments, Ashley got up, ejected the tape and put both tapes in their sleeves. "I'm going to show these to Darryl. And I've got to give this sex tape to the DA.

"So, you think they were both involved in her death?" Wyatt asked.

"I don't know," Ashley said. "The DA will investigate. But there's a real possibility. She was pregnant. There's no way Conright or my father could let her give birth. No way. It would have ruined both of them. This is not New Orleans before the Civil War, when having a black mistress and children was accepted. Yvette was murdered by a man or men who had enough money to hire those hit men. There's something I didn't tell you. I visited Yvette's apartment by myself. You're not going to believe this, but I know her spirit was there. The phone book opened by itself. The pages turned and stopped on Conright's page and then on my page. I thought Yvette was telling me Conright was involved in her killing and that she wanted me to help. I realize now that she stopped on my father's name, not mine. She was telling me that both he and Conright were involved. I can't tell that to the DA. But at least I can give him this tape. This is what Yvette wanted. She was with me tonight at Conright's house. That backdoor was locked but suddenly opened. And she opened the door to the secret room where I found the tapes. It was Yvette. I'm convinced. You don't have to believe any of this. The tape speaks for itself."

"They'll just deny any involvement and say they were just having consensual sex," Wyatt said.

"They can say what they want, but the connection with her is there," Ashley said.

"You're willing to turn in your father?" Wyatt asked.

Ashley paused and then said, "As much as I hate to admit it, the man on that tape is my father. And that's an ugly side of him I never knew existed. Yes . . . I have to do this. I promised Yvette." She turned to leave and then stopped and said, "It's sickening. I feel filthy."

"If I can do anything, let me know. I'll see you tomorrow. Try to get some sleep," Wyatt said.

"That's unlikely," Ashley said.

She put her arm around Wyatt and leaned her head on his shoulder. Surprised but pleased, Wyatt slipped his right arm around the small of her back. He felt her soft auburn hair on his face and smelled her lightly sweet perfume. He wanted to kiss her, not lustfully but lovingly. Though her actions and words were sometimes perplexing to him, he could not deny his attraction to her.

"You okay?" Wyatt asked.

"I'm tired. I'm so tired," Ashley said.

"You can stay here," Wyatt offered.

"You're kind," she said.

"I try," he said.

"And you're a good dad. I misjudged you. Sorry," Ashley said, looking into his eyes.

"Don't worry about it. And thanks for saving my ass — for coming to my rescue tonight," Wyatt said.

"Well, we are a team," she said.

"Yeah," he said.

They looked at each other, like lovers.

"Well, I'm going to go," Ashley said. "Again, sorry about misjudging you. For that, I am to blame. That's something I don't often do. Actually, that's something I never do. Get some rest. See you tomorrow."

"You, too. Watch yourself out there," Wyatt said.

"I will. For sure," she said. "I'm watching everyone and everything. I've never been so vigilant. It's exhausting."

Wyatt watched Ashley walk to her car, waved to her, closed the front door, and wondered.

CHAPTER 36

You Owe Me

A warm humid wind rose over the Gulf of Mexico and blew north to the choppy, muddy waters of the Mississippi River, and then across the vanishing wetlands and over vanishing towns, and onward through the long, gray beard-like moss hanging from old oak trees in New Orleans' Audubon Park, and up and down again to the Nashville Avenue wharf where longshoremen cried "Raymond!" in a plea for rain, where they worked all night in liquid heat to unload ships just arrived from around the world, and the wind twisting again into the city and wrapping around Ashley's beautiful but fatigued face as she slowly drove her convertible BMW up deserted Airline Highway, legendary U.S. Route 61, the "Blues Highway," that stretched to Minnesota and beyond.

It was 1:00 a.m. She pushed her hand through her long, tangled hair, sticky with humidity. She was exhausted. She was cut and bruised. Her designer clothes were torn and muddy. Her BMW was dirty, dented and the remaining bumper was about to fall off, as she made her way toward her home on Lowerline in the Black Pearl neighborhood.

She felt like turning the car around and heading up 61 all the way to Minnesota, away from work and worries of which there were many now. But her mother needed her now, like never before. And she needed her mother now, like never before. They were now alone, together. The image of her father with Yvette made her close her eyes in disgust and drift into the next lane. She opened her eyes, slowly pulled over onto the shoulder and stopped. She pushed both hands through her hair, as if to pull that horrible scene from her head. Then she leaned forward, put her head in her hands and cried. "How could you do that?" she whispered. "I can never trust you again. For all I know, you had her killed." She looked up at clouds drifting across the sky and moon. She turned around and saw clouds moving all around her. She felt dizzy and nauseous. She got out, fell down and vomited. She looked up at the moon, but it was no comfort. She felt like it was burning her skin. She felt unclean. She got back into her car, retrieved her anti-bacterial gel, and spread it all over her fingers, hands, arms, face and scalp in a futile attempt to reach her brain. She looked around. The quiet was disquieting. She felt as alone and empty as the highway. She stared at the bugs and moths sailing in circles within the beam of light from her left headlight. She grew sad, and then angry. She leaned her head against the steering wheel and then heard a rumbling behind her. Two young men in a red Pontiac Trans Am stopped alongside her.

"Hey, baby, don't cry. We'll take you home," the driver said, leaning over the steering wheel and smiling a Cheshire smile. "But maybe we'll stop for a few drinks first. Just the three of us." The image of Yvette, Conright and her father shot across her mind, making her head snap back. She slowly turned, stared at their leering faces, reached down, picked up her handgun and pointed it at them. "Jesus! She's got a gun!" the passenger said. "Hit it!"

The Trans Am peeled out. Enraged, Ashley hit the gas pedal and followed closely. She could see the driver looking in the rearview and the passenger frantically looking through the rear window. She wanted them to feel fear. And she could see that they did. Then she slowed down, not wanting to get caught in that web of fear and control. The Trans Am screamed down Tulane Avenue, but Ashley turned right onto Carrollton Avenue and headed toward her home on Lowerline, near St. Charles Avenue.

She pulled into her driveway, put the gun in her handbag, and got out of her car, and grabbed the videotapes. As she approached the house, she noticed it was dark inside, but thought for sure she had left the light on in the front room. She put the key in the door and heard something move inside the house. She thought it might be her dog, Georgina. The door squeaked open. She turned on the light. Nothing seemed out of place. Then she stepped on a small crystal angel that had been knocked to the floor by someone. She felt she had better leave. When she turned around, she heard heavy breathing. The front door slammed shut and stepping forward from the shadows was Frankenstein.

Ashley's eyes widened. Every muscle tightened. A shot of

adrenalin surged through her body and her heart skipped a beat. She backed up several steps, ran down the hall and into the kitchen but Les Himm, Conright's bodyguard, was right behind her, and tackled her. She fell to the floor, dropping the tapes and her purse. She shoved her Anne Klein high heel into his groin. That slowed him down for a minute, but then he continued to climb on and over her. She felt the stubble from his beard scrape her face and she could smell his sour beer breath. She began to scream but his fat belly fell on her face, as he crawled over her like a dinosaur. He was headed for the tapes. With her free right arm, she groped around on the floor for her purse and dragged it to her. She slipped her hand inside, slid her hand around the gun, and pulled it out. As the bodyguard grabbed the tapes, he felt the gun barrel in his crotch.

"Don't move," Ashley commanded. But he moved anyway, trying to bring his right leg over her head. She cocked the hammer. "I mean it!" He stopped. "Toss the tapes away from you." He tossed them on the floor toward the far wall. "Who sent you?" No reply. "Who sent you? Goddamn it!" She punched his thigh and buttock, but her hand slipped, causing her fist to crash against his testicles.

"Oww! Jesus Christ!" he cried.

"Tell me!" Ashley shouted. "I've had a bad day. My mother's dying. I found out my father is a pervert. You tried to beat me up. And now you're back! What the hell is going on? Who sent you?" He paused again, making Ashley push the gun deeper into his crotch. "I will blow it off. I swear to God I will. I have had it with you! Who sent you?"

"You're the one who broke into Conright's house. You should have stayed out of this," he said. She pushed the gun harder. "Watch it!"

"Who sent you?" she asked.

"Your father," he said.

"That's a lie. My father would never do such a thing," Ashley said.

"Maybe you don't know your father," he said.

"You're lying! It was Conright!" Ashley insisted.

"It was your father. He wanted me to scare you," he said.

"I know it was Conright. You work for him. How was he involved in Yvette's death?" Ashley asked.

"Don't know her," he said.

"She was murdered in front of Jackson Square. She's on that tape you want so badly. She was pregnant. Did he have her killed?" He wouldn't answer. "I'm calling the police," Ashley said.

"Call them. I'll just say I was trying to get back stolen items you took from Conright's home when you broke in. A reporter breaking into a mayoral candidate's home doesn't sound good, does it? And you hit me. I just defended myself. You'll go to prison," he said.

"Don't try to intimidate me. You tried to kill my cameraman, stupid." Realizing all she needed was the tape, she decided to end this and go to her parents' house to look through her father's belongings. "Get up slowly and leave. If you ever return to my home again, I will kill you. Get out!" Ashley commanded.

The bodyguard marched out, as ordered. He walked down the street, got into his 1973 lime green Oldsmobile Ninety-Eight sedan and pulled away.

Ashley locked the door and slumped to the floor. She felt a spike in her chest and stones in her stomach. A chill ran through her body, yet she was sweating. It seemed as if a glacier had descended over her body and then receded, all in a minute's time, leaving her to bake in heat and humidity.

How involved was her father in this, she wondered? That thought was a burning inflammation in her mind. She had to know.

She put the gun in her purse, grabbed the tapes and jumped in her car, looking all around her for Frankenstein's revenge. But that monster wasn't there, only the monster called "doubt" emerged, more fearsome perhaps.

As she drove down St. Charles Avenue, she felt strangely alienated and even embarrassed, as if the old oak trees that lined the Avenue knew what had happened to her family, and that they were now staring at her shamefully. And surely her friends would do the same and worse – ostracize her and her mother – unless she didn't pursue the matter. She looked down at the tapes on the seat. She was looking at history, and history in the making.

The Avenue was quiet. She gradually overtook a streetcar on the neutral ground with no one in it. It's humming sound filled her ears as she looked up to see the driver looking straight ahead toward nothing, beneath a swollen dark red-blue-black sky that looked like it was about to hemorrhage bags of blood.

She saw a white dog slowly walking between her car and cars parked on the Avenue. The dog eyed her suspiciously and then barked, turning its head toward the front of her car, as if to alert her to something. She looked forward and stopped short, just missing the same homeless man she had grazed in the French Quarter and had noticed on her way to the gun shop. He was standing in the middle of the Avenue.

Wearing a dirty white tee shirt with "Heaven's Gate" printed on it, baggy black pants and black high-top Keds tennis shoes, he limped over to a petrified Ashley and said, "It's a beautiful, disgusting world. Ain't it? And the night is full of betrayal." Ashley looked curiously at his dark eyes and weathered face with beard stubble, wondering who this strange man was and what was he talking about. "Can you give me a lift to the Quarter? Remember, you owe me." He smiled a crooked smile. She grasped her gun.

Ashley hit the gas and sped down the Avenue, looking in her rearview mirror at a lost soul, or a threat, or an omen, who was flashing the peace sign. She drove to her parents' house and pulled up behind her mother's Jaguar. Her father's Rolls Royce was not in the driveway. She knew he was still in the company of Nazis.

She unlocked the crystal door and entered a big, dark, silent house. She turned on the light, illuminating the checkered floor in the foyer that ran down the hall to the kitchen. It was an empty house in many ways now and she felt it – made empty by sickness, time and betrayal. She glimpsed herself in the hallway mirror as she ascended the stairs. For a moment she saw herself as the happy young girl she always was, on her way to Canal Street or a party with her mother, always with her mother who made her life the enjoyment that it was and helped to fill it with pleasant memories to be unwrapped later in life, like Christmas presents, or seen in mirrors, like ghosts.

She ran up the stairs and looked into her mother's bedroom, almost expecting to see her mother sleeping. The empty bed and silence sent a shiver down her spine. She entered her father's bedroom at the end of the hall. She opened all the drawers of his mahogany dresser. Looking through his underwear made her feel quite uneasy, but the news reporter in her told her to continue. She searched the suits and shirts in his closet. She stopped for a moment to run her fingers through a shirt pocket flattened by starch. It was something she loved to do to her father's dry-cleaned shirts when she was a child. She smiled, and then continued her search. She looked through small boxes on the top shelf of the closet and found receipts from nightclubs in the U.S., Europe and Eastern Europe. But these seemed inconsequential.

Her heart was racing as she sat on his mahogany four-poster bed and surveyed the room. This had once been the master bedroom her parents shared until six years ago when her mother moved into the spare bedroom next door, following the path of many aging marriages. Then she mysteriously became ill a month ago. She had many memories of climbing into this very bed to nestle between her mother and father. She remembered something her mother told her long ago that pleasant memories are like pillows against your head. She laid down and rested her head on a large down-filled pillow. She was exhausted. She thought of her past and smiled. She just wanted to be in her parents' bed again and not leave the past. Then she slid her hand under the pillow and over a gun. She quickly sat up and pulled out the gun, a black Walther PPK. She sat stunned momentarily and then realized she had another place to check. Before putting the gun in her pocket, she wondered why her father was sleeping with a gun under his pillow.

She ran downstairs and into her father's study, turning on the light as she entered. She looked through the drawers of his wide mahogany desk. She found only invoices, bills of lading, reports, real estate appraisals and photographs of buildings and homes for sale. Atop the desk were miscellaneous papers and framed photographs of Ashley and another of her mother in her cobalt-colored wool suit.

Then she looked down at the black safe in the corner to her right. Surely, if there was anything to hide, it would be inside, she thought. But could she remember the combination? She knelt down before the safe and searched her memory. She saw her father open the safe before. She remembered seeing the numbers turn, though she didn't focus on memorizing them. She began turning the numbers, to the left, then right, then left again. She kept seeing numbers in her head – birth dates, anniversaries, Independence Day. None worked. But "01" stuck in her mind. After a few minutes, "30" surfaced in her mind, and then "33". Indeed, she had seen her father open the safe, and then let those numbers sink to the bottom of her mind, like a sunken ship. She turned the handle and the iron door swung open to reveal papers, two videotapes and a small slender cobalt blue bottle.

The sight of the videotape sent a shiver down her spine, as if someone had whispered awful news in her ear. She removed the tapes and the papers. She looked inside the cobalt bottle and saw a liquid that looked like dark honey. She put it in her pocket and closed the safe. She turned off the light and exited the room into the hallway. She then noticed that the hallway light she had turned on was now turned off.

She stood there in silence, her eyes twisting left, then right. Her skin tightened. Then she looked straight ahead through the crystal front doors and saw her father's Rolls Royce in the driveway. She suddenly felt the return of the snakes in her bloodstream. She saw a reflection of someone in the glass of Jan Vermeer's "The Piano Lesson,"hanging on the wall next to her.

"You made the mistake of leaving these tapes in your car. Now give me those two and the papers you stole and we'll call it a night," her father demanded, holding the videotapes.

Ashley turned around to see her father standing ten feet behind her, bathed chiaroscuro-like in an eerie shaft of light from the hallway upstairs. This revered figure in her life had now become menacing. And for the first time in her life, Ashley did not trust her father, making her feel nauseous and frightened.

"No," she said defiantly. "I watched the tapes."

"Do not judge me," he said.

"They're disgusting! How could you?" she asked.

"Do not judge me, Ashley. Every man has needs and desires.

You just don't understand the nature of men," he said.

"Oh, what bullshit! Don't underestimate my intelligence. It's not unlike your own. And I do understand the nature of men. I understand it well. That's why I got divorced. But I thought you were different. How could you cheat on Mother? How could you associate with a Nazi?" she angrily asked.

"It's business. He may be the next mayor. And I want a city contract. It's that simple. If I have to salute an old Nazi to get it, that's what I'll do. Don't concern yourself with my business. It's a dirty world, Ashley. It's all about survival. I told you that you wouldn't like what you found if you became a reporter. I will not let you ruin what I've created because of your naiveté. Give me the tapes," he said, angrily, moving toward her.

"What do you know about the death of Yvette Lenieu?" she asked, bravely standing her ground.

Her father stopped and said, "Absolutely nothing."

"You're completely innocent? You know nothing about her death?" she asked.

"Nothing. She had sexual relations with many men. That's the way she lived her life. Maybe one of them wanted her dead. Or maybe it was a random shooting. In this city anything's possible," he said.

"And I suppose you know nothing about the man who assaulted me an hour ago in my home," she said.

"No! You should have called the police," he said.

"And embarrass you, father? He said you sent him to get the tapes and scare me," she said.

"That's absurd. Are you going to believe your own father or Conright's mutant bodyguard?" he asked.

"How did you know it was Conright's bodyguard? I didn't tell you who the man was. He could've hurt me! I'm your daughter, not a business deal gone bad! I am your flesh and blood!" Ashley loudly said. "I take it that these tapes are copies of the two tapes you stole from my car. So, call it an even swap."

"Yes. They're copies. I . . .," her father said, and then paused.

"You always told me, 'Never accept blame for anything.' But I think your time has come," Ashley said. Ashley took the cobalt bottle from her pocket. Her father's eyes widened, making the sclera of his eyes huge and bright. "Beverly said you fixed breakfast for mother, and then she became sick. If you did anything to harm Mother or Yvette, I will never speak to you again. It seems you can learn more about a person in the dark than you can in broad daylight. I'm learning a lot about you, Father, and it's not good news," she said, now noticing a fire in his eyes.

"You're not leaving this house with my possessions!" he commanded, as he walked toward her.

"I am leaving this house," she said. "For the first time, I am extremely uncomfortable in it."

"Ashley, I'm your father! You do what I say!" he shouted.

"No!" she said, standing her ground.

He walked vigorously toward her with his fists clenched. Ashley pulled out the gun.

"Are you insane, pulling a gun on your father?" he asked, disbelievingly.

"Don't touch me!" she commanded.

She backed up until she reached the front doors, turned the antique handle with her left hand and backed out onto the porch. She slammed the door and looked at her father whose sad face was obscured somewhat through the crystal pane, making him look like a relic under glass, a memory of what used to be, lost to the darkness of history.

Ashley made a U-turn on St. Charles Avenue on her way to Baptist Hospital. She knew she had to go straight to her mother and stay there all night. She no longer trusted her father. As she turned onto St. Charles, she looked across the Avenue at her parents' house. It suddenly hit her that life there, as she knew it, was over and that, indeed, the house might be sold because her father would need all the money he could get for his legal defense, if she gave the sex tape to the District Attorney. She saw the silhouette of her father in his bedroom window. She looked down at the tapes she had just taken, and then sped up on St. Charles.

Ashley entered the room on the eighth floor of Baptist where her mother had been moved. She was sleeping. Beverly was sleeping in a chair nearby. Ashley slid a chair close to the bed, near a table lamp, and looked at her mother experiencing the peace that sleep brings. She checked the blanket covering her mother's chest and watched for the slow rise and fall, to make certain she was breathing. She took her mother's hand as tears began to roll down her face. Like looking through a photo album, memories of birthday parties, trips to Canal Street and beautiful Christmases appeared in her mind. What a wonderful life her mother had given her. She desperately wanted the chance to thank her and create even more memories. She didn't want to believe that her father had caused her mother's illness and terrible suffering. But in the morning, she would give the cobalt bottle, which she clutched in her hand, to the doctor, and the tapes in her purse to the District Attorney. And she would soon know what that reddish honey-like liquid was.

CHAPTER 37

Roll Away the Stone

The French Quarter Jesus awoke in the city morgue located in the basement of the Criminal Courts building on the corner of Tulane Avenue and Broad Street. It was 5:00 a.m. The coroner had arrived early, eager to begin work on the pileup of bodies. They were literally stacking up in the cooler, due to death by murder.

The coroner opened one of the cooler's small steel doors and pulled out the tray on which Jesus was lying. He slid it onto a gurney and rolled it near a sink-work area. He then pulled back the sheet covering Jesus to look closely at the knife wounds inflicted by Dennis "the Menace" Mena, the young man who had badly beaten so many homeless men in the French Quarter. He and Jesus had taken their fight to another level. While the coroner was inspecting a long deep gash on Jesus' right side, Jesus opened his eyes. The coroner looked up. Startled, he closed Jesus' eyes. But they opened again, turned to the right, and looked straight at him.

"Jesus Christ!" the coroner exclaimed, falling to the floor, sweat dripping from his brow due to the broken air conditioning system.

Jesus sat up, wrapped the sheet around him, smiled at the coroner, put his bare feet to the cement floor, and walked calmly out of the room. When he stepped onto Tulane Avenue, outside the courthouse, the asphalt was hot but wet from a morning shower. He walked down the middle of Tulane, his reflection shining in the window panes of old, small businesses and motels that lined both sides of this avenue that had seen better days, but had become part of urban blight. He looked nothing like a dead man. He was luminescent. He was transfigured. He had seen Moses and Elijah, not on a mountaintop, but in a basement – the basement morgue at the Criminal Courthouse. He was a brilliant beacon on this old dark road leading to the central business district and nearby Canal Street. And he was an easy mark in a bad part of town. A drug addict in jeans and a tee shirt approached him and demanded money. Jesus stopped, put his hand on the man's forehead, looked deeply into his eyes and said, "Look to God for guidance. You don't need drugs. Go and sin no more. *Vade in pace.*"

The man looked at Jesus with a puzzled stare and replied, "I do need drugs. I need drugs to see God. I can see you ain't got nothing but shit in that big-ass diaper." Then the man stumbled away.

Jesus made it to Canal Street, which separated the central business district on his right from the French Quarter on his left. He walked down the middle of Canal, the main drag of New Orleans that cut the town in two and led straight to the River. This once vibrant area with large department stores and clothing stores on both sides of Canal was now in serious decline, characterized by white flight and the emergence of businesses catering to tourists, low-income families and those in need of a loan to light dark, desperate hours in the "City That Care Forgot."

A low-lying fog was breaking up as Jesus walked through it, making the fog look like the spirits of deceased New Orleanians crossing Canal and hurrying down its sidewalks, as if they were still alive with purposeful intentions. Then Jesus looked heavenward and saw Mother Mary ascending in flowing robes of white and blue. And he stopped to witness the brilliance of the sun rising over the fog and through parting clouds, that looked like the fingers of God embracing Mary's smiling face as she was assumed into heaven. And Jesus wept at the sight of the Womb of the Universe, Holy Mary Mother of God. In the light of day and behind the curtain of night was always Mary.

Jesus then turned left and entered the French Quarter by walking down the center of Bourbon Street where the smells of beer, garbage and urine wafted through the humid morning air, and the ruins of the night's revelry in the forms of cups, cans and Mardi Gras beads filled the gutters. Two policemen were asleep in the cruiser at the corner of Bourbon and Iberville. On the opposite side of the street was a young man lying on his stomach. He had been roughed up. Someone had obviously stepped on him, leaving a footprint on his white tee shirt. Jesus knelt over him, sat him up, and gave him a drink of water from a small, discarded Kentwood water bottle. He then poured water on his sheet hem and wiped drops of blood from the man's face. He made the sign of the cross on the man's forehead. He stepped into the corner bar and asked the bartender to call an ambulance. Though Jesus was an arresting sight, it was, after all, the French Quarter, so the bartender did not take notice for too long and called the ambulance.

Jesus continued down Bourbon which was deserted except for a few remaining pleasure seekers unable or unwilling to find their way home, two truck drivers unloading stacks of beer cans, and a lone long-haired shirtless youth with a peace symbol painted on his chest and a bull's-eye on his back, trotting up Bourbon, higher than Timothy Leary on LSD Appreciation Day. He flashed the peace sign as he continued his search for a psychedelic portal to the 1960s.

Jesus continued down Bourbon, passing jazz clubs, restaurants and strip clubs, one of which featured the bottom half of a female mannequin on a swing, swinging its legs into view over the sidewalk from a window above. He then encountered a homeless man who had rounded the corner at Conti Street. It was the old black man dressed all in brown who wanted Wyatt to bury him, if he found him dead by the curb. He was pushing his grocery cart full of his belongings. He hurried to Jesus, knelt down, and kissed his feet.

"Rise, my friend. Join me in my fight," Jesus said, with a smile. "I am the Light of the World. He that follows Me shall not walk in darkness, but shall have the Light of Life. *Creditis in me.*"

"Yes, Lord," the man said, rising.

Jesus looked down Bourbon and saw several disciples approaching him. They were, of course, all homeless men and included the man in red Wyatt had spotted on an Audubon Park bench while driving down St. Charles Avenue, and the same man who kept appearing to Ashley, seemingly everywhere she went, as if trying to collect on that debt he said she owed him. All four men knelt at the feet of Jesus and then rose in wonder. One man said, "Hosanna in the highest! Conqueror of Death, blessed is He who comes in the name of God."

"I have returned. I am resurrected to finish God's work," Jesus proclaimed. Each man then individually placed their hands over Jesus' heart. He looked them all straight in their eyes, each one, and said, "Where is he? Where is Satan?"

"He's asleep near the River," one said.

"Let us do God's work," Jesus replied.

They walked down Conti Street through a quiet, hungover French Quarter, crossed Chartres Street and turned left onto Decatur Street. After crossing to the other side of Decatur, the true believers soon encountered insomniac Tune, sadly blowing his sax across from Jackson Square. Dressed in black jeans, black New Orleans Saints tee shirt and Ray-Ban Wayfarers sunglasses, Tune was the sole survivor of the many people who walked Decatur the night before. And winding around the deep bluesy notes he blew, like a vine, was a distress signal from the heart of darkness.

"Jesus," Tune said in a low voice, after lowering his saxophone, "forgive me. Forgive me my sins." He lowered his head.

"What sin did you commit, my brother?" Jesus asked.

Tune hesitated and then said, "I've hurt some people."

"Are you truly repentant for what you've done?" Jesus asked.

"Yes," Tune replied sorrowfully, while wiping away tears. "I hurt those people. I've got blood on my hands."

"Follow me," Jesus instructed.

They all walked up the concrete embankment and over the walkway that led down to the River. The cool, crisp air rolling off the River filled their nostrils, sent chills down their spines, and awakened their spirits.

"There he is," one disciple said to Jesus, pointing to Dennis Mena, who was sleeping on the grass about a hundred yards away, down river.

Jesus replied, "Yes. The wrath of God shall be visited upon him this morning," eyeing the sleeping demon-man. He then turned to Tune and said, "My brother, you are a shattered man. I will make you whole. You are stained, but the waters of God Almighty's River will cleanse you."

The disciples prepared to lower Tune into the River by supporting his back with their arms. Jesus stood over Tune and breathed on him, saying, "Darkness, leave this man and give way to the Light and Breath of the Holy Spirit." Jesus placed his hands on Tune's head and said, "Father, drive out all blindness of heart and break this bond with Satan, so that his heart will see again. Set him free from the foulness of all wicked desires." Jesus then made the sign of the cross over Tune three times and said, "I exorcise thee, unclean spirit, in the name of the Father and of the Son and of the Holy Spirit, that thou depart from this servant of God. I command thee, accursed devil, give honor to the living and true God and leave this servant of God because he has found God's holy grace." Jesus looked into Tune's eyes and firmly stated, "Do you renounce Satan?"

"Yes," Tune replied.

"And all his works?" Jesus asked.

"Yes," Tune said.

Jesus dipped his fingers in the River and then made the sign of the cross on Tune's chest.

"Do you believe in God the Father Almighty, Creator of Heaven and Earth?" Jesus asked.

"I do," Tune replied.

"Do you believe in Me, Jesus Christ, His only Son, who was born, suffered, died and has risen?" Jesus asked.

"I do," Tune assured.

"Do you believe in the Holy Ghost, the Holy Catholic Church, the communion of Saints, the forgiveness of sins, the resurrection of the body and life everlasting?" Jesus asked.

"I do," Tune said.

Jesus poured water from the River over Tune's head three times, saying, "I baptize you in the name of the Father and the Son and the Holy Spirit. May Almighty God, My Father, who hath regenerated thee by water and the Holy Spirit, and who hath given thee the remission of all thy sins, may He Himself anoint thee with the Chrism of Salvation unto life eternal."

The disciples answered, "Amen."

"Peace be with you," Jesus said.

"And with your spirit," the disciples said.

Jesus ripped off a piece of the sheet he was wearing and tied it around Tune's arm and said, "Wear this unstained cloth that you may have life everlasting. Go and sin no more. God be with you. *Deus sit apud vos.*"

"Thank you, Jesus," Tune said.

Tune knelt before Jesus and kissed his feet. He then walked a few feet into the River, made a small cut on his hand with his pocketknife, bled into the River, scooped up the water mixed with his blood and drank it. He walked out of the River and over the embankment and then up Decatur.

Jesus looked at his disciples and said, "Draw your swords, my brothers. Today we battle Satan for the last time. He will not plague this city again."

Jesus led the way as the men pulled knives from their clothes and followed him to where Dennis Mena was sleeping on the ground beneath an oak tree, older than the city itself.

CHAPTER 38

Heat

Ashley Tarleton was a marked woman. Conright wanted her dead. Tune had always been the go-to man for dirty deeds. But Tune had a change of heart. His conscience would no longer allow him to do the work of Satan. He was now a servant of the Lord.

Tune sat on the damp floor of his Creole cottage, looking at the painting of Jesus hanging on his bedroom wall. He thought of Christ's suffering, and he thought of his mother and brother, all of whom died too young. Sweat and tears fell from Tune's face and dissolved into the Cypress wood floor, staining the wood dark like blood. Tune touched Jesus' flaming Sacred Heart which was emanating divine light and encircled by a crown of thorns. Tune mournfully said, "Forgive me, Jesus. I was the instrument of evil. But I am not that man anymore. I am not that man. Forgive me, Jesus. Forgive me. Forgive me. Forgive me." The cool air from the black 1935 Emerson oscillating fan felt like a woman's gentle hands on his naked body engulfed in tattoos of fire.

Tune picked up a pencil and paper and walked to the kitchen table. He sat down and thought for a few minutes. The breeze from the fan traveled down the hallway and wrapped around his bare feet. The rotational whisking noise from the large window box fan in the kitchen window was hypnotizing. He sat motionless for a few minutes with his eyes closed. The cool breeze encircled him, allowing him a few minutes of relief from the heat. Then the phone rang.

"Hi, Daddy. Pick up if you're there," his daughter said. After a few moments, she continued. "I guess you're not home. I just wanted to remind you about this weekend. Cece and I are going swimming at the NORD swimming pool. You promised to take us. Diving into the water is the only way to beat the heat. Call me back. Thanks. I love you. Bye."

Diving into the water is the only way to beat the heat, Tune thought. "The only way," Tune whispered, wiping tears from his eyes. He then spoke and wrote, "Please forgive me for leaving this way. A man has to pay for his mistakes in his life and stand before God in the next life. I have sinned. For that I am very sorry. I let you down and I am ashamed. I tried to teach you right and wrong and provide for you. But I haven't done such a good job lately. Now I'm the student. In these past few months I've felt like a man trapped in a burning house. And it doesn't help to know that I started that fire. And until now I didn't know how to put it out. Don't remember me as Tune. Remember me as Jack Rene Poirier, loving son, brother, husband and father. And remember that I always loved you. And we will see each other again in the next life. I love you. Daddy."

Tune wept. Tears dropped onto the note. He picked it up and walked into the bedroom. He took his saxophone and laid it on the bed. He set the note next to the saxophone. He looked at a photo of himself with his arm around his daughter; the two were laughing. He placed the photo on the bed. He then retrieved a white envelope from the dresser drawer. It contained ten-thousand dollars. He placed it under the photo. He stared at the collection of articles on the bed. The sum of my life, he thought.

He grabbed a pair of black jeans and a green tee shirt, and put them on. He slipped into a pair of sandals and opened the closet door. From there he pulled out a gas can and a sawed-off shotgun. He slipped ten shells into his pocket. He picked up the gasoline and the gun, took a last look around, and headed for the front door.

It was ten o'clock in the morning and already eighty-five degrees. Tune started to sweat in less than a minute as he approached his green Cadillac. He opened the trunk and deposited the gas and gun in full view of the children and neighbors on their front steps. He slammed the trunk down, sat down behind the steering wheel, shutting the squeaky door behind him. He revved the engine and put on his traditional black Wayfarers sunglasses. He waved to the children as he drove slowly up the street toward Lake Pontchartrain and Conright's house. He was saying goodbye to his impoverished, caged neighborhood where many of the shotgun houses and Creole cottages closer to Claiborne Avenue had iron bars on their windows and doors. When night fell, the residents retreated inside their meager homes, hoping to escape the wrath of the heavily armed vampires who freely roamed the city's streets. Only the rising sun could allay their fears. But with it came a hellish heat.

When Tune arrived at Keiffer Conright's house, he rammed the iron fence and shot Conright's dog, and the two German Shepherds belonging to the guest Nazis. He reloaded the shotgun, picked up the gas can, adjusted his Wayfarers, walked tall and upright like a man with God on his side, reached the kitchen door, and kicked it in. He immediately encountered Conright's Frankenstein bodyguard who fired twice at Tune but missed. Tune did not. He leveled the shotgun at the man and fired, striking the man in the face, neck and upper chest. The man fell backward like a sawed tree.

Tune stepped over him, looked left, down the hall, and saw Conright helping his father hurry up the staircase to hide in the closet. As he started down the hall, he encountered small-arms fire from the Nazis in the living room who had been watching archival footage of Adolph Hitler while they were playing Twister. Tune exchanged gunfire with the five men as they hugged the wall. Tune then took a bullet to his left shoulder, causing him to drop the gas can. While holding the shotgun with his left hand, he used his right hand to throw the gas can into the living room. He took the gun in his right hand, pulled the trigger, and hit the can, setting the room and the men on fire. Screams and the premature cuckoos from the cuckoo clock on the wall resounded throughout the house.

Tune reloaded and walked upstairs to the closet door in Conright's office. He blew it open and expected to see two corpses. But he saw no one. He stepped in, pushed aside splintered wood, boxes and some clothing. He then realized one of the three walls was false. He blew a hole in the one to his left but heard nothing. He reloaded and blasted the rear wall which then opened to the secret Nazi chamber. There were Conright and his father in the corner and dressed in Nazi black with red swastika armbands.

"Tune, are you insane? If you want more money, I'll get it now. Why are you doing this?" Conright pleaded.

"I was wrong. And all men must pay for their crimes. Nazis are the worst," Tune said.

Tune pointed the shotgun at them and fired, striking both in their heads. They sank to the floor as a large red Nazi flag descended on them from the shelf above.

The front half of the house was now ablaze, including the hall, down which Tune retraced his steps as though the flames could not affect a man already on fire. He started his car and watched the house go up in flames. One Nazi had jumped from the front window and was burning on the front lawn. All others were cremated in that house-size oven.

Tune drove for a few minutes as he tried to nurse his wound with a handkerchief. He crossed over West End Boulevard and then made a left turn onto Pontchartrain Boulevard which led to I-10. After a few minutes, he exited and turned left toward Airline Highway, Highway 61, which ran through a New Orleans suburb.

Tune drove twenty minutes, passing old motels, no longer postcard quality and now temporary homes for prostitutes, and small buildings that had housed numerous businesses since the highway's heyday in the 1940s, '50s and '60s, until it was eclipsed with the advent of Interstate 10. He finally turned onto a side street when he reached the area surrounding the airport and drove into a storage facility. He parked his Cadillac outside a storage unit large enough to accommodate a car. He got out, rolled back the aluminum door, and stepped inside.

Tune ripped off his tee shirt and threw it on the floor. He poured water from a Kentwood water bottle over the wound, the size of a pencil eraser. He saturated a towel with water and applied force to the wound which stung like a burn. He sat on an overturned white plastic bucket and watched the jets appear one after another from deep within the clouds, as if through a mysterious portal linking another world to this one. He watched and waited for the flight from Los Angeles. And he thought. And he knew what he was about to do, had to be done.

Tune checked his watch. An hour had passed. He walked to his car and opened the trunk. He wrapped the shotgun in an old dirty towel and returned to the storage unit. He took an old cloth and wiped the sweat from his face and neck. Because it was so hot, he walked outside the unit. He looked down the long concrete pavement road to the storage main gate. He then spotted the long black Mercedes-Benz sedan approaching the gate. He retreated inside the storage unit.

The two men had arrived from Los Angeles and had re-occupied the black Mercedes with the T-tag still in the rear window, that they had carjacked and left in the airport parking lot on their last visit to murder Yvette Lenieu.

The Mercedes pulled up near the storage unit. Two young black men slowly stepped out, both wearing black and silver athletic clothing, gold chains and sunglasses. One wore a Los Angeles Raiders jacket. They slowly walked into the garage.

"Tune, what is happening, my brother? Good to see you," said the man wearing the cap.

"What the hell happened to you?" the other man exclaimed, noticing the bullet hole in Tune's shoulder.

"Hey, man, is someone following you? Are you in trouble? Are the cops after you? If so, we got to split now," the other man said, adjusting his cap.

"No. I was cleaning my gun and shot myself. It was an accident. Come on in," Tune said, purposely not making eye contact.

The two men moved toward the middle of the floor as Tune pulled down the garage door.

"So, who's the bitch we supposed to off tonight?" one man asked.

"Hey, man, turn on the damn lights. I can hardly see you," the man wearing the jacket said, removing his sunglasses.

"The whole world is in darkness. Let Jesus light the way," Tune said in a calm tone.

"Jesus? What the hell you talking about, old man?" the other man said.

"Jesus said, 'I am the Light of the World. He that follows Me shall not walk in darkness but shall have the Light of Life,'" Tune said.

"Where's the damn money!?" the other man shouted.

"There's pain all around us. And we cause most of it because of our selfishness and greed and stupidity. Will you kneel with me and renounce Satan and his evil ways?" Tune asked.

"This old dude is crazy!" the man in the jacket said to the other.

"Yeah, man. This guy's whacked. We're gonna have to do him, too," the other man said.

Touching his stomach, Tune said, "Aren't you tired of feeding the serpent within you? We must kill the serpent, even if we die doing it. Don't you know that?" The two men looked at each other and then stepped forward. Tune quickly picked up the shotgun leaning against the wall and still wrapped in its towel. The two men split up, each slowly walking to the left and right of Tune. "It's all over for everybody. You just don't see, do you? Let Jesus light the way."

The man wearing the Raider's jacket, on Tune's left side, slowly lowered his left hand and pulled up his pant leg, revealing a large, clear plastic – metal detection resistant – knife in a sheath strapped to his leg. He quickly pulled the knife and threw it at Tune, lodging in his shoulder. Tune pulled the trigger. The shotgun blast hit the man in the chest, blowing him backward and down.

"Jesus Christ! You old . . ." the other man shouted, as he lunged toward Tune, who pulled the other trigger. That blast hit the man in the lower abdomen. He fell to his knees. He then began walking on his knees toward Tune. He reached Tune and tried to pull him down. As Tune sank to his knees, he pulled the knife from his chest and stabbed the man repeatedly in the neck. Blood erupted from his carotid artery and mingled with Tune's own blood on his chest. They both fell to the floor. Tune pushed away the body. He knew he had to act fast. He was bleeding profusely and losing strength. He feared he would lose consciousness, too.

He rolled open the garage door and backed in the Cadillac. After opening the trunk, he dragged one body toward the car using only his right arm. He felt intense, burning pain as he positioned the body in a seated posture against the rear bumper. Using mostly his right arm, he pulled the body up and into the Cadillac's huge trunk. He fell down twice, dragging the other body to the car. He had to hoist it onto his right shoulder and pushed it into the trunk.

He used a dirty rag to wipe the blood off the bumper. He pulled out of the garage. Shirtless and woozy, he drove up the facility's paved roadway toward his final destination where he could put out the flames, forever.

CHAPTER 39

Grevious Angel

It was 11:00 a.m. when Ashley walked into Darryl's office at TV-3 News, bringing with her the damning evidence on the videotapes that showed Conright wearing a Nazi uniform while speaking to a loyal following and the sex tape showing Yvette Lenieu having sex with Conright and Ashley's father.

"Hey! Morning," Darryl said, just before taking a bite of custard pie from McKenzie's Pastry Shop. "Want some? It's good."

"No. Thanks. I ate something at the hospital," Ashley said, taking the chair in front of Darryl's desk.

"How is your mother doing?" Darryl asked.

"Better now. But . . ." Ashley said, as her voice cracked.

"What is it? Bad news about your mother?" he asked.

"No," she said, taking a handkerchief from her Coach purse. "Bad news about my father."

"Oh, no. What is it?" he asked.

"I have reason to believe he poisoned my mother," Ashley confessed.

"What!? How do you know?" he asked.

"I found a bottle in his safe with a sort of red honey-like substance in it. I think he was adding it to my mother's food whenever he could to eventually kill her. And it was working," Ashley said, nervously wringing her hands.

"Why?" Darryl said, alarmingly, shaking his head.

"Greed. Some of his businesses are failing. He cannot stand to fail or take blame for anything. And he lost a lot in the stock market. Obviously, he sees my mother as an insurance policy, literally, to cash out," Ashley said.

"Money in the bank," Darryl unashamedly said.

"Yes. He's no better than the young thugs who run these streets," Ashley said, regrettably.

"Ashley, are you sure of this? This is as serious as it gets," Darryl said.

"The lab at Baptist Hospital is doing a test now. I'll know today if it's poison. But I don't doubt it. I had . . . an encounter with him last night at my parents' house. I've always respected him and looked up to him, even revered him. But last night, for the first time ever, I feared him. Darryl, I pulled my gun on him," Ashley said, shaking her head, while wiping away a tear.

"Jesus!" Darryl exclaimed.

"Last night my own father was a stranger to me," Ashley said. "I felt a chill run down my spine. I raced to the hospital and stayed awake most of the night, watching my mother breathe. I was so afraid she would stop. I didn't want to leave her unprotected."

"Well, sure. I understand," Darryl said.

"And I think my father and Conright had Yvette murdered," Ashley said. "She was pregnant. I'm sure one was the father. They're so arrogant that they could never father a child that was half black and half white. It would destroy them. Can you imagine Conright, the racist, admitting to fathering a black child, or my father who is a pillar of New Orleans society? So, they had her murdered, as if she was a runaway slave. And here's the evidence," she said, placing the two tapes on the desk. "One is a sex tape, and one shows Conright at a Nazi rally, addressing the troops. Don't ask how I got that one. Don't even ask."

"Wow!" he exclaimed.

"I'm bringing the sex tape to the DA. It will give him a reason to investigate Conright and my father. Will you run the other?" she asked, giving him the other tape.

"Yes. Of course. Good work, Ashley," Darryl said, with a surprised look on his face.

"If the DA hands down an indictment, I want to cover it,"

Ashley said.

"Are you sure?" Darryl questioned.

"Yes," Ashley quickly and forcefully said.

"Are you absolutely, positively sure? It will be incredibly stressful for you. You'll need to muster all the courage you can," Darryl said.

"I know," Ashley said.

"You'll testify against your own father?" he asked.

"Yes," she said, looking Darryl straight in the eye. "All men must pay for their crimes, no matter what position they hold in life or how old they are or who they are. I've learned a lot in a short time."

Cato stepped halfway into the room and excitedly said, "All hell has broken loose. Conright's house is in flames and the guy who torched it is threatening suicide on the GNO bridge. Wyatt's up there. He's doing a remote."

Ashley and Darryl exchanged wide-eyed stares.

"Are the police there?" Darryl asked.

"Yeah," said Cato. "They're trying to talk him down."

They all rushed into the studio to watch the scene unfold of Tune sitting in his Cadillac striding the four lanes, pointed north up river and the engine running. With the camera steady on his shoulder, Wyatt stayed wide and then slowly zoomed in on Tune who often closed his eyes and grimaced from the many flames of a fire raging within, so out of control that Tune's tears rolling down his face could not extinguish.

"Hey! Aren't you Tune? I've seen you in the Quarter," Wyatt shouted. Tune nodded. "You're a great sax player. Why are you doing this?"

"I've got to put out the fire," Tune said, enigmatically, looking straight ahead.

"What does that mean?" Wyatt said. No answer. "Why did you set Keiffer Conright's house on fire? Was he in it?"

"Him, his father, his bodyguard and four neo-Nazis," Tune

replied.

"Why?" Wyatt asked.

"I had to put an end to them, so they won't father any children to spread hate. I had to make things right before I leave this world," Tune declared.

"How did you know them?" Wyatt asked.

Tune looked at Wyatt and said, "Remember one thing. I want everybody in our great city to know that I did a bad thing. I'm confessing to you. And this is my punishment, my penance."

"Why did you kill Conright and the others?" Wyatt asked.

"Conright paid me to have Yvette murdered. I hired the hit men," Tune said.

"Where are they?" Wyatt asked.

"In my trunk," Tune said. "Asleep. I will deliver them to God. I hired them to kill Jacques Daniels. Conright wanted me to have Ashley Tarleton killed. He said she didn't know her place. But I had to put an end to it." In the studio, Ashley gasped. "So Conright had to die. And find Tarleton. He was in on it, too."

"George Tarleton, the businessman?" Wyatt inquired, astonished that Ashley's father was accused.

"Yeah. That's him. They all in it," Tune admitted, revving the engine.

"There's no need to end this way. Just give yourself up," Wyatt insisted.

"That won't stop the fire. Tell my little girl I love her," Tune said.

"Out of the way!" a police officer shouted, as he shot out the rear tires.

Tune floored the accelerator, thrusting the metallic green Cadillac forward and through the guardrail. The car was catapulted into space and then plunged into the River, like a knife of green obsidian stone slicing the neck of a victim of human sacrifice to please the ancient Aztec god of the sun, Huitzilopochtli, in an attempt to stave off the descent into darkness, except Tune's god was the God. Everyone stood stupefied by this senseless act. But

Wyatt quickly moved to the rail and caught the car descending and being swallowed by the muddy, rolling waters that churned like crushing teeth. Tune and his music were gone forever, and so was the fire.

In the studio, all were stunned after witnessing the suicide. They were all serious news gatherers, even news hounds. But they were never present to witness a murder or suicide. This tragedy left them all bewildered. What to do, they wondered.

"I'm sorry, Ashley," Darryl said softly as he leaned in. "We finally learned the truth about Conright."

"And the truth about my father," Ashley replied.

"Take the sex tape to the DA. We'll use the other for tonight's broadcast," Darryl suggested. "Did you want to do the story tonight?"

"I should do the story," Ashley said. "And I'm not afraid to do the story. But I want to be with my mother. I just want to be by her side and protect her and help her get better. I almost lost her, Darryl. I already lost one parent, so to speak. I'm going to stay with the one who always stayed with me. What I'm going to do in the future, I'm not sure."

"You're always welcomed here," Darryl offered.

"Thanks," Ashley said, hugging Darryl. "And thanks for trusting in me."

"Well, you proved yourself well. You're not just the entertainment reporter anymore. So, come back when you're ready," Darryl said.

"I will."

Ashley picked up her purse and videotaped evidence from Darryl's office and walked toward the spiral staircase. A white dove fluttering outside a window down a short hall caught her attention and was gone. She continued down the hallway, descended the spiral staircase and then proceeded into the garage. The large pull-up door was open. Standing in the driveway was the same little girl Ashley met previously. She was dressed in a white dress reminiscent of the nineteenth century and not wearing shoes.

"Ashley," the little girl shouted, while waving. "Come see."

Ashley stood and stared for a moment. "Come. My friend wants to meet you," she continued, motioning to her to come closer.

Puzzled, Ashley tossed the tape and her purse inside her car.

"Hi. I can't talk now. My mother is ill. I'm going to her now," Ashley said, bending down toward the girl.

"I know. But she's doing much better now. Isn't she?" the girl asked.

"Yes, how did you know?" Ashley asked.

"She'll be fine. Faith and prayer are the keys. My father told me," the girl said.

"Who's your father? Where is he? Is he a doctor?" Ashley asked.

"He's up there," she said, pointing to the sky. Ashley looked up at the buildings, not knowing what the girl was talking about. "Please. It won't take long." The girl took Ashley's hand.

"Wait! Where are we going? Where are your parents?" Ashley questioned, trying to keep up as they moved in front of St. Louis Cathedral where people were gathered talking about the bleeding statue of the Virgin Mary in the cathedral. Ashley gazed over to see three birds flying out of the cathedral. They trotted up St. Ann Street, next to the cathedral, crossed Royal Street and continued one block to Bourbon where they turned right and walked down a few doors to the Grevious Angel bar. The girl led her down an alley next to the bar until it ended in a courtyard that was once beautiful with banana plants, camellias and magnolias, but was now in disrepair like the city itself. "Wait!" Ashley exclaimed. "Where are you taking me?"

"He's here," the girl responded, pointing to the second story of the antebellum slave quarters at the opposite end of the courtyard.

The brown-gray-colored wooden slave quarters consisted of three small rooms on the ground floor and three rooms above with a leaning, wobbly staircase to the left. Each floor had one door with a wooden bottom half and six small panes of glass on the top. The whole structure leaned to the right, battered by hurricanes, and the weight of rot and time.

Ashley grasped the shaky wooden railing as she stepped onto

the thin boards that served as steps. She steadily, slowly climbed each step up to the second level with the little girl leading.

"Who's here? Who is your friend?" Ashley inquired, becoming more nervous with each step. "I thought you said your friend was dead."

"He has risen," the girl said, opening the door with squeaky, rusted hinges.

"Risen?" Ashely asked, perplexed.

They walked slowly to the room at the opposite end, passing two rooms with clothing, Popeye's fried chicken boxes, and paper bags on the floor. The floorboards creaked with each step. They then entered a dimly lit, L-shaped room where a pathway was lined with stolen stone angels that led Ashley into the longer part of the room around the corner. As she approached the turn, an unkempt man appeared.

"We've been expecting you," he said, revealing bad teeth behind a crooked smile. He wore a red tee shirt.

Ashley felt a waterfall of fear drop down her body. She recognized him as the red-shirted man sitting on the bench in Audubon Park and pointing toward heaven. She looked around for the little girl but she had disappeared. She wanted to run but felt paralyzed with fear. She looked down and to her right and saw three red and white Igloo ice chests and empty ice bags on the floor. And at the end of the room she saw the French Quarter Jesus sitting on a high back chair, flanked by his homeless disciples.

"Jesus!" Ashley exclaimed.

"Yes, my friend. We've been waiting for you to spread the Good News that the Beast is dead," the French Quarter Jesus said.

"No!" Ashley shouted, as she turned to escape but was restrained by the homeless man she grazed with her car that night when leaving the French Quarter.

"You owe me. Time to pay up," he said, with a firm hand on her arm, as he pushed her forward to the first ice chest. "It is glorious victory."

Another disciple opened the chest. Ashley looked down into the chest full of ice and the bloody severed head of Dennis "the

Menace" Mena, the young man who had terrorized the homeless. The face was wide-eyed and open-mouthed, as if shouting a forever-frozen cry for help.

"Oh, my God!" Ashley cried out, as she put her hand over her mouth.

Two disciples opened the other two ice chests which held his torso and his legs cut at the hip.

"We dismembered him so he could not transform again into Satan. His evil reign is over. The city is clean and free of fear. We have done this. We have captured and killed the Beast. As long as he remains in these three holy chests, which I have blessed, there will be no more killings. God's children are free. I have chosen you to spread the news," Jesus told Ashley, as if speaking the Word of God.

Her blood pressure and nausea rising, Ashley knew she was looking at the collective face of madness. Sweat cascaded down her face, neck and back. The heat and foul odor swirled around the room, making her dizzy. The pressure behind her eyes was making her see spots. Her fingers and toes were beginning to be numb as her stomach was rolling over. The room was like a furnace and Jesus and his disciples were the flames.

"You're all murderers," she said, backstepping.

"We're angels of God. Why can't you see that?" Jesus insisted. "I have chosen you to be the bearer of Good News."

"We are all slaves to fear. Precious souls are lost every day. We have put an end to slavery. We are not murderers. We are not criminals. We are liberators," a disciple said.

"Praise God on high!" the disciple in the red shirt shouted.

"Praise God on high!" repeated the others.

"Give thanks to the Lord for He takes away the sins of the world," one disciple said.

"May Almighty God cleanse us of our sins," another disciple said.

"Do not be afraid of the Lord. Embrace Him," said the man who Ashley hit with her car, as all the men walked toward her.

Ashley continued to backstep but fell over a stone angel.

"Stop! You're madmen! Stop!" she commanded.

She got to her feet and took one last look at the threatening, possessed group of orphaned men who apparently had no one else to turn to in life but the French Quarter Jesus who, himself, had no others but his ragged, haunted disciples. Ashley realized that in their crusade to stop murder in the city, they had themselves become murderers. They had become the beast they had devoured. The fact that they could not or would not recognize their crime made Ashley greatly frightened. She was in serious jeopardy of losing her own life. She knew she had to cage the liberators.

Ashley ran from the room and hit the wooden railing on the staircase with such force that part of it collapsed. Her heart was beating wildly as she ran up the alley and onto Bourbon Street, crowded with people who stared at this red-faced woman now in panic mode. She frantically looked left and right, her eyes darting about in search of a cop. She noticed two policemen standing on the corner of St. Peter and Bourbon in front of the Crazy Corner club.

"Please," she said, rushing over and catching her breath, "in the apartment behind that bar . . . there are men . . . there's been a murder!"

"How many men?" one cop asked.

"Six or seven," Ashley replied, trembling.

"How many were murdered?" the other policeman inquired.

"One young man . . . they cut his body into pieces. It's awful!" Ashley said, with a look of horror on her face.

"All right. Stay here," he told Ashley, as they called for backup.

The two policemen ran to the bar and down the alley. Tourists moved close to the bar, wondering what was happening. Ashley ran back to TV-3. As she was entering the garage, she saw Wyatt who was just returning from covering Tune's suicide leap off the bridge.

"Wyatt!" Ashley exclaimed.

"Jesus! What's wrong? You look white as a ghost," Wyatt observed.

"You've seen the French Quarter Jesus?" Ashley asked.

"Yeah, sure," Wyatt said.

"He and some homeless men killed Dennis Mena," Ashley said, trying to catch her breath.

"Dennis the Menace. You're shitting me!" he exclaimed.

"I'm not. Grab your camera. Let's go!" she shouted.

They ran back to the Grevious Angel where the crowd had grown. Two police cars and a police van had arrived. Ashley and Wyatt inched their way closer to the alley.

"This is an exclusive. We're the only press here," Ashley remarked. "You did a great job on the bridge. Excellent work."

"Thanks," Wyatt said, staring straight into her eyes a little longer perhaps than needed, as she returned the eye contact.

"Make way!" a polieman said, leading the first of the disciples through the crowd to the van.

The man Ashley hit with her car stared at her and said, "I'm not forgetting you. You owe me big time now."

The other disciples were then led to the van. The French Quarter Jesus followed last. Wyatt got a tight close-up.

"I am not a criminal!" Jesus exclaimed. "I am a warrior of God. Now Satan will rise again and plague this city. The murders will continue. This city needs a hard, hard rain to cleanse its soul. And it's coming! The tears of God will drown this city. Look to heaven above and see clouds gather. And remember this day when you let loose the Beast."

As the French Quarter Jesus stepped into the van, three employees from the Crime Lab came up the alley, each carrying an ice chest.

"Did Jesus or the other men say anything?" Ashley questioned a police officer.

"The followers didn't. But that Jesus guy said to keep Satan, who we believe to be Dennis Mena, so he could not rise again. And those stone angels in there were all stolen by his men to watch over the apartment. They were all stolen from local cemeteries," the officer said, as he closed the van doors.

"Thank you," Ashley said.

"This is incredible footage. I'm going to editing now. I always saw Jesus around here and always tried to stay away from him. But I never thought he would murder a man," Wyatt said, thoroughly astonished.

"But that's the point. To him, Dennis was not a man. He was the Devil himself," Ashley added, wiping sweat from her face.

"Who knows. Maybe he was. And we're just not paying close enough attention," Wyatt remarked. "It's hard to trust anyone these days. You never really know who you are talking to."

"Especially in this haunted city. Everyone wears a mask," Ashley added.

They looked straight into each other's eyes. They both knew each was thinking of Conright and Ashley's father.

"It's been one hell of a day. And it isn't even dark yet. Who knows what the night will bring. You're going to do the five o'clock, right?" Wyatt asked.

"No. I'm going to be with my mother now. You do it, you've got more talent than I gave you credit for. Tell Darryl that I recommend you," Ashley said.

"Thanks," Wyatt said. "And you have more talent and courage than I first thought."

"I agree with you," Ashley said. "And I'll need a lot more courage in the days to come."

"Feel free to call on me anytime . . . anytime at all," Wyatt suggested.

"I'll keep that in mind," Ashley replied.

"And I hope your mom is okay," Wyatt added.

"Thanks. I hope so, too," Ashley said.

"Watch out!" Ruthie the Duck Girl shouted, as she skated by the police van with her duck in tow. "Jesus is crazy! I always said that. This whole town is crazy," she added, lifting a can of beer to her mouth.

"Maybe she's right," Wyatt said, smiling.

"I hope not," Ashley said.

"Imagine what the national press is going to do with Conright's house in flames and Jesus arrested. They'll have a field day. To them, it will be the same old New Orleans: crooked and crazy," Wyatt said, as they walked toward the station.

"Yes. Sad but true," Ashley admitted.

"Only we know who we really are," Wyatt observed.

"I wonder what they'll say about us in the future?" Ashley asked.

"Who knows?" Wyatt questioned. "Maybe when they dig through the charred rubble of history, they won't even recognize us at all. They may see us as some ancient, primitive people who lived by the River and were forced to leave due to flood or fire."

When they entered the TV-3 garage, Ashley leaned against her white BMW convertible.

"Are you okay? You look pale."

"I'm okay," she said. "I'm a little nauseated. I've just seen a man cut in three pieces and I found out there was a contract on my life. I've had a dizzy bad morning. And my father . . . I don't know what to think about my father. But I've got to be strong for my mother. Her health is my top priority. No matter what I do, I must keep her alive."

"Do you want me to drive you?" Wyatt offered, helping her into her car.

"No. I'll be okay," she said. "I'll leave the top down. The fresh air will help. Do a 'Breaking News' story, so we can be first on the air. I'll be at Baptist Hospital, if you need me."

"Right. I'll call you later," Wyatt said.

Ashley backed out onto Chartres Street, just missing the old fish-eyed lady who was, as always, walking in circles in and around the French Quarter, looking for no one but observing all. Ashley turned left on St. Peter, maneuvered through the French Quarter and stopped at Decatur Street. She turned right and slowly moved up the street toward Canal Street, passing the gates to Jackson Square where Yvette was murdered. "I'm sorry. I didn't know you but I will always remember you," she whispered. She looked in her rearview mirror and saw Chicken George crossing Decatur on his 1959 black Phantom Schwinn bicycle with his large straw cowboy hat, his feathered staff and his *gris-gris* bag hanging from his belt. Then she noticed to her left two homeless men who were sharing a bottle of wine and looking for their Savior. She overheard them say that Jesus was in the French Quarter and that they must become his new disciples. To her, they looked like orphans from a terrible storm, with no direction home.

She crossed Canal and later turned up Poydras and then up St. Charles Avenue and soon passed Robert E. Lee atop the Doric column in Lee Circle, a deaf and dumb sentinel to the past that would soon be removed from its perch and placed in a warehouse to stand vigil over darkness and mold, as if the tragic events of the Civil War had never happened. She continued up St. Charles, driving beneath the oak tree canopy that looked less foreboding now and more sheltering. Then she crossed Napoleon Avenue and stopped in front of her parents' house. She saw her father's shadowy figure moving about his bedroom, like a spirit unaware of his own death. Ashley realized that she had to break away from her own father, almost as if he had died. She must close and seal that tomb. She stared a while longer and felt a chill run down her spine, though she had to wipe sweat from her brow.

Ashley made a U-turn on St. Charles and headed back to Napoleon Avenue where she turned left and traveled a few blocks to Baptist Hospital. She parked illegally on a side street and hurried to her mother's room where both her mother and Beverly were asleep. She sat down next to her mother's bed, clasped her hand in her mother's, and watched her mother breathe. She would sit awake all night long.

CHAPTER 40

A Toast to Life

Ashley and her mother sat on the blue-and-white striped French provincial couch in Ashley's cottage on Lowerline street. They watched the five o'clock news and a videotaping of Mayor Chenier as he took the oath of office in front of City Hall, earlier that day. At the top of City Hall was the city's golden emblem, the *fleur-de-lis*. Behind the mayor were members of his staff and good friend, Armstead. Next to the mayor were his wife and son. Judge Loretta Washington spoke the oath as the mayor repeated, "I solemnly swear that I will support the Constitution of the United States, and the Constitution of the State of Louisiana, and the Charter of the City of New Orleans, and that I will faithfully discharge the duties of the office of mayor of the City of New Orleans to the best of my ability, so help me God."

"Congratulations," the judge said, as she shook the mayor's hand.

"Thank you," the mayor said. He then kissed his wife and embraced his son. "Ladies and gentlemen," the mayor said, speaking into the eight microphones on the podium, "I am thankful to be your mayor for another term. I will do my best to perform my duties as mayor. We, as a city, have suffered greatly this past year and especially the last few months. We have had murders in this city at every turn, not the least of which was my opponent's, Keiffer Conright's murder. And he himself is under investigation for his alleged involvement in the murder that tragically took the life of a young woman not long ago. Let us remember her and all victims of murder. I promise that the NOPD, the DA's office and I will get to the bottom of all of these murders, every one. I ask for your patience again, even though patience is running thin. I am as bewildered and sick and tired of the crime in our great city as you are. But we will conquer this problem. We will win and the criminals will lose. I need your help, especially those who have witnessed a crime but are afraid to come forward and testify. Those people our city needs the most. Let's take back our streets, take back our neighborhoods and take back our city. And with God on our side, we will do just that. Thank you."

Before Ashley had a chance to turn off the television, Jack Randalls of TV-3 said, "That was the mayor's swearing-in which took place at noon today. He mentioned the murder of the young woman, Yvette Lenieu. That investigation is ongoing. Businessman, George Tarleton, is a suspect in this homicide. His whereabouts are unknown."

Ashley turned off the television and returned to the couch. She placed her arm around her mother's shoulders.

"I'm sorry you had to see that, Mother. Are you okay?" Ashley asked.

"I'll never be okay again. But the way to deal with bad news is day to day. I learned that dealing with my mother's death. Your father's disappearance feels like a death in the family," Ashley's mother said.

"I know. It feels that way for me, too," Ashley said.

"We've lost him, Ashley. And from all he was involved with, we apparently lost him a long time ago. You think the people you're closest to are on your side. And that's not always true," Ashley's mother said, looking straight into her daughter's eyes.

"You've got me, Mother. I'm glad I stayed with the one who stayed with me. We'll get through this, as you say, one day at a time," she said, giving her mother a kiss on the cheek. "And you've got to concentrate on getting stronger every day, birthday girl. Tonight, we celebrate your birthday and our new friends. Ready?"

"Yes. Thanks. You're so good to me," Ashley's mother said, embracing her.

"Oh, am I the world's best daughter, or what?" Ashley said, laughing.

"You are! You are the world's best daughter," Ashley's mother said.

"Mother, I learned it all from you. There were times when I took you for granted. And I apologize," Ashley said.

"You don't have to apologize," Ashley's mother said.

"Yes, I do. I've learned you were also the strong one in the family. I've learned my lesson," Ashley said, hugging her mother, and then caressing her mother's face, lightly moving her fingers over blanched, thinly wrinkled skin. "Now, we have to go or we'll be late."

"Where are you taking me?" Ashley's mother asked.

"Well, I was going to keep it a secret, but I'll tell you. Antoine's, your favorite," she said, smiling.

"Oh, wonderful! I haven't been in a long time. And who are these new friends? Not Paige?" her mother said, curiously.

"No. Not Paige. Mother, these are colleagues and people I have met around town,

people about whom I reported recently. Mother, I've asked a black family to join us. It's a mother and her two children, one of whom was wounded in a shooting in the St. Thomas housing project. Sadly, she lost her eye. I met them when Wyatt, my cameraman, and I did an interview there. They're good people but very poor, and they're my friends now. Is that okay with you?" Ashley hesitantly and nervously asked.

"My, how you've grown," her mother said, cupping her daughter's face in her hand. "If I only had your courage." She embraced Ashley and whispered, "If I only had your courage. I'm so proud of you."

"Mother, what's wrong?" she inquired, noticing tears on her mother's baby soft cheeks.

"There's something I have to tell you," Ashley's mother said anxiously, staring forlornly into her daughter's dark sienna brown eyes.

"What is it, Mother?" Ashley asked.

"I have a secret, and it's time that you know of it," her mother confessed. Ashley's chest and stomach tightened, her heartbeat quickened, and blood pressure rose. She and her mother never kept secrets. "I have a sister. Agnes. And our mother was a black woman. A Creole."

"Oh, my God," Ashley whispered.

"She was very light-skinned and passed for white," her mother continued. "No one could really tell, though some suspected. My father was white and we grew up in a white world. My sister's skin is a bit darker than mine. Just a bit. When your father found out, we were already married and he forbade me from inviting Agnes to the house or social gatherings. I should have had the courage to challenge him, but it was the 1950s and women didn't do that. After that, I was too settled in my marriage. Then I gave birth to you in '64, and I couldn't upset him. And, of course, I didn't want you to know because it was easier that way. Your father could have divorced me, and he probably thought about it. But your birth certainly changed his world. He all but ordered me to never tell you. But now I think you should know. Obviously, you know what this means."

"Yes. Your mother's blood is in my veins, too," Ashley said, shocked and feeling a sudden fatigue.

"She died young, so you never met her or suspected anything unusual. Did you?" her mother asked.

"No. Never. I don't see anything that would indicate black ancestry in you," Ashley remarked.

"I know. I am one of many in New Orleans who just 'pass' as white, and say goodbye to history. And if you remarry, you don't have to tell him anything, if you don't want. Let the River take the past and carry it far away. Let the churning waters pull it under and erase it from memory. I am very sorry for all of this. I'm very sorry," her mother said, wiping away tears.

"Mother, don't," Ashley said, quickly consoling her mother with a comforting hug. "Don't worry, Mother. You did nothing wrong. You've been the best mother. Where would I be without you? All the wonderful birthday parties and Christmases and the shopping on Canal Street. I have nothing but great memories, vivid memories, beautiful memories. And you made those possible. You created those memories. You gave them to me like gifts. And every day I unwrap another and I get to relive those days, those wonderful, carefree times. And I thank you for those times. You were proving to me every day how much you loved me. And I thank you for your love, your greatest gift to me. The poison has been washed from your blood, and your health has been restored. I'll make sure you stay healthy, forever."

She kissed her mother on the cheek and they both cried, their tears mingling as they rolled down their faces.

"Would you mind if I called my sister and invited her to dine with us?" her mother asked.

"Do that, Mother. Call her now and we'll pick her up. That's a wonderful idea. I want to meet her," Ashley said.

"Thank you for understanding," her mother said.

"We don't have to bury the past any longer. We should celebrate it," Ashley said. "And we will, starting tonight."

Ashley's mother rose and walked to the kitchen to use the phone hanging on the wall. Ashley walked to the aged Belgian blue mirror standing atop the mantel and leaning against the wall. As her mother spoke emotionally to her sister on the phone in the kitchen, Ashley stared intensely at herself, checking and questioning her makeup, but not her cosmetics.

They drove down St. Charles Avenue. Ashley drove slowly past her parents' house which had been padlocked, having been seized by the State of Louisiana for evidence and assets. Both looked at the dark house and then at each other. Ashley slipped her right hand into her mother's left hand. Then she picked up speed and continued down St. Charles Avenue. When they reached Nashville Avenue, Ashley turned right, drove down two blocks and pulled up in front of Yvette's apartment house. She took two yellow long-stem roses from the back seat. "These are for Yvette and her child," she said to her mother. She and her mother walked up the path and placed the roses next to many other colorful cut flowers lying flat near the door in the horizontal garden of roses, carnations and Gerbera daisies that sprang from sadness and sympathy, and watered by mourners' tears. "Rest in peace. I hope to meet you one day, but perhaps we already have. Thank you for your help." They returned to the car and found a pink Gerbera daisy on the windshield. Ashely picked up the flower and said, "Who put this daisy here, Mother?" They then just stared at each other.

Ashley and her mother continued down St. Charles, crossing over avenues and streets that provided Ashley access over the years to a rich life of exciting experiences like parties, receptions, teas, dances, dinners and diversions of all sorts, creating a multitude of pleasant memories on which to later reflect. She crossed over Arabella Street, down which was located Langenstein's where she often shopped for groceries. To the left on St. Charles at Octavia Street was Danneel Playground where she spent many Saturday afternoons with her friend Paige, watching Paige's young daughter run and play with the other children, and exchanging the latest gossip about their uptown neighbors and acquaintances, the equivalent of passing notes to each other as schoolgirls. They approached De La Salle high school on the right where Ashley attended several dances in the gym, and where she received her first kiss at sixteen on the side of her mouth because her date, Conrad Kruger whose family owned a luxury hotel, was too nervous to get it right. One block away on the right was the Milton H. Latter Memorial Library, extending the entire block between Duffosat Street and Soniat Street. The three-story mansion, built in 1907, stood distinctively on the Avenue as a prime example of neo-Italianate architecture. It changed ownership several times over the years until its last owners, Harry and Anna Latter, donated it to the city in 1948 for use as a public library in memoriam to their son, Milton, who was killed in action on the Pacific island of Okinawa during World War II, yet another New Orleanian lost but hopefully remembered by all patrons who ever entered this citadel of knowledge in their quest for clues to human behavior, angelic and demonic. It stood as a mammoth gravestone to Milton H. Latter. Ashley and her mother would often visit the library on Saturday afternoons to research school projects when Ashley was a student at Sacred Heart Academy, also located on the Avenue.

At the corner of Bordeaux a few blocks down on the left stood the distinctively memorable Aldrich-Genella mansion designed in the Second Empire architectural style with mansard roofs on the two-story house and its four-story tower. It was there on the second-floor balcony, where she first met her ex-husband at a party during Carnival season ten years ago. He was well dressed in a navy blue blazer and gray slacks, like her father often wore. He was very polite like a good uptown boy, came from a good family who lived on Carondelet Street, and his smile was quite alluring. He complimented her, paid attention to her needs, and treated her like the woman she was in the process of becoming. That is how he had been taught, but later in their marriage, he became demanding, possessive and cold, as he had been conditioned.

Ashley's stare lingered a few seconds on that balcony as she drove by and ten years passed in three seconds. She stopped at the red light at St. Charles and Napoleon Avenues where her vision drifted to the right, down Napoleon on which stood many beautiful mansions, some of which had been divided into apartments or doctors' offices. She remembered accompanying another friend, Priscilla, to a psychiatrist with an office on Napoleon. Priscilla had been suffering from postpartum depression and was experiencing numerous crying spells. Ashley and Priscilla had been friends since their days at Sacred Heart Academy. Ashley sat in the waiting room outside the rear exit of the doctor's office. When an hour had passed, Priscilla opened the door to avoid any patients in the front waiting room. Ashley quickly peered in to glimpse a single chair in front of a wide mahogany desk and a large box of Kleenex on a mahogany stand next to that chair in the room where emotions rose to the surface from the wellspring of human experience and memory, and tears fell as release and relief from the heat of the mind's shifting tectonic plates. These places and memories were all part of Ashley's uptown life and consciousness.

"Look, Mother, the Columns. Remember the many times we sat on that porch for Sunday brunch?" Ashley inquired, breaking the awkward and uncustomary silence between the two, as she glanced left at the beautiful Columns Hotel, built in the Italianate style with four wide white majestic columns facing the Avenue.

"I do. Many memories there. That was a tradition for us," her mother said.

"Well, we'll continue the tradition soon," Ashley quickly offered.

"Okay."

"Now that you're living with me, we'll have breakfast together every morning and Sunday brunch at the Columns," Ashley said.

"Sounds wonderful," her mother said.

"We'll have many good times together, Mother. You can be sure of that," Ashley said, smiling, and silently vowing to take care of her mother as long as she lived, and to remember her and honor her after her sojourn on this earth was over and her final embarkation had begun.

"You know there's sadness associated with the Columns," Ashley's mother said.

"Really?"

"Yes.," her mother said. "It was built in the late 1800s for Simon Hernsheim. He owned a cigar factory downtown on Magazine and Julia. Very rich man. But when his wife and sister both died in the same year, he was never the same. So, he committed suicide by ingesting cyanide."

"Oh, Lord," Ashley said.

"Yes. I saw it become a boarding house and then fall into disrepair. It was boarded up for a while until a couple bought it in the early '80s and saved it from demolition. I remember reading an article back then in the *Times-Picayune*. When it was shuttered, I would often wonder about the family that once made it their home. It's said that Mr. Hernsheim's ghost still haunts the house," her mother said.

"Seriously?" Ashley asked.

"Yes. Seriously. Connections to this earth are stronger than we know," her mother observed.

"And to each other," Ashley added, as she reached over and squeezed her mother's hand and smiled.

Ashley crossed over Louisiana Avenue and made a U-turn so she could turn right at the red light and proceed up Louisiana, away from the River. Louisiana Avenue on this side of St. Charles was not part of uptown that Ashley had ever frequented. In fact, this side frightened her. It was home to an all-black community with a few small shops, a night club, a liquor store, small houses and low-income apartments. She was much more familiar with the more well-traveled southern end of Louisiana from St. Charles to the River, but this corridor that led to South Claiborne Avenue was not welcoming to her in her mind. No grand homes or grand memories were ever constructed here for her. The farther up Louisiana she drove, the greater her anxiety grew. She knew this was a high crime area, and she realized she had forgotten her gun. She tried her best not to alarm her mother, but the snakes were making their presence known in her veins. She continued slowly up Louisiana, her eyes darting left and right, as she drove up this once splendid avenue, the ground of which had once been part of the Delassize family long-lot plantation in the 1700s and 1800s where blacks, who presently lived on this patch of earth, were then enslaved on it.

"Turn right here," Ashley's mother said, pointing to Loyola Avenue. Ashley turned right and proceeded down Loyola, noticing every front door and most of the windows of these pastel colored, narrow, one-story, wooden, shotgun houses had black iron bars on them, signifying a return to enslavement of sorts but under the whip of new masters. "You can pull over here."

Ashley pulled over to the right side of Loyola and parked next to a "No Parking Any Time" sign nailed to a telephone pole to which were also attached the street signs for Loyola and Franklin Court. Franklin Court was a narrow corridor but more of a walkway than a street because it could not accommodate cars, though there were a few homes like those on Loyola facing each other. To her, this was definitely unknown New Orleans.

"Are you sure this is it, Mother?" Ashley inquired, nervously looking all around her.

"Yes. I'm sure. I've been here before," her mother said.

"You came to this neighborhood by yourself?" Ashley asked, still perplexed by the day's revelations.

"Yes, Ashley. I have come here many times to visit my sister and reminisce. We are family, just like any other," she said, staring straight into Ashley's eyes.

"I'm sorry, Mother. Of course, you're right. I guess I'm seeing parts of New Orleans I never knew existed, or cared to know. I've received quite an education the last week or so. An unintended education. Please forgive me, Mother," Ashley replied, noticing that she had disrespected her mother.

"That's okay. Now come and meet your aunt," her mother said.

They opened a short, black wrought iron gate and walked up Franklin to a small pastel colored house looking somewhat like a quaint Creole cottage but without that architectural style's accouterments of a gabled roof and a French door and French windows; instead, black iron bars in front of the door and two windows greeted the morning sun and remained wide-eyed and vigilant during their night watch. Before Ashley's mother had a chance to ring the doorbell, Agnes opened the wooden door and then the iron one, and the sisters embraced. Agnes was as tall as her sister at five feet eight inches, slender and an aging beauty with light caramel skin and short black wavy hair with streaks of gray and a narrow flat nose. Though approaching sixty years of age, Agnes retained some of her youthful appearance, especially around her eyes. And the skin over her high cheekbones was still taut with a golden luster, like the sun that had not yet set. She stood elegant and statuesque in the wool, cobalt blue skirt suit that her loving sister had given her years before. She opened the iron door wider and smiled a bright, welcoming smile as if she had seen Ashley many times before. And, actually, she had. Over the years, Agnes would sometimes walk past the mansion on the Avenue and look through the crystal doors from the sidewalk of a family to whom she was related but with whom she was forbidden to associate, until now.

"Hello, Ashley. I'm your Aunt Agnes."

Ashley momentarily stood and stared, and then extended her hand. She felt a thin, gentle hand slide halfway into hers as the two women made eye contact.

"Hello. . . Aunt Agnes," Ashley softly said, adding a small smile.

Ashley was anxious. She didn't know how to act or what to say. Tenseness, like a claw, gripped the back of her head. The thought of using hand sanitizer even crossed her mind, as was her custom when she shook the hand of a stranger, but quickly dismissed it and wondered how it crept into her mind which was full of conflicting thoughts and emotions. She should have been happy and accepting, but, in truth, she was not. She should have given Agnes a big hug, but she could not bring herself to do that. Not yet. In the back of her mind, she hoped she could do that. But not yet. Ashley was a thirty-year-old white woman who was proud of her race and her privileged life. She had never examined her own prejudice, but now, like a psychoanalyst, she was suddenly forced to, though she didn't want to do it or face the pain it would inflict. She was headed for a change in her way of thinking that would be torturous in its coming. But to maintain her loving relationship with her mother, she knew she must accept her aunt for the good person she was without regard to race, without hesitancy, without prejudice, and only with love and acceptance, for Ashley was the head of the family now. She must take on this challenge and win. Not yet, but soon.

Ashley sat at one end of an attractive Welkin blue, French provincial sofa that she quickly recognized as having once been in her mother's home on the Avenue. She smiled just thinking of her mother's generosity and then noticed Agnes was sitting in a matching chair near her mother at the other end of the sofa. She watched the sisters softly chat and even giggle. Ashley could not quite hear what was being said, but she liked what she saw. Her mother was alive and again enjoying life. And Ashley knew she must keep her healthy and bring more joy into her life. At that moment, a little girl's face, much like the little girl in the French Quarter, crossed her mind. She looked at her mother and realized she needed to keep the family going. She needed to have a child, a girl, and name her after her mother. She then looked around the room and noticed a photo on a small mahogany table of her mother, Agnes and a young woman about Ashley's age. She walked to the photo and picked it up.

"She's my daughter, Arielle. She's thirty years old," Agnes said, standing alongside her.

"So am I," Ashley said.

"I know. Your birthdays are only seven days apart. And she's also in broadcast journalism in Houston," Agnes said.

"And all this time I never knew about you or my cousin," Ashley said, amazed.

"That's my fault, Ashley. I should have done something," Ashley's mother said, now standing next to Agnes.

"No, Mother, it's not your fault. Not at all," Ashley insisted. "The fault is Father's. . . and Society's. How do things become so twisted and families separated? Agnes. . . Aunt Agnes, I apologize for my father's behavior. You're welcome to my house anytime. In fact, I insist you and Arielle come to dinner often. I want to know all about your family."

"Our family," Ashley's mother added.

"Yes. Our family," Ashley agreed. "I have a lot to learn."

Ashley looked at her mother and aunt with wonder and amazement. Before her stood two quietly strong sisters and loving mothers who had stoically faced racism and survived on plots of land only a mile away but a world apart. Ashley realized how fortunate she was, and, like a good reporter, decided to spread the news. She knew she would file their story in the months to come and broadcast it to the world. Monuments, she thought, should be erected to people like her mother and aunt, the true heroes in life that are rarely honored, until now.

Ashley opened the passenger's door to her BMW and assisted Agnes into the back seat and her mother into the passenger's seat. She turned right on Toledano and left on South Saratoga, and continued south three blocks in this cloistered, impoverished neighborhood where all the houses were small, defenseless and forgotten. As she neared Washington Avenue, she passed Lafayette Cemetery No. 2 on the left. There, too, stood houses, houses of the dead in disrepair and greatly in need of prayerful remembrance and respect for the dearly departed. She turned right on Washington and drove five blocks to St. Charles Avenue, and then left onto the Avenue, noticing P. A. Chopin's floral shop with two large picture windows where she and other children would gaze in wonder at the bunny rabbits on display during Easter season. She then proceeded down the Avenue until she reached Lee Circle where a crowd of demonstrators and onlookers had gathered. Some demonstrators waved Confederate flags and other demonstrators held signs that read, "Take 'Em Down!" The mayor had made good on his promise to remove Confederate Civil War monuments from around the city. The most iconic, treasured monument by many, General Robert E. Lee, was slated to be the first to go, as a show of power. A tall crane stood adjacent to the statue of Lee atop the sixty foot Doric column as workers attached ropes around the statue. Slowly, the tarnished bronze statue of Lee was lowered to the ground as the "Take 'Em Down" supporters cheered and the Confederate flag wavers lowered their flags to the level of the statue, some wiping away tears. Some in the crowd yelled, "The Civil War is over!" while others screamed, "It has just begun again!"

As Ashley rounded Lee Circle, she noticed another horizontal garden of fresh-cut flowers had bloomed overnight on the corner of Howard Avenue where another young man had lost his life to violence.

Ashley completed the drive down the Avenue, crossed Canal Street, entered the French Quarter by way of Chartres Street and pulled into the Royal Orleans Hotel garage. The three women then walked down a sloped bottom floor of the hotel. They walked past a few shops and then climbed the staircase leading into the hotel lobby. They walked up the lobby past the open piano bar, then past the Rib Room restaurant, and then through the tall French doors leading to Royal Street.

"On second thought, Ashley, I'm embarrassed to be seen in Antoine's, considering your father . . .," her mother said.

"Father should be embarrassed, not you," Ashley said, holding her mother's hand and walking slowly.

Ashley noticed the old black man dressed in brown, who was sitting on the corner next to his shopping cart full of his belongings, hoping to collect quarters for his burial. Ashley gave him four.

They then walked a half block, and then down the alley next to Antoine's to the restaurant's side door, only used by locals familiar with the restaurant. Ashley picked up the phone next to the door and called her waiter who quickly appeared to open the door.

"Mrs. Tarleton, so good to see you, and you, Miss Ashley," Henry said.

"Thank you," Ashley replied. "And this is my Aunt Agnes."

"Good evening," Henry said.

Henry led them to a large table in the middle of the Red Room, a few feet away. Some patrons knew the Tarletons but purposely turned away, so they would not have to acknowledge or say hello to Ashley and her mother. Seated around the table were Beverly, Darryl, Bella, Wyatt, and Betty, Mark (known as "TheRe," until recently), and Alicia Johnson. Ashley knew she would be snubbed by some acquaintances there. But Antoine's was her and her mother's favorite restaurant and a family tradition. She thought if she was not well received by some, then so be it. She was just so happy that her mother had recuperated and was able to finally dine out. This indeed was a new beginning.

Beverly gave Mrs. Tarleton a hug.

"Mother, this is Darryl. He's my boss at the station," Ashley said.

"Mrs. Tarleton, it's good to see you again. We met at last year's Christmas party right after Ashley began working at the station," Darryl said, standing to shake her hand.

"Oh, of course. I remember you now," Ashley's mother replied. "You offered me a large slice of candy cane King Cake from Haydel's Bakery."

"Yeah. That was me. Love their King Cake," Daryl said, laughingly.

"And this is Wyatt Terranova. We worked together on the mayor's race," Ashley said, as she moved to Wyatt's side and placed her hand on his shoulder. "We didn't quite get along at first, but I know now he's quite a fella."

"How do you do?" Ashley's mother said.

"Fine. Thank you. And you're feeling better?" Wyatt said, as he stood to shake her hand.

"Thank you. I am," Ashley's mother replied.

"Well, this special evening is all about you. Enjoy yourself. And I hope to see you again," Wyatt said.

"You will. Mother, this is Bella. Wyatt and I did a story about Bella. She's a survivor of the Holocaust," Ashley said, moving next to her mother.

"Oh! How very nice to meet you," Ashley's mother said.

"Nice to meet you, too," Bella said.

"And these are the Johnsons: Betty, her son, Mark, and her daughter, Alicia," Ashley said.

"It's a pleasure to meet you all. Did you hurt your eye, Alicia?" Ashley's mother inquired, seeing the patch over her right eye.

"Yes. A stray bullet hit me and I lost my eye," Alicia said.

"Oh, no. I'm so sorry," Ashley's mother replied.

"She's doing much better now. But it's a strain on her. God's looking out for her. He guides her when she needs help," Betty reassured, as Mark leaned in and gave his sister a hug.

"Yes, He does. He guides all of us, sweetheart. You're a brave girl," Ashley's mother said, taking her seat.

"Wyatt and I are doing a story on Betty and her children, regarding their future and the future of New Orleans," Ashley said, sitting down.

"Oh, how wonderful," her mother exclaimed.

"Yes. For instance, Mark is working as a craftsman in a jewelry store," Ashley said.

"Yeah. I have sort of a flare for making crosses and rings and things. So, Ashley introduced me to a jeweler. And he's taken me on, like an apprenticeship. One day I want to own my own jewelry store," Mark said.

"What will you call it?" Ashley's mother asked.

"That's a good question. I already thought of that. I'll call it 'Marquis.' That's the shape of a stone cut a certain way and it's got my name in it, too," Mark said.

"Taking orders yet? I need a little cross for my daughter's Confirmation," Wyatt said.

"Hey, I'll make you the best cross you've ever seen. No problem," Mark replied.

"Good. You're on," Wyatt responded.

"It's a deal," Mark said.

"And I want to be a reporter like Ashley," Alicia said.

"And you can be one," Darryl said. "We'll give you a tour of the studio. You can sit in the big director's chair in the control room and run the whole show."

"Yes. It'll be fun," Ashley added.

"Oh, good! That's what I want . . . to run the whole show," Alicia said.

They all laughed.

"Oh, my goodness. This little child has ambition," Beverly said.

"What's ambition?" Alicia asked.

"The determination, drive and will to succeed, no matter what," Beverly said.

"Yeah. That sounds like me," Alicia replied.

They all laughed again, as a waiter served drinks and soufflé potatoes in a basket.

"And, everyone, I want to introduce my Aunt Agnes. She's like a long lost relative, to me, anyway," Ashley said.

"Until now," Ashley's mother added.

"Yes. We'll be seeing a lot more of each other now. We can't go back in time, but we can go forward, together," Ashley said, as the three women looked at each other.

The others looked on a bit bewildered but aware that something significant had occurred in Ashley's family. However, Agnes's facial features and slightly brown skin indicated to all that bloodlines in New Orleans were often of varying shades.

"Mrs. Tarleton . . ." Bella said, breaking the silence, as all sat down.

"Please, call me Evelyn," Mrs. Tarleton said.

"Evelyn, I would like to thank you and Ashley for giving generously to the Holocaust memorial now being built on St. Charles. Thank you, not only for your donation, but for remembering and caring about the victims of the Holocaust. This is very important in a time when some people are purposely trying to murder the memory of those people. From the bottom of my heart, I thank you," Bella concluded.

They all raised their glasses and toasted Ashley and her mother.

"We are very happy to help. And we will not forget them," Mrs. Tarleton said.

"They will live on in their children and in our minds," Ashley added. "They will not be forgotten. The man who insulted you, is gone and will be forgotten."

"Thank you," Bella responded.

"I would now like to make my own toast to my mother," Ashley announced. "You're an inspiration to me, Mother. Mothers are truly the unsung heroes of the world. And that is certainly true of you. When I think of all the good times I've had growing up and the pleasant memories, I realize they were all because of you. You nurtured me; you educated me; you guided me through life. I am the woman I am today because of all those yesterdays with you. My life would have suffered if you had not been there for me all these years. And one day I will give you a grandchild. And we will both love and educate that child like you did with me. And the greatest gift my child will ever receive will be having you as a grandmother. And even though some of our old acquaintances may no longer look our way, we still have each other. Mother, I should have thanked you more in the past. I'll make up for that in the future. Let us all toast my mother, the birthday girl, and my best friend and my hero. And after we eat, we will have a very special birthday treat, Baked Alaska for everyone."

"Thank you, Ashley, my beautiful daughter," her mother said. "I am so proud of you. You have brought me so much joy, to watch you grow and become the beautiful woman you are today . . . words cannot express what a blessing you are to me." Ashley hugged her mother. "And you're right. We have each other and our new friends here. Thank you. Thank all of you."

"Miss Evelyn, it's our pleasure. You are a true one-of-a-kind. And you have many more miles to go. And I'm going to walk those miles with you," Beverly said, as she hugged Mrs. Tarleton.

All at the table applauded, attracting the attention of everyone in the Red Room, especially Paige Hightower, Ashley's friend, who was making her way around the room, stopping to talk with families she had known for years. As she passed Ashley's table their eyes met but Paige said nothing and did not stop. Her look was one of searing condemnation while shaking her head. She then returned to her usual table where her husband and she whispered and intermittently stared, as if Ashley had committed the unforgivable offense of bringing strangers into the cloistered sanctity of the Red Room, and especially these strangers.

But Ashley could no longer be concerned about Paige or Paige-like apprentices to snobbery, a social crime of which Ashley was a guilty multiple offender. She looked at her mother and smiled, thankful that she was recovering from the neurotoxic effects of "mad honey" poisoning administered by her father in whom she had always confided as his loving daughter. This poison in combination with her mother's weak heart would have eventually killed her. But her mother was alive and that's all that mattered. And like many other victims and like the city itself, they would rebuild their lives in their city razed by the fires of crime and time. A new history had commenced.

The air outside was heavy with humidity as darkness slowly overtook the city, bringing some relief from the heat that slowed everyone down, like pain. Laughter, howls, and music from Bourbon Street could be heard, marking the spot of revelry and release. A warm wind sent the front page of a discarded Times-Picayune drunkenly staggering down Decatur street, announcing the same sad news as the days before, as it passed a young man placing a flower at the horizontal garden that honored Yvette Lenieu's memory in front of the south gate to Jackson Square. The wind then carried the page over cars crossing Decatur street and over the Moonwalk, down to the earth and rocks below, and finally into the River where its words were lost as it became one with the River's rolling repetition, one with history, and one with a world without end.

There on the bank of the River, appeared a little boy who was wet and barefoot. He was the same boy reported missing a few days before, leaving only his sandals on the rocks near the River. Thought for sure to be dead and carried away by the River, he was alive, as if the River had mercifully given him a new birth. He walked up the Moonwalk and down to the Café du Monde, a few feet away. He startled the patrons and Vietnamese waiters as he stepped into view. A waiter dropped her tray, breaking a cup. The

Vietnam War veteran, occupying his favorite corner seat, rushed to help her and the boy. When he asked the boy about his parents and why he was wet, the boy simply smiled and his eyes were aglow. Then the Angelus rang out from St. Louis Cathedral, the beating heart and spiritual soul of the city. For three centuries it stood firm and courageous in its conviction to rebuke Satan and all His works.

Noticing more people than usual entering the Cathedral, the Chicken Man riding his bike shouted to Ruthie the Duck Girl roller-skating toward him, "Why all these people?"

"Mary's bleedin' again," Ruthie shouted back, with her duck in tow. "And look up there. The spirits are loose," she said, pointing to three doves flying across the cloudless, pale blue sky above the Cathedral.

Inside the cool Cathedral many locals and visitors were congregating near the statue of The Virgin Mary to the left side of the altar where the crucified Christ looked down on them all. They were mesmerized by the thin red-rust colored liquid trickling down Mary's beautiful face. Some stood, while others knelt before the statue. Most were praying to the Virgin Mother. Among the prayers were the words, "Lamb of God, you take away the sins of the world, have mercy on us. Lamb of God, you take away the sins of the world, grant us peace."

Throughout the evening the faithful continued to send their whispered appeals to Heaven, every word a bird.

END

About the Author

Donald Patrick O'Callahan is an assistant professor of English at Delgado Community College in New Orleans, Louisiana.

He was born and raised in New Orleans. He very much enjoys his profession, and is dedicated to the success of his students. He is an avid reader, researcher, and supporter of the arts and sciences. He is also the author of several plays, two screenplays, numerous short stories and poems, and another novel, Toward Jerusalem. Horizontal Garden and Toward Jerusalem, were both shortlisted in the William Faulkner Literary Competition.

Contact: donaldocallahan@yahoo.com

9 781966 840831